THE CANDY KILLER

A DCI TYLER THRILLER

MARK ROMAIN

Copyright © 2021 Mark Romain.
All rights reserved.
ISBN-13: 979-8-5328-0015-1

The right of Mark Romain to be identified as author of this work has been asserted by him in accordance with sections 77 and 78 of the copyright, designs and patents act 1988.

This book is a work of fiction and any resemblance to actual persons, living or dead, is purely coincidental.

❦ Created with Vellum

For Carina 'Roo' Romain

For Andrew Romain

THE DCI TYLER THRILLERS

TURF WAR

JACK'S BACK

THE HUNT FOR CHEN

UNLAWFULLY AT LARGE

THE CANDY KILLER

DIAMONDS AND DEATH

WOLFPACK

READER ADVISORIES

Language and opinions

The DCI Tyler Thrillers are set in the late nineties and early noughties, which means most of the detectives they feature would have joined the police in the eighties. In the interests of realism, the books contain language and opinions that were commonplace and acceptable at the time, but which would now be considered inappropriate and offensive.

Spelling and Grammar

Please note that this book is written in British (UK) English, and that many spellings in the UK differ from those in the USA.

PROLOGUE

Wednesday 18th July 2001

The masked man ran out of the post office in Leytonstone High Road, his sawn-off shotgun clutched tightly in one hand, the two bags containing the proceeds of the robbery in the other. His name was Micky Harrington, but most people just knew him as Mad Micky.

Harrington was a big unit, over six feet tall, broad of shoulder and wide of neck. Behind his back, people speculated that his aggression issues were a side effect from all the steroids he'd taken over the years to help him get so big, but the sad truth was the sadistic bastard had just been born nasty.

A second masked man burst out of the doors a little way behind him. His loose-fitting clothing swamped his wiry frame, and an old Luger pistol was tucked into the front of his waistband. Unlike Harrington, he was struggling under the weight of the two cash-in-transit bags he carried. "Wait for me," he grunted, skinny legs pumping like pistons as he tried to keep up.

The stolen getaway car was parked fifty yards further along the road in the only free space that had been available on their arrival a few minutes earlier. As Harrington sprinted towards it, the masked driver leaned across and opened the front passenger door for him, shouting, "Get in! Get in!"

Behind the fleeing robbers, an audible alarm burst into life above the post office door, making enough noise to wake the dead. "Shit!" Harrington cursed, knowing that it would only be a minute or two before the first police units arrived.

As he reached the car, the driver started gunning the engine impatiently, and Harrington could tell that he was itching to get underway. Throwing both the money bags and his sawn-off onto the rear seat, Harrington screamed, "Go! Go! Go!" as he jumped into the front of the car.

The third man, who was still lagging a few yards behind, yelled at them in panic as Harrington's door closed with a loud clunk. "Wait for me!"

"Hurry up, you muppet," Harrington screamed back at him.

Skidding to a halt by the rear of the car, the second robber bundled the cash in and then threw himself on top of it. "I'm in!" he cried, pulling the door shut.

The S-Type Jaguar pulled away from the kerb with a squeal of tyres, leaving behind a thick cloud of smoke and the acrid smell of burning rubber. Swerving onto the wrong side of the road, the getaway driver rammed his foot all the way down to the floor, and the powerful V8 engine growled throatily as the stolen car surged forward, tearing past the slow-moving line of mid-afternoon traffic that was trundling north along the High Road, towards the Green Man roundabout.

The Jag's driver flicked his headlights onto full beam, so that oncoming motorists would see him in plenty of time to take evasive action. They would need to, because he had no intention of giving way. Thankfully, they didn't encounter many vehicles coming towards them, and the few they did had the good sense to move aside, rather than risk a head-on collision with the kamikaze Jag driver.

It unnerved Harrington slightly that his getaway driver, a skinny dweeb called Honest Steve Higgins, was getting off on playing chicken with the oncoming traffic. "Don't fucking kill us," Harrington growled, nervously placing his large hands on the dashboard and bracing for impact.

In the back, the third man, who was called G-Man, giggled at the big man's anxiety. Harrington ignored him; the twitchy-eyed fool was probably stoned out of his head.

"Relax, Micky," Higgins' muffled voice cooed from beneath his balaclava. "I know exactly what I'm doing, honest I do."

Micky Harrington tore his mask off to reveal a square-jawed face that was as hard as granite. Beneath the military style buzzcut, the forty-three year old's leathery skin was bright orange from overexposure to a sunlamp. Using a forearm that was the size of a small ham to mop sweat from his brow, Harrington laughed, low and mean. "Course you do, Stevie boy. That's why I brought you along."

―――

PCs Lee Bradshaw and Alan Dawkins were the late shift crew of Leyton's pursuit car, call-sign Juliet One. They were cruising along Cathall Road, just approaching the junction with Leytonstone High Road, when the armed robbery call came out over the Force Main-Set.

"Bloody hell, mate! We're only thirty seconds away from there," Bradshaw said, instinctively sitting ramrod straight and adjusting his grip on the steering wheel in readiness for a blue light run.

With a grin of youthful anticipation, Dawkins snatched the mic from the dashboard and toggled the press-to-talk switch. "MP, MP, show Juliet One responding," he told the Information Room operator at New Scotland Yard.

Bradshaw couldn't help but smile at the keenness in his junior colleague's voice; he had been that enthusiastic once, a long time ago.

As they pulled up at the junction with Leytonstone High Road, a red Jaguar flew by on the wrong side of the road, almost taking the front of their bonnet off in the process.

"Bloody hell!" Bradshaw exclaimed, flinching involuntarily.

Dawkins craned his neck to follow the speeding car. "Did you see that, Lee?" he spluttered, reaching for the mic again. "Two of the men in that car are wearing balaclavas."

Bradshaw nodded, grimly. "Yeah, I saw it, mate." Flicking the switches that activated the noise and lights, he pulled into Leytonstone High Road and set off in pursuit of the Jag.

Behind them, the jarring sound of a siren erupting into life wiped the cocksure smile from Harrington's face. Looking back over his shoulder, he groaned. A police car had just pulled out of Cathall Road, and it was closing in on them rapidly, with blue lights strobing and headlights flashing. Letting out a string of expletives, he leaned over and retrieved the shotgun from the back seat. "Put your foot down and lose the fuckers," he ordered, gruffly.

"I'm trying, Micky, honest, I am."

"MP, MP from Juliet One, active message," Dawkins said, raising his voice to be heard above the exhilarating wail of the siren. "We're behind a red S-Type Jaguar, heading north along High Road Leytonstone. We're just passing Juliet Sierra on our offside..." Juliet Sierra was the phonetic code for Leytonstone police station "...Speed approaching seventy – that's seven-zero – MPH."

"*Received by MP. What's the vehicle concerned in?*" The male operator's voice was reserved, almost bored, and Bradshaw had to admire him for it. It couldn't be easy, being that calm and composed while a high-speed chase was going on.

Dawkins quickly rattled off the Jag's registration number. "MP, the vehicle's failing to stop for us. It's now doing seventy-five in a thirty speed limit, travelling on the wrong side of the road and forcing oncoming traffic out of the way." Dawkins was trying and failing to sound as chilled as the operator at Information Room. "The vehicle contains three men, two of them masked, and is believed to be concerned in the armed robbery we were just assigned to."

"*All received, Juliet One. Keep it going,*" the operator said, as casually as if he were asking Dawkins if he wanted milk and sugar with his tea.

Other Main-Set units were volunteering to assist in their droves. In their eagerness to get assigned to the call, they were all talking over each other, clogging up the airwaves so that Dawkins was unable to get a word in. "*All units wait!*" the MP operator ordered with scary firmness. "*Units offering assistance, please make your way, but do NOT transmit. Keep the commentary going, Juliet One.*"

"MP from Juliet One, we're now heading towards the Green Man roundabout, speed down to forty MPH ... Standby for a direction of travel."

Up ahead, a centre island divided the two streams of traffic, with a 'Keep Right' bollard warning drivers which side of the island they needed to be on. Beyond the bollard, a long row of waist-high metal railings ran all the way up to the roundabout, some fifty yards further along the road. Just before it reached the bollard, the Jag's driver braked sharply and swerved to his right. There were no gaps for him to squeeze into, so he simply smashed into the side of the nearest car, bumping it up onto the pavement. Thankfully, there were no pedestrians in its path, but there was a red telephone box, and the out of control saloon smashed straight into it. With an almighty bang, the front of the car crumpled inwards, and the phone box toppled over, coming to rest at a forty-five degree angle. As he drove past the smoking wreckage, Bradshaw prayed that the demolished phone box had been empty.

Sitting beside him, Dawkins squeezed the PTT. "MP from Juliet One, the bandit's just rammed a car off the road, causing it to crash into a phone box."

Up ahead, the bandit's path to the roundabout was impeded by two slow-moving lanes of traffic, each about six vehicles deep. The

Jag's driver was honking his horn in frustration, trying to bully the obstructing cars into moving aside.

"Maybe we should try and drag them out of the car now, while it's blocked in?" Dawkins suggested.

Bradshaw shook his head, vehemently. Sod's law dictated that the bandit would take off again the moment they stepped foot outside their vehicle.

Sure enough, the Jag suddenly accelerated, smashing into the rear bumper of the last car in line and shunting it forward several feet. The driver then swung the Jag's steering wheel violently to his right, pushing the car completely out of its way. The sound of glass breaking and metal folding in on itself was audible, even over the siren. Almost immediately, the Jag's crazy driver repeated the move, this time swerving to his left.

Witnessing the mayhem behind them, the other vehicles blocking the bandit's path started hurriedly moving aside, but the getaway driver was too impatient to wait, so he accelerated heavily, scraping against the sides of the cars in his way. Leaving a trail of smashed glass and displaced bumpers in its wake, the Jag powered forward, towards the roundabout.

As the pursuit car cautiously followed, Dawkins raised the mic to his lips. "MP from Juliet One, the bandit's literally smashing slower moving cars out of its way on the approach to the Green Man roundabout." He turned to Bradshaw, shaking his head in wonder. "It's like the Red Sea parting for Moses."

Bradshaw's mouth compressed into a thin line. He was too busy concentrating on not hitting anything to reply.

Up ahead, the Jag finally burst onto the roundabout, pulling straight into the path of an oncoming Heavy Goods Vehicle, which immediately locked up and slewed sideways.

"Oh my God!" Dawkins gasped.

"This bloke's a raving lunatic," Bradshaw growled, wondering how much longer the Chief Inspector at Information Room would allow the chase to continue before deciding that it was too dangerous and ordered them to break it off.

There was a horrendous crashing together of metal as the side of the articulated lorry slammed into several cars in the next lane, trapping them underneath the trailer unit and shoving them sideways across the road.

Bradshaw was torn between stopping to check for casualties and continuing the pursuit but, in the end, the thrill of the chase proved too strong to ignore. "Call it in," he told Dawkins. "Get units here quickly."

Dawkins glanced over his shoulder at the mayhem behind them, and swallowed hard. "MP, we'll need units to attend the Green Man roundabout ASAP, to deal with a multi-vehicle pile-up."

"All received by MP. Juliet One, be advised that the bandit car is reported as being lost or stolen from Newham section since yesterday evening. Are there any Stinger equipped Traffic cars available to assist Juliet One stop the vehicle?"

A Stinger was a hollow spiked tyre deflation device that, when deployed across the road just before the bandit vehicle arrived, would puncture the tyres and bring the stolen vehicle to a controlled stop. Unfortunately, only specialist TPAC – Tactical Pursuit And Containment – units were equipped with Stingers and, at the moment, none of them were responding to the request.

In his rearview mirror, Bradshaw spotted the reassuring flicker of blue lights, but they were only the size of pinpricks, which meant they were still a long way back. "Looks like the cavalry's on its way," he observed, relieved that officers would be on scene at the accident within a couple of minutes.

Giving him a thumbs-up, Dawkins continued with his commentary. "MP, the bandit's going right, right, right, taking the fourth exit onto Bush Road," he yelled into the mic, all attempts at calmness now forgotten. "We're now heading towards Wanstead Flats, speed increasing to sixty-five – that's six-five – MPH."

"Can't you go any faster?" Harrington demanded. "The Old Bill is still on our tail, and we need to lose them before we get to the changeover point."

"I know that, Micky, honest, I do," Higgins responded, tetchily. He was annoyed that he hadn't shaken them off at the roundabout. He would just have to try something else to get rid of them, but that wasn't a problem; he had lots of tricks up his sleeve.

The changeover point, where they planned to swap the Jag for another stolen car, was roughly a mile away. To get there, they would have to drive straight through Wanstead Flats, which was a wide expanse of open grassland surrounded by trees, and that was where he planned to lose his pursuers once and for all. Grinning beneath his mask, Higgins knew that the police wouldn't dare follow him off-road, especially not in a low-slung vehicle like the high-performance Rover that was chasing them. The Jag wasn't exactly suited to off-roading either, but as long as it held together long enough for him to lose his pursuers, he didn't give a toss about fucking up the sump.

They were approaching a four-way junction at a frightening speed, and Higgins stamped on the brakes, causing the wheels to lock and the back end to drift out. "Hang on tight," he shouted as he yanked the steering wheel to the right, simultaneously jerking the handbrake up and inducing a controlled skid that dragged the car sideways into Blake Hall Road.

Higgins whooped in joy as the car careered through the turn. Unfortunately, unlike G-Man in the back, who was hanging onto the overhead grip for dear life, Harrington didn't heed his advice in time, and the sideways inertia slammed him into the passenger door, causing his head to bounce off the window with a loud thunk.

The driver of an oncoming delivery van was forced to stamp on his brakes to avoid T-boning the Jag as it sailed through the junction. Unfortunately, the old man at the wheel of the Morris Minor chugging along behind him wasn't as quick to react, and he drove straight into the back of it, catapulting the van into the path of a double-decker bus. The resulting crash completely blocked the crossroads behind them.

Glancing in his rearview mirror, Higgins sniggered in satisfaction; that would hold the police up for a while. As the Jag straightened, he floored the gas pedal, enjoying the exquisite sensation of being pushed back into his contoured seat.

Having been thrown all over the place, Harrington was still cursing as he finally straightened himself up, and he instinctively raised his right hand to lash out at his driver.

Higgins cowered. "Sorry, Micky, honest, I am," he said, hastily.

Harrington grunted, withdrew his hand. "Fucking idiot. Give me more of a warning, next time," he complained, gingerly rubbing his head.

"It won't happen again, Micky," Higgins assured him. "Honest it won't." Beneath his mask, he couldn't resist a little smirk. After all, it wasn't as if there was anything inside Harrington's thick cranium to damage.

Approaching a sweeping left hand bend, Higgins positioned the car towards the white centre line, powering it through the road's apex at maximum speed. Clearing the bend, the Jag emerged into a long stretch of straight road, and he was about to give it some more welly when he spotted a herd of cows huddled together in the middle of the carriageway, about five hundred yards ahead. "Shit!" he exclaimed, reluctantly feathering on the breaks.

"Don't slow down, you soppy twat," Harrington ordered. "Just sound your horn and frighten them out of the way."

Higgins immediately leaned on the horn, but this had no effect. A few seconds later, he was forced to start breaking heavily.

"What did I tell you?" Harrington screamed, his face inches away from Higgins' ear.

Higgins flinched. "I've got no choice, Micky, honest."

The cattle, which were owned by the commoners of Epping Forest, had grazing rights in the area, and they regularly wandered the grasslands of Wanstead and Whipps Cross, bumbling along the busy roads whenever the urge took them, blissfully ignorant of the havoc they were causing to the traffic flow. Once they decided to stop, there was nothing that anyone could do but wait patiently until such time as they decided to move on of their own accord.

Doing a quick headcount, Higgins estimated that there were about fifteen cows in all, and a good two-thirds of them were clustered together in the middle of the road, completely blocking both lanes. Cursing their bad luck, he reluctantly brought the Jag to a halt a few feet short of a large, docile animal that appeared to be eyeing them with mild curiosity.

Ignoring Harrington's churlish rant, he thought about using the grassland to their left to circumnavigate the herd, but there was a deep trench between that and the tarmac, and any attempt to cross it would lead to them becoming irrevocably stuck.

He glanced over his shoulder, wondering whether to wait it out until the cows moved on or do a U-turn and look for an alternative route. Then he heard the faint wail of a siren approaching from behind and realised that going back wasn't viable. "We need to get them to move or we're fucked," he said, trying to ignore the anxiety that was starting to eat away at him.

A few of the cows had wandered onto the grassland, and they were now chewing away contentedly, but several more had joined the cow who had taken to staring at them, and this particular group of bovines showed no inclination to go anywhere.

Harrington leaned over and pressed the horn, but the cows, who were probably used to the histrionics of impatient humans, didn't even bat an eyelid at the noise.

Walking along the verge towards them in an orderly line, Higgins spotted a group of young school children in burgundy blazers. There were four adults scattered amongst them, presumably teachers, and the man leading the line stopped and pointed at the cows. As the others concertinaed to a halt behind him, he smiled and said something to the children, who all started laughing.

"Wait here," Harrington instructed.

"Where are you going?" Higgins demanded as the wail of the siren grew steadily louder.

Harrington glared at him. "I said, wait here," he shouted, sending little specs of spittle flying from his mouth.

Swallowing nervously, Higgins checked his rearview mirror. His heart sank as a police car appeared as a tiny dot in the distance. "But Micky, the Old Bill are–"

Harrington angled the shotgun resting on his lap upwards until the barrel was pointing straight at Higgins' midsection. "Don't make me say it again," he warned, sliding his finger inside the trigger guard.

There was something about the unstable look in Harrington's eyes that made Higgins' sphincter twitch. "Okay, Micky. Whatever you say. Honest."

Harrington opened his door and alighted. With an angry glance at the approaching police car, he tucked the sawn-off against his right leg so as not to draw attention to it.

Higgins opened his door and followed Harrington out, going as far as the Jag's bonnet before stopping. "Please, Micky..." he begged.

Ignoring him, Harrington strode towards the nearest cow.

To Higgins' dismay, the teacher leading the line started walking purposefully towards Harrington, waving his hands like an air traffic controller to get his attention.

"There's nothing you can do, I'm afraid," the man called out, smugly. "The cattle have right of way here."

Jarring to a halt, Harrington turned towards the approaching man. "That a fact?" he demanded, staring at him with contempt.

The teacher placed his hands on his hips and broke into an annoyingly superior smile. "I'm afraid it is," he said, as though addressing the class simpleton.

Mad Micky Harrington raised the shotgun so that it was pointing at the cow's stomach. "Not a problem," he said, pulling the trigger.

The cow bellowed in pain and collapsed in a crumpled heap on the floor. Terrified by the sudden deafening noise, the rest of the herd immediately dispersed, effectively unclogging the road.

"You vile man!" the teacher screamed as Harrington turned to walk away.

Harrington stopped in his tracks, spun to face him. "What did you say?"

The teacher had pulled out his mobile phone and was in the process of dialling 999. "Nothing," he said in a trembling voice. As he spoke, he slid the phone behind his back.

Harrington's eyes narrowed. "Who were you just calling?"

All colour had drained from the teacher's face. "N-no one. I just–"

Harrington aimed the shotgun at the man's lower legs and fired. "I fucking hate grasses," he snarled.

Dropping like a stone, the wounded teacher began writhing around on the floor in agony, clutching at his shattered, blood-soaked legs and screaming for help.

Laughing at him, Harrington quickly ejected the spent cartridge cases and inserted two fresh ones. He was using buckshot rounds, and each shell contained ten 9.1mm ball bearings.

Having watched in stunned disbelief, Higgins ran back to the car, jumped in and slammed the door behind him. "Micky, get back in the fucking car, now!" he bellowed as Harrington drew level with the vehicle.

Ignoring him, Harrington calmly walked forward to meet the approaching police car, which screeched to a halt thirty feet behind the stationary Jag.

In the distance, the steadily increasing volume of multiple sirens told Higgins that numerous police units were converging on them. If they didn't leave straight away, Higgins knew they would be trapped, and they would all end up facing a very long stretch in prison.

Higgins felt a gloved hand on his shoulder. "Stevie, we need to go," G-Man said from the back.

"Be quiet," Higgins snapped, shrugging his hand away. He thought long and hard about abandoning Harrington to his fate, and every fibre in his being screamed at him to do exactly that. The only thing stopping him from driving off was the sure and certain knowledge that, no matter how long it took him, Mad Micky would hunt him down and kill him for deserting him.

Pushing the Rover to its limit, Bradshaw powered the car through the sweeping bend, straight-lining it as much as he possibly could. The Jag had been long gone by the time that the flustered bus driver reversed clear of the junction, and he hadn't held out much hope of catching it up so, when the road straightened out to reveal the stationary getaway car just a few hundred yards ahead, he was absolutely gobsmacked.

Dawkins spoke into the mic. "MP, MP from Juliet One, we've just reacquired the bandit vehicle. It's now stationary in Blake Hall Road, unable to proceed because a herd of cows is blocking the road."

"All received, Juliet One. Are the suspects still with the vehicle?"

Dawkins squinted. "Not sure, MP," he replied. "I'll give you an update as soon as we get closer."

Suddenly, the Jag's passenger door flew open, and a huge white male with a buzzcut lumbered out. With a backward glance at the approaching police car, he strode towards a large cow that was standing in the middle of the road.

"What the hell's he doing?" Dawkins wondered aloud.

Bradshaw had no idea, but he certainly wasn't doing a runner, and that made him feel a little uneasy. "Why isn't he having it on his toes?"

Dawkins toggled the PTT again. "MP, the front passenger's just decamped from the car. He's a stocky IC1, over six foot tall." As he spoke, he unclipped his seatbelt ready to jump out and go after the man as soon as their vehicle stopped.

Up ahead, the robber stopped by the cow and extended his right arm in front of him. The boom that followed was audible, even above the noise of the siren, and the startled cow staggered back a step and dropped to the floor.

"Jesus!" Bradshaw gasped, immediately slamming on the brakes. As neither of them were armed, he couldn't risk going any closer. The Rover skidded to a halt, stopping about thirty feet behind the Jag.

Beside him, Dawkins stiffened. "Oh my God!" he exclaimed, nearly dropping the mic in shock.

Powerless to do anything, the two constables watched in strained silence as the shooter – they could now see he was holding a sawn-off shotgun – turned towards a group of people standing on the left verge. They were mainly school children, but there were a few adults, too. With the barrel still smoking, the gunman pointed his weapon directly at the man who appeared to be in charge.

"Run," Bradshaw implored the man, gripping the steering wheel so hard that his knuckles whitened. "For fuck sake, run."

The robber discharged a second round, which hit the man in the legs, knocking them out from under him. With an agonised scream, the victim toppled to the floor and began writhing around in agony.

Dawkins made to open his door.

"Stay where you are," Bradshaw ordered.

"But we need to help him," Dawkins insisted.

"We won't be able to help anyone if we're dead too," Bradshaw snapped.

The radio crackled. *"Juliet One from MP, can we have a sitrep?"*

With a shaking hand, Dawkins pressed the PTT. "MP, shots fired! Shots fired! We require urgent armed assistance!"

Turning towards the pursuit car, the shooter calmly ejected the spent shells and replaced them with fresh ones.

"Shit!" Bradshaw exclaimed as the gunman suddenly broke into a trot, raising the shotgun to his shoulder as he ran towards them. Ramming the selector into reverse, Bradshaw stamped on the gas pedal and began reversing at high speed.

In films, cops often drove towards an advancing gunman, but in real life that was a suicidal thing to do. There were two bangs in quick succession, and the windshield shattered, spraying Bradshaw with glass fragments. He instinctively ducked down, which caused the rear of the car to fishtail. The Rover was picking up speed, and Bradshaw kept his foot nailed to the floor until he was satisfied that they had put a safe distance between themselves and the madman with the shotgun. Bringing the car to a screeching halt, he squinted through the spiderweb of cracks that now littered the windshield. Punching out a tiny segment of glass, he watched as the gunman ran back to the getaway car and climbed in. Leaving a cloud of smoke in its wake, the battered Jag took off like it was competing in a speedway event.

As soon as it drove off, a woman in her mid-twenties disentangled herself from the frightened children, who were now all huddled together behind a large tree, and rushed over to the injured man, who was still rolling around on the floor.

The Rover's windscreen was too badly damaged for Bradshaw to risk driving it in that state, so he hammered at it with his open hands, trying in vain to push out the glass.

Nothing happened.

"Fuck!" he cursed, pressing the horn on the steering wheel to cancel the two-tones. "Don't just sit there, Alan," he yelled at Dawkins, who had stopped transmitting. "Inform MP that the bandit's on the move again and–"

Dawkins was lying back in his seat, head slumped to one side, eyes half-open. A hole the size of a small coin was clearly visible in the centre of his forehead.

For a moment, Bradshaw couldn't move, couldn't speak, couldn't even breathe. "Oh, my God," he whispered, feeling tears prickle his eyes. Unclipping his seatbelt, he leaned over and examined his colleague, gently placing a hand on the back of his head to check for an exit hole. When he removed it a moment later, it was bright red.

Bradshaw's heart sank. "Hang in there, mate," he said, barely able to speak. With a trembling hand, he gingerly placed two fingers on the side of Dawkins' neck, hoping to find a pulse.

Nothing.

"*Juliet One, Juliet One from MP. Can we have a sitrep, please?*" Was it his imagination, or had a note of anxious tension crept into the operator's usually calm voice?

Bradshaw gently removed the mic from Dawkins' dead hand. "MP from Juliet One, we need an ambulance urgently. Shots fired, shots–" his voice broke off, and he choked back a sob. Taking a deep breath, he shook his head to fight back the tears. "MP, we have two casualties here, one fatal."

Wiping his eyes, Bradshaw looked up in a barely suppressed rage, just in time to see the Jag disappear from sight.

1

Tuesday 24th July 2001
THE RELEASE

John Anthony Spencer had been counting down the days to his release since his incarceration first began, eight miserable years earlier. And now, after having been institutionalised for what seemed like an eternity, he could hardly believe that he was less than an hour away from regaining his freedom.

Although Spencer had served several short terms at Youth Offender's Institutes as a teenager, this had been his first long stretch. It had also been his first time in a high security prison. Looking back now, he realised how easy the YOI regimes of his youth had been in comparison to the gruelling hardships that he'd endured here at Strangeways.

As a convicted rapist, Spencer's early days in general population – or gen-pop as it was known within the system – had been fraught with danger. The other prisoners, who had made it very clear they didn't approve of rapists and kiddie fiddlers, had given him two severe beatings in quick succession, sending him to the hospital wing with broken bones on both occasions.

Fearing that he would find himself on the receiving end of more violence when he returned to gen-pop, Spencer had swallowed his pride and requested a transfer to the Vulnerable Prisoner Unit, more commonly referred to as the nonce's wing. There were no words to describe the hatred he felt for all the sickening paedophiles and other nut-jobs that were housed in the VPU but, as much as they made his skin crawl, none of them posed a threat to him.

Spencer had never been much of a morning person, but he had awoken full of energy and optimism today. Lying on his narrow bed, hands contentedly clasped behind his head, he had spent the last hour and a half running through his plans for the coming days. The reunion was going to be glorious, and he couldn't wait. The thought of seeing her again was the only thing that had kept him sane these past few years.

The VPU's cells were normally unlocked at 7.45 a.m. in order to allow the unit's residents sufficient time to perform their morning ablutions and prepare themselves for their daily activities, which commenced at 8.30 a.m. come rain or shine. However, lockdown always ended slightly earlier for the lucky few who were being shipped out.

On most weekday mornings a trickle of inmates departed HMP Strangeways in order to appear at court, attend medical appointments or be driven to nearby police stations by bored looking detectives who wanted to interview them about outstanding crimes. The vast majority were returned to their cell at the end of the day, but a lucky few, like him, had served their time and were leaving the establishment for good.

At 7.31 a.m. Spencer heard footsteps approaching, and then a key was noisily inserted into the lock of his cell door. He sat up expectantly as the double bolts of the locking mechanism unlatched with a loud clank, and the heavy metal door was opened by a sour-faced screw. Standing ramrod straight, the guard eyed him suspiciously, and then consulted the movement list in his hand to make sure that he had the right convict. Sure enough, Spencer's name was on it, marked up as 'time expired'.

"Come along Spencer," the man said, impatiently beckoning him to stand up and gather his belongings. "Let's be having you."

As someone detained under Prison Rule 43, Spencer had been allocated a cell all to himself, and not sharing had enabled him to minimise his interaction with the loathsome creatures around him. He had deliberately avoided forming friendships of any kind on the VPU because, to his mind, fraternising with *their* kind would have been tantamount to admitting that he was one of them, and that was something he could never accept.

Standing up, Spencer eagerly chucked the few items he deemed worthy of taking with him into a small cardboard box. Without a backwards glance, he followed the burly prison officer through a seemingly endless series of locked doors and gates down to the main reception area.

After being strip-searched, he was placed in a holding cell while the reams of paperwork required for his release were completed. Fortunately, as he was one of only two inmates being shipped out that morning, the process was completed relatively quickly.

Thirty minutes later, he had changed out of his drab prison attire into the new clothes that had been ordered in for him a few days before, and he was back in reception, fidgeting impatiently as he waited to be shown out.

The world-weary officer sitting behind the raised counter shoved a form in front of him and indicated three separate places where he needed to sign, once for his £46 prison discharge grant, a second time for a brown envelope containing a debit card with what remained of his commissary account on it, and a final signature for a travel warrant that could be exchanged for an off-peak ticket at Manchester Piccadilly before making the tiresome journey back to London. He was warned that if he didn't make it to the halfway house by the allotted time it would be considered an escape, as he was still technically in custody whilst out on licence.

"We'll be sure to keep your room vacant for you," the jaded prison officer sneered as Spencer was led away.

"Don't bother," Spencer replied over his shoulder, "I won't be coming back."

The screw rolled his eyes theatrically, before fixing Spencer with a contemptuous glare. "You'll be back," he said with absolute certainty. "You're a predator, Spencer. You like abducting and raping little girls, and you'll soon slip back into your old ways."

Spencer bristled at the insult, but he managed to hold his tongue. There was no way he was going to give the ignorant tosser the satisfaction of provoking a reaction. Besides, whatever anyone else might think, he knew that he hadn't done anything morally wrong. He hadn't abducted Phoebe; they were kindred spirits, and she had been a very willing participant in the elopement. And yes, she had only been fourteen at the time, whereas he had been twenty-four, but age was just a number and they had been deeply in love. Once she had overcome her initial shyness, the sex had been consensual, even though she had given evidence very much to the contrary during his trial. He forgave her for that; her father and the police had obviously conspired to brainwash her until she no longer realised what she was saying.

A wave of cold anger engulfed him as he thought about Phoebe's father, and the cruel pleasure the man had derived from poisoning his daughter's loving relationship with Spencer. Well, the tide was about to turn, and Spencer would soon be in a position to give the vindictive bastard a taste of his own medicine.

As the gate slammed behind him, Spencer emerged into a beautiful July morning. Stepping into the street, he felt as though he was being transported out of an old black and white film into glorious Technicolor. The sun, already toasty warm on his skin, shone down from a velvety blue sky, and it looked as though his first day of freedom was going to be a real scorcher.

The air outside Strangeways smelled noticeably different; it was fresher somehow, less tainted. He paused for a moment, staring up at the high, barbed-wire walls that surrounded the Victorian prison, thinking what a splendid job they did of containing the vile stench of criminality that was so noticeable to those stranded on the other side.

He crossed the road and walked a hundred-yards until he came to a glass panelled bus shelter. After checking the time-table, which wasn't easy to read through the mindless graffiti that had been scribbled over it, he made himself comfortable and waited for the next bus, which was due at eight-thirty.

When it arrived, the green, single-decker was bereft of passengers. The driver was a greasy-haired, middle-aged man with a pale, stubbly face. He gave Spencer a judgemental look as he paid for his ticket, no doubt trying to work out what he had been inside for. Spencer stared back defiantly while he waited for his change, and he felt a petty twinge of satisfaction when the other man broke eye contact first. He stared at the driver, who was starting to get a little nervous, with utter contempt.

Mug. Don't give me no dirty looks. I'm not the one with the dead-end job.

Sitting at the very back of the bus, Spencer studied the outside world with interest during the twenty minute ride. Although everything looked pretty much the same on the surface, he knew that things had moved on and attitudes had changed. For a starter, people had become ultra-sensitive about what poofs and wogs were called, and you couldn't even tell a joke about a thick paddy without being called a racist. What was that all about?

Inevitably, his mind turned to Phoebe Cunningham, and the changes that would have occurred in her life while he'd been away. She would be twenty-two now, which was only a couple of years younger than he'd been when they'd first met. He imagined that the pretty little girl he adored so much had matured into a real stunner. She hadn't contacted him once while he'd been inside, which had really hurt. He forgave her though, knowing that the blame rested solely on her spiteful father's shoulders.

Still, if all went according to plan, he would be seeing Phoebe again soon enough, and there was no doubt in his mind that, once she got over the initial shock, their relationship would pick up exactly where it had left off.

And this time it would be legal.

Ben Cunningham put down the telephone with a heavy heart and turned to his wife, Jessica, who was staring up at him anxiously from the cream leather sofa she was sitting on.

"That was a detective from the police Sapphire unit, calling to inform us that the bastard was released from Strangeways prison a couple of hours ago." He shook his head slowly and then let out a woeful moan. "My God, Jess, what are we going to tell Phoebe?" He had been having nightmares about this moment for weeks now, waking up in the dead of night drenched in sweat, his stomach twisted in knots. The monster who had kidnapped and raped his little princess – not just once, but multiple times during the seven days that he'd held her captive – should have been hanged, or at the very least been given chemical castration. Instead, in their infinite wisdom, the spineless parole board had seen fit to reward his depravity by releasing him when he still had four whole years left to serve on a sentence that, in Ben's opinion, hadn't been anywhere near long enough in the first place. Despite all their objections, and the privately funded campaign they had run to keep him locked up, this disgusting piece of human flotsam was now free to torture another innocent family the way he had the Cunninghams.

"I don't know," Jessica admitted, running her fingers through her long brown hair the way she always did when she was stressed. "Maybe we shouldn't say anything at all."

Ben pressed his lips together in barely contained annoyance. That was so typical of Jessica. When an unpalatable situation arose, her default settings were to either pretend it didn't exist or bury her head in the sand and hope that it would go away. Phoebe was just the same.

The Cunninghams were both in their early fifties, with him a year older than her. He was a successful music mogul with a string of big hits by well-known recording artists under his belt, while she ran a beauty salon franchise in East London.

"We have to tell her something," Ben fretted.

Jessica gave a dismissive wave of her hand. "Oh Ben!" she chided him. "There's no rush. It's not as though the wretched man knows where we live and is going to turn up on our doorstep unannounced." For Phoebe's sake, as soon as the trial had been concluded, they had relocated from Barnsbury in Islington, where they had lived all their lives, to Wanstead in order to make a fresh start.

"So?" he demanded, staring down at her and folding his arms belligerently.

"So," she said, taking a deep breath to centre herself. "I don't want our baby having to think about the piece of shit who..." She couldn't bring herself to use the word 'rape' "...who hurt her any sooner than she has to."

"Neither do I," he said, trying not to let his exasperation show.

"Then we should leave her in peace until she gets back to London on Thursday morning, and then we can tell her all about it." Phoebe was spending a few days at the family's country retreat, a delightful little cottage just outside of Diss in South Norfolk.

"But what if she needs someone to look after her?" he agonised.

"She'll be fine. Besides, Martin's driving up there tomorrow evening. He's going to take her out to dinner and spend the night with her, so stop worrying." Martin was Phoebe's fiancé. They had been together for almost three years now, and Ben knew that he absolutely idolised her.

Ben opened his mouth to object, but she stopped him with a raised hand. "Ben, she's ninety-five miles away from London. They're hardly likely to bump into each other, are they?"

"I suppose," Ben allowed.

"And I can't imagine his release making the national news, can you? It might be of monumental importance to us, but it's not a story that would interest anyone else."

Ben grunted. He knew Jessica was right – she usually was – but it went against the grain to keep secrets from their daughter. Phoebe was their only child, and she was their world. Her suffering was their suffering – and God knew, the odious creature who had abducted and raped her had already caused them all several lifetime's worth of that. The terrifying ordeal had sent Phoebe, who had not been without issues to start with, completely off the rails.

If the truth be told, despite the small fortune that Ben had coughed up for professional counselling, Phoebe had never fully recovered. You only had to look at some of the disturbing paintings she had produced over the years to see that she still carried a great deal of emotional baggage, and he was terrified that Spencer's early release would derail all the hard won progress she had made. "We ought to say something," he insisted, stroking his neatly trimmed beard thoughtfully. "She always knew that he'd get out sooner or later, but now that it's actually happened, she's going to be devastated, and she'll need a lot of support to get through this."

Jessica's mouth formed a perfect O, the way it often did when something caught her by surprise. Unlike Ben, the eternal pragmatist, she hadn't considered the situation from that perspective. "Yes, I suppose you're right," she conceded with a heavy heart. "Maybe I'll call her later this morning."

Ben stiffened, visibly ruffled that his wife intended to exclude him from the conversation. "Shouldn't we drive up there now, and break the news in person?"

Jessica reached out and squeezed his hand affectionately. "Ben, my darling," she said tenderly. "You're a wonderful husband and a loving father, really you are, but sometimes you can be a little *too* intense," which was a polite way of saying that he sometimes behaved like a bull in a china shop when it came to his dealings with Phoebe. "Let me handle this. I promise I'll give you an update as soon as I've spoken to her."

Ben nodded slowly, reluctantly, at the same time pulling his hand away from hers. "Okay," he said, gruffly, "but make sure you tell her I love her, and that I'm right here if she needs me."

2

HAT CAR WEEK

The Homicide Command was part of the Met's Serious Crime Group, having replaced the old Area Major Investigation Pools during the organisational restructuring that had occurred in the wake of the Stephen Lawrence Enquiry in 1999.

The new command was split into three distinct geographical areas: Homicide South, Homicide West, and Homicide East. Each area had nine teams, and each team was led by a Detective Chief Inspector who performed the role of Senior Investigating Officer. Unlike the old AMIP teams, where a small core of permanent staff was supplemented by detectives drafted in from the host division, the new Major Investigation Team – or MIT – model was completely self-contained and relied on having much bigger and better-trained teams.

At one o'clock that afternoon, DCI Jack Tyler, a Senior Investigating Officer for one of the East teams at Hertford House in Barking, emerged from the air-conditioned building into the bright sunlight of a glorious summer's day.

Tyler had just spent an extremely tedious morning sitting in the Police Room on the third floor of The Central Criminal Court, waiting for the verdict to come in on a murder that he'd dealt with in Enfield the previous September. The victim, an elderly man, had been stabbed to death by three teenagers he had disturbed while breaking into his flat during the night.

The jury had retired to consider the evidence at lunchtime the previous Friday, and Tyler was beginning to worry that it didn't bode well if they still hadn't reached a verdict.

Wishing that there was some shade to shelter in until his ride arrived, Tyler loosened his tie and undid the top button of his shirt. That did little to diminish the effects of the early afternoon sun and, within seconds, his shirt was sticking to his back.

Slipping his sunglasses on, Tyler checked his watch impatiently, wondering how much longer she would be. They had arranged to meet at one p.m., which was when the court broke for lunch, and he had expected her to be outside, waiting for him when he emerged.

As if on cue, he spotted a dark blue Volkswagen Sharon driving along Old Bailey towards him, coming from the direction of Ludgate Hill. He raised a hand in greeting and the driver gave a brief flash of the headlights in return. The people carrier stopped outside the Bailey's main entrance, and Tyler jumped into the passenger seat to escape the searing heat. Mercifully, the air conditioning had been cranked up to its maximum setting, and the inside of the car felt wonderfully cool.

"Has anything of interest happened while I've been stuck at court?" he asked the driver, Detective Inspector Susan Sergeant.

"Nothing, so far," she informed him. Today was the start of their latest round of Homicide Assessment Team duties, which came around every ninth week. The role of the Homicide Assessment Team – or HAT as everyone referred to it – was to provide expert advice to divisional officers attending the scenes of potentially suspicious fatalities, or dealing with situations in which someone had been seriously injured and were likely to die. When called out to a crime scene, the HAT car crew – usually a DS and two DCs – would carry out an initial assessment in order to decide whether or not the death was suspicious. If it was, the Homicide Command would take responsibility for the ensuing investigation and the HAT would hold it until the in-frame Murder Investigation Team took over. If it wasn't suspicious, the incident would normally remain with the host borough.

HAT week was always so unpredictable; if Tyler's team were lucky, they might only have a handful of callouts to deal with. If not, they could find themselves being run ragged from start to finish, literally fielding one call after another. It wasn't uncommon for teams to pick up a couple of jobs during busy HAT weeks.

"Where do you want to go for lunch?" Susie asked in her soft Irish lilt. She had just come from New Scotland Yard, where she'd spent the morning obtaining a new warrant card. Although it was nearly three months since she had been promoted to the dizzy rank of Detective Inspector, this had been the first opportunity that she'd had to trade in her trusty old warrant card for one that reflected her new status.

"Let's pop over to Snow Hill. The food's good there and I can get back quickly if I need to."

Susie drove them the short distance to Snow Hill and parked the Sharon in one of the bays opposite the City of London police station, making sure the MPS logbook was visible on the dash. They crossed the road and entered the old-fashioned front office. Susie smiled at the blue shirted constable on desk duty and showed her shiny new warrant card. "Hi, we're Met officers with an ongoing trial at The Bailey. We've parked our vehicle in one of the bays opposite while we grab some lunch. Is that okay?"

The young man behind the counter smiled back at the shapely DI with the pretty face and green eyes, whose strawberry blond hair was worn in a braided ponytail. Slightly taller than average, Susie was wearing a dark blue pinstripe business suit over a light blue blouse and a pair of sensible black shoes. Even in her drab work attire, and without the benefit of make-up, it had to be said that Susan Sergeant was very easy on the eye.

"As long as the logbook's visible, that will be fine, Ma'am," he said.

They thanked him as he buzzed them through.

City of London canteens were generally far superior to their Met counterparts, and this one was no exception. The quality of the food on offer was higher, and the cost of eating was lower. After purchasing their food – he went for the chicken chasseur with plain boiled rice, and she grabbed a tuna salad – they found a table and sat down to eat.

"That's not going to fill you up for long, is it?" Tyler observed, pointing to the salad.

Susie smiled and patted her stomach. "I'm on a new diet and a strict exercise regime," she told him, proudly. "I've cut out alcohol, and only healthy food passes my lips these days."

Susie had recently separated from her husband of six years and, although he would never say it, Tyler suspected that her sudden obsession with training and healthy eating had more to do with a nagging insecurity that her husband had dumped her for another woman because she was no longer attractive than it was about getting fit. He didn't like the idea that she might be punishing herself because she felt the need to impress someone who was clearly unworthy of her affection.

They had just started eating when DS Steve Bull and DC George Copeland strolled into the canteen. Steve was the Case Officer for the job they had at trial, and George was his exhibits officer. After purchasing their lunch, the two men joined them at their table.

Like Susie, Steve had opted for the tuna salad. Predictably, George's tray was fuller. He had purchased a bowl of vegetable soup for starters, a giant portion of lasagne and two slices of garlic bread for his main course, and a large slice of Bakewell tart, which was swimming in a sea of custard, for dessert.

"Are you sure you've got enough food there, George?" Tyler asked, shaking his head in awe.

"I'm a growing lad," George replied, affectionately caressing his bulging stomach, which promptly wobbled like a waterbed.

"That's what I'm worried about," Tyler confessed. "If you grow any bigger we might not be able to get you out of the door and back to court."

"You really could do with losing a few pounds, George," Susie told Copeland, and then her eyes lit up as an idea struck her. "I could write you up a diet plan," she offered. "I've been looking into it lately, and it would be no trouble at all."

George shuddered. "Thanks, but no thanks," he replied, shaking his head emphatically. "I already watch my diet carefully. Besides, as my old mum used to say, celery and lettuce are better suited to bunny rabbits than grown men."

Steve Bull chortled. "George, your idea of watching your diet is to look in the mirror while you shovel doughnuts down your throat."

Responding with a crisply executed two-fingered-salute, George promptly stuffed some more food into his mouth.

The others laughed and, for a while, they all ate in companionable silence.

"So, who's still in with a chance of winning?" Susie asked after finishing her meal. The exhibits officer was running a book on when the verdict would come in. For a pound a go, punters got to predict the day and the hour in which the jury would return. Whoever was nearest won the lot.

"Neither of you, I'm afraid," George gloated. "You predicted the verdict would come in between eleven and twelve today, and the DCI said between twelve and one. Mr Dillon bet it would come in between two and three this afternoon, and I've gone for between three and four. Everyone else is already out, so if the jury doesn't return a verdict by the end of play today the bet's off and everyone gets their quid back."

"Let's hope they don't decide until tomorrow, then," Steve said, grinning.

Susie turned to Tyler. "How much longer do you think the judge will wait before he indicates a willingness to accept a majority?"

Once it became apparent that the jury was unable to reach a unanimous verdict, the judge would have no choice but to instruct them that he was prepared to accept a majority of ten against two. If that failed, and the outcome was a hung-jury, they would be left facing the unpleasant prospect of a retrial.

Tyler had been wondering the same thing all morning. "I think he'll give the instruction first thing tomorrow if there's no verdict before then," he said. "My gut feeling is that the jury are already agreed on the first two defendants, but are struggling with the third."

The third defendant, Jared Henshaw, had been seventeen years old at the time of the murder, and he was the youngest of the three boys standing trial. His defence had been that, although he had broken into the flat with his co-defendants intending to steal, it had come as a complete surprise to him when they stabbed Eric Lane, a seventy-eight-year-old war veteran, after he woke up and tried to stop them.

The Crown had countered that this was a classic case of joint enterprise. Henshaw, an unsavoury character who, despite his youth, already had a string of convictions for robbery, burglary and carrying offensive weapons, had been fully aware that his companions were carrying knives, and it must have been obvious to him that they would resort to violence if disturbed. If that were the case, the rule of joint enterprise meant that he was equally complicit in the murder, despite not having been one of the actual stabbers.

"Hopefully, we'll get all three down," Steve Bull said, doing his best to sound positive.

They were all patiently waiting for George to finish his dessert when Tyler's mobile went off. He answered the call, listened pensively for a few seconds, glanced at his watch, which told him it was one-fifty, and then hung up. "That was Debbie," he told the others. Debbie Brown was the Family Liaison Officer, and she had remained over at The Bailey with the victim's family. "The usher just gave her a tug and said that the jury's reached a verdict. It looks like we'll be going back into court at two-o'clock sharp, so we'd better make a move."

As everyone stood up, Steve Bull grinned nervously. "I always hate this bit," he said to no one in particular.

"You know what I hate?" George responded, hurriedly spooning the last of his Bakewell tart into his mouth. "I hate the fact that Tony Dillon's going to win twenty-five quid."

———

Spencer stood in the open doorway, surveying his new abode and feeling somewhat underwhelmed. The small room on the second floor of the halfway house was dull and tatty, and the mish-mash of furniture it contained had definitely seen much better days. Overall, it didn't feel like much of an upgrade from the prison cell he'd vacated that morning. On the bright side, there were no obvious signs of damp and everything appeared spotlessly clean.

A UPVC window was set in the far wall of the oblong shaped room. It was fitted with blinds instead of curtains and, unlike everything else in the room, they appeared relatively new.

A single bed, consisting of a wafer-thin mattress on top of a cheap metal frame, took up the wall space beneath the window. Spencer turned his nose up, thinking that a bed of nails would probably be more comfortable.

There was also a shoddy bedside table on which an archaic reading lamp with a wonky purple shade had been deposited, a medium-sized chest of drawers, and a lopsided wardrobe that seemed to be leaning against the wall for support.

Closing the door behind him with his heel, Spencer dumped his cardboard box on top of the chest of drawers and then hung his jacket up in the wardrobe, which rocked unsteadily as he opened it. He would need to place something underneath one end to even it up, he realised, scouring the room for something he could use. In the end, he tore off a section of cardboard from the box he'd brought with him and folded it into the shape of a wedge. Once he'd attended to the wobbly wardrobe issue, Spencer sat down on the bed, which was even harder than anticipated. He prodded it several times, but there was no give in the lumpy mattress. "Don't think I'll be getting a comfortable night's sleep on you," he said with a grimace.

Looking up, he noticed a chipped washbasin in the corner, hidden in a recess behind the door. That was good. At least he could have a wash and a shave – or a piss if he was feeling particularly lazy – without having to traipse all the way down the other end of the corridor to use the communal bathroom.

Stifling a yawn, Spencer eased himself to his feet and ran his fingers through the bristles of his number two haircut. He spent a few pointless seconds staring out of the window onto the street below, then ambled over to the sink. He turned the cold tap, which was stiff from lack of use. At first, nothing happened. Then there was an ominous rattle in the pipes, followed by a gurgle in the tap. After several seconds, a strong jet of dirty brownish water gushed out. Spencer let it run until the water's colour returned to normal, then cupped his hands together and splashed his face several times.

A good sized mirror hung above the sink, but a previous occupant had punched it at some stage during their tenancy, creating an intricate web of cracks that radiated out from the central impact point. Spencer stared at his fractured image, which he thought provided a poignant reminder of how broken he had felt inside since being separated from Phoebe.

With no towel in sight, Spencer dried his face on his sleeve and his hands on his trousers, before returning to the lumpy bed. This place might not be the Ritz, he decided, but it was free, and it would do him for a few nights while he got his life in order. Closing his eyes, he decided to take an afternoon nap and recharge his batteries.

An hour later, he was rudely awoken by a loud knock on his door.

Dragging himself into a sitting position, Spencer wiped his bleary eyes with his knuckles, yawned, and then slowly stood up.

There was another knock, followed by an impatient shout. "Oi, open the bloody door."

Scratching his head, which felt irritatingly itchy in the heat, Spencer slouched across the room and cautiously opened the door a couple of inches. Peering through the narrow gap, he was confronted by the miserable looking guy from reception. Staring in at him with shifty eyes, the sour faced man informed Spencer that there was a visitor waiting for him in the office downstairs.

Spencer's visitor turned out to be his newly assigned probation officer, a runt of a man called Clive Dibney, whose ridiculous comb-over and disgusting habit of nervously licking his lips in a lizard-like manner every few seconds made him look more like a sex offender than Spencer ever could.

Inviting Spencer to take the chair opposite, Dibney explained that he'd called around to introduce himself and go through the long list of 'dos' and 'don'ts' of being on licence with him.

Leaning back in his chair, Spencer cracked his knuckles, making the air inside his joints pop as loudly as the chewing gum bubbles he'd blown as a kid. "You didn't waste any time, did you?" he observed, sullenly.

Dibney opened his notebook. "I try to be efficient," he said, ignoring the dig. He then proceeded to explain that, under the Sex Offenders Act, Spencer was required to register with the police within three days of being released from prison. In addition to providing his new address, he was also obliged to supply the authorities with a host of other information, including his national insurance number, his banking details, and even his passport number if he had one. Once registered, Dibney explained in his unpleasant orotund voice, a member of the Public Protection Unit would make an appointment to visit him at home to verify that he was actually living there, and to conduct an informal assessment. They would want to know if any children under the age of twelve were living at the address, Dibney told him, as if that were a likely scenario in a halfway house for ex-convicts.

"Yeah, the paedophile in room four is keeping one as a pet," Spencer responded with a cruel smirk, only to receive a lecture on how inappropriate such unsavoury comments were, especially coming from someone whose current position in society was so precarious.

When the tedious meeting was finally over – Spencer felt like it had gone on forever – Clive Dibney's parting words were ominous. "Remember," he warned, waving an admonishing finger at Spencer. "You're out on licence. If you don't toe the line, it *will* be revoked, and you *will* be recalled to prison."

The stinging words that the cynical screw had taunted him with that morning came flooding back, making Spencer's blood run cold.

We'll be sure to keep your room vacant for you...

———

"I'm delighted that the jury saw through the defendants' lies and unanimously convicted all three," Jack Tyler told the assembled group of reporters, who were clustered around him on the pavement opposite the Bailey's main entrance. It was nearing five, but the heat was still surprisingly oppressive. He had removed his sunglasses to make the address, and was now fighting the urge to raise a hand to shield his eyes from the bright sunshine. "This result won't bring Eric Lane back, but at least it will help his grieving family to take their first painful steps towards finding closure."

Cameras clicked away as photographers jostled for the best position. Jack Tyler was six-foot-four inches tall, with a strong jaw, broad shoulders, short brown hair, and bright blue eyes. He had great presence, and the cameras liked him.

"Sadly, the victim was frail and elderly, and therefore unable to defend himself but, in his prime, I suspect Eric Lane would have made short work of all three assailants. He was a brave man, a war hero who risked his life to protect the rights and freedoms of people like you and me. It's a travesty that a man who did so much for his country should come to such an untimely end, stabbed to death inside his own home by these vile cowards. Thankfully, today's conviction will prevent them from terrorising the public for many years to come."

Standing a few feet away from the reporters, George Copeland turned to Susie Sergeant and Steve Bull. "You've got to admit," he said with undisguised admiration, "he certainly knows how to work the crowd, does our Jack."

"He does," Susie agreed, "but he's far too forthright."

Steve Bull shook his head. "Nah, he just tells it the way it is. The press loves him for it."

"The press might," Susie said, "but the Mandarins at The Yard don't. The world is changing, and he's not politically correct enough for their liking. It's why he's still only a DCI when he should be at least one rank higher."

When Tyler finished speaking, he handed over to Debbie Brown who, in her capacity as the Family Liaison Officer, began reading an impact statement from the deceased's family.

Satisfied that he was no longer needed, Tyler slipped away to rejoin the others. "Right, apart from my not winning the money for guessing when the jury would come in, I think this has been a pretty good day," he said with a smile.

"It has," Steve Bull agreed enthusiastically. "So let's indulge ourselves in a time-honoured tradition and pop over the road for a quick celebratory drink."

"I'm up for that," Copeland beamed, earning a look of disapproval from Susie.

"George, do you have any idea how many empty calories there are in a pint of beer? It won't do your diet any good."

Tyler screwed his face up. In his experience, there was no such thing as a quick celebratory drink, not when coppers were involved. "I'd love to, Stevie. But, unlike you, the three of us are on call tonight."

As Case Officer, Bull had been excused from HAT duties until the weekend.

George's face dropped and, when he spoke, there was an air of desperation in his voice. "But on the duty roster we're shown as being at court tomorrow," he protested, sounding absolutely crestfallen. "Surely we won't be expected to come back into work if anything happens tonight?"

Bull couldn't hide his disappointment, either. "Surely one won't hurt?" he pleaded. "Tony Dillon's on his way up to meet us. I phoned him earlier to arrange it, and he'll have the right hump if only I turn up."

Tyler sighed. "Alright, but it will literally only be for one. After that, everyone who's on HAT week goes on the lemonade."

"Deal," Bull said, smiling.

"I hate lemonade," George muttered under his breath.

3

SKIPPY

In need of some fresh air, Spencer followed the jobsworth probation officer into the street. As the man got into his car, a little Renault Clio, Spencer leaned against the wall and lit up a smoke.

Dibney waved at him as he pulled away, and Spencer acknowledged this with a grudging nod of his head. Taking a long drag, he closed his eyes and enjoyed a few peaceful moments basking in the late afternoon heat while he pondered his next move. He needed to find out what was going on with Phoebe, which meant touching base with Skippy. After finishing his cigarette, he took a slow walk down to Shoreditch High Street. From there, he caught a bus over to Stratford.

Alighting the bus outside the Stratford Centre, Spencer crossed the road and set off along West Ham Lane. He turned left when he reached the junction with Adworth Road, which was directly opposite the local cop shop, a dour unfriendly building that brought back a host of unpleasant memories.

About halfway along Adworth Road, he came to a mid-terraced

house that had been converted into two flats. There were two street doors. The one on the right, which belonged to the upstairs flat, was a shiny new PVC jobbie, whereas the door on the left, which led into Skippy's ground floor flat, was a manky old wooden thing that looked like it was infested with woodworm and would fall off its hinges if anyone knocked too hard.

A small clump of weed-infested grass masqueraded as a front garden, but it had mostly withered and died from the extreme summer heat. Opening the rickety wooden gate, which creaked like an out of tune violin, he rapped out a tune on the flaking wooden door and waited.

When no one answered the door, Spencer cupped his hands against the grimy bay window and peered in. There was no sign of movement in the living room, and no sound coming from within, which was highly unusual because Skippy had always hated silence.

Cursing under his breath, Spencer rapped on the ancient wooden door again, only louder this time. He was on the point of giving up and heading back to Hackney, when he heard a metallic rustling coming from inside as the security chain was slipped off its latch. A second later, the door creaked open a couple of inches and an eye cautiously appeared in the gap. It then opened wider to reveal an unhealthy looking man with short brown hair and a badly pock-marked face. On seeing Spencer, he broke into a wide grin, exposing a row of crooked teeth.

Spencer winked at him. "Alright, Skippy?"

With a loud whoop, Tommy 'Skippy' Skipton lunged forward and wrapped his spindly arms around his cousin's shoulders. "Spence! I can't believe it!" he said, pulling him in tight. Then, pushing him away, he held him at arm's length to get a better look. "You're finally out!"

Before Spencer could reply, Skippy started dragging him inside, glancing nervously over his shoulder as he went. "Let's get away from prying eyes," he said, slamming the door behind them the moment they crossed the threshold.

Spencer noticed how jittery his cousin seemed. "What's the matter, you afraid to be seen with me or something?"

Skippy shook his head. "Nah, nothing like that. It's just that I owe money to some pretty scary people at the moment, and I don't want them seeing me until I've got the readies to pay them back."

Spencer grinned. Some things never changed. "I was beginning to think that you'd gone out and I'd had a wasted journey," he admitted, patting his cousin on the back.

"Nah," Skippy said as he led Spencer into the cluttered kitchen, which looked like it hadn't been cleaned or tidied in months. "I was just having an afternoon nap before starting work this evening."

Spencer grinned knowingly. "Yeah, right. You were just knocking one out, more like," he said, jerking his hand up and down quickly several times.

Skippy looked away, shamefaced.

"I knew it!" Spencer cackled. "I hope you washed your hands before opening the door."

"Leave it out," Skippy said, trying his best to sound indignant. "I was having a nap, not a wank."

"Whatever you say," Spencer retorted, still laughing.

Skippy put the kettle on and removed a couple of chipped mugs from a cupboard above the cooker. The insides were heavily tea stained and clearly in need of a good scrub. "Still take your tea white with two sugars?" he asked, flinging a teabag into each cup.

Spencer shook his head. "I've given up sugar," he said, proudly. "Just a dribble of milk will do for me."

Once the kettle had boiled, they carried their drinks through to the cramped lounge and settled down to catch up. Whatever Skippy's failings were, he was the only person who had bothered to visit Spencer during his incarceration. More importantly, Skippy had been keeping tabs on Phoebe for him during the months leading up to his release.

They spent a little time reminiscing about the good old bad old days; boasting about the crimes they'd gotten away with, and ruing the ones they'd done time for. The banter made Skippy feel so nostalgic that he suggested they pop along to the nearby Stratford Centre to celebrate Spencer's newfound freedom properly with a little spot of shoplifting.

An hour later, Skippy was the proud owner of a pair of Wrangler jeans, next season's West Ham United football jersey, and an expensive pair of Adidas training shoes, all of which were now crammed into the sports holdall that he'd pilfered from the first shop they'd visited.

Spencer hadn't been anywhere near as prolific as his light-fingered cousin, and the only two items to have caught his eye were a large kitchen knife and a one-litre bottle of Jack Daniels.

"Are you hungry?" Skippy asked as they emerged from the artificial glow of the shopping centre into the bright glare of the late afternoon sun.

Spencer shrugged. He hadn't really thought about food. "A bit, I suppose."

Skippy, who was always hungry, patted him on the back. "Good. Let's go and grab some nosebag."

Skippy guided him to a rundown pizzeria that was nestled between two equally unappealing fast food establishments in a little parade of shops about halfway along the High Road, explaining that this was where he spent his evenings working as a delivery driver.

Pausing by the entrance, Spencer shot Skippy a questioning look. Not only did the place have filthy windows and peeling paintwork, but the pungent smell of stale urine coming from the doorway was overpowering.

"Don't look at me like that," Skippy admonished. Then, with a conciliatory shrug: "I know it don't look like much, but the food's not *that* bad, and I get a whopping staff discount."

As he pushed the door open, Spencer mumbled something under his breath about breaking Skippy's legs if he contracted food poisoning, but it was all bluster. The truth was, with only his discharge grant to keep him going until he could sign on and start claiming unemployment benefit, he really couldn't afford to be fussy about where he ate.

The unshaven Turk behind the counter looked up as they entered, frowning when he spotted Skippy. "Bit early for your shift, aren't you?" he said in heavily accented English.

Skippy grinned. "Not here to work," he replied, ushering Spencer over to a dirty Formica table at the back. "Thought I'd treat my favourite cousin to a spot of grub at the best pizza place in Stratford."

The man behind the counter snorted at the empty compliment. "The cheapest, you mean," he complained under his breath.

After eating their fill of pizza, which Spencer reluctantly admitted had actually been quite nice, Skippy took him to a nearby council estate, where they clubbed together to purchase a bag of ganja from a local supplier. The deal done, they wandered into a nearby park and found themselves a nice quiet bench in the shade, where they settled down to enjoy their weed in peace.

"God, I've missed this stuff," Spencer wheezed, exhaling a thick plume of smoke.

Skippy seemed genuinely surprised to hear that. "Are you seriously telling me you couldn't get your hands on a bit of blow while you were inside?"

Spencer responded with a non-committal shrug. It wasn't too difficult if you were in gen-pop, as long as you knew the right people to ask, but it was nigh on impossible in the VPU, where security was much tighter. As he didn't want Skippy knowing that he'd been on the nonce's wing, he promptly changed the subject. "Come on then, tell me what's been going on with Phoebe."

Skippy quickly brought him up to speed, telling him what Phoebe had been doing with her life since his last visit to Strangeways, three weeks earlier. When he finished his narration, he withdrew a tatty exercise book from the back pocket of his jeans and handed it to Spencer with something akin to reverence. "I've been saving this up as a present for when you got out," he announced.

"What the fuck is it?" Spencer demanded, eyeing the grubby, dog-eared book suspiciously. A cursory examination revealed that it contained page after page of Skippy's barely legible scrawl.

"Those are my notes," Skippy replied, as though it should have been obvious. "Everything you need to know about the Cunninghams is in there. Their new address, the registration numbers of all their fancy cars, even the details of the stupid cottage they've got in Norfolk, which is where your girlfriend is now by the way, and all the remote places she visits to do her stupid painting."

Spencer's face darkened. "I thought Phoebe was here, in London."

"Nope. She buggered off to Norfolk three days ago."

"How quickly can you get hold of a set of wheels for me?"

Skippy seemed puzzled by the question. "Dunno, Why?"

"Because I want to find her as soon as possible, you dickhead. Why do you think?"

Skippy placed a hand on his arm. "Spence, you've only just come out. Trust me, mate, I'm as keen as you are to get on with this, but we need to wait until next week before making our move, just in case the Old Bill's watching you."

Spencer shrugged the hand, and the advice, off. "Fuck the Old Bill. I ain't afraid of them."

"I know you're not, but if you do something rash now, we'll both end up doing porridge, not just you."

Spencer glared at him. "Listen, Skip, the only thing that kept me going while I was doing bird was the thought of holding Phoebe in my arms again. It's been eight years, mate. Eight-fucking-years!" Spencer bared his teeth in anger. "Don't you think that's long enough?"

"I suppose so," Skippy conceded, "but I still think it would be better to wait until next week. By then, that tosser from the probation service will have forgotten all about you."

"No point in waiting," Spencer said, tersely. "I want her back in my arms before the week's out. Speaking of the job, have you found us somewhere quiet to hide up until her old man coughs up the ransom money?"

"Well..." Skippy began, but then floundered.

Spencer's eyes narrowed. Folding his arms, he levelled an accusatory stare at his cousin. "Well... what?" he demanded.

"I've found somewhere that would be perfect."

"But...?"

Skippy swallowed hard. "But it's not exactly local."

Spencer could feel himself getting angry. "What the fuck are you talking about?"

"Okay, so, here's the thing," Skippy said, speaking so quickly that his words all seemed to merge into each other with no discernible breaks. "Most weekends, Phoebe buggers off to that poxy cottage in Norfolk. Sometimes her fancy boyfriend goes with her, but mostly she goes alone. Over the last couple of months, I've got to know the area pretty well from following her, and I'm telling you, Spence, it's a hell of a lot quieter out in the sticks than it is down here in London."

Spencer opened his mouth to protest, but Skippy cut him off with a raised hand. "Just hear me out," he insisted. "That cottage of theirs is in the middle of nowhere. There are no other houses anywhere near it, and there's no Old Bill for miles around. If we grab her there, we won't have to worry about making a noise or being interrupted. I've done a bit of snooping around, and I've found a deserted barn a couple of miles away from the cottage. There are dozens of similar places scattered around the countryside, to be fair, but this one is by far the best. Honestly, Spence, it's bloody well perfect for what we've got in mind. It's all there in my notes."

Spencer shook his head. Skippy was a good lad, and he meant well, but he really wasn't equipped for thinking. That was Spencer's job. "I don't give a toss how quiet it is up there, I don't like the idea of grabbing Phoebe from a place I've never even seen."

"Yeah, granted, but if we don't grab her until next week, I can take you up there beforehand, show you around the place."

Spencer didn't like the sound of that. "Nah, I reckon we'll be better off snatching her from the family gaff, here in London."

Skippy hawked up a huge goblet of phlegm, chewed on it for a moment, and then spat it out. "At least have a think about it," he pleaded. "Truth be told, Spence, I'm not comfortable with the idea of breaking into the Cunningham's place in Wanstead. I mean, it's a fucking fortress, mate. It's got electric gates and a fancy CCTV system, and there's probably a panic alarm inside, too."

"Fair point," Spencer accepted grudgingly, "but, how do you know this little cottage of theirs ain't got CCTV and panic alarms fitted as well?"

"Trust me, it ain't."

Spencer spat contemptuously. "Oh yeah, and how would you know?"

A sly smile crept onto Skippy's face. "Because, when she went out for a walk one night, I broke in and had a little mooch around. I'm telling you, Spence, there's fuck all security, and the locks are ancient. The back door was a piece of piss to open. And, like I said, there's no nosey neighbours around to raise the alarm, so even if she kicks off when we grab her–"

"My Phoebe won't kick off," Spencer insisted, indignantly. "If anything, she'll be over the moon to see me." At least he hoped that would be the case. "Do you know when she's coming back to London?"

Skippy inserted a grubby finger into his right nostril, had a good rummage around. "She's due back the day after tomorrow," he said, removing his finger and examining the glob that was now affixed to the end. "Why?"

"Why?" Spencer spluttered, wondering if his idiot cousin had just picked the remaining bit of his brain out through his nose. "Because I want to bloody well see her again, that's why." He snatched the joint from Skippy's hand and took a long drag on it. When he spoke again, his voice was a smoke-induced rasp. "Look, I ain't making no promises, but I'll think about what you've said, okay?"

Skippy was delighted. "Trust me, Spence, we've got a much better chance of getting away with this job if we pull it in Norfolk. I really don't fancy our chances if we try and nab her here, in London."

"Maybe you're right," Spencer conceded as he passed the joint back to his cousin, "but I don't want to wait another week." As he exhaled the smoke from his lungs, he broke into a coughing fit. "I don't think I can."

Skippy shuffled across to him and patted his back until the coughing stopped. "Look, Spence, I know it ain't been easy for you, but you've already waited eight long years; surely you can hang on for a few more days?"

Spencer shrugged once, a short sharp movement. "Like I said, I'll think about it."

Squeezing his shoulder, Skippy glanced down at the cheap Casio on his wrist and grimaced. "Fuck, is that the time already? I've got to go mate or I'll be late for work."

———

Left alone with his thoughts, Spencer found himself becoming increasingly morose. As much as he hated to admit it, he knew that Skippy was right, and that it made far more sense to wait a week before going after Phoebe, but the urge to be reunited with her was so all-consuming that he doubted he'd be able to wait another day, let alone a whole bloody week.

A creature of habit, Spencer decided to do what he always did when things got him down; he would go on a bender. While drowning his sorrows wouldn't solve anything, it would take his mind off things for a few hours, and that was better than nothing. As he unwrapped the bottle of JD and stared at it longingly, a little voice in the back of his mind cautioned him against drinking in public. If he was going to get bladdered, it would be much wiser to do it in the safety of his room, where he couldn't get himself into trouble. He always became punchy when he was drunk, and he couldn't afford to get himself nicked for fighting, not on the day that he'd been released from prison.

You'll be back in your room within the hour, just hang on till then...

Like that was going to happen. With a heavy sigh, he unscrewed the lid and gulped down several large swigs in quick succession. He paused for breath, knowing that he ought to stop while he was still in control, but he really didn't want to.

Fuck it!

He guzzled down some more, letting the whiskey stoke his anger.

When he lowered the bottle, Spencer was surprised to discover that he'd already consumed over a third of its contents. Against his better judgement, he allowed himself a final mouthful before reluctantly returning the bottle to its carrier bag.

It was getting late, and Spencer decided to make his way back to the halfway house in Hackney. He stood up, tottered unsteadily for a moment, and then set off towards the bus stop.

As he wandered along West Ham Lane, he spotted a little olde worlde confectioners that had been there for as long as he could remember. Wedged between a stationers and a dry cleaners, it seemed totally out of place, like a throwback to a bygone age. He had often popped in there after school to purchase – well, to steal – sweets and cigarettes.

Crossing the road, he stood outside the shop and stared at the old fashioned display inside the window. Childhood memories came flooding back, drowning him in nostalgia, and he found himself wondering whether the grumpy old git who had owned the shop when he was a kid was still alive. It seemed highly unlikely. The cantankerous old codger was almost certainly six feet under by now, feeding the worms.

For old time's sake, he decided to pop in and have a quick nose around.

The middle-aged woman standing behind the counter glanced up as the bell above the door tinkled, and smiled a polite greeting at him. "Evening," she said as the door closed.

"What happened to the old bloke who used to own this place a few years back?" he slurred.

The woman's brow creased in thought. "Mr Weissenberg, you mean? He's been dead for years now, gawd rest his soul."

Spencer grunted. "Figured as much," he said.

The shop hadn't changed one bit inside; not the layout, not the décor, not even some of the stock from the looks of it. Everything was just as he remembered it, right down to the old-fashioned till. The shelves behind the serving counter were stacked with jars of sweets: Dolly Mixtures, Sour Dummies, Milk Bottle Gums, Large Foam Shrimps, Rock Fruit Candy. There were even some strips of Oor Wullie's Highland Toffee. He broke into a wide grin when he spotted the Crazy Dips, giant Gobstoppers and Pez dispensers, complete with refill packs.

Moving on, he spent a few moments browsing through the various magazines, and was disappointed not to find any copies of *Mayfair* or *Penthouse* hidden amongst the other reading material on offer. Then, turning his mind to the subject of snacks, he ummed and ahhed over whether to get an extra-large bag of his favourite candy coated chocolates or a super-sized bag of crisps. In the end, he decided to live dangerously and purchase both.

With a final glance at the top shelf, just to satisfy himself that there really were no girlie mags lurking beneath the issues of *Model Railway Weekly* and *Knitting For Beginners* on display, he paid for his items and left.

4

MR BEARDY

There were already half a dozen people standing in a loosely formed queue when Spencer arrived at the bus stop. He slotted into place behind two teenage girls who were having an animated conversation about boys and fashion, giggling every few seconds in a manner that he found extremely annoying. Phoebe had never been that immature – or that shallow.

To ease the boredom, he ripped open the bag of cheese and onion crisps and began noisily munching his way through them.

Just beyond the giggling girls, three scruffily dressed Eastern Europeans were talking in a language he didn't understand. Judging from the dried paint and plaster splashes on their clothing, he guessed they were heading home after a hard day's labouring. They looked completely shattered, and he shook his head at their stupidity, wondering why anyone would bother putting themselves through such purgatory, especially as they were probably only being paid the minimum wage.

Mugs.

That was no way for a man to live his life, flogging himself into an early grave just to make some rich bastard like Ben Cunningham even richer.

Standing at the front of the queue, a fragile old lady with a wrinkly face and blue rinse hairstyle was squinting at the timetable like a female version of *Mr Magoo*. She reminded Spencer of his dearly departed mother, who had worn her hair in a similar fashion.

Raising the bag to his lips, Spencer poured the last few crisps into his mouth and then, ignoring the nearby bin, casually tossed the bag onto the floor. He gave each of his fingers a good suck, but they still felt greasy, so he wiped them down the sides of his new trousers.

Bus stops are transient places, with people constantly coming and going, and the latest arrival was a harried looking man in a dishevelled pinstripe suit. Looking like a heart attack waiting to happen, the obese man was panting heavily from having just waddled across Romford Road. Full of self-importance, he cut in front of the old blue rinse, who was still trying to decipher the timetable. Ignoring her indignant, "Well, really!" the fat man stood with his back to her, running a pudgy finger down the bus timetable until he found the information he sought. Having read it, he glanced at his fancy watch and let out a frustrated huff.

A double-decker glided to a halt, and its electric doors opened with a soft hiss. The diesel fumes spewing from its rattling exhaust were so overpowering that they set Spencer off on a prolonged fit of coughing. At least, during his incarceration, the chronic asthma that he'd suffered from since his childhood had improved. He would have to remember to take his inhaler everywhere with him now that he was out.

The two giggly girls and the Eastern Europeans clambered aboard the bus, and a dribble of people alighted from the exit doors halfway along. Spencer watched in fascination as they dispersed to go their separate ways.

A few moments later, the doors closed with a gentle swish and the bus pulled away, kicking out more pollution. Spencer fanned his nose as he watched it go.

The unrelenting heat was giving him a hellish thirst. Wiping his brow, he removed the whiskey bottle from its carrier bag, unscrewed the top, and took a large swig. Letting out a satisfied 'Ahhh,' he wiped his mouth along the back of his hand.

The obese man had wandered away from the bus stop and was now talking loudly into his mobile. His plethora of chins wobbled furiously as he complained about the injustice of having had to work late. He sounded like a petulant child, and Spencer was sorely tempted to give him a slap and steal his phone, just because he could. Instead, he let out a long, loud burp, which he projected in the fat man's direction.

The blue rinse granny immediately gave him a sharp look of disapproval, and Spencer responded with a mischievous grin, which he hoped she would reciprocate. Instead, she looked away, raising her chin in haughty disdain.

The smile faded from his face. *Jesus! It's a good job I didn't fart*!

Removing the bag of candy coated chocolates from his pocket, he ripped a corner off with his teeth and stumbled over to join her. "Have a sweet, granny," he slurred, holding the bag out and hoping to make amends for his earlier crudeness. He hadn't meant to offend her. He actually liked old people. "Try a red one," he advised. They were his favourites.

"No, thank you," she replied, wrinkling her nose at the strong smell of whiskey wafting off of him.

"Go on," he insisted, nudging her encouragingly. "You'll like them." He shoved the bag right in her face.

The old woman recoiled in alarm. "I said, no thank you," she replied, frostily.

With a 'suit yourself' shrug, Spencer lowered the sweets. Then he remembered that his mother had always enjoyed a little tipple during the evening. Tucking the sweets back into his pocket, he held up the whiskey bottle and grinned at her. "Perhaps you'd prefer a little drop of this, instead?" he said with a conspiratorial wink. "It'll put hairs on your chest."

"Leave the poor woman alone," the obese man barked from behind. "Can't you see you're upsetting her?"

Spencer whirled on him. Holding the bottle by its neck, he raised it threateningly, and took a half-step towards the man. "I'll upset you in a minute, you fat fucker," he snarled.

As Spencer had known he would, the man immediately backed down.

Laughing drunkenly, Spencer staggered over to a low-level wall a few feet behind the bus stop and slouched down against it. "Wanker," he muttered under his breath.

An old AEC Routemaster pulled up, its 1960s built engine chugging loudly. The fat man gave Spencer a look of pure hatred as he dragged his great bulk onto the iconic London bus, barging his way through a small group of passengers who were trying to get off. As it pulled away, the man raised his middle finger at Spencer and shouted, "Drunken tosser!"

Spencer glowered back at him with malevolence.

The blue rinse granny was all alone at the bus stop now, and he caught her shooting him the odd furtive glance, clearly worried that he might bother her again.

A few seconds later, a portly man with reddish-brown hair and a matching beard joined her at the bus stop. He was like a bearded version of the Mr Men, and there was something about him that made Spencer think of the *Flash Gordon* actor, Brian Blessed. Clad in a dark suit, Mr Beardy carried the obligatory office worker's briefcase like a personalised ball and chain. Taking up station behind the blue rinse granny, he nodded politely when she glanced back at him.

Spencer experienced an irrational twinge of resentment at the warm smile she gave the newcomer. *I bet she would have accepted a sweet from him.*

Finally, the bus he was waiting for arrived.

As soon as the doors opened, old blue rinse and Mr Beardy shuffled aboard, their travel cards held at the ready. Spencer lazily pushed himself away from the wall and followed them on. As he was purchasing a ticket from the driver, a scruffy couple in their twenties got on behind him and, from the sound of it, they were in the middle of a heated domestic.

"If you're so fed up with me making you the same sandwiches for lunch every day, you should get off your big fat arse and make your own," she scolded, "instead of sitting there every night with your feet up, watching bloody television while I slave away in the kitchen. Your mum might have been soppy enough to put up with that shit, but don't you kid yourself that I will."

Spencer would never have permitted a woman to speak to him that disrespectfully, but the timid man just seemed to soak up the abuse without batting an eyelid.

"All I said was that it would make a pleasant change to have something other than cheese and ham," he said, patiently. "It doesn't mean that I'm *not* grateful."

Spencer briefly glanced over his shoulder at the man, willing him to stand up for himself and stop acting like a doormat.

Give her a slap and put her in her place, you mug.

The blue rinse granny and Mr Beardy had already gone up to the top deck, and Spencer joined them there a few seconds later. To his relief, the henpecked man and his bullying wife opted to remain below.

There were eight other people on the upper deck when Spencer arrived. Two teenage boys were sitting at the front, talking quietly. A middle-aged Sikh in a dark blue turban sat a couple of rows behind them, reading an evening paper. Mr Beardy had taken the seat directly opposite the stairs, and he was staring out of the window, content to watch the world go by. The blue rinse granny had taken the seat directly behind him and was busy tucking her purse back into her bag.

Sitting on the right, behind the stairs, two young women who were discussing make-up, which seemed befitting as their faces were plastered with the stuff. Both were attractive, but the brunette in the aisle seat had the edge over her red-haired companion.

After eight long years without a woman, the muskiness of her scent was making him feel dizzy with desire. Allowing himself a lascivious grin, Spencer decided that he would store that smell, along with an image of her pretty face, in his wank bank for later.

Lastly, an elderly, unshaven man in a flat cap was slumped against the window in one of the rear seats, snoring loudly. Spencer wondered how long ago the old codger had dozed off, and he found himself fretting that the poor old boy would miss his stop if he didn't wake up.

Spencer slid into a seat on the left side of the bus, directly opposite the girls. Resting the whiskey bottle on the seat beside his left leg, he made himself comfortable. A few seconds later, the bus moved away with a sudden lurch.

With nothing more interesting to occupy his mind, Spencer found himself becoming more and more intrigued by the girl's banal conversation, and he wondered if this was the sort of tripe that Phoebe and her friends discussed. If it was, he'd soon put a stop to it. Once he was back in her life, Phoebe would have no further need of her shallow friends, or her tiresome family.

The bus was held up by a red light for a couple of minutes at Stratford Broadway, but then it continued on its way again. Almost immediately, the two boys at the front stood up, and one of them rang the bell, indicating that they wanted to get off at the next stop.

Spencer watched them jog down the stairs, laughing and joking as they went. Moments later, the bus glided to a halt.

As it pulled away from the stop, the old man sitting behind him jumped to his feet, looking flustered, and rushed towards the stairs, cursing that he had missed his stop. Spencer caught a faint whiff of alcohol as the man stumbled past him, and he couldn't help but smile. *It's not just me who's been on the sauce, then!*

With the old man now gone, Spencer's attention quickly returned to the two girls, who were dressed in the identical uniforms of shop assistants. He listened, transfixed, as they gossiped about their co-workers. Eventually, the redhead caught him staring at them and nudged her companion. The brunette turned around, curious. When he winked at her, she turned her nose up at him, and the frosty expression on her face, before she turned back to her friend, translated to: 'not in your wildest dreams!'

Spencer pulled out the bag of candy coated chocolates and sidled over to the edge of his seat. He knew she was just playing hard to get, as Phoebe had done at first. "Want a sweet?" he asked, leaning forward and nudging the girl's bony shoulder.

"No thanks," she said, not even bothering to turn her head.

Spencer bristled at the coldness of her tone. "They're candy coated chocolates," he said, pushing the bag forward again.

She stared at him with open animosity. "Look, we don't want a sweet, okay," she said, getting all gnarly. "We're having a private conversation, and we'd like to be left alone if that's not too much to ask." Turning back to her friend, she made a point of tutting loudly. "Honestly, why do I always attract the pissheads and fruitcakes?" she declared, deliberately speaking loud enough for him to hear.

The redhead leaned into her friend and whispered something that he couldn't quite hear, and they both sniggered nastily.

Spencer's face flushed with anger and embarrassment. All he'd done was offer them a sweet, and now they were making fun of him. He pulled a handful of sweets from the bag and threw one at the side of the brunette's head. When she spun around to glare at him, he threw another one, which hit her in the centre of the forehead.

Grinning spitefully, he punched the air with his fist. "Bullseye!"

"Piss off, will you?" she yelled, instinctively raising a hand to her head.

Underneath all the bluster, Spencer could tell that she was scared of him, and he responded by throwing some more sweets at her.

By now, everyone on the top deck was staring in his direction, their expressions ranging from mild curiosity to deep concern.

The girl's eyes were brimming with tears as she stood up. Trying not to cry, she rubbed the side of her face, where a dozen angry dots had broken out from being peppered by the confectionery. "Prick!" she yelled, angrily.

Spencer tilted his head back and laughed uproariously. "You look like you've got a bad case of the measles," he mocked, thinking that it served her right for having no manners.

The redhead had also risen. "Come on, Liz," she soothed. Wrapping a protective arm around her friend's shoulder, she started nudging her towards the stairs. "Let's go down downstairs, away from this drunken idiot."

In an instant, Spencer was on his feet. His nostrils flared in anger as he threw the remainder of his sweets at her. The redhead gasped in shock as they bounced off the back of her head and shoulders and scattered on the floor around her feet.

"You need to watch your mouth and show a little respect," he snarled, taking a threatening step towards them.

The girls sank into each other's arms, terrified.

Their fear was intoxicating, and Spencer found himself becoming sexually aroused. "Not so quick to shoot your mouth off now, are you?" he sneered.

"Please!" the redhead said, glancing nervously down the stairs. "We don't want any trouble."

A cruel laugh escaped his lips. "Should've thought of that before you upset me."

———

With great reluctance, David Bannister stood up and moved into the aisle, inserting himself between the two frightened girls and the gangly man who was abusing them. He raised his hands in what he hoped would be seen as a placatory gesture. "Please," he said, speaking softly so as not to agitate the man further. "Let's all just calm down."

"Fuck off, you bearded twat," the drunk replied, trying to squeeze past him.

Although the drunk was a few inches taller than him, Bannister was easily a couple of stone heavier and, in the narrow confines of the aisle, he was able to use the extra weight to his advantage.

"Get out of my way," the drunk snarled.

Out of the corner of his eye, Bannister noticed that the old lady sitting behind him was now cowering against the window, clutching her bag to her chest as though it were a shield. "For God's sake, man," he pleaded, "can't you see that you're scaring this poor woman half to death?"

The bellicose drunk responded by giving Bannister a firm, two-handed shove. "What are you going to do about it?"

Bannister pulled his mobile from his inside jacket pocket and flipped it open. "I'm warning you," he said, holding it up to make his point, "I'll call the police if you don't sit back down, right now."

After eight years in prison, Spencer had had a belly full of people who thought they were better than him telling him what he could and couldn't do, and when he could and couldn't do it. Now that he was a free man, he had no intention of taking any shit from anyone. "Make me," he growled, shoving the bearded man a second time.

Caught off guard, the stranger staggered backwards, tripped, and landed clumsily on top of the old woman, trapping her beneath him.

Spencer was upon him in an instant, wading in with a succession of wild punches.

Somehow, Mr Beardy managed to block the first blow with his forearm, but Spencer's second punch caught him smack on the nose, jarring his head backwards. This was swiftly followed by another right, which bounced off the top of the stunned man's head and was harmlessly deflected into the seat padding behind.

Breathing heavily, Spencer took a step backwards and raised his left foot high into the air, intending to stamp on the man's face but, at that precise moment, the bus braked unexpectedly. Thrown off-balance, Spencer tumbled forward, landing awkwardly in his lap.

Squashed by their combined weight, the terrified woman was now shrieking hysterically.

The lower half of Bannister's face was covered with blood from his splattered nose, and his vision was a little blurry from the blow to the head, but he had suffered worse injuries playing rugby and, while he was nowhere near as fit or as strong as he'd been in his prime, he could still mix it up in a scrum when the need arose. Wrapping his right arm around the drunk's skinny neck, he leaned over him and delivered a quick flurry of rabbit punches to the man's face.

———

Luckily for Spencer, none of the blows landed with any real force. He wriggled and bucked, trying to pull free from the headlock, but the man holding him was too strong, so he changed tact and reached for his beardy face, clawing at his eyeballs in an attempt to gouge them out.

That did the trick. Screaming in pain, Mr Beardy pushed Spencer away, catapulting him onto the empty seat opposite, where Spencer landed heavily, banging the back of his head against the window.

Mr Beardy was clutching his face, and Spencer saw that he was bleeding from a deep gash along the outside of his left eye, which had been inflicted by a dirty fingernail slicing open the flesh.

For a moment neither man moved, but then Mr Beardy was talking hurriedly into his phone. "Police… I need the police, urgently."

Spencer stiffened. If the police came, they would arrest him – they *always* arrested him – and his licence would be revoked; if that happened, he could kiss his long-awaited reunion with Phoebe goodbye. The leering face of the screw who had processed his release papers that morning popped into his head unbidden. *We'll be sure to keep your room vacant for you…*

Without conscious thought, Spencer reached behind his back, fumbling for the hard plastic handle of the kitchen knife. Curling his fingers around it, he pulled it free from his waistband. Keeping the blade tucked against the side of his leg, Spencer heaved himself to his feet, desperate to get off the bus before the Old Bill turned up.

Mr Beardy stood up too, moving forward to block his path. There was a strange glint of determination in his one good eye. "The police will be here soon," he announced triumphantly, "and when they arrive I'm going to make sure you get exactly what you deserve."

Spencer's face contorted with rage. There was no way he was going to let anyone prevent him from being reunited with the love of his life. "You're the one getting what he deserves, you fucking cunt," he snarled, driving the blade deep into the other man's stomach.

As Mr Beardy collapsed against him, Spencer grabbed hold of his hair and leaned forward so that he could whisper in his ear. "That'll teach you for poking your nose into other people's business."

―――――

It was eight-thirty when Tyler's Job mobile rang. He looked at the incoming number, grimaced, and then moved away from the table that he and his raucous friends had occupied for the past three hours. "DCI Tyler speaking," he said, pressing the phone tightly against his left ear, and plugging the right with a finger.

"*Boss, Colin Franklin here. Sorry to spoil the party, but there's been a murder on Forest Gate's ground.*" Colin was the acting late turn DS on the HAT car. Having passed the sergeant's exam earlier in the year, he was standing in for Steve Bull until the court case finished.

Tyler cursed under his breath. They hadn't even managed to make it through the first day of HAT week without picking up a murder. It was obviously going to be one of *those* weeks.

"What exactly have we got?" he asked, stepping outside the pub so that he could speak more freely. Perhaps it would turn out to be a simple Category C case: a domestic with one crime scene, one victim and one suspect who had already confessed everything to the locals.

"*Fight on a bus. Our victim's a middle-aged man who tried to play the Good Samaritan when a drunk started annoying a couple of girls. Unfortunately, his chivalry got him killed.*"

Visualising how the all-too-familiar scenario had played out, Tyler shook his head at the senseless waste of life. "How many times was the victim stabbed, Colin? And did he die at the scene or in hospital?"

"The victim was stabbed multiple times, and he died at the scene. From what I can tell from talking to the locals, he put up a hell of a fight."

"Has the suspect been detained?"

Please say yes!

A moment's hesitation. "*Afraid not, boss.*"

Of course not! That would make life far too easy.

Tyler sighed. "What do we know about the stabber?"

"*The stabber's a white male in his late twenties to early thirties. He decamped from the bus straight after the incident.*"

"Do we at least know his name?"

"*No, we don't. At the moment, all we have is a very basic description.*"

Tyler groaned out loud. So, this was going to be a manhunt. "What about the murder weapon? Has it been recovered?"

"*There's no obvious sign of it, but the bus hasn't been searched yet, so perhaps we'll be lucky and find he discarded it on board.*"

Tyler wasn't going to hold his breath. "Is the bus equipped with CCTV?" he asked, crossing his fingers that it was.

"*It is, and Paul's on the phone to Transport for London now, trying to find out how quickly we can access the footage.*"

DCs Paul Evans and Dick Jarvis were posted to the late shift HAT car with Franklin.

"That's good news, at least," Tyler said, rubbing his chin thoughtfully. "Tell him I want that footage tonight. What about witnesses?"

"*I don't know if we even have any, yet. The call only came through to us five-minutes ago. I'm just waiting for Dick to get me a printout of the incident log, and then we'll be setting off from KZ. I'll be able to give you a better update once we arrive on scene.*"

KZ was the phonetic code for Hertford House, and Tyler knew it wouldn't take the HAT car long to reach Stratford from there. "Who's the on-call CSM?" he asked.

"*It's Juliet Kennedy, and she's here in the office with me now.*"

That was a relief. Juliet was one of the best Crime Scene Managers they had. "Okay, mate. I'll grab Susie, and we'll meet you there in about twenty-minutes. Phone me straight away if there are any significant updates."

As he walked back into the pub, he found himself regretting his earlier moment of weakness when, under pressure from Dillon and Bull, he had agreed that George Copeland could stay and have a proper drink with them, and that he would be exempt from coming back into work if anything happened.

When he returned to the table, all conversation stopped, and the five people sitting around it eyed him expectantly.

"Well," Tony Dillon said, stoically, "from the look on your face, I'm guessing that phone call has just terminated what was turning into a very enjoyable evening?" Dillon was a bear of a man. With his hulking physique and glowering countenance, he looked more like a professional wrestler or a bouncer than a homicide detective.

Tyler smiled, wanly. "It has for me and Susie. Steve, you and Debs can stay here and keep the big lug company a little while longer if you want but, seeing as George is already completely bladdered, one of you needs to put him straight in a cab and send him home. And make sure he knows that I expect to see him in the office at eight o'clock sharp tomorrow morning for the office meeting."

Dillon glanced across at Copeland, who had stood up unsteadily and was now swaying from side to side like he was on the deck of a ship during a particularly rough storm. "I don't think we'll be getting much work out of poor old Georgie Porgie tomorrow, Jack," he confidently predicted.

Copeland was trying to flatten his hair, which was sticking up like Ken Dodd's. "I'll be right as rain once I grab a coffee," he assured them, slurring every word. When he finished with his hair, he turned his attention to the front of his shirt, which was heavily stained with ketchup and spilt beer. He attempted to button his jacket up to hide the evidence, but his stomach was so big that the two sides wouldn't meet in the middle.

"Don't worry about George," Steve said. "Seeing as we've taken a job, I'm gonna call it a night now, anyway, so I'll make sure he gets home safely."

Debbie Brown, a short, buxom woman in her late thirties, with collar-length auburn hair and a plain but not unattractive face, reached up from her seat and placed a hand on Tyler's arm. "Guv, I've only been drinking orange juice, so I'm more than happy to tag along if you think you can use me."

Tyler considered this. "Well, that would be very helpful. Are you sure?"

Debbie smiled at him. "You know me, always happy to get stuck in."

Debbie had only been on the team for a couple of months, but she had impressed Tyler in that short time. Not only was she ultra-efficient, but she never complained, and she never tried to cherry-pick cushy roles for herself, unlike some he could name.

"In that case, you're very welcome to join us," he told her.

"I'll just pop to the ladies first if that's alright?" she said, standing up and grabbing her handbag.

"Of course," he said, moving aside to let her squeeze by. As soon as she had gone, Tyler turned to Susie. "Are you okay to drive?"

Susan Sergeant arched an eyebrow in mild surprise, as if to say, 'I can't believe you even needed to ask me that!' "To be sure, not a single drop of the demon liquor has passed these fair lips," she told him, laying on the Irish accent thickly.

"Good. In that case, as soon as Debs gets back we'll be on our way. Steve, make sure he gets home safely." He pointed at Copeland, whose bleary eyes were worryingly vacant, even though his brow was creased in fierce concentration as he tried to follow the conversation. "And tell him I'll have his balls on a platter if he's late for tomorrow morning's office meeting."

"Well, that's one way of helping him to lose weight, I suppose," Susie observed, drily.

5

THE CRIME SCENE

The crime scene was a Dennis Trident long-wheelbase double-decker bus with an Alexander ALX400 dual door body. It was a big unit, fitted with sixty-eight seats and certified to carry a further twenty standing passengers, and it was parked a short distance away from the Magistrates Court in Stratford High Street. An inner cordon had been set up around it, with an outer cordon some twenty-five yards further back.

A half dozen police vehicles were parked in the immediate vicinity, their blue lights still pulsating brightly. There was also an LAS ambulance and a rapid response Subaru, which had deployed a specialist trauma team from The Royal London Hospital in nearby Whitechapel.

Susie pulled over in front of the bus and flicked a switch to kill the flashing blue lights concealed within the Sharon's grill. After removing the magnetic strobe light from the roof, she and Tyler set off to find Colin Franklin, while Debbie Brown went in search of the first responders to get the low down on potential witnesses.

They stopped at the outer cordon in order to sign in with the female PC running the scene log. Tyler flashed his warrant card. "We're from the Homicide Command," he informed her. "I'm Detective Chief Inspector Tyler and this is Detective Inspector Sergeant."

The officer hesitated. "Sorry," she said, sounding a little embarrassed. "Was that Detective Inspector or Detective Sergeant?"

"It's Detective Inspector Sergeant," Susie said with studied patience.

Pen poised, the constable looked from one to the other, clearly wondering if this was a wind-up.

"No, really," Tyler said. "My colleague's a DI whose last name happens to be Sergeant."

"If you say so, sir," the officer replied, filling in the log.

"Trust me," he said, leaning in conspiratorially. "It was even more confusing when she was Detective Sergeant Sergeant. People used to think she had a terrible stutter."

The PC grinned broadly, or at least she did until she caught Susie giving her daggers. Trying to keep a straight face, she cleared her throat, thanked them, and raised the tape for them to duck under.

They spotted Franklin, a tall, athletic black man in his late twenties, talking to the uniformed Duty Officer. Franklin looked weary, which was hardly surprising as he and his wife, Carmen, had recently had their second child, a little girl they had named Dawn because she'd been born at sunrise.

As soon as he saw Tyler, Colin Franklin excused himself from the Duty Officer and made his way over. "You made good time," he said, impressed. "We've only been here five minutes ourselves."

Tyler smiled. "And hopefully, in those five minutes, you've already solved the case and nabbed the killer?"

Franklin shook his head ruefully. "I wish," he said, handing Tyler a copy of the Computer Aided Dispatch printout.

Tyler accepted it with a grimace and started reading.

The gifts kept on coming as Franklin handed over a blue A4-sized daybook. "A little something for you to make some notes in," he said, passing an identical book to Susie.

"Have you received any updates since last we spoke?" Tyler asked, looking up from the CAD printout.

"The victim's a white male in his forties. His name's David Bannister. A paramedic found his driving licence on the floor beside his body, reckons it must have fallen out when he took a tumble. We've located two key-witnesses. The first is an old lady who was sitting directly behind Bannister when the fight kicked off. The second is a Sikh gentleman who was sitting at the front of the bus. It looks like the old lady got on the bus at the same stop as our victim and the suspect. Apparently, he'd been bothering her at the bus-stop, offering her sweets and whiskey. Oh, and before Bannister arrived, he nearly got into a fight with another office-wallah type."

Tyler raised an eyebrow. "Do we have that man's details?"

"No," Colin said. "Unfortunately, he got on a different bus to the others."

"It sounds to me like the stabber was looking for trouble, even before he met our victim," Susie opined.

"It does, doesn't it," Franklin agreed. "Anyway, all three went upstairs. The suspect sat down two rows behind the old girl, which means that he was three behind Bannister. Almost immediately, he started throwing sweets at two shop workers who were sitting opposite him. Naturally, they got upset and moved away. Bannister stepped in when it started to get out of hand, trying to calm the situation down–"

"Sorry," Tyler interrupted. "These two shop workers, do we have their names?"

Franklin shook his head, and his expression became melancholy. "Considering that Bannister died trying to protect them, you'd have thought they'd have had the decency to remain at the scene but, no, they were long gone by the time the first responders arrived."

"So, what happened when Bannister intervened?" Susie asked.

"In a nutshell, the suspect steamed into Bannister, who somehow managed to fight him off and call the police; the 999 details are on the CAD printout, and we'll request a copy of the recording first thing in the morning. When he started losing the fistfight, the suspect pulled out a blade and buried it in Bannister's gut. Incredibly, despite having just been stabbed, Bannister chased the bastard down the stairs and grabbed him again as he tried to decamp from the bus. During that struggle, the suspect stabbed Bannister a further six or seven times in his abdomen, chest, and neck."

Susie winced.

"Miraculously, the poor man was still clinging to life when the LAS and trauma team arrived six minutes later, but they couldn't save him. He's still lying in situ by the exit doors in the middle of the bus if you want to have a look." Franklin knew that Tyler liked to study the body while it was still at the scene whenever possible. He claimed it helped him to visualise what had happened and get a feel for the killer.

"That would be most helpful," Tyler said, nodding gratefully. "Has life been pronounced extinct yet?"

Franklin checked his notes. "Yep. The doctor called it at 8.17 p.m."

At that point, Juliet Kennedy joined them, carrying several sets of cellophane-wrapped Tyvek suits under one arm.

Although the petite blond was in her late forties, she routinely dressed like a wayward teenager on her way out clubbing, and Tyler wondered how outlandish tonight's outfit would be, not that he could see it beneath the heavy-duty coveralls she was wearing.

Sagging under the weight of the forensics bag draped over her right shoulder, Juliet came to a halt and awkwardly adjusted the strap, which was cutting into her. "Fuck me, this bag is heavy," she complained, handing a Tyvek suit to Tyler. "There you go, Jack, a double XL for you."

He took it with an affectionate grin. "Thanks, hon."

Juliet smiled back and then handed another set to Susie. "And you're a medium if I'm not mistaken," she said, dropping the forensic bag on the floor. It landed with a dull thud, and she immediately breathed a small sigh of relief. As she straightened up, her face twisted into a painful grimace. "Help yourselves to gloves, overshoes, and Victoria Masks," she told them, massaging the small of her back.

"Are you alright there, Juliet?" Tyler asked, noticing her obvious discomfort.

"Pulled a muscle playing badminton over the weekend," she told him. "It's been giving me gyp all day. Think I'll stick to bingo and gin rummy from now on."

"Probably wise at your age," he teased.

"Fuck off, you cheeky sod," she said, nudging him in the ribs.

As soon as Tyler and Susie had slipped into their protective clothing, and pulled their hoods and face masks up, Juliet led them over to the middle doors of the bus.

It was a warm, humid night, and Tyler was already beginning to perspire. To make matters worse, the air-conditioning had stopped working the moment the ignition had been switched off, so climbing aboard the bus was a bit like stepping into a blast furnace.

The victim lay on his back, eyes half-open, legs akimbo. His clothing had all been cut away by the LAS, and he was still intubated.

Staring down at Bannister's pale corpse, it struck Tyler that there really was no such thing as dignity in death, and he was profoundly grateful that the victim's family would never have to see him like this. The debris from all the emergency medical kit that had been used littered the floor around the body, and there was a lot of blood, as one would expect to find in a case where the victim had been stabbed multiple times.

Up close, the coppery smell of blood was accentuated by the oppressive heat inside the bus. Tyler could see that most of the injuries were located in the lower right quadrant of the body, but there were a couple of jagged incisions higher up, and one on the right side of the neck. Leaning forward to get a better look, he saw that, although it was a nasty flesh wound, the jagged gash in Bannister's neck appeared to have missed the artery.

Presumably, the fatal blow had been the one in the upper right quadrant, which had pierced the heart. It was difficult to be sure though, as the trauma team had carried out a pre-hospital thoracotomy. The procedure involved making a transverse incision across the patient's chest, literally opening it from one side to the other, and then cutting through the breast bone with a pair of shears. After that, the build-up of blood that had leaked from the punctured heart into the sack around it was drained. Patients were technically dead at that point, as pressure from the leaked blood surrounding the heart had stopped it from beating. Once the excess blood was removed, the hole in the heart had to be stitched up so that the trauma doctor could attempt to massage it back into life. The procedure was extremely risky, and only ever attempted when it was abundantly clear it was the patient's last and only chance of survival.

Tyler looked at Juliet, questioningly. "Looks like they attempted open-heart surgery," he observed.

Juliet nodded. "I spoke to the trauma specialist when I arrived," she told him. "He said that, as soon as they opened the victim's chest up, it became glaringly obvious that his injuries were too extensive, and there was nothing they could do to save him."

"I don't think I'd be able to do it," Tyler said, staring into the open chest cavity with a mixture of dread and awe. "I mean, can you imagine what it must feel like to reach into the very centre of a human being and take their heart in your hands? It's brutal, and I imagine it would affect you profoundly afterwards, emotionally speaking."

Juliet stared down at the corpse dispassionately. "The doctor, who's quite dishy by the way, was telling me that the trauma team performs one of these procedures every couple of weeks on average."

Tyler stared at her, wondering how she could be so blasé about it. Then he reminded himself that, in her line of work, she saw gruesome sights such as this, and many that were far worse, on a daily basis. "Does it ever work?"

Juliet responded with a lackadaisical shrug. "The technique's still relatively new, and the survival rate isn't that great at the moment, but it'll improve with time."

Tyler shuddered, and his face took on a cynical expression. "What really pisses me off is that, if the victim had been a low-life scumbag, he would have probably survived, irrespective of how serious his injuries were."

"Probably," Juliet agreed.

Tyler had seen a lot of dead bodies during his career as a policeman. Some of them had died peacefully; for others, the end had been drawn out and painful. The lucky ones had slipped away during their sleep after having lived a long and fulfilling life; others had met their demise as a result of tragic accidents, long illnesses or misadventure. He didn't remember the names or faces of any of those people. He did, however, vividly recall the names of every murder victim that he had ever dealt with and, when he closed his eyes at night, he could picture their faces clearly. He could also remember the names and faces of their killers, for he had been charged with bringing those people to justice, and it was a responsibility that he had always taken very seriously.

Tyler had a 100 per cent solve rate as an SIO, but he was deeply conscious that his perfect record couldn't last forever. The thought terrified him, not because he was vain, but because an unsolved case would mean that he had failed a victim and their family. If that happened, he wasn't sure that he would ever be able to face himself in the mirror again. The thought sent a shudder of apprehension through him and, as he did every time he took on a new job, he found himself hoping that this one wasn't destined to be the case he couldn't crack.

Tyler stared at the body for several long seconds, his face becoming increasingly grim as he contemplated the injustice of David Bannister's murder. Then, being careful not to step in the trail of blood that ran down the stairs, or accidentally lean against the wide red smears that plastered the walls, Tyler ascended to the top deck.

He stood there for a moment, trying to visualise the tragic sequence of events as they had unfurled.

Walking to the front of the bus, Tyler stood where the Sikh had been sitting, to get an idea of what he would have seen. Then he walked to the rear of the bus and studied the area where the fight had occurred. A discarded item on one of the seats immediately caught his eye. "Where do we think our suspect was sitting?" he asked Susie, who had remained at the top of the stairs so that he would have plenty of space to move around unhindered.

She came over to join him. "Not sure exactly which seat he was sitting in, but he was definitely behind Bannister and Mrs Bradley, somewhere on the left of the bus. Why do you ask?"

Tyler pointed at the object, which was lying on a seat five rows back from the staircase. Although it was wrapped in a white carrier bag, the distinctive shape of the bottle was unmistakable. "I was just wondering who that belonged to," he said.

Susie stared at the object for a moment, then looked him straight in the eye. "We couldn't be that lucky, could we?" There was a note of excitement in her voice.

Tyler could only shrug. "Well, Colin did say the suspect was drunk, and that he'd offered the old woman some whiskey when they were at the bus stop, earlier."

Letting out a low whistle, Susie set off towards the stairs. "I'll get Colin to check with her and confirm exactly where they were all sitting," she called back over her shoulder.

Tyler turned to the CSM, who had now joined him. "Juliet, once everything's photographed, I want that bag and its contents rushed straight up to the lab to be examined for fingerprints and DNA."

"Your every wish is my command," Kennedy replied with mock subservience. "Now, if you've finished having a look around my scene, kindly piss off and let me get on with my job."

It was a relief to get back into the fresh air, and Tyler lost no time in removing the uncomfortable layer of barrier clothing. He scrunched the paper suit, gloves, and mask into a ball and tucked it all into one of the overshoes, making it less cumbersome to carry around until he could find somewhere suitable to dispose of it.

Wiping a bead of sweat from his forehead, he set off to join Susie and Colin, who were standing near the outer cordon's perimeter, talking to Dick Jarvis, a tall, fresh faced young man with fair hair.

"I've finished having a nose around inside the bus," he told Susie, "so unless you want to go back in for any reason, you can do away with that getup."

"I'm good," Susie said, and immediately started to remove her white suit. "Dick's already spoken to the old woman, Mrs Bradley, and it looks like the bottle in the carrier bag is the one our suspect was carrying."

"That's excellent news," Tyler said, winking at her. He turned to young Jarvis. "I've already told Juliet, but just so you know, I want that bottle sent up to the lab first thing tomorrow."

"I'll get it sorted," Jarvis promised.

Jarvis was the designated advanced exhibits officer for this case, but he'd only completed the course a few weeks earlier, so this would be his first time performing the role in a live investigation. Tyler decided that when George came in tomorrow – if George came in tomorrow – he would have a quiet word with him, and ask him to keep an eye on Dick for the first few days, just to make sure that he wasn't struggling.

"Dick, Juliet has just started examining the bus. You'd better go see what she wants you to do."

"Okay, boss," Jarvis said with an eager smile. "I must say, I'm rather looking forward to getting stuck in."

Dick Jarvis was a Cambridge University graduate with a first in something or other, and he was frightfully posh. When he'd first arrived on the team, a little over two years ago, Jarvis had seemed far too nice to be doing anything as grubby as police work, and Tyler had wondered if the naïve youngster with the plummy voice would survive the constant brutality of working murder investigations. He needn't have worried; Dick had not only survived, he had positively thrived in what must have been a very alien environment for him and he had blossomed into a really good detective under the tutelage of his more experienced peers.

Tyler turned to Franklin, deep in thought. "Colin, if possible, I want Mrs Bradley and the Sikh gentleman who was sitting at the front of the bus to be interviewed on tape tonight. Debs can take the lead on that. Tell her I want them to draw detailed diagrams of who was sitting where on the top deck and then produce their drawings as exhibits."

"Will do," Colin said, making a quick note in his daybook. "Is there anything else?"

Tyler nodded. "Can you ask Paul to make contact with the local CCTV control room for me? I want footage from all the cameras in the vicinity of the bus stops where the suspect got on and off seized – two hours either side of the incident should suffice for now. I also want a detailed list of every camera they have within a one mile radius of the two bus stops. Hopefully, we can use the CCTV network to track where the suspect came from beforehand, and then show us where he went afterwards. Meanwhile, I'd better phone the Reserve at The Yard and let them know we're off watch for the foreseeable now that we've taken a job. The West Hat car will have to cover any call-outs that occur overnight, and I'll speak to George Holland in the morning to see who's going to cover our HAT duties for the remainder of the week."

6

Wednesday 25th July 2001
OPERATION JACKSONVILLE

Tyler's MIT was based on the first floor of Hertford House in Barking, East London, and by eight o'clock that morning, the main office was buzzing with frenetic activity as twenty-five detectives and a handful of civilian support staff waited eagerly for Jack Tyler to kick off the briefing for the new job.

A few minutes later, flanked by Tony Dillon and Susie Sergeant, Tyler emerged from his office, one of two smaller rooms branching off from the main open plan area. "I hope you've all had time to grab a hot drink," he said, taking a seat with his back to the office doors so that he could face everyone.

Susie Sergeant, today clad in a grey suit and black blouse, took a seat to his immediate left, while Tony Dillon, wearing a blue, light-weight summer suit by Pierre Cardin, plonked himself down in the chair to Tyler's right.

While doing a quick headcount, Tyler's eyes lingered on George

Copeland, who was slumped over his desk with his head buried in his hands. The Yorkshireman's complexion was a couple of shades greener than Herman Munster's, which was actually a significant improvement on how he'd looked when he'd first arrived, a half hour earlier. Luckily for George, the girls in the Major Incident Room had rallied around him like a group of old mother hens, rustling him up some strong coffee and paracetamols. They had nursed him into a semi-functional state, but Tyler was far from convinced that George would see out the day, and he made a mental note not to assign him with anything too arduous.

I bet you're regretting last night's over-indulgence, now!

As if reading his mind, Copeland glanced up at him, and Tyler quickly looked away, feeling petty.

At that moment, the door flew open and Juliet Kennedy breezed in, coffee in one hand, a chaotic bundle of notes in the other. "Sorry I'm late, she said, breathlessly. She looked around, spotted an empty seat, and made a beeline for it.

"Right," Tyler said. "Now that we're all here, let's make a start. As you all know, we've taken a new job. It's a fatal stabbing that occurred at approximately 8.10 p.m. yesterday on a bus in Stratford High Street. The trauma doctor in attendance pronounced life extinct at 8.17 p.m. As far as we can tell, neither of the parties involved knew each other before the incident. We don't know the killer's identity yet but, once we've identified him, Mr Dillon will take charge of the manhunt, leaving DI Sergeant free to focus on the reactive side of the investigation."

Once he'd finished giving them a general overview of the case, Tyler asked Debbie Brown to run the team through the key-witness testimony, which she did expertly, concentrating primarily on the account provided by Mrs Bradley.

"It sounds to me like we're looking for a retarded fuckwit who doesn't like being told what to do," DC Kevin Murray observed after she had finished. The skeletally thin detective was in his mid-thirties, and he sported a goatee beard and moustache that took some of the sharpness out of his features.

"Pot calling kettle," Dillon observed, cattily.

Murray blushed profusely but said nothing. The two men shared a mutual antipathy that went back many years.

Tyler raised a finger to his lips to hush the pockets of giggling that had broken out. "Does anyone have any questions for Debs about the witnesses?" he asked, staring at them pointedly.

Jarvis put his hand up. "Would either of our witnesses recognise the suspect again?"

Debbie nodded, emphatically. "Yes, Dick. They're both confident they'd pick him out in a line-up."

It seemed there were no other questions, so Tyler cracked on. "The locals deployed a Family Liaison Officer last night, but Debs will be introduced to the family later today, and she'll take over that role for us." Tyler swivelled in his chair to face her. "What time's the handover arranged for?"

"I'm meeting the family at one o'clock," Debbie replied.

Tyler made a note of that. "What do we know about the victim and his family so far?"

Debbie's eyes dropped to her lengthy notes, and she began reading from them. "David Bannister was a forty-three year old lawyer, married with two kids in their early teens. He was a Senior Prosecutor at the Stratford branch of the CPS. From what I can gather, he was a hard working professional who was tipped to go far. He had no enemies that his family or colleagues were aware of. In fact, he seems to have been a very popular guy. When the attack happened he had just finished work and was on his way home. He only lives – sorry, lived – a short distance away, in Leyton."

"Right," Tyler said, turning to Paul Evans, a fiery Welshman whose two main passions in life were rugby and football. "Let's view the CCTV."

Evans stood up and walked over to the TV–video combo mounted on the wall, above and slightly to the right of Tyler's head.

"Paul managed to get the bus footage downloaded last night," Tyler explained, "and he's put together a basic compilation, which he's going to play for us now. Over to you, Paul."

After turning the TV on, and inserting a VHS tape into the video player beneath it, Evans turned to address his colleagues. "This is only a rough edit, mind you," he told them in his rich baritone, "so bear with me if it jumps a bit."

When he pressed the play button, the screen flickered and then burst into life. The footage they were viewing came from a camera mounted high inside the front of the bus, providing a fish-eye view of the entry doors and driver's cubicle. The picture quality was extremely good, which wasn't always the case with CCTV.

As soon as the clip began, the doors opened and an elderly woman and a bearded man in a suit boarded the bus. Each swiped their travel card before moving out of shot. "The old biddy is Mrs Bradley, and the man behind her is our victim, David Bannister," Evans explained. A few seconds later, a tall, gangly male, dressed in a thin, tan jacket and khaki trousers, staggered into view and climbed aboard. He was carrying a bottle-shaped object in his right hand. "This odd looking chap here," Evans tapped the screen with his pen, "is our suspect."

The man's shoulders seemed to slump forward unnaturally and, with every step, his head wobbled on its long neck, accentuating the prominence of his Adam's apple.

"Och, he looks like a giant turkey," DS Charlie White cackled in his thick Glaswegian accent. He had sticky-out ears and a nose that had once been so badly broken that it almost sat at a right angle to the rest of his face, making his voice sound perpetually nasal. "Perhaps we should check with Bernard Matthews to see if any of the wee fuckers have escaped from his farm."

Ignoring the spontaneous laughter that had broken out, Dillon leaned in to address Tyler. "It looks like the suspect used cash to pay for his ticket," he observed. "I'm guessing that means he doesn't use public transport a lot, otherwise he'd have a travel card like the others."

The last people to board the bus before it moved off were a scraggy, mid-twenties, white couple, who were engaged in a heated argument, making them oblivious to everyone and everything around them.

"Actions are being raised to trace everyone who was at the bus stop with the suspect, along with all the unidentified passengers on the bus," DS Chris Deakin informed Tyler. Deakin was the Office Manager, and he ran the team's Major Incident Room.

On screen, the view changed to a shot of the upper deck, and this time the footage was provided by a camera located at the rear of the bus. "There are several other cameras that record the incident from different angles," Evans informed them, "but, in my opinion, this one affords us the best view of what happened upstairs."

The team watched in silence as the various players appeared. Mrs Bradley was first, followed by Bannister. Both took seats on the left side of the bus.

"The two females you see sitting on the right, behind the stairs, are the shopworkers our suspect picked on, as you'll see for yourselves in a minute," Paul Evans told his audience.

Within seconds, the suspect appeared, carrying the bottle in his right hand. He flung himself onto an empty seat two rows behind Mrs Bradley, clearly having chosen it so he could sit opposite the girls. Evans fast-forwarded the tape a few seconds, until an elderly black man sitting at the back of the bus suddenly got up and rushed towards the stairs. The sweet throwing started fairly soon after his departure. This was followed by a heated verbal exchange between the suspect and the girls. And then Bannister was standing in the aisle, and it was obvious from his body language that he was simply trying to diffuse the situation.

"I wish we could hear what they were saying," Jarvis said, mesmerised by the unfolding drama.

On screen, Bannister was suddenly knocked backwards, landing on top of Mrs Bradley. The suspect immediately started hitting him about the head and face, but Bannister fought back, eventually dragging the suspect down on top of him.

"The victim certainly made a fight of it," Colin Franklin remarked.

"Didn't get him anywhere though, did it?" Murray pointed out.

The two men were suddenly thrown apart, ending up on opposite seats. For a long moment, they sat facing each other, and then the suspect jumped up.

"Right, this is where it all goes drastically downhill," Evans said.

On screen, Bannister was trying to detain the drunk. "Look at the suspect's right hand," Evans instructed them, pointing towards the screen as he spoke. There was a blur of movement, a brief glint of steel, and then Bannister dropped to his knees, grabbing onto the suspect as he fell.

"Poor sod," Debs said, her voice thick with compassion.

The two men remained entangled for a second or two, and then the suspect managed to pull the knife free. The blade, which they could now see clearly, was about six inches long.

To Tyler's astonishment, as the suspect ran down the stairs, Bannister forced himself to his feet and gave chase.

"Oh, you poor brave man," he heard Debs whisper. "Why didn't you just stay where you were?"

The screen flickered for a moment, and the view switched to another fish-eye camera covering the bottom of the stairs and the exit doors in the middle of the bus. As they watched, the suspect came hurtling down the stairs, barging aside a man who was standing by the exit doors. While looking in the general direction of the driver and shouting something, which Tyler presumed was an order to pull over and stop, the suspect started jabbing at the bell. Then, as the bus began to slow, he grabbed the emergency release and tried to prise open the doors.

"Where are the two wee lasses he was arguing with upstairs?" Charlie White asked. "The bus is still moving, so they couldnae have got off."

Paul Evans clicked the pause button and the screen froze. "They're at the front, with the driver, trying to persuade him to stop. It's all captured on a different camera." He pressed play again. On screen, just as the suspect was forcing open the doors, Bannister appeared, half falling down the last few stairs. The front of his shirt was stained bright red, and his face was pale from blood loss. He launched himself upon the suspect, wrapping his arms around him and trying to use his weight to pin the other man against the half-open doors.

"None of the other passengers came to his aid," Evans said, stating the obvious.

The suspect's right arm was pumping like a piston as he repeatedly drove the knife into Bannister's body, and Tyler counted a total of seven strikes. Then, with sickening slowness, Bannister's arms slid down to his sides, his head slumped forwards, and his knees buckled under him. The terrible footage ended with the suspect pulling free and decamping from the bus.

"Game over," Evans said with a sad shake of his head.

"Wait," Tyler instructed as Evans moved to turn the TV off. "Can you rewind the tape and replay the bit where the suspect disentangles himself for me?"

"What did you see?" Dillon asked as Evans rewound the tape.

"I might have imagined it," Tyler admitted, "but I thought the suspect scooped something up from the floor as he stood up."

Everyone in the room stared at the screen intently as Evans restarted the tape. About halfway through the stabbing frenzy, Tyler stood up. "Pause it there!" he ordered. Moving forward, until his face was only a couple of feet away from the screen, he tapped it with his pen. "Look, as the victim falls to his knees, something falls out of his jacket pocket. Advance it a frame at a time from this point onwards, if you would, Paul."

Sure enough, with the tape now being played in slow motion, they were all able to see the suspect snatch something from the floor as he stood up. Clutching the item in his left hand, he turned and fled the bus.

"Could anyone tell what it was that he just picked up?" Tyler asked, glancing around the room expectantly.

"It looked like a wallet to me," Murray said, "but it could just as easily have been a mobile phone or a packet of cigarettes."

Evans played the sequence for a third time.

"I agree with Kevin," Tyler said, thinking that there had to be a first time for everything. "It looks like a wallet, and it's probably where the driving licence we found by the body came from." His eyes sought out Jarvis. "Dick, can you check the inventory of the victim's belongings to see if he had a wallet with him when he was shipped off to the morgue?"

"Will do."

Tyler's head swivelled towards Debbie Brown. "Can you speak to his wife and find out if he normally carried one?"

Debbie acknowledged the instruction with a sombre nod.

Tyler returned to his seat and checked his notes. "Debbie, when you spoke to the first responders last night, was there any suggestion that the victim made a dying declaration?"

She shook her head, sadly. "No, the LAS were already working on the victim by the time the first police units arrived, and he was dead by the time they were allowed access to him."

"Who spoke to the medical staff?" Tyler asked, this time seeking out Colin Franklin.

"The locals did," Franklin confirmed. "They gave Dick all the details of the LAS and trauma team personnel in attendance, but we haven't spoken to any of them ourselves yet."

"When we do, let's make sure we ask them about dying declarations."

There were nods all around the room.

"Right, Juliet," Tyler said, turning his attention to the CSM. "Let's talk forensics. Where are we with the SPM and the scene?"

"The body was photographed in situ last night and removed to Poplar mortuary during the early hours. The special post mortem won't take place until tomorrow, but that's not going to tell us anything that we don't already know. The bus has been forensically sealed, and taken to Charlton car pound. I'll be going over there straight after the meeting to continue the forensic sweep, which I anticipate will be completed by the end of the day. I believe that Tricky Dicky's provisionally booked a POLSA team for tomorrow morning. Is that right, Dicky?" She was referring to one of the Met's specially trained search units that were led by a Police Search Advisor – or POLSA.

Jarvis nodded but said nothing, and Tyler noticed that he'd flinched both times Juliet had referred to him as 'Dicky'. He hoped that none of the others had spotted his reaction, or the tormenting bastards would all start calling him that, just to wind him up.

"Some of you may have noticed that the killer was holding something in his right hand when he boarded the bus," Tyler said, and he was rewarded by half a dozen nods. "It was a bottle of Jack Daniels wrapped in a white carrier bag. Luckily for us, he left this on the seat when he decamped. Dick, how long will it take you to knock out a lab form?"

"I've already done one, boss," Jarvis responded, proudly.

Tyler was impressed. "Good man. Juliet, can you forewarn the lab that it's coming, and make sure they know how important it is?"

Juliet nodded. "Consider it done."

"Getting the bottle up to the lab is our top priority, today," Tyler told her. "That goes without saying."

Murray leaned into Jarvis, placing a hand on his shoulder. "If it goes without saying, why the fuck did he say it?" he whispered into the younger man's ear.

Jarvis irritably brushed his hand away.

Tyler noticed the interaction and narrowed his eyes. "Is there something you two want to share with the team?" he asked, annoyed that they weren't paying attention to the briefing.

"Well," Dick said, looking extremely uncomfortable, "Kevin asked me... URGH –"

A hard elbow from Murray cut him off mid-sentence. "I asked him if he needed a hand, boss," Murray said, quickly. "As it's his first exhibits job, I thought I'd let him know he can rely on me if he needs any help."

Tyler considered this. "Do you need any help, Dick?" he asked, weighing up Murray's offer. After all, Murray had been an advanced exhibits officer for some years now, and it might make sense to pair them for the day, especially as George clearly wasn't up to helping the youngster out.

"I'm fine, boss," Jarvis said through gritted teeth.

Tyler nodded. "Fair enough, but let me know if you start getting bogged down."

"Will do," Jarvis promised. He glared at Murray, who responded by giving him a smarmy smile.

"Today, we need to focus on CCTV," Tyler told them. "I want to know where our suspect came from, and where he went after the attack. Paul, at some point this morning, you need to sit down with me and Susie to discuss viewing parameters."

Evans nodded and gave him a thumbs-up.

Tyler then turned to DC Jim Stone, a seasoned detective in his late thirties whose facial expression never seemed to change, and whose philosophy was to never use a sentence when a single word would do. "Jim, you're the house-to-house co-ordinator for this job. I suspect, given the layout of the area where the incident occurred, house-to-house will be minimal, but it still needs to be done, so it might make sense for you to join us when we discuss parameters with Paul."

Stone nodded. "Gotcha," he said.

Next, Tyler turned his attention to Dean Fletcher, the lead researcher on his Intel Cell. "Dean, I'll need a research docket started on the victim, and I'd also like you to prepare a briefing slide for the local plod. In fact, thinking about it, we should probably circulate it to all the surrounding stations, not just the one where the murder occurred. It needs to include a really good photo of the suspect, and I want to be informed immediately if anyone recognises him."

"Can I suggest that we burn off a short video clip of the suspect walking, and also get that shown?" Dillon added. "As Whitey pointed out earlier, he does have a very peculiar gait and, if anyone's ever dealt with him, they're just as likely to remember that as they are his face."

"Good call," Tyler said. "Dean, can you get that sorted, please?"

Fletcher, a taciturn man with a mop of salt and pepper hair, nodded. "Leave it to me."

"I've spoken to DCS Holland," Tyler informed them, "and he's agreed to take us off HAT duties until we've wrapped this case up. West and South will cover for us, so let's hope they don't end up taking any jobs for the next few days."

Tyler nodded to Susie, indicating that she should take over.

She flashed him a smile and cleared her throat. "Apart from pursuing forensic and CCTV opportunities, the reality is that we're likely to be treading water until we identify the killer. Hopefully, that won't take too long. In the meantime, the MIR will start issuing actions to trace potential witnesses from the bus stop and top deck, especially the two shop girls, so let's try and work our way through those as quickly as possible so that we can crack on with trying to catch the bugger as soon as we know who we're after."

Tyler checked his watch and then stood up, indicating for Dillon and Susie to follow suit. "Right, Colin, I'll leave you and Steve to start tasking people while the DIs and I adjourn to my office for a quick brainstorming session. Paul, Jim," he nodded at Evans and Stone respectively, "I'll be calling you both in to discuss the CCTV and house-to-house parameters shortly, so don't wander too far away."

"Have we got an operation name, yet, boss?" Charlie White asked. "You know, for overtime claims."

Tyler raised a cynical eyebrow. "Well, it's good to see you've got your priorities right, Whitey," he said with a wry smile.

"It's Operation Jacksonville," Chris Deakin informed them. Operational names were randomly generated by the HOLMES computer, an acronym that stood for Home Office Large Major Enquiry System. At the moment the machine was picking them from towns and cities in North America.

There was a sudden flurry of activity as everyone in the room eagerly jotted down this vital piece of information.

Leaving Franklin and Bull to task the team, Tyler led the two DIs over to his office and indicated for them to sit in the comfy chairs clustered around a small coffee table in one corner of the room. After closing the door behind him, he joined them. "As I see it, this is actually not too difficult a job," he said without preamble. "The murder's captured on film, and the suspect's intent to kill or seriously injure is so clear as to be irrefutable. We have two very good witnesses who saw what happened on the bus and, in Mrs Bradley's case, at the bus stop beforehand. I'll be amazed if we don't get something – either fingerprints or DNA, but hopefully both – from the carrier bag and the bottle. Then we'll have forensic evidence to physically link the suspect to the crime. All we've got to do then is identify the fucker and nick him. What are your plans for the manhunt?" he asked Dillon.

"As soon as we've got a name to work with, I'll task the Intel Cell to look at his movement history and known associates," Dillon promised. "We'll also start a financial profile, and try to identify any phones he's been using. In addition, I'll get the Dedicated Source Unit to see if any of their registered informants know him. If they do, I'll explore the possibility of having them tasked to find him for us."

"It might be worth letting the DSU show a photo of the suspect to some of the people on their books anyway, just to see if they can name him," Susie Sergeant suggested.

Tyler shook his head. "Let's wait and see if we can identify him via fingerprints or DNA before going down that route."

"I agree," Dillon said. He stood up and stretched expansively. "Chances are, our suspect's holed up in a dingy little flat somewhere local to the scene. He's probably shitting himself with worry and wondering what to do next. From the look of him, he hasn't got a pot to piss in, so he's unlikely to have strayed very far. Hopefully, we'll have identified him through his fingerprints by the end of the day, and then we can really get the ball rolling. Until then, there's not a lot I can do from a proactive perspective." As he spoke, Dillon crossed the room. Opening the door, he turned to address his friends. "Right, unless there's anything else you need from me, I'm going downstairs to get some breakfast in the canteen. Don't suppose either of you fancy joining me?"

"I can't," Tyler said. "I've got way too much to do here to even think about eating."

"Fair enough," Dillon said. "Susie, what about you? Can I tempt you?"

She shook her head. "Sorry, Tony. Like the boss said, I'm too busy to think about eating right now."

"Pity," Dillon said. "Right, I'll be back in twenty minutes. If anything happens before then, give me a call."

7

A NICE LITTLE TRIP TO NORFOLK

The previous night, Spencer had run as though a pack of hungry wolves was snapping at his heels as he fled the scene. The moment the wail of approaching sirens reached his ears, he ducked into a darkened side street to avoid being spotted by the three police cars that whizzed past a few moments later.

Shaking with fear, Spencer tore off his bloodstained jacket, wrapped the kitchen knife in it, and dumped them both in a refuse bin sitting outside the front of an unlit house. Rifling through the victim's wallet, he was surprised to discover that it contained two hundred pounds in cash, which he greedily tucked into his pocket before tossing the blood-soaked wallet into the bin to join the other discarded items.

Keeping to the back streets, Spencer gradually worked his way over to a minicab office he knew of in Waterden Road, not far from Hackney Wick Dog Stadium and, from there, he took a cab to Old

Street. He made a point of telling the disinterested driver that he was planning to catch the Northern Line over to Morden, where he was going to stay with some friends for a few days. It pleased him to think that, if the police somehow managed to track the cabbie down, and if by some miracle the man actually remembered anything, the information that he passed on would send the Old Bill off on a wild goose chase to the other side of London.

Having been dropped off near Old Street roundabout, Spencer stopped at the first phone box he came across and called Skippy.

"What's wrong with you, you daft cunt?" Skippy yelled at him on hearing the news. *"You ain't even been out a day yet, and you're already a wanted man! You've fucked me over good and proper by shivving that bloke. I was relying on that ransom money to get myself out of the shit with Jonas Willard."*

Willard was a well-known face in the area. Apart from running a string of betting shops, which were a legitimate front for his other activities, he was a high-end fence and a loan shark, and he was most definitely not a man to get on the wrong side of.

"Don't worry," Spencer assured him. "I got away, so it's all cool."

"Don't fucking worry? Are you having a—"

"Look, I know what I did was stupid, but it's done now, so let's just forget about it."

At which point, Skippy flew into an apoplectic rage, shouting obscenities until he became so hoarse that he could hardly speak. Ignoring Spencer's futile attempts to reassure him, Skippy was still swearing when he hung up on his cousin.

Back in his room, still sulking over Skippy's unreasonable reaction, Spencer decided that the safest thing he could do – at least in the short term – was carry on exactly as normal, so as not to arouse his probation officer's suspicion.

After cleaning himself up, he fell into his lumpy bed and slept like a log.

Spencer awoke feeling rested and refreshed and, after washing his face in the sink, he took himself off to a local café to treat himself to a full English fry-up. After eating his fill, he set off for Shoreditch police station to register with the Public Protection Unit. Along the way, he stopped off at a shop that sold mobile phones. Skippy had told him that everyone had one these days, and that he would definitely need one for what they had planned.

Going in, he was greeted by a junior assistant who was desperate to make a sale. Wearing a suit that was a size too big for him, and had probably been handed down by his father, the spotty boy showed him a variety of handsets. Spencer settled on a very basic model, paying for it with some of the money that he'd liberated from Mr Beardy. He also put a fiver's worth of credit on the Pay-As-You-Go phone, which the sales assistant assured him would be more than enough, unless he planned to use it frequently, which he didn't.

Mobile phones hadn't been commonly available or affordable for most people when Spencer had been imprisoned eight years earlier, and even the rudimentary model that he had chosen was capable of performing functions beyond his understanding, like sending text messages. Thankfully, the obliging salesman carefully set everything up and explained exactly how the clever little contraption worked.

While he sat in the reception area at Shoreditch police station, waiting for an officer from the Public Protection Unit to come down and see him, Spencer christened his shiny new purchase by making a quick call to his probation officer. Dibney was surprised to hear from him, and delighted that he had taken such prompt action.

Within fifteen minutes of leaving the police station, Spencer was putting his larceny skills to good use by breaking into a 3 series BMW that was parked at a meter in one of the quiet roads adjoining Moorfields Eye Hospital. He knew it was a little extravagant, and that he ought to have chosen something a little less conspicuous, but he had a long journey ahead of him and he wanted to make it in style. Besides, he figured that turning up in a flash new Beamer would impress Phoebe, and that was very important to him.

John Anthony Spencer was a man who lived in the moment; it simply wasn't in his nature to dwell upon the mistakes of the past or worry about the consequences of his actions. As far as he was concerned, the stabbing was yesterday's news; today, he was going to be reunited with Phoebe and, if everything went according to plan, they would both be rolling in money within a week, thanks to a generous – albeit involuntary – donation from her moneybags father. As he drove along the A14, listening to the radio, all he could think about was how happy Phoebe would be to see him again.

'It wasn't me!' by Shaggy was playing, and he sang along, thinking that's exactly what he would tell the police if they ever questioned him over the stabbing.

When the song finished, the DJ asked his listeners who they thought would be at number one that weekend, and told them to make sure they tuned in to the chart show on Sunday afternoon to find out.

I'll give that a miss, thanks.

With any luck, he and Phoebe would be far too busy rekindling their relationship to worry about who was going to be top of the pops. After the obligatory string of boring adverts, the news came on, and the bus stabbing was the headline story.

The announcement that the victim had died from his injuries hit Spencer hard. Up until then, he had foolishly allowed himself to believe that Mr Beardy would pull through, and that the injuries were nowhere near as bad as he remembered them. This was now a murder enquiry, and he knew that the police would throw everything they had into solving it.

The media were calling him 'The Candy Killer,' which he thought sounded a little effeminate. Why couldn't they have chosen something darker, more masculine? 'The Stratford Stabber' or 'The Bus Butcher' would have been far better.

The police were appealing for witnesses to come forward, and a Scotland Yard spokesman, speaking in a dull monotone, said that the Homicide Command were investigating the murder and pursuing a number of enquiries.

He experienced a tiny stab of anxiety.

Enquiries? What enquiries?

It was midday and Tyler was sitting in his office, sleeves rolled up, collar undone and tie worn at half-mast. The little radio on his windowsill was playing quietly in the background. The large tinted windows in Hertford House were sealed units, and he missed not being able to open them and listen to the noise of the birds singing outside, as he'd done when he worked at Arbour Square. The upside to that was that the building was air-conditioned, so at least his office was always nice and cool.

Tyler was so ensconced in the towering mountain of paperwork in front of him that he almost didn't look up when Detective Chief Superintendent George Holland strode in.

Holland was accompanied by an impeccably dressed woman in her mid-twenties, who was struggling under the weight of a big shoulder bag that bulged at the seams. The sunlight streaming in from the window behind his desk bounced off her shoulder-length blond hair, which was so shiny it could have been used in a shampoo advert.

Tyler's eyes narrowed when he spotted the large notepad tucked under her arm.

She's a bloody reporter.

"Hello, Jack," Holland said, smiling warmly. "While I'm in the building, I thought I'd stop by and see how the new investigation's progressing."

In his early fifties, Holland was a man of medium height and build, with slightly receding fair hair that was in the process of turning grey. Without waiting for an invite, he sat down opposite Tyler's desk and indicated for his guest to pull up a chair beside him.

Tyler stared at the young lady for a long moment, still wondering who she was and, more importantly, what she did for a living. The lanyard she wore around her neck proclaimed her as a visitor, but it provided no other useful information, not even a name. Then he turned to face Holland. "It's going okay," he said, guardedly. He wasn't about to discuss the fine details of a live investigation in front of a stranger, especially not one who bore all the hallmarks of an investigative journalist.

As if reading his mind, Holland grinned indulgently and said, "Allow me to introduce my young guest. This is Imogen Askew. She's a researcher for a television company who are making a documentary about one of my old cases. I've agreed to let her shadow me for a while, in order for her to get some background information for the programme."

"Pleased to meet you, Imogen," Tyler said, leaning forward to shake her hand, which was soft and delicate. He had never met anyone called Imogen before, and he wondered if her voice would be as posh as her name. The green eyes staring back at him revealed a formidable intelligence, and he got the distinct impression that she was evaluating him like a shark does its prey.

"Likewise," she said, treating him to a smile that exposed a perfect set of teeth.

Yep. Posh.

"Imogen and her colleagues have signed a confidentiality agreement, which is legally binding and prohibits them from revealing any information about sensitive matters or live investigations that they may become privy to while accompanying me, so you can rest assured that we can speak freely."

A privacy agreement – what the hell did that mean? Tyler frowned, immediately sceptical. "With all due respect, sir," he began, only for Holland to hold up a hand.

"Let me stop you there, Jack. The legal eagles at the Yard have gone over the agreement with a fine-tooth comb. Nothing we discuss in front of Imogen will be leaked or reported, so you really can speak freely."

"If you say so, sir," Tyler said, shooting a doubtful glance at Askew. Was it his imagination, or was she staring back at him in one-upmanship? He swallowed the disapproving growl that was building in the back of his throat.

"I do," Holland said, pointedly. "Now, why don't you get one of your staff to make us a brew, and then you can run me through what we've got so far."

Just then, Chris Deakin popped his head around the door. "Sorry to interrupt," he said, nodding respectfully at Holland, "but I thought you'd want to know, we've just received a call from a lady who lives in Carpenter's Road, a few streets away from the where the stabbing occurred. Apparently, she's found a kitchen knife wrapped in a blood-stained jacket that someone dumped in her dustbin overnight. Colin's sent Kevin Murray down to retrieve it."

Diss was a very pretty market town, but its rustic charm was completely wasted on Spencer. After grabbing some lunch at a pub in Mount Street, which he paid for with more of Mr Beardy's money, he donned a pair of Ray-Ban sunglasses that he'd conveniently found in the stolen Beamer's glove compartment and took a slow walk along the High Street to scope it out.

He took an instant dislike to the place. It was too quiet, too quaint, too picture perfect, too... nice. He felt as out of place here as a cat would do if someone tried entering it at Crufts.

Stopping at a little souvenir shop, he grabbed a white floppy hat off the rack and plonked it on his head. Studying his reflection in the mirror, he thought that he looked like a right prat in it, but that was a small price to pay if it prevented people from recognising him. Now that he was a famous murderer, he couldn't afford to take any chances.

After leaving the shop, Spencer continued his journey down to the Diss Mere, a six-acre lake that Norfolk folklore proclaimed was the bottomless crater of an extinct volcano although, in reality, it was actually about sixty-feet deep and consisted mostly of mud.

Thanks to Skippy's childlike notes he knew that, when she was in Norfolk, Phoebe spent most of her days painting landscapes, but her early evening routine invariably involved taking long, solitary strolls along a route called the 'Diss Circular Walk'. According to a frayed and faded tourist map that Skippy had thoughtfully stapled into the back of the book, the trail started at Mere's Mouth, led over to Roydon, then across to Fair Green and up to Palgrave, before eventually returning to Diss.

Skippy's notes had turned out to be surprisingly informative, even describing the car park behind the shops where Phoebe parked her car.

Spencer took a leisurely stroll around the lake. It was a quiet and peaceful place, ideal for what he had in mind. When he was satisfied that he'd seen enough of the landscape, Spencer stopped at a quaint little café overlooking the Mere and ordered coffee.

It struck him that people in this part of the world were far too friendly for their own good. The talkative young waiter was more than happy to answer all his questions, and even went on to offer some useful rambling tips to help him get the most out of his stay, not realising that the inquisitive visitor was contemplating something far more sinister than a bit of hiking.

After finishing his coffee, Spencer set off in search of the car park Phoebe used. When he reached it, a few minutes later, he decided to check out the footpath at the far end, just to see where it brought him out.

Susie Sergeant popped into the stairwell at the back of the building to use her phone. It wasn't the ideal location to make a sensitive call, but it was probably the only place where she could guarantee that she wouldn't be disturbed halfway through by someone barging in with an urgent request or wanting to discuss some complicated facet of the new job.

As she dialled her estranged husband's number, the demented butterflies in her stomach were performing an acrobatic routine worthy of the Red Arrows. "Please answer this time," she mumbled under her breath. She bit her bottom lip waiting for a dialling tone. "Come on, you bastard, please don't ignore me again."

Since Dan had abandoned her in favour of a young probationer ten years her junior, the two-timing swine had been doing his utmost to avoid her. It was incredibly cruel of him to treat her this way, and the stress of not being able to sort out their future was literally making her ill.

Dan still worked as a PC on a relief at Leyton, which is where they had originally met eight years earlier. She knew, from friends who worked the division with him, that he was turning up for work as usual every day, and that he seemed absolutely fine in himself. Of course he was fine, she thought cynically. He was probably having the time of his life.

It quickly became apparent that he wasn't going to pick up, not that she had realistically expected any other outcome. Of course, there could be a perfectly legitimate reason for this; he could be dealing with a prisoner or responding to an emergency call. With a heavy heart, Susie ended the call and tapped out a text message, asking him to contact her as soon as he received it. Tucking her phone away in her shoulder bag, she returned to the MIR, a fake smile plastered across her face to mask her inner sadness.

At five-o'clock, Dillon popped his head around the door to Tyler's office. He had spent the afternoon at a case conference with Queen's Counsel, discussing an upcoming trial. "Any updates before I head over to the gym?" he asked cheerfully.

"Only that we've recovered the murder weapon. After he fled the bus, the suspect dumped it, along with his blood-stained jacket and what we think is the victim's wallet, in a bin in the front garden of a house in Carpenters Road."

"That's really good news," Dillon said, flopping into a chair and clasping his shovel-sized hands behind his head. "Between the carrier bag and JD bottle recovered from last night's crime scene and these new items, we're bound to get his fingerprints and DNA. If we get a hit on his fingerprints, I reckon we'll have him identified by the end of the day. If we have to rely on DNA, it might take a little longer."

Tyler nodded his agreement. They would almost certainly get wearer DNA from the discarded jacket, and victim's DNA from the blood it was drenched in. On top of that, there was an excellent chance that the lab would find the suspect's fingerprints on the knife's handle, and the victim's DNA on its blood encrusted blade.

Tyler rolled his neck, which ached from spending the afternoon hunched over his Decision Log.

Dillon picked up on this. "Are you sure you can't spare an hour to join me over the gym?" he asked, his face plastered with concern. "The break would do you good."

Tyler responded with a wan smile. "I'd love to," he said, "but I can't – way too busy."

"Pity, I'm doing a chest workout today, and I could do with you there to spot me while I bench press." Dillon mimed doing a few reps. "Out of interest, have you seen the little hottie that Holland's been parading around the building all day?"

Tyler scowled, remembering the annoyance he'd felt earlier, as he'd been forced to bring Holland up to speed on the bus killing with her sitting there, taking in every word he said. "Yeah, I've seen her," he admitted.

"Do you know who she is?" the big man asked.

Tyler nodded. Unfortunately, he did, and he didn't approve. "She's a researcher for a TV company who've decided to make a documentary on one of George's old cases," he explained. "She's shadowing him to get some background information." He made air quotes to accompany the last two words.

Dillon smiled, lasciviously. "I wouldn't mind her shadowing me for a week."

Tyler rolled his eyes. Dillon had a one-track mind.

"Seriously though, what old case are they interested in?" Dillon asked.

Tyler responded with a lazy shrug of indifference, and then allowed himself a self-satisfied grin. "I didn't ask. I could tell that

George was desperate for me to show an interest, but I was so pissed off at having to brief him about this current investigation in front of her that I made a point of blanking him every time he dropped a hint."

Dillon chuckled. "I bet he hated that."

The telephone on Tyler's desk chirped into life. Turning his nose up at the unwanted interruption, he scooped it up. "DCI Tyler speaking." He listened carefully, jotted down a few notes in his daybook, and then asked the caller to pop through with the details. "That was Julia in the MIR," he said as he cradled the receiver. "The two shop workers our killer threw sweets at have just phoned the helpline, offering to make a statement."

Dillon gave a little nod of approval. "It sounds like the case is coming together nicely."

Tyler snorted. "I think I'll wait till we've got the fucker banged up in a cell before I allow myself to start thinking like that."

"Don't be such a pessimist," Dillon admonished him.

Tyler raised the middle finger of his left hand. It seemed the most suitable response.

Dillon chortled. "And the same to you, with bells on it." He stood up and headed for the door. "Right, Captain Grumpy, as you've obviously got everything well under control here, I'm off to pump some iron. I'll see you in an hour or so."

Within seconds of Dillon's departure, Paul Evans poked his head around the door. "Can you spare a minute, boss?"

Tyler lowered his pen. "Sure. Go ahead, Paul."

"I've obtained all the CCTV we requested from the local authority. In light of the fact that we now know the suspect made off along Carpenters Road, I've widened the radius slightly, just to be on the safe side."

"Okay, sounds reasonable. Make sure you let Susie know, so that she can update the CCTV strategy to reflect the new parameters."

"I will do. Also, I obtained the CCTV footage of Bannister leaving the CPS building." He handed over a black and white still that he had recently printed off.

Tyler studied the shiny photograph with a sad frown. It was hard to believe that, just twenty-four hours previously, the man it depicted had been alive and well, full of hopes and aspirations, with his whole life ahead of him. Now he was just an inanimate slab of meat being preserved in a mortuary freezer until the pathologist got around to slicing him up. Once that was done, he would be placed in a wooden box and either buried or cremated, leaving a great void in the lives of all those who had loved him. "Good work, Paul," he said, placing it on his desk.

Tyler's third visitor in a row showed up as Evans was leaving, and they smiled an acknowledgement at each other in passing.

Julia Prestwick was a long-standing member of the team, having joined in the days when they had still been based over at Arbour Square. She held a sheet of paper in her left hand and a red mug in her right. "I thought you might like a cup of coffee to keep you going," she purred, placing the mug down in front of him.

"Julia, I don't know what I would do without you," he said, smiling appreciatively.

"And here are the details of the two girls who were on the bus," she said, handing over the paper. "Susie was in the MIR when the call came in, and she asked me to let you know that she's sorting out someone to interview them both this evening."

"Thanks, sweetheart," Tyler said, studying the information she'd given him. Just then, the phone rang. It was Juliet Kennedy, calling from Charlton car pound.

"*Thought you'd want to know*," she said without preamble, "*I've just found a beautifully clear thumbprint in the victim's blood on the inside of the emergency exit handle, by the lower deck middle doors. Am I good or what?*"

"You're better than good," Tyler assured her, waving at Julia as she left. "Can you make sure it goes up to The Yard as quickly as possible?"

He heard Juliet tutting at him down the line. "*Jack, give me some credit. Dicky's here with me. As we speak, he's on the blower to Colin Franklin, arranging for someone to fly it up to NSY on blues and twos. As long as the suspect's known to us, and I'll be amazed if he's not, we should get an ident back later tonight."*

Tyler hung up and immediately dialled Dillon's number, hoping to catch the big lug before he started training. Maybe Dillon had been right after all? The case was coming together nicely and, with a bit of luck, the killer would be safely behind bars within a day or two.

8

I'VE MOVED ON AND I'M GETTING MY LIFE BACK

Phoebe Cunningham was feeling jittery as she double-locked the cottage door and gave the handle a little tug to check that it was secure. It was a few minutes before seven and, thankfully, the cloying heat that had made the day so unbearable was finally starting to dissipate.

For her dinner date with Martin, she had elected to wear a loose-fitting, yellow summer jacket with a vibrant flowery lining, and a flowing red dress that was covered in little yellow flower buds. Martin constantly teased her over her obsession for buying clothes with a flowery theme, but she didn't care; she had always liked flowers, they somehow made her feel happier.

Gravel crunched underfoot as Phoebe purposefully strode across the drive towards her car, a gleaming red Alfa Romeo Spider. As she unlocked it, her eyes darted nervously to the overgrown shrubbery that surrounded the house, fearful that an intruder might be lurking within its dense foliage.

Sliding behind the wheel, she hurriedly started the coupe and pulled away, churning gravel into the air as she went.

Ever since her mother had called to break the news of Spencer's release, yesterday morning, her emotions had been all over the place, tumbling around inside of her and depriving her of the ability to think straight. She had been a bundle of nerves all day, seeing things that weren't there, jumping at shadows, and constantly looking over her shoulder in case the man – no, the monster – who had abducted and raped her all those years ago suddenly reappeared.

Her imagination had completely run away with her earlier in the day, while she'd been in town doing some shopping. At one point, much to her chagrin, she had become convinced that she'd just spotted Spencer crossing the road a little way ahead of her. Stopping dead in her tracks, oblivious to the tutting pedestrians swerving around her, she had dragged herself into a nearby shop doorway to hide. Paralysed with fear, Phoebe had felt as though all her weaknesses had suddenly been exposed for the world to see, and that everyone passing by was looking down their noses and thinking how pathetic she was. Afterwards, when she finally stopped shaking, she had angrily berated herself for falling apart like that in public.

Although the part of her mind that remained rational had told her there was absolutely no way that Spencer could have tracked her down, she had been unable to shake the irrational fear that he was nearby and, in the end, she had abandoned her shopping trip and returned to the cottage in a state of restless anxiety.

That afternoon, for the first time in years, Phoebe had felt compelled to commit the disturbing images to paper. Hurriedly setting up her easel in the garden room that ran off the kitchen, she had manically sketched a tortured figure cowering in a shop doorway, surrounded by a horde of faceless demons.

The evening drive through the winding country lanes into the town centre took just over ten minutes, and she spent the time repeatedly checking her rearview mirror to satisfy herself that she wasn't being followed.

Unlike her physical injuries, which had healed relatively quickly, the emotional and psychological harm she'd suffered at Spencer's hands, all those years ago, was every bit as raw as a freshly opened wound.

It was hard to believe that her relationship with Spencer had started as an innocent friendship. They had met while he was working as an odd job man for her father, doing a spot of gardening, washing his car and running the occasional errand for him. One day, when Phoebe returned home from school, he had been sweeping leaves in the front garden. Out of politeness, she had said hello, and he had responded by asking her name.

At first, Phoebe had taken pity on Spencer because of the offhand manner in which her father always treated him; he was just so horrible to the poor man, constantly criticising everything that he did. No matter how hard Spencer tried to please him, her father always found something in his work to pick fault with. When she got to know him better, she found herself beginning to like Spencer as a person, and she started looking forward to seeing him. As their unlikely friendship grew, Phoebe started finding reasons to be around the house whenever he was working there, just so that they would have an excuse to chat. One afternoon, when both her parents were out, she even persuaded him to pose for her, and she had given him the sketch when it was finished. He had been thrilled by it, claiming that it was the best present he had ever received.

When the summer holidays came, Phoebe found that she had time on her hands to kill, so she started accompanying him while he did other odd jobs in the area. He was always so nice to her, so respectful, and he always seemed genuinely interested in her welfare, unlike her parents who were always far too wrapped up in their business affairs to give her the attention she needed. Phoebe particularly liked the fact that Spencer listened attentively to everything that she said, and that he was always interested to hear her views on whatever news stories were doing the rounds.

One afternoon, as she had done several times previously, she accompanied him to the local park while he ate his lunch. He habitually drank a bottle of beer with his sandwiches, and on this particular occasion he surprised her by bringing an extra one along for her. She had been touched by the gesture, and it had made her feel very grown-up. Unaccustomed to alcohol, she had become a little tipsy, and she had told him some things that, in hindsight, she probably shouldn't have, like how domineering her overprotective father was towards her, and how he had never allowed her to have a boyfriend or go to parties in case a sex-mad boy tried to take advantage of her. On hearing that, Spencer had leaned over and hugged her. He had then kissed her on the forehead and told her how pretty she was, and how lucky any boy would be to have her as his girlfriend. Phoebe had been incredibly flattered to hear this; he was the first boy to have ever made her feel attractive and desirable and, when he started clumsily flirting with her in the aftermath of that conversation, she made no effort to discourage him.

They had already known each other for several months by that time, and she felt very comfortable with him so, when he invited her to accompany him on a day trip to Kent, she was more than happy to accept. Knowing that her parents would never permit it, Phoebe had lied to them about where she was going, pretending to be visiting a schoolfriend instead. It had been very wrong of her to mislead them, but it had also been very exciting.

Driving through the Kent countryside on their way to the cottage, Spencer had explained that his gran had recently died, and that it had fallen to him to clear out her bungalow before it could be sold. When they reached the bungalow, Spencer had given her a guided tour, and then he had kissed her. She had been expecting this, hoping for it if truth be told, and she had responded willingly, excited to finally be experiencing her first kiss. However, it had quickly become clear that he wanted far more than an innocent snog from her. She had refused, explaining that she wasn't ready to have sex with him or anyone else yet. Instead of respecting her wishes, as she had expected him to, his response had been to drag her into the bedroom and force himself upon her.

After defiling her, Spencer had kept her a prisoner at the bungalow for seven long days. Ignoring her constant pleas to be released, he had somehow convinced himself that she wanted him as much as he wanted her, and that her continued reluctance to have sex with him was purely down to her being afraid of her father's reaction. "Stop playing hard to get, you little prick tease," he had shouted, forcing her legs apart and ramming his engorged manhood into her. "You know you want this as badly as I do."

If it hadn't been for a concerned neighbour, who had called the police because he thought the empty bungalow had been broken into by squatters, she might have been trapped there for weeks.

At some point during the period she'd been held captive, something deep inside Phoebe's psyche had snapped.

By the time that she was reunited with her parents, Pheobe had gone from being a sassy extrovert who yearned to travel the world in search of romance and adventure to a broken girl who was too afraid to leave the house, let alone jump on a plane.

Phoebe would never forget the weeks she had spent locked away in her room in the wake of her ordeal, either staring listlessly out of the window or curled up in a ball on her bed, crying uncontrollably; the terrible nightmares that had plagued her sleep, or the graphic flashbacks that tortured her waking hours, becoming more intense with each unwanted replay.

As painful images of Spencer's grunting body, grinding away against her own, flooded her mind, Phoebe squeezed the leather steering wheel until her manicured nails dug sharply into her palms. She shook her head to dispel the disturbing memories.

I'm strong. I've moved on and I'm getting my life back.

Phoebe hated the fact that, even now, she still suffered from debilitating panic attacks like the one she'd experienced earlier; and that they were capable of reducing her to a gibbering wreck within seconds of coming on.

I'm strong. I've moved on and I'm getting my life back.

Phoebe checked the mirror again, and her eyes lingered on the pretty girl staring back at her. They had so many things in common: the same blue eyes that sparkled whenever the light caught them at the right angle; the same heart shaped mouth that melted men's heart's when it smiled; they even had the same wavy, brown hair. Despite these striking similarities, the girl in the mirror wasn't the real Phoebe. Sure, they had the same laughter lines around their eyes and an identical set of dimples in their cheeks, but the girl in the mirror was a charlatan and a fraud. The real Phoebe – the tortured soul behind the reflection's carefree smile – spent most of her time mentally screaming in anguish. No one ever heard those cries, of course, because she had become so adept at keeping the pain bottled up.

Phoebe knew that dwelling on the past like this was unhealthy, and that it always ended up with her spiralling into a morbid state of depression. She desperately wanted to be in a happy state of mind when she met Martin for dinner, so she decided to switch the radio on and see if some music would lighten her mood. Instead of an upbeat tune, all she got was the news.

"...Meanwhile, the search continues for the man known as The Candy Killer, who brutally stabbed CPS lawyer, David Bannister, to death yesterday evening during a disturbance on a bus in East London. Mr Bannister, who leaves behind a wife and two teenaged children, had attempted to intervene after his attacker began hassling two fellow passengers. Stunned witnesses say that..."

Phoebe was feeling lugubrious enough without having to listen to heart-wrenching tragedies like that, so she leaned forward and switched channels.

Dancing Queen. That was more like it! There was nothing like a bit of ABBA to brighten the mood.

Traffic through the town proved to be extremely light and, before she knew it, Phoebe was pulling into the car park behind the shops. Climbing out of her car, which she lovingly called her *Tesoro* – it was the Italian word for treasure – Phoebe turned her mind to tonight's dinner date with Martin. Like the faithful servant he was, her shamelessly ambitious fiancé had chosen to remain in London, where he worked as an executive producer at her father's record company, rather than accompany her on this trip. Although the decision had left her disappointed, Phoebe had long since come to understand that nothing came before

Martin's career, not even her, so she supposed she ought to be grateful that he'd agreed to finish work early today, and that he was driving all the way up from London to share her final night in Norfolk with her.

Deep down, she suspected that Martin had only acquiesced to that because her father had indicated it would please him. Martin was a shameless toady who would do anything to further ingratiate himself with daddy. Still, to celebrate Martin's 'sacrifice', she had booked them a table for eight-thirty at one of their favourite restaurants.

Before meeting him, she intended to enjoy her customary evening walk around the Mere. These solitary strolls always seemed to raise her spirits and reinvigorate her, even when she was at her lowest ebb, like now, and she would miss them dearly when she returned to London.

As she set off towards the path that led from the car park down to the Mere, she glanced over her shoulder at her Tesoro, thinking that it was possibly the cutest car she had ever seen – far better suited to her character and temperament than the garish BMW her snobbish father had wanted her to have. Speaking of BMWs, some inconsiderate arsehole, who obviously had far more money than sense, had thoughtlessly parked a silver three series right across the narrow entrance to the footpath. Cursing under her breath, Phoebe had to suck in her tummy and shuffle sideways in order to squeeze through the piddling gap that the braindead moron had left her.

It was nearly eight-fifteen by the time Phoebe returned to the car park. She hadn't intended to be gone so long but, as usual, she had become totally absorbed in the antics of the cute little Mallard ducklings down by the lake and she had lost all track of time. Even though she was now running late, Phoebe found herself smiling as she recalled how sweet the tiddly ducklings had looked as they'd copied their mother – a fine-looking hen with mottled brown buff plumage and a bright orange bill smudged with black – foraging around the shallow waters by the edge of the lake in search of food.

The smile faded when she saw that the badly positioned BMW was still blocking the gate back into the car park. Why would anyone choose to park their car like that? She might have been a tad more understanding if the place had been super busy and there had been no alternative, but it wasn't and there was, and it really grated on her that some inconsiderate douchebag had parked across the entrance out of sheer bloody ignorance.

As she drew nearer, she noticed that the passenger door was slightly open, and a Black Sabbath track was blaring out from within. Her mouth formed a tight little moue. "Excuse me," she called as she approached the car. "I'm in a bit of a hurry, so would you mind moving your car back a bit so that I can squeeze through without having to perform a bloody contortionist's act?"

No answer was forthcoming, which was hardly surprising, given that it would have taken a minor miracle for anyone to be able to hear her over the racket coming from inside.

Hands on hips, Phoebe tutted impatiently. Enough was enough; she had tried being polite, but that hadn't worked, so now she would let him have a piece of her mind. Squeezing through the gap, she aggressively pulled the door open and thrust her head inside. "I said, can you...Oh!"

The car was empty.

As she stood up, something heavy thudded into the base of her skull, causing an explosion of pain. As the world started to spin out of control, there was a terrible sensation of falling, followed by blackness.

Susie Sergeant barged into Tyler's office, with Colin Franklin riding her slipstream. Both were grinning triumphantly. "We've got a name for our suspect," she announced breathlessly.

Tyler raised an enquiring eyebrow. "And where did we get that from?"

"Someone from The Yard just phoned in the results from the blood-stained fingerprint Juliet found on the bus," Colin explained, grinning like he'd just won the lottery.

Tyler's weariness was instantly forgotten as he found himself getting caught up in their euphoria. "That's great news," he said, breaking into a wide smile.

Susie handed over a sheet of paper with the suspect's details scribbled on it. "His name's John Anthony Spencer. I've asked Dean to run him through the PNC to see what he's known for. If you like–"

Tyler held up a hand, cutting her off mid-sentence. "Sorry to interrupt you," he said, reaching for the phone, "but I need to pass this information to Dill." He felt mean for raining on her parade like that, but the sooner Dillon knew about this development, the sooner he could get the manhunt underway. Hanging up, two minutes later, he looked up at Susie and smiled apologetically. "You were saying?"

"I was about to ask you if you wanted to accompany us over to Dean's desk to see what he's managed to dig up?"

"I'd be delighted to," Tyler said, easing back his chair.

Thirty seconds later, all three of them were crowded around Dean Fletcher, staring down at him expectantly. "Come on then, Deano. What dirt have you uncovered so far?" Tyler asked.

Dean responded with a noncommittal grunt. He had logged into the Police National Computer and was working his way through Spencer's criminal record. "I've literally only just started looking at his PNC record, but I can already tell you that he's not a pleasant bloke," he announced in his usual dour tone. "He's thirty-two years old, with a string of convictions dating back to his teens, mainly for car theft, burglary and carrying offensive weapons... looks like there are a few minor assaults as well." Scrolling down to the next page on his screen, Dean suddenly paused. "Hello, what's this?"

Behind them, the office door swung open and Dillon strode in. "What have we got?" he asked, joining them at Dean's desk.

"Well, on top of everything else," Dean said, "it looks like this

Spencer bloke's a paedo. Eight years ago, he was convicted of the kidnap and rape of a minor, and he was sentenced to a twelve stretch."

"Interesting," Dillon said, leaning forward to get a closer look at the screen. "When did he get out?"

Dean scrolled down, trying to find this information. "Hmmm, there's nothing on the system to suggest that he's been released," he announced a few seconds later.

"Well," Tyler said, folding his arms tetchily, "fingerprints don't lie, so he obviously has been."

"Perhaps the PLO hasn't had a chance to update the PNC yet," Franklin suggested.

Tyler snorted. "How long would it have taken the Police Liaison Officer to fire off a quick e-mail to the PNC Bureau? A minute or two? Five at the most."

"Perhaps the PLO's off sick?" Franklin offered as an alternative explanation.

"Maybe," Dillon allowed. "Whatever the reason, it's too late to do anything about it now."

Tyler wasn't impressed. The information should have been readily available on the system. "Dean, I'll need you to get straight onto the prison Security Governor first thing tomorrow morning. With a bit of luck, they'll have a release address for Spencer, especially if he's been let out on licence."

"If he's on licence, he'll also have a probation officer assigned to him," Susie pointed out.

"Good point," Tyler said, nodding thoughtfully. "Can you chase up the probation service and see what info they can give us?"

"Will do," Dean said, jotting his instructions down on a sheet of scrap paper.

"In the meantime, I'll need you to get Spencer circulated on the PNC and, I know it's a royal pain in the arse, but you'll also need to update the briefing slide you created earlier to include his name, and then resend it to all surrounding stations. I want it to be made available for the night shift when they come on duty at ten."

"I'll get straight on it," Dean promised, calmly adding the latest instructions to his ever growing list of things to do.

―――――

Ben Cunningham was beside himself with worry. Martin had just phoned him from the restaurant, where he was still waiting for Phoebe, who should have been there twenty-five minutes earlier, to see if they had any idea why she was so late.

"Maybe she just lost track of the time," Jessica suggested, ever the optimist.

Ben shook his head, emphatically. "Martin reckons he's been ringing her mobile non-stop, but the bloody thing keeps going straight to voicemail."

Jessica dismissed this with a shrug. "Perhaps her battery's died?"

Ben glared at her, annoyed that she wasn't taking what was clearly a very disturbing development seriously enough. "No, something's definitely wrong." He was pacing up and down now, growing more agitated with every passing second.

Jessica countered by offering a more rational explanation. "You know how she likes to go for long walks down by the Mere of an evening. It's one of her coping mechanisms. Perhaps she just walked further than she meant to, and she's now running late." Despite her optimism, Jessica was conscious of a little niggle of anxiety that had started to form in the pit of her stomach.

"She would have phoned him if that were the case," Ben snapped.

"Not if her battery were dead, or if she simply forgot to take her phone with her," Jessica insisted. "It wouldn't be the first time she's done something harebrained like that, after all."

Ben fidgeted, restlessly. "I can't just sit here and do nothing," he growled. "I've made up my mind. I'm going to drive up to the cottage. Are you coming with me?" It was more of a demand than a request.

Jessica's forehead wrinkled in consternation, which took some doing after all the Botox injections she'd had. "Don't you think that driving all the way up to Norfolk, just because she's twenty-five minutes late for a dinner date, is a little extreme?"

Ben shrugged, forlornly. "Maybe – I don't know." A long sigh of frustration. "All I know for sure is it's a hell of a coincidence that the day after that raping bastard was released, our daughter goes missing."

"We don't know that she has gone missing," Jessica said, stubbornly clinging to the hope that Phoebe had just forgotten the time. News of Spencer's release had clearly unsettled her, and there was a distinct possibility that their daughter just needed some time alone, and that she would reappear at any minute, completely oblivious to all the panic she had created.

Please God, let that be the case, Jessica prayed.

———

Phoebe's eyes flickered open to find the world swathed in stygian blackness. She was lying on her left side, and the unyielding surface beneath her body was extremely uncomfortable. It took her a moment to work out that she was on a dusty concrete floor, and not a bed. Raising her head, Phoebe gasped at the unexpected pain that exploded in the base of her skull. "Hello...?" she whispered, her voice barely rising above a croak. "Is anyone there?"

Silence.

Afraid and confused, Phoebe lowered her aching head back onto the floor. Her brain felt sluggish, like a car engine constantly being cranked over but refusing to start. It was the same heavy feeling that she'd had when her doctor put her on a course of strong antidepressants. Despite the fug that was dulling her mind, she sensed that something was very wrong.

As the echoes of her rasping breath came back at her in the darkness, she suddenly became aware of the vile-smelling hood covering her head. Overcome by a feeling of intense claustrophobia, Phoebe violently shook her head in an attempt to dislodge it. As she drew in breath to scream, the foul-tasting material was sucked deep into her mouth, making her choke. Beneath the hood, her eyes widened in fright, and she could hear the blood pounding in her ears. Convinced that she was suffocating, Phoebe frantically tried to force the material out of her mouth with her tongue. Coughing and spluttering, she finally expelled the alien object and sucked in air. She was so stressed that her body started shutting down. She couldn't think; she couldn't move; she couldn't make a sound. Her chest spasmed and tightened and it became difficult to breathe.

Very difficult...

And then she blacked out.

The faint only lasted a few seconds. When she came too, her limbs were so unbelievably heavy that all she could do was lay there, feeling completely drained. Gradually, Phoebe's breathing returned to normal and, as if the spell had been broken, she found herself able to think again.

What the hell was happening to her?

Where was she?

How long has she been there?

Phoebe remembered walking along the footpath that led up from the Mere to the car park behind the shops but, after that, everything was hazy.

And then the chilling reality of her situation struck her. "Oh, God! No!" she whispered, biting her bottom lip so hard that her teeth broke the skin.

It was *him*.

It was Spencer!

He had found her, and he had abducted her again.

A stream of hot bile immediately rushed into her throat, but she somehow managed to swallow it back down, knowing that she couldn't afford to throw up inside the hood. Thankfully, after a moment or two, the bout of nausea passed.

"No, no, no!" Phoebe sobbed as she lay on the ground, trembling with fear. "Please God, no!" She couldn't go through *that* again; her sanity had barely survived the first ordeal.

An overwhelming sense of dread descended over her, covering

her like a death shroud. Phoebe screwed her eyes shut and repeated the mantra her therapist had taught her: *I'm strong, I've moved on and I'm getting my life back.*

The first ordeal had changed Phoebe in unimaginable ways, eroding the person she was born to be beyond all recognition. Her fear of Spencer had driven her to forsake her morals and perform degrading acts with a man she hated in order to survive. The ignominy of having done that had haunted her ever since, and it had taught her that death was infinitely preferable to living with the burden of such unbearable shame. As she lay there, shivering despite the heat, Pheobe vowed to herself that she would never permit that monster to violate her again, not even if she had to pay for her defiance with her life.

But Phoebe had no intention of dying.

I'm strong, I've moved on and I'm getting my life back.

Forcing all other thoughts from her mind, Phoebe repeated the simple intonation. Before long, her fear receded and another emotion asserted its dominance. To her surprise, it was hatred, pure and undiluted, and it was fuelled, not by her desire to survive, but by her hunger for revenge.

As she lay there, it spread through her like an all-consuming fire, burning away everything in its path. Empowered by this strange new feeling, Phoebe took a deep breath and forced herself to concentrate.

Come on, Phoebe! You might not be able to see, but you've still got all your other senses! Make use of them! Don't let that bastard get the better of you again!

She was laying on a concrete floor with an abrasive surface, which probably ruled out her being kept inside a house. Could he have taken her to an industrial unit or a warehouse, perhaps?

There was a warm breeze blowing gently from behind, which suggested she was being kept in a well-ventilated room, but there was no sound of passing traffic, and nothing to indicate the nearby presence of other people. Had he taken her somewhere remote?

Ignoring the dull throbbing in her skull, Phoebe lifted her head and sniffed the air, cautiously at first, but then with more gusto.

Through the heavy material that covered her face, she identified the distinctive smell of old grass. Buried beneath that, she thought she detected the musk of animal fur and dried dung, and there was something else, possibly the oily smell of old machinery?

Her lips narrowed to a thin slit. Was the depraved bastard holding her prisoner at a farm? Phoebe cocked her head to one side and strained her ears, listening for the tell-tale animal noises that would confirm her suspicions, but there was nothing at all.

She knew that she had to do something, so she attempted to sit up. To her alarm, she was unable to move her limbs. Had the attack left her paralysed? She wriggled her fingers and toes, and then flexed both her knees and her elbows, which was how she discovered that her ankles had been bound together, and her hands had been securely tied behind her back.

"Oh no..." The realisation left her feeling utterly powerless.

Salty tears pricked her eyes.

Get a grip on yourself, you silly girl! You can do this!

She could, and she would!

Rocking herself from side to side to build up momentum, she tried again.

And failed again.

"Come on... you can do this..." She hissed through gritted teeth.

This time, accompanied by much grunting and groaning, Phoebe clumsily forced herself into a sitting position. Beneath the hood, her face was becoming flushed with perspiration, and she irritably blinked away the sweat that was stinging her eyes. It took her several seconds to get her breath back, but then Phoebe began wriggling backwards on her rump, not having the slightest clue where she was going, and not particularly caring.

Eventually, her back collided with something solid and she came to a jarring halt. Tentatively exploring the unseen obstacle with her fingers, she pulled out several clumps of what could only be straw.

It's a bale of sodding hay!

Spencer was leaning against the side of the stolen car, enjoying a cigarette. He loved these warm summer evenings when the sun didn't set until late and, having missed out on so many during his incarceration, he fully intended to make the most of this one. He could hardly believe that, just a couple of days ago, he had been cooped up in his little cell, staring at the opaque window and pining for freedom, just as he had every night for the past eight years. Smiling inwardly, he only just about resisted the urge to give himself a good hard pinch, just to make sure that he wasn't dreaming.

As much as he hated to admit it, Skippy had done incredibly well to find this old barn. It was literally in the middle of nowhere, located within a large natural dip that was accessed by a winding dirt track and completely hidden from the main road above. Even if Phoebe went into one when she saw him, there was no one around for miles to hear her screams.

Spencer was still smarting over the way that that Skippy had abused him for stabbing Mr Beardy the night before. If his cousin thought that treating his own flesh and blood that way was acceptable, then he didn't deserve to be included in Spencer's plans any longer, and he would have to forgo his share of the ransom when Ben Cunningham coughed up a million quid in exchange for his daughter's safe return.

Taking a final lazy drag, he threw the butt on the floor and stamped it out underfoot.

Spencer's stomach was tying itself in knots as he set off towards the barn to check on Phoebe. He knew that he was being daft, getting himself all worked up like this, but he just couldn't help it. They had been apart for eight long years and, even though his heart told him that everything would be fine, what if it wasn't? He didn't know how he would cope if the unthinkable happened and she rejected him. Just the thought of that happening was enough to bring him out in a cold sweat.

With nothing but a crumbling, disused well to keep it company, the ramshackle barn was a sorry sight to behold. Surrounded by overgrown weeds, the countless cruel winters and hot summers had taken a heavy toll on it. Numerous tiles were missing from the sagging roof, and some of the wooden panels that made up the walls looked fragile enough to disintegrate if anyone leaned against them. In fact, the abandoned building seemed on the verge of imploding, and he was a little surprised there were no warning signs proclaiming that it had been condemned as hazardous.

Spencer tugged at the heavy doors, and the rusted hinges protested worse than a cantankerous old man as they reluctantly swung open. Inside, slithers of daylight streamed in through the myriad holes in the roof, each one creating its own little spotlight to showcase the millions of dust motes floating in the stale air.

He paused just inside the entrance to let his eyes acclimatise to the dimness within, turning his nose up at the rancid stench of mouldy hay and dried dung that immediately assailed his nostrils. "I hate the fucking countryside," he cursed under his breath.

A long line of foul-smelling wooden stalls, which he assumed had once contained livestock, spanned the entire left side of the barn. A large hayloft was suspended above them, and Spencer could see that the floor was covered in a thick layer of dirty straw. A rickety ladder led up to the hayloft, but he had no intention of ascending. Even if the rungs didn't break when he put his weight on them, which they undoubtedly would, the worryingly bowed ceiling was bound to give way the moment he stepped onto it.

On its own in the middle of the barn, like the centrepiece in a car showroom, there sat the sad shell of an old tractor. It had probably been quite an impressive piece of machinery in its day, but that day was long gone. He could see that, over time, it had been stripped for parts, leaving nothing but a russet coloured husk.

At the back of the barn, in the shadowy area beyond the tractor, he could just about make out the silhouette of a small mountain of hay bales. It looked as though they had been piled high for storage, and then forgotten about.

Spencer wondered if bats were living in the rafters. He had heard that the flying rodents liked old buildings like this. He had also heard that they sometimes carried Rabies, and that, he knew, was fatal to humans. Keeping one eye peeled for bats, he crossed the barn to the spot where he had laid Phoebe to rest fifteen minutes earlier, only to find that she was nowhere to be seen.

"No!" he gasped.

Heart in mouth, he frantically swivelled his head in search of her. A moment later, he detected a slight movement deep within the darkness. As he rushed across the barn towards it, he was relieved to find the woman he loved had propped herself up against the hay bales by the rear wall. The sight of her sitting there, head bowed onto her chest, took his breath away. Even with a hood covering her head, she was still breathtakingly beautiful and, for a moment, all he could do was stand there and stare at her, completely transfixed. He had dreamed of this moment for so long, acting it out in his mind on an almost nightly basis before going to sleep, but now that it was actually here, he suddenly felt awkward and tongue-tied.

What would he say to her?

How would she react?

Like an idiot, he hadn't thought to bring her flowers or chocolates to demonstrate his love, and he was still wearing the same crusty clothing that he'd worn the day before.

Raising his arms, Spencer tentatively sniffed his armpits, one after the other. With a grimace, he recoiled from a smell that was every bit as unpleasant as the barn's pervading odour of animal dung. Suddenly, feeling very self-conscious about his lack of hygiene, Spencer turned and bolted back towards the car. He didn't have any deodorant with him, but there was a large bottle of mineral water on the back seat, and he could splash some of that over his festering armpits to freshen them up. He decided to take a quick peek in the vanity mirror while he was at it, just to make sure there were no embarrassing food stains around his mouth or unsightly clumps of gooey sleep in the corners of his eyes. Girls tended to notice little things like that, and he desperately wanted to make a good impression on Phoebe, to show her what she had been missing.

9

WORST FEARS CONFIRMED

Martin Whitling had waited at the restaurant for the best part of an hour before reluctantly conceding defeat and driving over to the cottage.

He had half-hoped to find Phoebe sitting there waiting for him but, of course, the place was empty. Kicking his shoes off, Whitling paused on his way through the lounge, dumped his phone and keys, and poured himself a large shot of Glenfiddich before opening the patio doors and stepping into the expansive rear garden.

Unlike Ben Cunningham, who had been pestering him for updates every five minutes since he'd called to say that Phoebe was a no-show, he wasn't remotely worried about her failure to turn up at the restaurant. As far as he was concerned, not that he would ever dare admit this to either Ben or Jess, Phoebe was just doing her usual pampered princess routine. There was absolutely no doubt in his mind that, right now, Phoebe was having a quiet drink in a nearby pub, revelling in the thought of getting everyone all worked up over her disappearance, and heartily looking forward to basking in the attention they'd all lavish upon her when she finally deigned to show her face again.

They had been together for the best part of three years now, and he had popped the question six months earlier, asking her to marry him in a drunken moment of madness that he had bitterly regretted ever since.

Although Martin still genuinely cared for Phoebe, he was no longer in love with her. The harsh reality of the situation was that he had grown to dislike the conniving way that she constantly manipulated the people who cared for her, himself included. Yes, he unreservedly accepted that the terrible ordeal she'd been through eight years earlier had been indescribably hellish, and he didn't for a single moment doubt that the PTSD she still suffered from was very real, or that the dreadful experience had scarred her for life. However – and he felt guilty for even allowing himself to think this – that didn't excuse her for constantly milking the situation for all it was worth, or for shamelessly encouraging the endless adulation that her doting parents heaped upon her in their never-ending quest to compensate for the horrors she'd endured. It was clear to him, as a relative outsider, that they blamed themselves for her abduction, and that Phoebe was perfectly content to let them do so.

He had fallen into the sympathy trap himself at first, and he had mollycoddled Phoebe for the first two years of their relationship. Gradually, over time, he had come to realise that Phoebe actually liked being a victim, and that she had no intention of giving up her prized status and moving on with her life. It was a discovery that had injected poison into their relationship, souring his feelings for her until they withered and died.

The sad truth was that Martin had been trying to find a way to end the relationship for a while now but, whenever he worked up the courage to broach the subject, Phoebe's mental health conveniently relapsed and, as much as he wanted out, he just couldn't bring himself to pull the plug while she was feeling depressed.

She was toying with him; he knew that but–

The sound of his mobile ringing inside the house shattered his reverie and, with a sullen curse, he rushed into the lounge, snatching it up from the trolley where he'd swapped it for a much-needed drink. There was no time to check caller ID and, as he thumbed the green button, he prayed that it was Phoebe, calling to let him know she was okay, and not Ben, making a nuisance of himself again.

"Hello?" he said, a little breathlessly.

"Have you heard from Phoebe, yet?" the woman at the other end of the crackly line asked, skipping straight past the pleasantries. Her name was Anna Manson, and she was Phoebe's best friend.

Martin's face hardened. "Not yet," he said, irked by the directness of Anna's tone. Then the penny dropped, and he let out a long sigh. "I take it Ben's been on the phone to you?" As he spoke, Martin tucked the handset into his chin and poured himself a refill from the decanter on the side

"I just finished speaking to him," Anna confirmed. *"The poor dear's worried sick."*

Martin rolled his eyes. "When it comes to Phoebe, Ben's always worried sick." He knew it was an incredibly crass thing to say, but Phoebe's shenanigans were starting to wear very thin, and he couldn't believe that he was the only one who could see that she was playing them.

There was a sharp intake of breath. *"Oh, Martin, don't be like that,"* Anna rebuked him, her tone becoming unusually harsh. *"Surely, you can understand why he's fretting so much? I mean, poor Phoebe's gone missing a day after the monster who kidnapped and raped her was released. You have to admit, it's a very troubling coincidence."*

Poor Phoebe! Martin inwardly scoffed at that. "Leave it out, it's classic Phoebe, playing mind games with us to ensure we keep pandering to her every whim when she eventually shows up."

Anna's voice softened, became laced with guilt. *"You don't think... You don't think that she's doing this because of us, do you?"*

Martin stiffened. "What do you mean?"

"Well, she's been acting a little strange around me lately, and I've started to wonder if she suspects something's going on between us."

Martin closed his eyes and placed the cool glass against his forehead.

Not this again. Not now!

"Anna, please!"

Anna brushed the plea aside. "*No, Martin, I won't be fobbed off this time. I just think the kindest thing to do would be to tell Phoebe the truth about us, and put her out of her misery,*"

Anna was starting to sound like a broken record but, rather than antagonise her, Martin took a deep breath and forced himself to speak calmly, knowing that the conversation would quickly deteriorate into another argument otherwise. "Anna, you *know* I can't do that. How do you think she'll react to the news that her fiancé and her best friend are having a secret relationship behind her back?" He had been tempted to say 'affair' – a word he knew she hated – out of spite, but then he'd thought better of it. Her injured gasp told him that, even without the A word, his comment had stung. He knew he was being petty, but he couldn't help but feel a small twinge of satisfaction.

"*You make it sound like something sordid,*" Anna protested, and he visualised her hanging her head in shame.

"I didn't mean it like that," he lied.

"*I know. And I know you're really worried about hurting Phoebe, but she's going to find out at some point anyway, so why not tell her now? Surely, that's the kindest thing to do?*"

Martin pinched the bridge of his nose, feeling a headache coming on. Was he just swapping one demanding woman for another? Maybe he should dump them both and be done with it. Another deep breath. "Anna, it's not that simple. I need to pick a time when Phoebe's emotionally stable, and the fact that she's buggered off tonight suggests to me that this clearly isn't it." He consciously softened his tone, trying to inject the intimacy of a caring lover into it. "I just need you to be patient for a little longer, my angel. I'll tell her as soon as I can, I promise."

Silence.

"Anna?"

"*Okay,*" she said, sounding terribly hurt. "*I'd better go. Will you let me know as soon as you hear anything?*"

"Of course."

She hung up without even saying goodbye.

He knocked back a large gulp of whisky. "Bloody women!" he complained into his now empty glass.

Almost immediately, the phone started ringing again.

Wiping his mouth on the back of his hand, Martin glanced down expectantly. Surely this had to be Phoebe?

His heart sank as he recognised the incoming number: It was Ben-bloody-Cunningham again.

Phoebe froze the instant she heard the barn's protesting doors creak open again. A moment later, there came the sound of dirt crunching underfoot. Someone was approaching her. Was it the same mysterious person who had entered the barn a little while ago, only to leave without saying anything?

Was it him – Spencer – or someone else entirely?

The few paltry seconds it took the newcomer to traverse the barn seemed to stretch into eternity.

Suddenly, without warning, the hood covering her head was whipped off. After the absolute darkness of the filthy sack, even the half-light of the dilapidated barn seemed blinding, and she instinctively screwed her eyes shut to block out the glare of the evening sun, which was shining in through the open doors of the barn, silhouetting the person standing in front of her.

Blinking rapidly, Phoebe could just about make out the blurred shape of a tall figure looming over her. Her eyes were stinging, but she forced them to stay open and watch as the figure moved forward and knelt down beside her. Her heart lurched as the man's face came into focus, confirming her worst fears. It was *him*, the loathsome man who had stolen her innocence and ruined her life. Spencer was so close that she could feel his breath caressing the side of her face. He looked older, more haggard than she remembered, but she supposed eight years in prison could do that to a person.

His features broke into a goofy smile, exposing a mouth full of bad teeth. "Hello Pheebs," he whispered, staring at her like a lovesick puppy. "Have you missed me?"

When she didn't answer, a troubled crease knitted Spencer's brow, and his mouth turned down in a reverse smile. He ran his eyes over her, allowing them to linger on her breasts, and she could feel him undressing her with them. The sensation made her skin crawl.

After a moment, he shifted on his haunches. "You don't look very comfortable. Let me help you," he said, reaching for her legs.

Phoebe instantly recoiled, feeling the stress build in every sinew of her body as he came nearer. *Don't touch me, you disgusting monster!*

Spencer's hands froze, mid-air, and there was an awkward moment's hesitation while he considered how best to put her at ease. "Please don't be afraid," he begged in a voice that sounded pathetically needy. "I would *never* do anything to hurt you."

If she hadn't been so afraid, she might have laughed at the perverse irony of his words. *You already have, you heartless bastard!*

Moving with exaggerated slowness, which she supposed was his way of demonstrating that he intended her no harm, Spencer gently took hold of Phoebe's ankles and straightened her legs out.

She went rigid at the contact but didn't try to resist, in case it angered him.

"There," he said releasing them with a lingering caress. "Isn't that better?"

She found herself nodding, just to appease him.

Spencer reached behind his back and withdrew a nasty looking knife from his waistband.

On seeing it, Phoebe drew back in fear, sinking onto the hay bale behind her.

"It's okay, Pheebs," he assured her with a crooked smile. "I'm just going to untie you." He mimed the motion of sawing to demonstrate his good intentions.

Initially, she was too mesmerised by the sight of the blade to respond, but then she tore her eyes away from it and looked up at him, slowly nodded her understanding.

"That's it, just relax," he soothed. Gently sliding the blade between her ankles, he began carefully slicing through the thick gaffer tape. "There," he said, as it gave way with a soft ripping sound.

Standing up, Spencer tucked the knife back into his waistband, adjusting it so that it was nestled comfortably against his spine. "I'm gonna help you stand up now," he informed her, before leaning forward and placing his hands under her armpits. "On three, okay. Ready? One, two, three." With a grunt, he hauled her to her feet.

The moment he released her, her knees gave way, and she would have dropped like a stone had he not stepped forward to catch her. "It's all right babes, I've got you," he grunted as he wrapped his scrawny arms around her waist.

Phoebe's blood ran cold at the contact, but she felt powerless to resist. It was as though she were in the clutches of an energy vampire; a Satanic creature capable of draining her life force merely by touching her.

Spencer dragged her backwards, not caring that her expensive shoes were scraping along the rough concrete floor, until he reached the old livestock area. Wrapping an arm around her waist to support her, he hoisted her into a standing position and leaned her against one of the wooden frames. He continued holding her until it was obvious that she could support herself unaided.

"It's been a long time, eh?" he said, grinning bashfully.

Phoebe nodded, still too numb to speak. Her legs still felt like jelly, and she was afraid they would give way again at any moment, but she didn't want him to see in case he touched her again.

"I got out yesterday," Spencer casually informed her. "They've put me up in some shit-hole of a halfway house till I can find a place of my own. It's not much, but it'll have to do, I suppose."

Phoebe cleared her throat. "My hands," she managed to say.

Spencer seemed baffled by her remark. "What about them?"

Phoebe twisted her torso around so that he could see them tied behind her back. "They've gone numb, and they're *really* hurting me. Can you untie them, please?"

Spencer squirmed uncomfortably. "I dunno about that, Pheebs," he said, looking down at his feet and shaking his head. "No offence, but I need to be sure I can trust you first."

"What do you think I'm going to do?" she asked, struggling to remain calm.

Spencer just shrugged, a deflated motion that signified he didn't have an answer.

Phoebe wanted to yell at him, but she knew doing that would achieve nothing. Spencer wasn't the type to respond to histrionics. Instead, she forced herself to draw in a deep breath and release it slowly. "Spence?"

He shrugged again, but it was more belligerent this time, as if he didn't like being put under pressure. "I dunno, run away, or scream for help."

"But I could just as easily do either of those things now," she pointed out, trying her utmost not to sound patronising.

There was a childlike simplicity about Spencer and, for the first time, she realised just how intellectually stunted he was. In that instant, a microscopic bud of hope blossomed inside Phoebe's heart. Maybe his inherent stupidity was something that she could exploit to her advantage? If she could somehow persuade him that she wanted to rekindle their relationship, he might lower his guard enough for her to make a break for it. She decided to test the waters with a little flattery. "You're looking very well," she said, forcing a rigid smile onto her face.

That got his attention. "Am I?"

"Uh-huh. And I really like what you've done with your hair." She didn't; it looked as though someone had gone at it with a blunt lawnmower.

Spencer self-consciously raised a hand to his head, stroking his prison buzz cut. "I think it makes me look old," he confided, "but it's easier to look after when it's short like this."

"It suits you," she insisted. "You should keep it like that."

Spencer blushed at the compliment. "Maybe I will, Pheebs, if you really like it."

She nodded insistently, hoping that she wasn't overdoing it. "I do. Now, how about you untie my hands so that we can sit down together and talk?"

The frown was back in place. "I don't think that's a good idea," he said, wringing his hands together apologetically.

She remembered how stubborn he could be once he'd made his mind up about something, so she decided not to push her luck, just in case he became suspicious of her motives. "Fair enough, I don't blame you, but if you're not happy untying me, can you at least re-tie my hands in front of me? They're so painful like this."

Spencer thought about that for a moment. "Okay," he eventually said. Without another word, he spun on his heel and set off towards the barn door.

"Wait!"

Spencer turned to look at her, his face expectant. "Yes?"

"Where are you going?" She didn't care; she just wanted to know how long she would have until he returned.

He grinned at her. "I'm just going to get my roll of gaffer tape from the back of the car. Why, are you missing me already?"

Like a hole in the head, you pathetic freak!

She forced out a little chuckle that sounded more like she was choking on something. "Of course I am," she replied, doing her best to sound upbeat. He seemed so pleased by her response that she decided to turn the charm up a dial. "I don't suppose you have any water, do you? Only I'm terribly thirsty."

Spencer nodded, just the once. "I've got some in the car. I'll bring it back with me."

Tyler was halfway through writing up his latest Decision Log entry when his telephone rang. It had been doing that a lot, and it was getting on his nerves.

Lowering his pen with a little growl of frustration, he scooped it up, thinking that he could well and truly do without the constant distraction. He could feel a headache coming on, and he knew he ought to take a five minute break to rest his eyes, stretch his legs and get some much needed fresh air, but there was still so much to do, and he was determined to push on and get as much of the laborious paperwork out of the way as he could before finally calling it a day.

"DCI Tyler," he said with a weary sigh.

"*Hello, handsome!*"

Tyler's face lit up. "Kelly! What a lovely surprise. I wasn't expecting to hear from you until Friday."

DC Kelly Flowers was Tyler's significant other, and she was currently in Lyon, France, halfway through the first week of a three-week exchange programme that had been organised through the European Police College, or CEPO as it was more commonly known.

She chuckled, throatily. "*Well, you know me. I like to keep you on your toes!*" Her voice became coy. "*Then there's the fact that I was missing you like crazy.*"

A warm fuzzy feeling ran through him when she said that. "Yeah, I'm missing you, too."

Kelly laughed. "*I should hope so, too. So, come on then, tell me, what you've been up to while I've been away?*" Her voice suddenly became mock stern. "*I hope you've been behaving yourself, eating proper food instead of getting takeaways every night, and not staying up till the early hours binging on Bond movies?*"

Tyler had a weakness for Bond, especially the Sean Connery incarnation, and he could happily get through a couple of films a night if left to his own devices. He grinned. They had been together now for almost twenty months and, in that time, she had learned to read him like a book. "Well, I've had a couple of takeaways," he confessed guiltily, "but we took on a new job yesterday, so I doubt I'll get to watch much TV for the foreseeable future."

"*A new job? Anything interesting?*"

Tyler pulled a face. "Not really. Some drunken idiot on a bus stabbed another passenger after an argument. We already know who he is, and the evidence seems pretty strong, so it's just a matter of catching him. It shouldn't prove too challenging." A thought suddenly occurred to him. "What time will you be getting back on Friday evening?"

Kelly was supposed to be catching the Eurostar straight after work, returning to the UK for the weekend so that she could accompany Tyler to a dinner party on Saturday evening. Truth be told, he was dreading the event, which was being hosted by his ex-wife, Jenny, and her new husband, Eddie but, as they had recently asked him and Kelly to be godparents for their son, Ralph, he felt compelled to go. He really hoped that she wasn't calling to drop a last-minute bombshell on him by saying that she couldn't get away.

There was an awkward silence. *"Ah. About that,"* Kelly eventually said, confirming his suspicions. *"I've been invited to participate in a massive anti-terrorism raid during the early hours of Saturday morning, and I'm not sure what time I'll get off duty afterwards, so I might struggle to get back in time for the dinner party."* There was a moment's hesitation, and then she continued, speaking hurriedly. *"Obviously, I'll tell them that I can't go on the raid if you don't want me to, but it's a very good opportunity for me to network."*

Tyler closed his eyes. *Of course I don't want you to go!* Taking a deep breath, he tried to hide his disappointment by injecting a large dose of buoyancy into his voice. "No, don't be silly. You go. I'll explain to Jenny and Eddie. I'm sure they'll understand." He doubted that either of them would mind. Jenny didn't particularly like Kelly, although he couldn't work out why, and Eddie was far too self-absorbed in himself to care about anyone else. Tyler had wanted her there purely for his sake, not theirs.

"Obviously, I do want to come," she said, sounding conflicted, *"and I promise I still will, if I can get away in time, but it's all going to depend on how the operation pans out."*

Tyler knew how these things went. The chances of her making it were minuscule, so he might as well start resigning himself to the fact that he was going alone. "Don't sweat it," he said, suddenly feeling very disheartened. "As long as you're back the following weekend, for the christening."

"*Of course I will be,* " she promised. "*Otherwise, you'd have to take Tony with you as your plus one.*"

Tyler shuddered at the thought. "God, can you imagine that?" Dillon was his closest friend, and he had never forgiven Jenny for leaving Jack and shacking up with Eddie Maitland. The big lug was hardly subtle at the best of times and, once he got a couple of drinks inside him, there was a very real risk that he'd say something inflammatory, especially if either Jenny or Eddie rubbed him up the wrong way, which they seemed able to manage just by breathing.

"That's definitely not an option."

"*I'm really sorry about this, Jack, but don't worry. Whatever happens, I'll be back for the christening,*" Kelly promised.

Tyler pinched the bridge of his nose, feeling his headache go up another notch. "Listen, Kelly, I'm in the middle of something, right now, so I'm going to have to say goodbye. Call me again on Friday, and hopefully, by then, you'll have more of an idea."

"*Oh, okay,*" she said, clearly surprised that he was ending the call so quickly. "*I love you.*"

"I love you, too."

———

Phoebe began examining her surroundings in earnest the moment that Spencer stepped out of the barn. Now that she could actually see, she was able to take in much more information, and she drank it down greedily. The place was a lot bigger than she had imagined, and it was in a truly dreadful state of disrepair.

How the hell did he find this place? He's only been out a day!

There were double doors at both ends of the building, but the ones at the rear were almost completely blocked by an eight foot high wall of stagnating hay bales, so she discounted them as a possible means of egress.

Casting a nervous glance at the front doors, which he had closed after him, Phoebe set about exploring her makeshift prison. She knew that she would have to tread very carefully because he would fly off the handle if he returned to find her snooping around.

As frightened as she was of getting caught, Phoebe knew that she had to press ahead if she was going to get the better of her captor and see him brought to justice.

I'm strong. I've moved on and I'm getting my life back.

Conscious that she didn't have much time, Phoebe darted between the wooden framed animal enclosures, checking them out one at a time, and hoping to stumble across an old sickle or a rusty pitchfork that she could use as a weapon. Anything would do, even a big lump of wood, as long as it was heavy enough to cave the bastard's empty head in.

Unfortunately, there was nothing even remotely suitable.

As soon as she finished in the stalls, Phoebe hurried over to the tractor in the middle of the barn. Maybe, if she were really lucky, a few tools had been abandoned with it. A large adjustable spanner would be perfect. It was an old John Deere, one of those old-fashioned things with a single bucket seat, massive steering wheel, and no roof, and it looked like it had been around since the Second World War. Buried beneath all the rust and grime, she could just about make out the last remaining traces of its original green paint.

Phoebe quickly circled the ancient tractor. Then, dropping to her knees, she bent forward – not the easiest thing to do with her hands tied behind her back – and peered underneath. Apart from all the dust and dirt, and a dried oil patch, there was nothing of interest. It suddenly occurred to her that, even if there had been, she would never have been able to pick it up, not with her hands tied behind her back.

Fuming at herself for having wasted precious seconds on a pointless exercise, Phoebe slowly clambered to her feet. As she stood up, her left foot slid on some loose straw and lost traction. Unable to stabilise herself, she tottered sideways, clattering into the engine compartment with a loud thud. Phoebe cringed as the noise reverberated around the barn. Worried that Spencer might have heard, and knowing that he would come straight in to investigate if he had, she quickly moved away from the tractor's filthy carcass. As she did, her yellow summer jacket snagged on a sharp piece of metal protruding from the engine casing. There was a horrendous ripping sound, and then she was jerked to an abrupt halt.

Phoebe glanced down to find that a jagged edged pipe had pierced the material, effectively impaling her. "Damn it," she cursed, giving her jacket an experimental tug. It was immediately obvious that the garment was ruined beyond repair, so she yanked it free, fuming that Spencer had ruined something else that she loved.

To her surprise, a cylindrical piece of metal, about eighteen inches in length, came away with it, and she watched as it tumbled to the floor and rolled to a stop a few feet away.

Firing a nervous glance at the barn doors, Phoebe rushed over to where the pipe had landed and flung herself onto the floor. Landing heavily on her posterior, the way that cops in movies do when they throw themselves onto car bonnets, she ignored the jarring pain that shot up through her buttocks and into her lower spine. Rotating her body so that her hands were facing towards the pipe, she began blindly fumbling for it. A moment later, her fingertips brushed against the cold, hard metal, knocking it just out of reach. Cursing her clumsiness, she shuffled backwards on her aching behind and tried again, this time wrapping her fingers firmly around it.

To her delight, it felt reassuringly solid.

She nodded in satisfaction. This would do the job.

Now, all she had to do was stash it out of sight before Spencer returned. Breathing heavily, she rolled onto her knees, scraping her bare flesh on the rough floor. Wincing in pain, she unsteadily forced herself up onto one foot, and then onto both. Thankfully, she had chosen to go out in flats this evening, because she would almost certainly have twisted an ankle had she been wearing heels.

Checking the door again, she ran over to the hay bales at the rear of the barn. To her horror, just before she got there, she heard the harsh screech of protesting hinges, and the barn doors began to open.

Reaching the hay bales, she spun around to face Spencer, who was now walking towards her, a roll of gaffer tape in one hand and a large bottle of water in the other. The pipe was still in her hand, and she knew that she would be in serious trouble if he spotted it.

Leaning back against the nearest bale of hay, and acting as nonchalantly as she could in the circumstances, Phoebe tried to shove it in.

Nothing happened, It was as though the bale was made of wood, not straw.

Shit!

Phoebe smiled at Spencer, who had almost reached the tractor, at the same time casually shuffling to her left. She stopped when she reached a gap between two bales and eased the pipe in.

The bloody thing became stuck when it was about halfway in.

Phoebe leaned back, using the rocking motion to give it a push. Nothing. The stupid thing didn't budge an inch.

"Alright, Pheebs?" Spencer asked as he took another step closer.

"Fine" she replied, forcing a welcoming grin onto her face. "Just thought I'd stretch my legs, get the circulation going again."

She jiggled the pipe until she felt it free itself of whatever was in its way and, under the pretence of shifting her weight, pushed again. The pipe slid in another couple of inches, and a final shove was enough to complete the job.

With a sigh of relief, she rushed forward to intercept him, stopping directly in front of him to prevent him from going any further.

Spencer frowned, and then looked over her head towards the hay bales.

Suspicious bastard!

Knowing that she needed to distract him before he cottoned on to the fact that she was up to something, Phoebe took another step forward, intent on creating the impression that a sexual tension existed between them. Leaning inwards, so that their faces were only inches apart, she stared him straight in the eyes. "You were ages," she pouted.

Spencer's face reddened, and he swallowed hard. "I've – I've got the water," he stammered. Taking a backward step, he unscrewed the top and held it out towards her mouth so that she could take a sip.

Instead of doing so, Phoebe turned her back towards him and wriggled her fingers. She knew she had him flustered, and she was determined to make the most of it.

"Before I have a drink, would you mind retying my hands in front of me? They're very uncomfortable like this." As she spoke, she smiled at him over her shoulder. "That way, I can wrap my arms around your head and give you a hug."

Spencer almost dropped the bottle in his eagerness to oblige.

10

ESCAPE

Now that Spencer had retied her hands in front of her, Phoebe's movements were far less restricted, and her newfound mobility made her feel even more hopeful of engineering an escape.

As promised, even though it made her flesh crawl to do so, she gave him a big hug as a reward for repositioning her hands. The startled look on his gormless face, as she wrapped her arms around his scrawny neck, might have been amusing to behold had the situation not been so ghastly.

When she released him, Spencer led her over to one of the bales and indicated for her to take a seat. To her horror, he sat down right beside her, encroaching her personal space as he took her tethered hands in his. Phoebe found the unwanted intimacy utterly repugnant and, as he droned on about how much he had missed her, and how much she meant to him, she found herself really struggling to keep her emotions from getting the better of her.

"What was prison like?" she asked him at one point, just to feign interest.

"It was really bad," he admitted, lowering his voice a couple of octaves to emphasise that it hadn't just been bad, it had been *BAD*!

Good! The obvious discomfort that he showed, while telling her about his trials and tribulations in prison, gave her a warm glow of satisfaction.

"But I'm out now," he said, drawing her hands to his face and smothering them with a series of passionate kisses. The grotesque display of affection was so repulsive that she nearly threw up. Somehow, she managed to conceal her true feelings and play the part of the doting girlfriend, pretending to be interested in his mindless drivel, smiling dutifully, and nodding sympathetically every time he paused for breath.

They remained that way for well over an hour, with him doing all of the talking, and her faking the interest he expected her to show. She found every second excruciating and, beneath her outwardly calm façade, Phoebe could feel herself slowly going insane.

As she watched his pasty lips move, not really comprehending the distorted noises that came out of them, she promised herself that, one day, whatever the personal cost, she would make him pay for everything that he had done to her.

It was ten o'clock and, apart from one or two stragglers who were still tying up loose ends, the rest of the team had gone home for the night. Dillon had offered to remain behind and give him a lift home, but Tyler had declined, telling his friend not to worry.

Wishing the dawdlers a good night on his way out of the office, Tyler took the stairs down to the ground floor. He was absolutely shattered, and he couldn't wait to crawl into his bed. It had been a long, gruelling day, and he suspected that tomorrow would go much the same way. Still, on a positive note, at least they now had an identity for their suspect and, starting first thing tomorrow morning, Dillon could start the manhunt in earnest.

As far as the reactive side of the investigation was concerned, they were well ahead of the game. The CCTV viewing and statement taking were all in hand, and the special post mortem examination was being carried out the following morning. Susie would be attending that, along with Dick Jarvis as exhibits officer and Juliet Kennedy in her capacity as Crime Scene Manager.

Dean was going to chase up the prison and probation services and, hopefully, they would be able to provide a current address for Spencer. With a bit of luck, when the arrest team made their entry, they would find him cowering in a cupboard, and it would be job done.

Swapping the building's air-conditioning for the sultry weather outside, Tyler found his thoughts returning to Kelly Flowers. Putting aside the fact that this was the first time they had been apart since she'd moved in with him a little over a year ago, and he was missing her so much that it hurt, he had been relying on having her by his side on Saturday evening to help him struggle through Maitland's tedious dinner party. He didn't want to sound ungrateful, but that sort of thing really wasn't his cup of tea. If memory served, this was the fourth – no, fifth – one that he'd been invited to since Eddie had decided that he and Jack should become friends and, although he had managed to duck out of them all so far, he had finally run out of plausible excuses.

Even though he hadn't actually been to one yet, he just knew that Eddie's dinner parties would be awful, pretentious affairs, attended by a bunch of wealthy, opinionated, not to mention incredibly boring, businessmen and their showpiece wives – basically clones of Eddie and Jenny – with whom he and Kelly had absolutely nothing in common.

Maybe he could tell a little white lie and pretend to be ill, although, now that he thought about it, he had used that excuse once already. Maybe, the manhunt would still be ongoing and he could–

Tyler's mobile phone rang before he could finish the thought.

"Shit!"

He fumbled in his pocket, pressed the green button, and hoisted it to his ear. "DCI Tyler speaking," he said, staring at the Barking gas works, a monstrous eye-sore that dominated the skyline on the opposite side of the A406 dual carriageway.

"Boss, it's Colin. Have you left the building yet?"

Tyler glanced up at his office, which overlooked the front car park, an area exclusively reserved for officers of DI rank and above. "I'm just about to jump in the car, why?"

Franklin appeared at the window a couple of seconds later and waved down at him. *"You might want to pop back up,"* he said. *"I've just fielded a very interesting call from a skipper at Wanstead nick."*

Phoebe had lost all track of time, but it was dark outside now, so she reasoned that it had to be quite late, although she was fairly confident that it was still this side of midnight.

The barn was without electricity, so there was no lighting. Fortunately, Spencer had thought to bring a torch along with him, and it now stood upright on the dirty floor, with its thin beam shining up towards the high ceiling. The glow it gave off was fairly weak, but it was better than nothing.

She wondered how her parents were coping. She was confident that Martin would have called them when she failed to turn up at the restaurant, and it comforted her greatly to know that they would have put two and two together and contacted the police immediately. Her father, being her father, would have kicked up a massive fuss about her disappearance, and there was no doubt in her mind that he would have people out searching for her by now.

But how long would it take them to find her?

It had taken seven unbearably long days the last time around. Even then, the police had only stumbled across Spencer's hiding place by accident, because a concerned neighbour had thought they were squatting and had reported them.

She knew that the searchers would be methodical, which meant they would start at the cottage. When they drew a blank there, they would turn their attention to Diss town centre and the area around the Mere. God alone knew how much time they would waste traipsing around there? Realistically, she knew, it could take them several days, or even several weeks, to widen the search radius this far into the countryside. Phoebe couldn't afford to wait that long. At best, she only had a couple of–

Her train of thought was broken by Spencer, who suddenly released her hands and stood up. Snatching them back from him, Phoebe protectively tucked them between her thighs. In the darkness, they felt hot and unclean, having been contaminated by his foul touch, and she experienced an overwhelming desire to scrub them until they bled.

"I need to take a quick leak," Spencer informed her. "Then I'm going to phone Skippy and give him the good news about us getting back together. When I've done that, I'll sort us out some grub. You must be bloody starving by now. I know I am. I saw a little garage a couple of miles back. I'll grab us something from there to tide us over for tonight."

Phoebe twitched with suspicion. "Who's Skippy?"

"He's my cousin. My best friend, too. We're like that." Spencer crossed his fingers in front of her face to indicate their closeness. "You'll like him," he added as an afterthought. Then a look of guilt flashed across his face, and he flopped back down on the hay bale beside her. Leaning in, as if he were about to reveal a great secret, he said: "To tell you the truth, Pheebs, he's pretty pissed off at me at the moment over something that happened yesterday evening, and his reaction made me so angry that I decided to cut him out of a job we've been planning together. Now that I've had time to cool off a bit, I'm feeling really guilty, so I'm going to see if we can make up and get things back to normal."

"What happened yesterday evening?"

He gave her an evasive shrug, which his dancing shadow

mirrored. "Nothing really. Some mug on a bus gave me a bit of attitude, so I had to take care of him."

"And where was this?" she asked, suddenly feeling uneasy. Something about what he had just told her was ringing an alarm bell at the back of her mind, but she couldn't quite put her finger on it.

"It was in Stratford," he informed her and left it at that.

And then the penny dropped, and she recalled the news bulletin from earlier.

'*...Meanwhile, the search continues for the man known as The Candy Killer, who brutally stabbed CPS lawyer, David Bannister, to death yesterday evening during a disturbance on a bus in East London...*'

Stratford was in East London.

Phoebe's blood turned to ice. She had always known that Spencer had a violent streak in him, but to kill a man? "Okay," she said, nodding emphatically. "You go and phone your cousin, then drive to the garage, and I'll wait here till you get back."

Spencer suddenly seemed troubled. "Look, Pheebs, it ain't that I don't trust you," he said meekly, "and I don't want to upset you, but I can't leave you here alone."

Her heart sank. "Why not? I'll be perfectly okay on my own for a little while, and it's not like you'll be gone long."

Spencer shook his head, apologetically. "Sorry, babes, but I'll have to take you with me."

Phoebe let out a deflated sigh. "I see," she said, her voice small and brittle. For a wonderful moment, she had dared to hope that this might be her chance to make a break for it.

"You ain't gonna like this," he said, wringing his hands together, "but I'll have to put you in the boot so that no one sees us together."

Phoebe reacted with a sharp intake of breath. Her head shot up, and when she spoke, her voice was full of trepidation. "You're not putting me in the boot. I don't do confined spaces, especially not in this heat. No, no, no. There's no way I'm doing that."

He raised his hands to pacify her. "It's for your own good, babes," he insisted. "Listen, I'll take out the rear parcel shelf, so you don't feel trapped, and that'll give you plenty of air. It's a good size boot and I promise you won't be stuck in there for long."

Phoebe knew him well enough to grasp that this was going to happen whatever she said and, if she tried to put up a fight, all the trust that she had worked so hard to build up would be instantly undone. With a sickening sense of inevitability, she realised that there was nothing else to do but grit her teeth and pray she survived.

"I really don't want to do this to you," he was telling her, "but your old man's bound to have reported you missing by now, and we don't want the rozzers to find us and ruin our plans, do we?"

"No, I suppose not," she lied, feeling numb inside.

"I'm glad you understand," he said, sounding enormously relieved. "Let me have a quick piss, and phone Skippy, then we'll be on our way."

———

Susie stripped out of her suit, hung it up, and threw on her dressing gown. She was tired, but she wasn't ready for sleep, so she went down to the kitchen to grab a beer. Not the best thing to have right before she went to bed, especially as she had done so well by abstaining for several weeks now, but this was just one of those days when she needed to indulge herself.

"Surely, just the one won't hurt?" she said as she prised the lid off the bottle. After taking a quick sip, she set about loading the dishwasher up and then turned it on. With only her in the house, she was finding that she only needed to run it every other day.

It began chugging and churning away in the background, making a right old racket. The machine was getting old now, and she should probably think about replacing it, she decided as she pulled the door closed behind her. For a moment, she wondered if that was how Dan had seen her: old and in need of a replacement. Was the reason for their split really that simple?

Feeling glum, she crossed into the lounge, switched the TV on, and flopped down on the sofa, tucking her feet up underneath her.

The late-night news was playing, and the first story she saw related to the bus murder they were investigating. Holland appeared on screen, looking suitably stern. *"We're currently pursuing several lines of enquiry and are confident of making an early arrest,"* he was saying.

"Don't tempt fate by telling them that, Georgie boy," she warned her boss, toasting him with her beer.

When the segment finished, she turned the TV's volume right down and tried ringing Dan. As expected, it rang until his voicemail cut in. She thought about leaving a message, decided against it, and hung up. "Useless wanker," she mumbled under her breath.

Susie checked the time. It was getting very late, and she had an early start in the morning, so she glugged down the remainder of the beer and went upstairs to get ready for bed.

Dan was working late shifts this week and, as she brushed her teeth, she wondered what he was doing right then. He was probably in the pub with his colleagues and his floozy, knowing him, enjoying a quick one before heading back to her place for a quick one of another kind.

———

"Right, take me through this saga of yours slowly," Tyler said. He was sitting in his office, nursing a freshly made cup of coffee that Franklin had kindly prepared for him.

The uniform PC standing in front of his desk fidgeted uneasily. He was a tall man in his early fifties, with rounded shoulders and a little beer belly that sagged over the edge of his belt. A dishevelled bush of thick grey hair sat atop his potato-shaped head, and a pair of matching eyebrows took up most of his large forehead. The nametag on his chest read: PC Simon Carter.

"Well, sir," Carter said, nervously glancing sideways at Colin Franklin, who nodded for him to continue. "It's like this. I was posted as late turn station officer at Wanstead nick today. It was a fairly quiet shift until about half nine, when a bloke called Ben Cunningham and his missus ruined it by coming in to report their daughter missing."

Tyler raised a disbelieving eyebrow. The nerve of some people! Fancy someone having the audacity to ruin Carter's quiet shift just because their daughter had vanished!

Carter was too busy consulting his notebook to notice Tyler's reaction. "Her name's Phoebe, she's in her early twenties, and she's been staying at the family cottage in Diss for a few days. Anyway, when she didn't show up for a meal that she'd arranged with her fella this evening, her parents came into the station in a bit of a flap, claiming that she'd been abducted by some weirdo who's just got out of prison."

Tyler and Franklin exchanged subtle glances.

"Did they give you the weirdo's name, by any chance?" Tyler asked.

The constable's eyes flickered down to the notebook in his pudgy hand. "Yes, sir. John Spencer. Apparently, he kidnapped and raped Phoebe when she was fourteen. Got twelve years for it, but the blighter was released on licence yesterday, after only serving eight of them."

Tyler felt his heart rate spike. When Colin had called him back up from the car park, half an hour earlier, he hadn't known what to expect, but it certainly hadn't been anything like this.

"And what exactly did you do about this allegation?" Tyler enquired of PC Carter, who clearly wasn't the sharpest tool in the proverbial toolbox.

Carter's worried frown suggested that he thought this might be a trick question. "Well, the alleged incident happened in Diss, not London, so I told them they needed to notify the Norfolk Constabulary, not us."

Carter's words, uttered so defensively, confirmed what Tyler had suspected from the man's slovenly appearance: He was a bone idle slob who had tried to fob the Cunninghams off to avoid having to put pen to paper.

"Can't think why," Carter said in a tone that suggested he had been done a grave injustice, "but Mr Cunningham got a bit grumpy when I told him that, and he threatened to make a complaint." Carter cleared his throat. "I could see they were upset, so I offered to take the report, even though it wasn't technically a crime, here in the Met."

"Very generous of you," Tyler said, coating each word with stinging sarcasm. It had taken the threat of a complaint to get this lazy git to do his job, and he wasn't impressed. "What did you do then?"

Wilting under Tyler's fierce stare, Carter folded his notebook and tucked it into his shirt pocket. "I phoned it straight through to Norfolk Force HQ, gave Mr Cunningham the crime reference number they'd provided, and told him someone would be in touch in due course."

"And was Mr Cunningham satisfied with that?" Tyler asked. He most certainly wouldn't have been.

Carter shook his head, and a look of righteous indignation appeared on his ruddy face. "No, he wasn't. He had the cheek to tell me that I hadn't done my job properly, and then he stormed off with the raging hump. Can you believe that?"

Tyler could. Easily.

Carter tutted imperiously, as though he had never heard anything so preposterous in all his days. "Anyway, after he left, I thought I'd best cover my arse and let a supervisor know, just in case. My skipper had already gone home, but the night duty bloke, Sergeant Peabody, was briefing his troops, so I waited until he finished and then informed him. When I told him the suspect's name, he got all excited and told me not to go off duty until he'd spoken to you lot. Next thing I know, I'm being told to hotfoot it over here to brief you in person."

"For which I'm very grateful," Tyler said, drily. "I'm going to need you to sit down with my colleague, here," he indicated Franklin, "and make a detailed statement. But first, I'd like you to photocopy your notes for me so that I've got them to hand when I ring Mr Cunningham."

Carter seemed a little confused. "If you don't mind me asking, sir, what are you going to ring him for? You're not taking his ridiculous story seriously, are you?"

Tyler's mouth tightened into a thin angry line. "My colleague will show you where the photocopier is. Once you've copied your notes and completed your statement, you can head off home. I think we've deprived your village of its idiot long enough for one day, don't you?"

When Spencer returned from speaking to Skippy, who was still sulking and had given him the cold shoulder yet again, he saw that Phoebe had moved from where they had been sitting together and was now standing over by the stack of hay bales at the far end of the barn.

She had her back to him, and her head was bowed as though she were praying. He wondered if she was thanking God for reuniting them? That would be nice, and very fitting, he decided. Out of respect, he gave her a moment to finish.

He had found a coil of nylon rope in the boot of the BMW, and he planned to tie Phoebe's wrists and ankles together with this instead of using the gaffer tape. It would give her a little more flexibility and it would be easier to remove once they got back to the barn. He hoped that she would appreciate his being so considerate.

Spencer didn't like the dark, and he was starting to find the old barn a bit spooky. Dismissing this as nonsense, he shone the weak beam from his torch around the barn, just to make sure no monsters were lurking in the darkness. Or bats. After satisfying himself that there were none, he directed it back in Phoebe's direction, illuminating her in a flickering pool of light. She was still just standing there, strangely immobile, like a zombie from a horror film.

Christ! How long does it take to say a few prayers? "You ready to go, Pheebs?" he called impatiently, at the same time walking as far forward as the tractor.

She didn't move. She didn't answer. She just stood there staring down at the hay bale in front of her.

The way she was acting was a little creepy. "Pheebs?" he said, taking a cautious step towards her. Nothing; no response at all. Her odd behaviour was starting to give him the heebie-jeebies, and the fact that it was, made him react angrily. "For fuck sake, don't ignore me," he warned, striding across the barn towards her.

The instant before he reached her, she glanced over her shoulder to stare at him, and there was something about the vacant look in her eyes that made him hesitate. "Phoebe, what's wrong with–"

She spun around, her face contorting into a mask of hatred as she raised the thin, heavy object in her hands and swung it like a cricket bat, aiming for the side of his head.

Spencer's eyes widened in shock but, before he could react, the pipe slammed into his temple with a dull thud, knocking him two steps sideways and spinning him around. Dazed, his hands instinctively cradled his head. He cowered away, expecting further blows, but none came, for Phoebe was already running for the barn door.

"Argh," he cried out, stooping to retrieve the torch and nylon cord, which had both fallen from his hands when she'd hit him. Spencer stood up unsteadily, head throbbing, vision blurred. He tentatively rubbed the side of his head and then winced in pain. "Motherfucker," he cursed, feeling both shocked and betrayed. Why had she hit him like that? He loved her and wanted to give her everything. How could she be so ungrateful?

The barn doors screeched horribly as she pulled them open.

The realisation that she was trying to get away focused his mind. "Come back here, you cow," he called out as he staggered after her. His hand felt wet and, in the bouncing light from the torch, he saw that it was covered in a glistening red substance.

I'm bleeding!

The barn doors protested furiously as Phoebe tried to close them behind her.

Fuelled by anger, Spencer lowered his shoulder and charged the doors without slowing down. As he cannoned into them, he heard a satisfying 'oomph' from outside, as the air was expelled from Phoebe's lungs.

"What the fuck are you playing at?" he demanded as he thrust his head and shoulders through the narrow gap he had created.

Her response was to bring the heavy pipe crashing down onto his forehead with all her strength.

After debriefing PC Carter, Tyler called Ben Cunningham to see if he could shed any light on Spencer's release from prison. He knew it was getting late, but he figured the poor man would be far too worried about his missing daughter to sleep, and wouldn't mind the intrusion.

"*Have you found her yet?*" Cunningham demanded before Tyler had even finished identifying himself.

Tyler took a deep breath, realising it was going to be one of *those* conversations. "Mr Cunningham, the search for your daughter is being carried out by Norfolk Constabulary, not by the Met, so I'm afraid I don't have any information on how that's progressing."

There was a sharp intake of breath, followed by some indignant spluttering. "*What is it with you lot?*" Cunningham yelled down the phone when he eventually found his voice. "*All trying to pass the buck onto someone else, instead of getting off your fat, lazy arses and looking for my poor Phoebe. I'm sick of it, and I demand that you put me onto someone who knows what's going on immediately.*"

"Mr Cunningham," Tyler said, doing his best to remain calm, despite the other man's antagonistic comments, "I know you're very upset, and you're probably going out of your mind with worry, but you really need to listen to what I say, otherwise this conversation will just end up going round in circles."

Cunningham huffed, then grumbled an obscenity under his breath. "*Fine. I'm listening. What do you want?*"

"As I said, I don't know what's happening in Diss, but I promise you this: as soon as we finish speaking, I'll ring Norfolk HQ on your behalf to see if I can find out who's running the investigation. I suspect I'll be told that the Duty Officer, that's the inspector in charge of all the uniform officers patrolling the area for the shift, will be handling the initial enquiries, ably assisted by night duty CID, and that a Senior Investigating Officer won't be appointed until the morning. That's how these things usually work. Rest assured though, I'm confident that the Duty Officer will be taking your daughter's disappearance very seriously," at least Tyler hoped they would be, "and will have every available officer out searching the area for her."

Cunningham seemed marginally appeased by that. "*I should bloody well hope so, too.*"

"I can't get involved directly because the incident occurred in Diss, which is Norfolk's jurisdiction, not London's. To be perfectly honest, it's a moot point as far as I'm concerned because, as it happens, Spencer's also wanted here in London, albeit for an entirely different matter, and we're already doing everything that we possibly can to apprehend him."

As the conversation continued, Cunningham gradually climbed down from his soapbox. He told Tyler all about the courtesy call he'd received on Tuesday morning from a detective who was based at Islington's Sapphire Unit. The call had been made to warn him of Spencer's release from HMP Manchester, the high-security prison more commonly known as Strangeways.

Tyler thanked him for the information. Having the name of the prison would, hopefully, save Dean a little time in the morning.

True to his word, as soon as he finished speaking to Cunningham, Tyler put in a call to Norfolk Police HQ. He was put straight through to the Duty Officer, whose name was Fiona Terry, a very bubbly lady who was eager to help in any way that she could. She confirmed that she would nursemaid the case overnight, and that an SIO would be appointed the following morning. Terry spent a few minutes walking him through the enquiries she had initiated so far, which were all the standard things that Tyler would expect in a situation like this.

Armed with this information, Tyler called Cunningham straight back to update him, promising that he would check in with Norfolk again first thing in the morning.

Having done everything that he possibly could, Tyler dragged himself out of the office, and set off for home to get some much needed rest.

11

Thursday 26th July 2001
AFTER A STORM THE SUN ALWAYS SHINES

It was four o'clock in the morning and, although sunrise was still a little over an hour away, it was already starting to get lighter outside. Leaning back in his swivel chair, PC Peter Warren, the night duty Station Officer at Diss police station, checked his wristwatch and stifled a yawn. It had been a very dull shift, with nothing more exciting for him to deal with than the odd person coming in to produce their driving documents following accidents or traffic stops, and even that had dried up by midnight.

With only two hours of his shift remaining, he was really looking forward to going home and grabbing some shut-eye while it was still cool enough to sleep. He toyed with the idea of making himself another brew, but decided against it, having already consumed so much tea that he could literally hear it sloshing around inside him every time he stood up.

The muffled sound of a woman's crying reached his ears from the foyer outside. Groaning inwardly, Warren assumed that he was about to receive an unwelcome visit from a drunk, a junkie, or someone with mental health issues. After all, who else would be bothering him at that time of night in sleepy Diss? Most respectable people were safely tucked up in their beds, as he dearly wished that he was.

Closing the newspaper he was reading with an agitated sigh, Warren glanced up in time to see a pretty girl in her early twenties push open the door and approach the desk. Her clothing was torn and dishevelled, her hands and face were covered in mud and grime, and she seemed on the verge of collapse. Warren's expression instantly changed to one of deep concern. "Are you alright, miss?" he asked, wondering what could have happened to reduce the poor girl to such a dreadful state.

"Help me," the woman sobbed, her red-rimmed eyes staring at him imploringly. "Please help me." With that, she sagged against the counter and began to cry uncontrollably.

Her words confirmed Warren's fears that something terrible had happened and, as he sprung out of his chair to comfort her, he found himself hoping that someone from night duty CID was still around to take charge.

Warren stabbed at the security keypad with a slender finger but, in his haste, he got the combination wrong and had to repeat the process. When the door finally clunked open, he crossed into the public side of the counter and approached the victim – he had already categorised her as such, even though he didn't have a clue what had actually happened yet.

He sincerely hoped that he was wrong, but Warren's gut reaction was that she had been raped. He had never dealt with anything as serious as rape before, and he racked his brains trying to recall the proper procedure. He would need to take a first account from her, arrange for an officer trained in dealing with sexual offences to chaperone her, and inform a supervisor and the CID. Was there anything else? Oh yes, he should discourage her from using the facilities, just in case she flushed away any semen while having a pee.

"Why don't we go and sit down in one of the waiting rooms,

where we can have some privacy while we get you sorted out?" he suggested. Gently taking hold of her arm, he directed the distraught woman towards one of the station's little side rooms. She initially stiffened at his touch, but then relaxed and allowed him to guide her.

The small, starkly furnished waiting room contained a wooden table, which had been bolted to the floor, and three plastic wing-back chairs. Although the walls had recently been treated to a fresh coat of magnolia, sections of it had already been covered in dirty, kiddie sized handprints and defaced by the odd smattering of graffiti. At least it was clean, with the sweet-sharp smell of lemon cleaning products permeating the air. A small window overlooked the car park outside, which was illuminated by a nearby streetlamp.

Warren indicated for her to take a seat. "You're safe now, miss," he assured her. "No one can get at you or hurt you in here." He frowned when she stared into space without acknowledging him. Had she even heard him? "Miss? Did you hear me?"

"Yes," she replied, staring straight ahead, as though in a daze.

Shock, he decided. She was going into shock. Perhaps he should offer to make her a cup of tea? First though, Warren needed to find out what had happened, so he perched himself on the edge of the table, leaning forward to rest his notebook on his knee. While he was busy patting his pockets for a pen, the mysterious woman sat there sobbing quietly, with her arms wrapped protectively around her body.

Warren noticed that her nose was dripping, and he quickly removed a small, crinkled packet of disposable tissues from his trouser pocket. "Here, take these," he offered.

The woman gave him a grateful smile, revealing the cutest dimples. "Thank you," she said, unfolding a tissue and dabbing her nose in a ladylike manner.

Her hands were shaking badly, he noticed.

"Now, miss," Warren said, flashing her a little smile of encouragement. "Why don't you take a nice deep breath, and then tell me exactly what happened."

"I'll try," the woman said, running a trembling hand through her messy hair.

"Let's start with your name, shall we?" Warren asked.

"M-my name's... My name's Phoebe. Phoebe C-Cunningham," she told him in a quivering voice.

Warren could tell that she was fighting a losing battle to hold back the tears, and his heart went out to her.

Phoebe suddenly looked up at him, eyes glistening. "Can you call my parents and let them know I'm okay?" she pleaded. "They'll be worried sick about me." And, with that, she burst into tears again. Burying her head in her hands, her whole body became wracked by a series of gigantic, heart-rending sobs, each of which was punctuated by a long wail of anguish.

Feeling uncomfortably awkward, and not really knowing what else to say, Warren reached out a tentative hand and patted her shoulder. "I'll go and put the kettle on, and give you a couple of minutes alone," he told her. He turned to go, and then paused. "My mum used to say that after a storm the sun always shines, and that crying's much the same, so don't be afraid to let it all out."

As often happened during the first few nights of a new job, when his mind was stuck in overdrive, instead of sinking into a catatonic slumber the moment his head touched the pillow, Tyler had slept fitfully, and he arrived at the office at seven-thirty, bleary-eyed and still half-asleep.

Feeling like a bear with a sore head, he was glad that he hadn't accepted Dillon's offer to bring him into work this morning. His friend was always so full of beans when they had an early start, and Tyler thought that he would have probably ended up strangling the big lug if he'd subjected him to one of his 'mornings are the best time of the day' lectures today.

No one else was in yet but, in fairness, Tyler hadn't expected them to be. As he dumped his shoulder bag down on the floor behind his desk, he wondered if this drained feeling was what insomniacs experienced every day of their lives.

Resisting the urge to make a bee-line for the urn, and grab a coffee to kick start his day, he collapsed into the high-backed chair behind his desk and picked up the phone. Two minutes later, he was speaking to a friendly switchboard operator from Norfolk HQ.

Susie arrived just as Tyler was being transferred through to Diss CID. She popped into the office and made a C shape with the thumb and forefinger of her left hand. Tyler responded with a thumbs up and a smile of gratitude.

A couple of minutes later, she was back, and she placed a mug of steaming hot coffee on the desk in front of him.

"Thank you," he mouthed.

The call to Norfolk lasted for just over fifteen minutes, during which time Tony Dillon arrived. After making himself a hot drink, he pulled up a chair next to Susie, and the two of them sat in companionable silence, trying to work out what was going on from the one side of the telephone conversation that they were privy to.

When Tyler finally lowered the phone to its cradle, he let out a low whistle and turned to face the two DIs sitting opposite him. "Well, that all sounds a bit intense," he told them, leaning back in his chair and steepling his fingers.

"Spill the beans, then," Dillon said, rubbing his hands together in gleeful anticipation. "What did the County Mounties say?"

"Well, it looks like Spencer abducted Phoebe Cunningham from a public car park behind the shops in Diss town centre yesterday evening."

That wiped the smile from Dillon's face. "How the hell did he manage that?" he asked, leaning forward.

Tyler stifled a yawn. "Apparently, he was lying in wait, and he grabbed her as she was returning to her car after taking her evening constitutional. As we speak, the local plod are checking the CCTV cameras to see if they can identify the car he was using, but they're not overly hopeful."

"I take it that the car was nicked?" Dillon ventured.

Tyler responded with a half-hearted shrug, then stared at his empty mug, longing for a refill. "I'm guessing it was, but we don't have an index number yet. The good news is that the girl escaped and made her way to Diss police station unharmed."

"What about Spencer?" Dillon asked.

Tyler pulled a face. "He's still at large."

"Were there any witnesses to the abduction?" Susie enquired.

Tyler shook his head, still thinking about coffee. "None. According to Phoebe Cunningham, Spencer sneaked up behind her when she wasn't looking, hit her over the back of the head, and then bundled her into his car. When she eventually came round – she doesn't know if it was minutes or hours later – he'd whisked her off to a remote barn in the arse end of nowhere. Her wrists and ankles had been securely bound, and a hood had been placed over her head. At some point, Spencer removed the hood and retied her hands in front of her to make her more comfortable–" he made air quotes with his fingers "–while they talked."

"How very thoughtful of him," Susie observed, drily.

Dillon smiled. "If only all kidnappers were that considerate."

Tyler picked up his mug. If neither of them was going to offer, he'd have to make his own coffee. "God knows how, but when he wasn't looking, she managed to whack him over the head with a length of pipe she'd found and, while he was writhing around on the floor in agony, she did a runner."

"Good for her," Dillon said.

"Sounds like she had a very lucky escape," Susie observed, holding out her mug as Tyler walked by. "If you're in the chair, I'll have another coffee," she said, smiling sweetly.

Tyler grunted, took the mug from her. "What about you?" he asked Dillon. "Want a refill?"

"Might as well," the big man said.

With Tyler in the lead, they all wandered into the main office. People were starting to arrive in dribs and drabs, and Tyler nodded to each of them as they walked past the urn.

"Anyway, after getting away, the girl blindly traipsed through an endless procession of fields in the darkness, eventually stumbling out onto a winding country lane," Tyler informed them. "She had absolutely no idea where she was. Apparently, she managed to free her hands by sawing through the gaffer tape with some broken glass she found in the road, and then wandered around for what seemed like hours before stumbling across somewhere that seemed vaguely familiar."

"That must have been hellish," Susie said, "like one of those anxiety nightmares where you run and run, but never get anywhere."

Tyler yawned, then set about making the coffee. "Eventually, she found a busier road, managed to flag down a passing car, and blagged a lift into Diss. She stumbled into the local nick at four o'clock this morning, looking like she'd been dragged through a hedge backwards."

"I don't suppose the Turnip Pullers know where Spencer is?" Dillon asked.

"No, sadly not," Tyler said, spooning coffee into each of their mugs. "In fairness, it took them a while to get any sense out of the girl, which is hardly surprising, given how shocked she must have been, and by the time they drove her out to the barn, which took them ages to find, there was no trace of Spencer or the car."

"Did he sexually assault her?" Susie asked, suppressing a shudder.

Tyler poured some milk into each mug. "Thankfully, she escaped before he had a chance to lay a finger on her."

"It probably wasn't his finger she was worried about," Dillon said, keeping his face deadpan.

Susie elbowed him, hard. "Not funny." Leaving Dillon to massage his ribs, she turned to address Tyler. "Have the girl's parents been informed yet?"

"Yes. The local plod called them. They're on their way to Norfolk as we speak."

Hot drinks made, they all retreated to Tyler's office.

Within seconds of sitting down, there was a brisk rap on Tyler's office door, and Dean Fletcher wandered in. "Morning all," he said.

"I'm still waiting to hear back from the probation service, but the prison Security Governor's e-mailed me a copy of Spencer's file. It contains the address of the halfway house he was released to on Tuesday morning."

Tyler held out his hand. "Well done, Deano," he said, taking the note and reading the address. "Looks like he's been staying in Hackney, not far from Old Street," he informed the others. After copying the details down in his daybook, he passed the note over to Dillon. "Can you get an arrest team ready to hit it? He's probably not going to be there, but we have to proceed on the basis that he is. If nothing else, his room is a crime scene, and we might find important trace evidence linking him to Bannister's murder when we process it."

"Leave it to me," Dillon said. Standing up, he knocked back his coffee in three large gulps and then left.

"Susie, in case he's not there, we're going to need a Section 8 PACE warrant to search it," Tyler said. "I know you're going to be tied up with Bannister's special post mortem all morning, so can you ask Steve to get that organised, ASAP?"

"I'm all over it," she said, gathering her things to leave.

It was getting on for nine o'clock when a uniformed constable showed Phoebe Cunningham back into the same drab waiting room that she had occupied earlier in the day.

"If you wait here, miss," he said in his thick Norfolk burr, "DC Stebbins will be back down to see you shortly."

Upon their return to the station, Stebbins, the surly detective who had taken her on a lengthy drive through the Norfolk countryside in search of the barn that Spencer had held her captive in, had popped upstairs to report his findings to his boss.

Phoebe pulled a chair out from under the desk and wearily plonked herself down onto its hard plastic surface. She gave in to a jaw-splitting yawn, and then dry washed her face, feeling mentally and physically exhausted. All she wanted to do was close her eyes and allow sleep to wash over her, but she knew that wasn't going to be possible until the police had finished with her. To keep herself awake, she turned her chair around to face the window, and her eyes quickly settled on a little blue hatchback, which she followed along the road until it disappeared from view. The car had contained a smiling woman and a little girl with pigtails. Probably a mum doing the school run, she decided, envying the simplicity of childhood and wishing that it was still hers.

Her stomach rumbled, and Phoebe suddenly realised that she was ravenously hungry. She hadn't eaten since lunchtime the previous day and, apart from the strong cup of tea that PC Warren had made her upon her arrival in the early hours, she hadn't had anything to drink either.

The past few hours had passed in a blur. As soon as PC Warren, whom she had thought sweet and attentive, had finished taking a brief account from her, he had rushed off to find DC Stebbins. The surly detective had been openly sceptical at first, and was clearly suspicious that she had made the whole thing up. After giving her the third degree for the best part of twenty minutes, Stebbins had called the Force Medical Examiner in to examine her.

Dr Frobisher, who must have been seventy if he was a day, had prodded the base of her skull, tutting when she flinched in pain, shone a torch into her eyes to see if her pupils were equally dilated, and instructed her to follow his moving finger with her eyes to make sure she was able to focus and track properly. After that, he'd tested for cognitive impairment by asking a number of memory related questions, like what day of the week was it? Who was the prime minister? What did twenty minus four equal? She had passed this test with flying colours, answering each question without the slightest hesitation.

At the conclusion of his exam, Frobisher's liver-spotted hand had jotted down his findings in an illegible scrawl, while she watched in fascination as the veins under his parched skin wriggled like sluggish worms. Although there were no obvious signs of concussion or internal haemorrhaging, Frobisher had advised her to attend A&E

for a more thorough examination, pointing out that it might be advisable to carry out an x-ray, bearing in mind that she had been rendered unconscious for a short period of time.

"I feel fine," she had insisted, bracing herself for a lecture. Surprisingly, instead of kicking up a fuss, Dr Frobisher had pragmatically noted her response, and then prescribed some painkillers to help with the headache. Before taking his leave, the unfriendly septuagenarian had reeled off a list of tell-tale signs and symptoms to look out for, and advised her to go straight to A&E if she developed any of them during the next twenty-four hours.

Phoebe's reminiscence was cut short by the sound of the waiting room door opening behind her, and she glanced over her shoulder to see who was there.

DC Stebbins strutted into the room, looking a little smarter now that he had tidied himself up. He was followed by an older, more distinguished looking man who possessed an unmistakable air of authority. The newcomer, a large man in a three-piece tweed suit, was in his mid-fifties, with a florid complexion, a torrent of red hair, and a bulbous nose that drew the eye like a Belisha beacon. Beneath his out-of-control eyebrows, a pair of amused green eyes twinkled mischievously.

"Good morning, Miss Cunningham," he said, treating her to a warm smile. "My name's DCI Bartholomew Craddock and, for my sins, I'm the man who's been put in charge of finding the bugger who abducted you."

Craddock pulled out a chair, dragged it over to where Phoebe was sitting, and then deposited his considerable bulk on it. The plastic chair creaked ominously, as if its load-bearing capacity was being tested to its limits, but it somehow held firm.

Stebbins remained standing by the door, like the lackey he was.

Craddock adjusted the creases of his trousers and then crossed his thick legs. "Now then," he said in his broad Norfolk accent, "let's get down to business. In a minute, I'm going to ask young Frank here to take a detailed statement from you."

Phoebe reacted without enthusiasm. "But I've already gone through everything with *him,* and with PC Warren," she objected.

Craddock nodded, sympathetically. "I know, my dear, but that was just to give us a snapshot of what happened to you. Now, we need to go through your account in far more detail, picking the bones from it, as it were."

Phoebe could feel her eyes prickling with tears, and she let out a little moan of distress. What Craddock was asking of her would take forever, and she was so close to exhaustion. She bit her bottom lip in an effort to conceal her growing desire to escape.

Craddock picked up on this, and his craggy face softened. "Phoebe, I know you've been through a lot, and I know you're probably feeling tired and cranky. I appreciate that you're desperate to get home and get some rest, truly I do, but we really need a statement from you now, while it's all fresh in your mind."

Her bottom lip quivered. "Can't I just come back later, after I've had time to rest?" she begged.

Craddock smiled, sympathetically. "I'm afraid it doesn't work that way," he told her. "Now, before Frank takes you away from me, I need you to rack your brains and see if you can think of anywhere this rogue, Spencer, might have sloped off to in order to lick his wounds?"

"How could I possibly know that?" she bristled.

Craddock leaned forward in his chair, fixing her with a piercing stare. "He didn't say anything to you about where he was staying, or where he planned to take you?"

Phoebe shook her head, wearily. "No... Although come to think of it, he did mention that he was staying at a halfway house in London."

The two detectives shared a glance. "I'll get someone to check with the probation service," Stebbins volunteered. "If he's out on licence, they should have a record of where he's living."

"It might be nothing," Phoebe said, "but he phoned someone called Skippy late last night." She glanced from one detective to the other as she spoke. "I don't know if that helps?"

"It might well do," Craddock replied with an encouraging smile. "Who exactly is this Skippy character, if you don't mind me asking?"

Phoebe responded with a hostile shrug. It annoyed her that they should automatically assume that she knew any of Spencer's friends. As far as she was concerned, the less she knew about Skippy, or anyone else connected to Spencer, the better. "I don't know, and I don't care," she replied, testily. There followed a brief pause while she replayed the conversation from the barn in her head, and then a thoughtful frown creased her forehead. "All I can tell you is that Spencer said they were cousins, and that they were very close."

Craddock considered this for a few moments. "Interesting," he eventually said. "There was no trace of your mobile phone at the barn, Miss Cunningham. You say that he took it from you after he'd abducted you. Is that right?"

Phoebe sighed her impatience. "I assume so," she replied, becoming increasingly agitated by the constant bombardment of questions. "It was in my jacket pocket when I went for a walk down by the Mere so, unless it fell out while I was unconscious, I'm guessing he must have it. Why do you ask?"

"Well, my dear, we have the technology to track mobile phones these days," Craddock explained. "Every time the handset makes or receives calls or text messages, it communicates with the nearest phone mast. We don't know his mobile number yet, so we can't track that particular handset, but if he's still in possession of your phone, we can run some checks and see if there's been any activity on it overnight. If there has been, we might be able to narrow down the area he's hiding in."

Despite her weariness, Phoebe sat up straight. Her parents, Martin, Anna; she was confident they would all have repeatedly tried ringing and texting her after she went missing. "So you can follow someone by their phone?"

Craddock nodded, indulgently. "I've given you a simplified version of how it all works but, basically, yes."

"And they don't have to answer the calls, or open the messages?"

An amused smile. "No. As long as the phone is switched on, and it receives the incoming alert, we can work our magic."

Phoebe processed this information. So, the phone had to be turned on. *Interesting.*

There was a muffled commotion outside: raised voices becoming steadily louder; the sounds of an argument developing, followed by hurried footsteps.

Craddock glanced over his shoulder at Stebbins. "Frank, pop out there and tell them to keep the blasted racket down, would you? I can hardly hear myself think–"

The door was thrown open, clattering into the wall with a loud bang, and Ben Cunningham charged in like a man possessed. "Phoebe!" he exclaimed on seeing his daughter. Arms extended, he rushed over to embrace her, hoisting her out of the chair and wrapping his arms around her so tightly that she could hardly breathe.

Phoebe closed her eyes and let herself sink into the hug, feeling the intensity of her father's love wrapping itself around her like a warm blanket keeping out the cold.

Jessica Cunningham followed her husband in, with the flustered uniformed constable on desk duty bringing up the rear.

"I'm so sorry, sir," he said, glancing nervously across at Craddock, who had half risen from his chair. "These people are the girl's parents. I asked them to wait outside, until you were finished speaking to her, but they wouldn't listen."

"It's quite alright, Constable Parsons," Craddock said, ushering the man outside. "Why don't you return to your duties and let me sort this out."

"Yes, sir," Parsons said, clearly relieved that he hadn't been given a reprimand for letting the Cunninghams barge in, uninvited.

Phoebe was beginning to feel a little claustrophobic as her parents continued to smother her with hugs and kisses. They were both talking at once, trying to outdo each other, and they were pulling her all over the place in the process. She knew that they meant well, and she was incredibly relieved to see them, but she was finding the onslaught a little overwhelming. She came over all hot and clammy, and her aching head started to spin. "I need some air," she gasped, trying in vain to disentangle herself from their grasp.

Ben Cunningham suddenly held his daughter at arm's length and stared straight into her eyes. "Did he molest you?" he demanded, nodding towards her nether regions. "You know, down there."

Phoebe was horrified by the uncouth directness of the question, which had been blurted out with no thought for her feelings. "No! He didn't," she responded, pulling away angrily.

Things got a whole lot worse as the door flew open again, and this time Martin Whitling blew in like a whirlwind. In an instant, he had crossed the room and thrown his arms around her, crushing her to his chest and making Phoebe feel even more trapped than before. Not to be outdone, her parents joined in with the group hug.

A second later, PC Parsons appeared, red-faced, feathers ruffled. "Sorry," he said, breathlessly. "This one slipped by me while I was–"

Craddock held up a hand to cut him off. "It's alright, constable," he declared, although the daggers he was giving Parsons made it abundantly clear that it wasn't. With a dismissive wave, Craddock signalled for him to leave.

Face glowing with embarrassment, Parsons turned to go.

"Try not to let anyone *else* in," Craddock's scathing voice boomed after him.

Parsons' shoulders slumped. "I'll try, sir," he said, closing the door despondently.

With one arm still wrapped around his daughter's shoulders, Ben Cunningham turned on Craddock. "Why is my daughter still here?" he demanded. "She should be at hospital, receiving treatment, not stuck in this dump being interrogated like a common criminal."

Craddock was too old a hand at the game to be intimidated by an aggrieved parent, even one as combative as the man now shouting at him. Raising himself to his full height, he took hold of his lapels, one in each hand, and fixed Cunningham with an icy stare. "Mr Cunningham, I'm Detective Chief Inspector Bartholomew Craddock, and I'm the man in charge around here, not you."

Cunningham's jaw dropped. "How dare–"

"Mr Cunningham," Craddock said, speaking with such authority that Ben Cunningham froze mid-sentence, "your daughter *was* advised to attend the local A&E by the Divisional Police Surgeon, but she refused. As *you* pointed out, she is *not* a prisoner, and, therefore, we cannot force her to do something she doesn't want to do."

"But she's–"

Craddock did it again, quickly drowning out Cunningham. "What she is, sir, is an adult, capable of making her own informed decisions. We are treating her as such. May I suggest that you do the same."

Ben Cunningham's face had turned the colour of beetroot. "Who do you think you're talking to?"

Jessica placed a warning hand on his arm, but he angrily shrugged it off. "You have no idea what this poor girl has been through," he said, refusing to back down.

"Please, dad!" Phoebe intervened, but Cunningham was too riled to listen.

"I will not have my daughter's mental health jeopardised by some country yokel who's keen to make a name for himself."

"Dad!" Phoebe exclaimed, staring at her father in shame.

"Oh, Ben," Jessica said, cringing with embarrassment.

Whitling had the decency to stare at the floor.

Craddock merely laughed. "A country yokel, you say? Tell me, Mr Cunningham, how many degrees have you got? Because this country yokel has two."

Cunningham looked around the room and, from the expression on his face, it was clear that he realised he'd overstepped the mark by calling the detective a yokel. "Look," he said, making a conscious effort to show contrition, "I'm sorry for being a tad rude, but I tend to be fiercely protective when it comes to Phoebe. I didn't mean to cause offence –"

"None taken."

"–but she hasn't had it easy, and I don't want her being put through any more pain than is absolutely necessary."

"On that, at least, we agree," Craddock said. "Now, here's what's going to happen. It's non-negotiable, so please don't bother wasting my time with useless objections," he warned, cutting off the words that had already started to form in Cunningham's mouth. "Phoebe is going to go off with my colleague, and she's going to make a detailed statement about what happened. When that's done, she can go home and get some much needed rest. The quicker we start, the quicker we finish. You're all very welcome to wait here, in this room, as long as you don't start making a nuisance of yourselves with my already overworked staff. Alternatively, you can go back to your cottage and wait in comfort there. Rest assured, DC Stebbins will call you the moment she's done. Isn't that right, Frank?"

"Yes, sir," Stebbins replied, dutifully.

"How long do you think it will take?" Martin asked, taking hold of Phoebe's hand and squeezing it tight.

"How long is a piece of string?" Craddock responded with a question of his own. Then: "At a guess, I would say a couple of hours."

"We'll wait here," Cunningham said, crossing his arms resolutely.

"No, Ben, we won't," Jessica contradicted him. "We'll go back to the cottage."

Cunningham was horrified by the suggestion. "But what if Phoebe needs–"

"Ben!" Jessica snapped. "You've already embarrassed me quite enough for one day. The Chief Inspector is right: Phoebe's an adult. If she needs us, she'll call."

12

THE SEARCH WARRANT

A liveried police carrier pulled up at the front of the building, and seven men alighted briskly, leaving only the driver on board. They all belonged to the Territorial Support Group, the Met's elite public order unit, and they were dressed in full public order attire, which included NATO helmets, flameproof overalls, combat boots, and body armour.

Their leader, a short, stout man with the three chevrons of a sergeant on his epaulettes, carried a round shield that was made from transparent acrylic and had the word 'POLICE' plastered across the front.

The first three constables to jump out after him were similarly equipped, but the next two carried larger, rectangular shields, more commonly known in law enforcement parlance as 'long shields'. These two would be the first to enter Spencer's room, while the rest of the TSG crew followed behind, ready to step forward and make the arrest once the suspect was under control.

The last man to appear was lugging a bright red battering ram, officially known as an Enforcer but often referred to as 'the big red key'.

"Hurry up, Ron," the sergeant shouted.

Hoisting it over his shoulder with a loud grunt, PC Ron Steadman nodded to let the others know that he was ready to go.

Tony Dillon and DC Gurjit Singh, a slightly tubby Asian male in a turban, emerged from the battered Astra that had pulled up directly behind the carrier. Leaving Gurjit to lock the car, Dillon ambled over to the TSG skipper, who smiled a warm greeting at him from beneath his visor.

"Are your boys happy that they know exactly what's expected from them today, Bobby?" Dillon asked, conversationally.

PS Bobby Beach chuckled happily. "Simple, gov. We go in and detain the fucker, then hand the room over to your guys to search. It's pretty basic stuff for my lot."

Dillon nodded approvingly. That was pretty much exactly what the briefing had stipulated. "And you've all had sight of the search warrant?" he asked.

Beach's helmeted head bobbed up and down, and the sight made Dillon think of a dancing Teletubby. "Yep, Steve Bull produced it at the briefing." The head bobbing abruptly stopped, and a thoughtful expression appeared on Beach's face. "I take it you've remembered to bring it with you, because we haven't got it?"

Dillon was seriously tempted to say no, just to wind the other man up, but he resisted the urge. "Yep, Gurjit's got it." As he spoke, a look of uncertainty flashed across his face, and he quickly glanced sideways at Singh for confirmation. "You *do* have it, don't you?"

"Never fear, Gurjit's here!" Singh announced in his thick Brummie accent, and he tapped the battered blue clipboard nestling under a chubby arm to indicate that the warrant was safely tucked away inside.

Dillon groaned. "Is that a yes or a no?"

Gurjit grinned up at Dillon, who towered above him. The two men were old friends, having previously worked together on a

Special Projects Team before Dillon's promotion to DI. "It's a yes from me!" he replied, doing his cheesy impression of an American game show host.

A second unmarked car, this one a blue Ford Escort, pulled up behind the Astra. DC Kevin Murray clambered out, looking all hot and bothered, while the two detectives who had accompanied him remained where they were. He wandered around to the boot and removed an exhibits bag. "I don't like this bloody heat," the slender detective complained.

Closing the boot, Murray returned to the front of the car, and Dillon could see that he was miffed to find that neither colleague had moved.

"Let's go," Murray barked, putting his hands on his slender hips and scowling in at them. "Sometime today would be nice."

The two officers alighted the car lethargically and, with Murray chivvying them on from behind, skulked over to join Dillon and Gurjit.

"Are we going or what?" Ron Steadman complained. "This thing isn't exactly light, you know, and I'm sweating my cods off in all this kit."

"Stop complaining," Beach told him, then indicated for his crew to form up in single file behind him, "Right, let's get going before poor hard done by Ron collapses from heat stroke."

Dillon and Gurjit accompanied the TSG officers and, as soon as they were all safely inside the building, the two detectives peeled off to intercept a startled looking man standing behind the receptionist's desk. He was an unsavoury looking character, with shoulder-length brown hair that was in dire need of a good wash, shifty eyes, and the sallow complexion of a drug user, and he was already lifting the counter hatch in his eagerness to confront the uniformed officers.

"Oi! Where do you think you're bloody well going?" he demanded, waving his arms angrily to get their attention. There were large wet patches under his armpits, and the unpleasant stench of body odour heralded his impending arrival.

Wrinkling his nose in disgust, Dillon stepped into his path and thrust his warrant card into the approaching man's face. "I'm DI Dillon from the Homicide Command. My colleagues and I are here to execute a search warrant. Can you tell me who's in charge?"

Out of the corner of his eye, he saw Beach leading his team towards the staircase at the far end of the foyer. That was good. The plan was for the TSG officers to head straight up to Spencer's room on the second floor while Dillon located the manager. Hopefully, they would be able to borrow a master key and let themselves into Spencer's room without them having to use the Enforcer, which would save them a bit of extra paperwork.

"What's your name?" Dillon asked.

"Gerry Mangrove," the agitated man said, although he seemed far more interested in watching the TSG officers than answering Dillon's questions.

Gurjit smiled amicably. "Well, Gerry, why don't we go back to the counter and have a chat?" he said, gently placing a hand on the man's arm.

Gerry brushed it off, and his demeanour instantly became confrontational. "Don't touch me," he warned Gurjit. "I'm allergic to bacon."

Dillon tutted, then rolled his eyes for good measure. If he had a penny for every time someone had called him 'pig' or 'bacon' during his career, he would be a rich man by now. "If you're going to resort to insults, you could at least try coming up with something original."

Gerry suddenly developed a nervous tick, and his left eye and the left side of his mouth started twitching in unison: mouth up, eye down.

It was very off-putting.

"Are you alright?" Dillon asked, fanning his hand in front of his face to disperse the unpleasant pong coming from Mangrove.

Balling his fists, Mangrove squared off against Dillon, even though he only came up to the detective's nose and was built like a garden rake. "What are you doing that for?" he demanded, puffing his pigeon chest out. "Are you trying to say I smell or something?"

"You *do* smell," Dillon pointed out, still fanning his face.

"No, I don't," Gerry insisted, taking his eyes off Dillon long enough to have a quick sniff.

Dillon glanced sideways at Gurjit and sighed, which only seemed to exacerbate the situation because Gerry started bouncing up and down on the balls of his feet like a boxer getting ready to enter the ring and start trading punches. The exertion was making him sweat even more. "You wanna watch what you say," he growled. "Copper or not, I ain't having anyone tell me I stink. Now, get out of my way."

Dillon rolled his head from side to side, causing the huge muscles of his neck and shoulders to bunch and ripple. "Gerry, you're giving me a headache," he said quietly. "Why don't you be a good boy and fetch the duty manager for us?"

Gerry had other ideas. Lunging forward, he attempted to shove the big man out of his way, but it was like trying to move a wall. "I said, get out of my way, pig," he yelled in frustration.

Dillon calmly placed a hand on each of the man's bony shoulders and shoved him back a step. "Now, pack it in and behave," he admonished, "before you end up getting yourself arrested."

Trying to defuse the situation, Gurjit Singh stepped in between them and opened his clipboard. Holding it out in front of him, he tapped the warrant. "Look, Gerry, here's the search warrant. It authorises us to enter and search the room of one of your residents, using force if necessary. As my colleague just said, if you keep trying to interfere, you'll only end up getting nicked for obstruction, and then you'll probably lose your job, so why don't you just calm down and call the duty manager?"

Gerry turned on Singh. "Which bloody resident?" he snarled, not showing the slightest inclination to back down.

"His name's John Anthony Spencer," Singh told him, patiently, "and he was released on licence from prison on Tuesday morning."

Gerry's face was twitching even more violently as he reached for the warrant. "Show me that," he insisted.

Gurjit drew it back. "Please don't touch the warrant," he said. "I'll happily sit down and talk you through it, but I'm afraid I can't hand it over."

Gerry sneered at him. At least Dillon assumed it was a sneer, although it could just have been a variation of his twitch.

"I bet it ain't even a real one," Gerry said. Without warning, he tried to snatch the warrant from the clipboard.

Dillon was far too quick for him. Wrapping one of his shovel-sized hands around the other man's wrist, he squeezed it and twisted his arm into a Gooseneck hold. Gerry's face contorted in pain as he was forced up onto tiptoes.

"Aaargh!"

"What part of 'don't touch' are you struggling to understand?" Dillon asked, smiling pleasantly at the man, who was now hopping from foot to foot in acute discomfort.

"Excuse me, what's going on?" an ebony-skinned woman, who had just emerged from the back office, demanded in a scathing tone.

The three men froze. As one, their heads spun guiltily to look at the newcomer, who was about five-eight or five-nine tall and slim, with straightened hair that fell halfway down her back.

"Well?" she demanded when no one spoke immediately, and there was a distinct chill to her voice.

Dillon eased the pressure on Gerry's wrist, allowing him to stand straight. Then, grabbing him by the scruff of the neck, he unceremoniously frogmarched Gerry over to the counter. "I'm DI Dillon from the Homicide Command," he told her, gruffly. "This is DC Singh. And you are?"

The woman ran glacial eyes over him. "I'm Naomi Masters, the duty manager," she replied coldly. "Would you mind telling me what you're doing here? And why you're manhandling one of my residents?"

Dillon glanced sideways at Gerry, who was standing there meekly, like butter wouldn't melt in his mouth. "Resident? Doesn't he work here?"

Gerry's eyes flickered between the woman and the two policemen flanking him. "I never claimed to work here, Naomi," he said, hurriedly.

For a second, Naomi stared at him, saying nothing. Then she

turned to address Dillon. "Unless Gerry's under arrest, would you mind releasing him?"

With a small huff of frustration, Dillon complied with her request.

A triumphant sneer appeared on Gerry's face as he distanced himself from the big man, and he made a big show of massaging his right wrist. "Police brutality, that was," he said, licking his lips nervously. "I could sue you for that."

Dillon noticed that the palm of his right hand was stained purple, and wondered if he worked in the print industry.

"Be quiet, Gerry," Naomi snapped.

Dillon spread his arms in a gesture of peace. "Look, Mr Whiffy was standing behind the counter, going through some drawers when we arrived, and he kicked off as soon as we asked to speak to whoever was in charge. Then the idiot decided to fight us, so I was forced to restrain him until he calmed down."

"That's not true!" Gerry bleated. "I didn't do anything."

Naomi stared accusingly at Gerry, who immediately wilted under her penetrating gaze. "What were you doing behind the counter, Gerry? You know that's off-limits to residents."

Gerry didn't answer at first. He was too busy trying to conjure up an excuse. "I... er... I was looking for a pen to fill in my unemployment forms..." he eventually said, not convincing anyone.

"He certainly wasn't searching for deodorant," Dillon observed, po-faced.

"Stop saying I smell," Gerry snapped, glaring up at the big man angrily.

Naomi's mouth tightened into a thin line. "Wait there," she told them.

Gerry let out a low, pitiful groan as she retreated behind the counter, and his discomfort rapidly intensified when she started checking through the drawers beneath it.

Dillon and Gurjit exchanged mystified glances. "Anything you want to tell us, Gerry?" Dillon asked him.

Gerry huffed. "Not without my solicitor present."

Naomi let out a little sigh of disappointment, muttered a barely audible, "Oh, Gerry," and then came back to join the others, carrying a small, black cash box in her hands.

Gerry seemed to shrink in size when he saw this. Swallowing hard, he started to back away, but Dillon grabbed hold of his elbow. All the fight seemed to have gone out of him, and he made no effort to resist.

"Hand over the money," Naomi demanded, holding her hand out.

Reluctantly, Gerry reached into his jeans pocket and withdrew a crumpled wad of notes. Unable to meet her eye, he passed it across without saying a word.

Naomi's eyes were tinged with sadness as she took the money from his outstretched hand, counted it, and then returned it to the cash box it had been stolen from.

"We've been having a few petty thefts lately," she told Dillon as she closed the lid, "but I would never have suspected Gerry." She shook her head sadly. "If you needed money, why didn't you speak to me, instead of stealing it?"

Gerry fidgeted uncomfortably. "Didn't like to say anything," he told her, sullenly. "And, anyway, I wasn't nicking it, I was just borrowing it."

Dillon sighed. This was all very touching, but it was getting in the way of what he'd come here to do. It was time to cut to the chase. "I take it you want to make a formal complaint, and have us arrest him?"

Naomi surprised him by shaking her head. "No. That's what our policy stipulates I should do but, in this instance, I'm going to deal with the matter internally."

Gerry's head shot up, and from his bemused expression, it was clear he hadn't expected her to say that. "Thank you, Naomi," he gushed. " I promise I won't do it again."

Dillon thought she was mad, but he bit his tongue. Of course Gerry would do it again. The first opportunity that he got.

Propped up by a small selection of pillows, Skippy lay spreadeagled across the top of his bed, puffing away at a joint. All he had on were his Y-fronts and a pair of odd socks. The left one had a hole in it, and a dirty big toe was poking through. He wiggled it, thinking that his nails badly needed cutting. He had been wearing the same underwear for three whole days now, having run out of clean stuff earlier in the week. Still, it wasn't as if anyone was going to be getting close enough to notice, so he figured that he could probably postpone the arduous trek to the launderette for another couple of days yet.

The radio was blaring away in the background, and he joined in as Robbie Williams belted out *Eternity*. As he sang along, he shoved a hand down the front of his shreddies and scratched his balls, which felt unpleasantly hot and sticky to the touch. He knew he needed a shower, but he really couldn't be bothered. Instead, he decided to go and make himself a brew.

Stubbing the joint out in an ashtray that rested on his stomach, he swung his bony legs over the edge of the bed. After coughing his lungs up for several seconds, he started hunting for yesterday's T-shirt. He grabbed a pillow, looked underneath it, and then launched it across the room when he didn't find what he was searching for. As he pulled back the quilt, his mind turned to Spencer. What the hell had his idiot cousin been thinking, grabbing the girl on his own like that? Of course, the answer was obvious; he'd done it because Skippy had dared to tell him a few home truths after he'd stabbed that bloke on the bus. Spencer had never been able to handle criticism, and now he was punishing Skippy for speaking his mind.

He finally found the creased T-shirt he'd been looking for under the bed, where it had been kicked last night. "Got you, you little bugger," he said, snatching it up from the floor and slipping it over his head.

Skippy decided that he'd had enough of Spencer's temper tantrums. He would have to eat humble pie for now, just to make sure that he didn't miss out on his share of the ransom, but once they got their hands on the money, Spencer could go and fuck himself.

Scooping his mobile phone off the bedside table, he dragged

himself through to the kitchen and put the kettle on. At some point, he was going to have to ring Spencer and apologise for having a go at him, so he might as well get it over with.

Dean Fletcher strolled into Tyler's office carrying three mugs. "There you go," he said, handing one to Tyler and another to Steve Bull.

"That's very kind of you, Deano," Tyler said, looking up in surprise. It wasn't often that this happened. "To what do we owe the honour?"

Dean indicated a chair opposite Tyler's desk. "May I?"

Tyler nodded. "Of course." He took a sip of the coffee Dean had just made him and suppressed a shudder. It was so strong that he could feel it eroding the enamel on his teeth. "Delicious," he said, placing the mug on his desk. He would get rid of it later, once Dean had left.

Bull, he noticed, had done likewise.

Dean took a long slurp from his own drink before addressing them. "After I spoke to Clive Dibney at the Probation Service earlier, I started doing some thinking,"

Tyler smiled. "I thought I could smell burning."

No smile in return. Just an inverted eyebrow.

Tyler made his face serious again.

"Dibney told me that Spencer signed on with the Public Protection Unit at Shoreditch nick yesterday morning, so I put in a quick call to them to confirm this. The skipper in charge kindly faxed me over a copy of his paperwork, and guess what I found on it?"

Tyler performed an eyebrow shrug. "The mind boggles."

"Spencer gave them a contact number, which means he's got a mobile phone that we didn't know about," Dean said, removing a scrunched-up note from his shirt pocket and sliding it across the desk to Tyler. "There you go."

Tyler glanced at it for a moment, then picked up his phone. He tapped in a five-digit internal number and waited patiently for his call to be answered. "Ah, Reg, can you pop into my office, please. I have an urgent assignment for you," he said.

Less than fifteen seconds later, a fair haired man with a cherubic face walked through the door. "You summoned me, oh illustrious leader?" DC Reg Parker said with a frivolous smile.

Tyler passed him the note. "Dean's uncovered a mobile phone number for Spencer, and I want you to submit urgent subscriber, call data, and cell site applications to the TIU."

The Telephone Intelligence Unit were based at New Scotland Yard and dealt with all the Met's phone related enquiries.

Reg examined the note carefully. "I can certainly do that," he said, turning to go.

"Thanks, Reggie," Tyler said with a weary smile. "Let me know as soon as you hear anything back."

Skippy tried ringing Spencer's mobile again but, as it had done every other time, it went straight to voicemail. "Spence, phone me as soon as you get this," he growled, leaving his fourth message of the day.

Killing the call, Skippy tossed the phone on the kitchen table and cursed his idiot cousin, who was probably having so much fun with the girl that he'd switched his phone off to prevent anyone from interrupting their rapturous lovemaking. The thought of them going at it like a pair of rabbits made him shudder.

As he walked back to the living room, the hourly news bulletin came over the radio.

"*As the hunt for the man dubbed The Candy Killer continues, police have released new information. They have named John Anthony Spencer as a man they would like to speak to, both in relation to the murder of David Bannister and a botched kidnapping that occurred in Norfolk yesterday evening. In that incident, an unnamed woman was abducted from a car park in Diss town centre and taken to a remote location, from which she subsequently managed to escape. Police have stressed that the woman is someone who was previously known to her abductor, and that there is no suggestion that any other women are at risk. Let's go over to our reporter outside Diss police station for more..."*

"What the fuck...?" Skippy spluttered. He rushed over to the radio and twiddled the dial clockwise, turning the volume all the way up. For the remainder of the segment, he remained glued to the spot, shaking his head with growing incredulity.

"Fuck! Fuck! Fuck!" he muttered, turning the volume back down as the anchor-man moved onto the next segment. His mind was reeling. Spencer had boasted that the girl had been over the moon to see him again, and that everything was all lovey-dovey between them. Clearly, it wasn't, not if she'd escaped and dobbed him straight in to the police.

How would that affect the kidnap plan?

Spencer had assured him that he hadn't said anything about that to her. As far as she knew, he had grabbed her purely so that they could be together again.

That was something, wasn't it?

He reached for the phone, aggressively thumbing in Spencer's digits. Voicemail again. "Spencer, you useless mug, I've just heard about the girl on the radio. What the fuck are you playing at? Call me back as soon as you get this. I'm not joking, Spence! Call me back." Only after he'd hung up did it occur to him that, if the police ever got their hands on Spencer's phone, they would find all five of his messages stored on it. Would they then accuse him of helping his cousin? "Fuck," he moaned, slapping his forehead angrily. Why hadn't he thought of that *before* he'd made the calls?

13

BANISHING DEMONS

Susie Sergeant had always found mortuaries to be rather depressing places. They were dark, foreboding buildings in which the dead were stored pending examination by a pathologist. Only then, after suffering that final ignominy, could their remains be released for burial or cremation.

Irrespective of whether it was a gothic-styled edifice dating back to Victorian times or a more contemporary design, every single mortuary that she had ever set foot inside had been filled with the same pervasive smell of death and Trigene. At least, unlike Tony Dillon, who was a little squeamish around cadavers, the actual process of dissection – along with some of the truly revolting smells that came with it – had never bothered her in the slightest.

Susie was sitting patiently in the office upstairs, awaiting the arrival of the Home Office Forensic Pathologist who was going to perform the special post mortem on David Bannister. The Coroner's Officer, an ancient PC who had worked there for longer than anyone could remember, and had probably joined The Job during Queen Victoria's reign, had kindly made her a cup of instant coffee, and she was now flicking through June's edition of Private Eye, which she had found on one of the vacant desks, to occupy herself while she waited.

She flicked through the pages without paying much attention to the contents. Dan still hadn't responded to the endless succession of messages she had sent him, all imploring him to contact her so that they could sort out their finances. She had lost count of the times that she'd tried to ring him since he'd walked out on her, and it was getting to the stage where she was beginning to feel like a bloody stalker!

The more Susie thought about their failed marriage, the more convinced she became that the break up was her fault. After all, she and Dan were very different creatures when it came to what they wanted from their careers. He had absolutely no interest in climbing the promotion ladder, while she was desperate to emulate her father, who had retired as a Chief Superintendent. Perhaps her naked ambition had been too much for him to cope with? Perhaps it had gotten in the way of their marriage? Irrespective of that, she had always loved Dan unreservedly, and she hadn't deserved the treatment she had received from him.

Of course, divorce was a depressingly common phenomenon amongst police officers; even Jack Tyler had fallen foul of it. Susie liked and admired Tyler, and she was glad that he had managed to weather the storm and emerge from the other side unscathed. He had even found love again with Kelly Flowers. Maybe, in a year or so, Susie would find herself in a similar position, sharing a new life with a wonderful man, and all the pain that she was now feeling would be relegated to a dim and distant memory?

She certainly hoped so.

Susie had always prided herself on being a very practical person, and she didn't like her life being this disordered. Apart from all the emotional turmoil of the split, there were some very difficult logistical issues that needed to be resolved, and she wanted these addressed sooner rather than later. The house and their savings were in joint names. They needed to sit down and discuss the situation like adults and work out how they were going to divide the spoils. With regards to the house, did they sell up and split the proceeds, or should one of them buy the other one out? Susie had already done the maths, and she was confident that she would be able to keep up the mortgage repayments without Dan's help.

The question was, did she want to?

Perhaps it would make more sense to sell up or let him have it, rather than carry on living in a house that was full of uncomfortable memories?

Although Susie felt incredibly angry with Dan for cheating on her, she was equally livid at herself for having neglected their relationship. Would this have happened had she been more attentive to his needs instead of putting The Job first?

Surely, even if she was to blame for their relationship turning to rat shit, that didn't excuse him for running off with another woman? He should have been upfront about it and told her that he was unhappy, and he should have given her a chance to put things right, not taken a lover to make himself feel better.

"DI Sergeant. I believe I'm to have the pleasure of your company for the next few hours," a very well educated, but slightly sinister voice announced from the doorway.

Startled from her reverie, Susie looked up to find Creepy Claxton standing there, evaluating her with cold, unblinking eyes. A little chill ran down her spine, and she half expected the pathologist's arrival to be accompanied by forked lightning and an outbreak of spooky organ music. "Good morning, Dr Claxton," she said, standing up to shake his hand. It was cold, just like a corpse's. "I've got the briefing document here for your perusal," she said, digging into her shoulder bag and removing the form. "I'll let you have a read through that, and then I'll try and answer any questions you have."

"Excellent," Claxton said, accepting the document with a formal little bow.

The TSG officers had stripped out of their public order overalls and were now loading all the shields back onto their carrier in readiness for a quick departure.

After sending Gerry away with a flea in his ear, Naomi Masters had escorted Dillon and Gurjit up to Spencer's room, opening the door with her master key. As expected, the room had been empty, and a cursory search had revealed that there were no clothes in either the wardrobe or chest of drawers. Apart from a cardboard box containing a few low-value personal items, the most interesting of which was a hand-drawn sketch of a much younger Spencer, there was no sign that he had ever been in the room. It was impossible to tell whether the unmade bed had been slept in overnight, but they very much doubted it.

Leaving DC Murray and his two perspiring companions to carry out a more thorough search, which would probably take them all of ten minutes, Dillon and Gurjit returned to the street.

"Where now?" Gurjit asked as he climbed into the old Astra, with its creaking springs and coffee-stained seats. "Do you want me to take you straight back to the factory, or are we going on a mystery tour of London?" As he spoke, he wound down his window to release some of the heat that had built up in their absence.

Dillon was doing likewise and, as soon as he finished, he stuck his large head out to get some fresh air. "Pity this heap doesn't have air conditioning," he complained.

"It's got nature's air conditioning," Gurjit replied with a happy-go-lucky smile.

Dillon raised a lazy eyebrow at the stupidity of the statement. "If I didn't know you better, I would swear you were a retard, coming out with crap like that."

Gurjit laughed indulgently. "I'm not the one sticking my head out of the window like a dog," he pointed out. "I told you we should have taken one of the newer motors but, for some bizarre reason, you insisted on using the oldest car in the office, so you've only got yourself to blame if you're cooking in your own juices."

"You know, no one likes a smart arse," Dillon pointed out.

"You didn't answer my question," Gurjit reminded him. "Are we going back to the factory or not?"

"Yes," Dillon told him, drawing his head back inside and folding his arms sulkily, "but only for long enough to swap cars. Then we're heading off to sunny Diss to spend a nice afternoon in the countryside."

The family flocked to Phoebe's side the moment that she walked through the cottage door, all talking over each other in a bid to have their questions answered first. In the end, unable to bear it any longer, she shouted at them to be quiet and give her some space.

The silence quickly became deafening, and Jessica disappeared into the kitchen to put the kettle on, while the others sulkily retired to the lounge. After taking a moment to compose herself, Phoebe followed them in.

As she entered the room, her father looked up from his pacing. "As soon as we've all had a nice cup of tea, you need to go and pack your bag," he told her. "The sooner we get back to London, the better. If the police can't protect you, I bloody well will, of that you can be assured."

Phoebe had wondered how long it would take for him to start harping on about DCI Craddock's refusal to provide around-the-clock protection.

Not long at all, it seemed.

"I'll hire a couple of heavies from the company we use to look after our artists," Ben said. "They're all ex-military types, so they know what they're doing." He paused long enough to harrumph, and then resumed his ill-tempered stomping. "I'd like to see that cretin, Spencer, try and get past any of those guys."

Phoebe groaned in exasperation. "Dad, please don't do that. I really don't want any of your paid gorillas following me around." She flopped down on the couch, exhausted.

Ben brushed her concern aside. "Nonsense, you won't even know they're there."

With a groan of despair, Phoebe buried her head in her hands. "I just want to lay down for a little while and get some rest, then I'll be fine," she said, wearily.

After a moment, Martin sat down beside her, nursing the large Scotch whisky that he'd poured himself as soon as she'd walked through the door. "Don't feel you've got to put on a brave face for our benefit, sweetheart," he told her. "I know you must be all churned up inside, after what you've just been through, but as soon as we get back to civilisation, we'll get you an appointment with Dr Abingdon, and he can prescribe you some sedatives or something to calm you down. Then, tomorrow morning, we'll book you some therapy sessions and, before you know it, you'll be right as rain again."

"Martin's right," Ben said, and then raised his voice, directing it towards the hall door. "We won't let this little setback destroy all the progress Phoebe's made, will we Jess?"

"Of course not, darling," she shouted back from the kitchen.

Phoebe shook her head. "Dad, you don't get it, do you? I'm not falling apart. I'm just tired. Don't ask me why, but what I went through yesterday didn't affect me in the same way that it did last time. I know this sounds strange but, if anything, the fact that I escaped from his clutches without anyone's help has actually helped me to banish some of my demons."

Ben and Martin exchanged glances. This wasn't the timid, indecisive girl they were used to dealing with. Martin responded with a perplexed shrug, but Ben's jaw merely tightened with resolve. "I knew it," he said, slamming his fist into his open palm. "You're in denial."

Inside her head, Phoebe screamed. This was a classic example of how they had taken to controlling every aspect of her life, bulldozering her objections aside and insisting that they knew better. Phoebe felt like pulling her hair out in frustration but, instead, she took a deep breath, paused for a moment, and then released it slowly. "I'm going to go upstairs and take a nap," she told them, calmly. "You can stay here if you want to but, if you do, you need to understand that

I'm not coming back to London with you. Not yet, anyway. I feel like I need a little time alone to get my head together, and I'd prefer to do that here, where it's nice and quiet, rather than in London, where everything always seems so chaotic."

The two men stared at her in stunned silence as she stood up and headed towards the hall door. "But you won't be safe here," Ben protested. "What if Spencer makes another attempt to grab you?"

"He won't," Phoebe responded without turning her head. "Chief Inspector Craddock said that he'll be running for the hills with his tail between his legs."

"Gah!" Ben spluttered, staring up at the ceiling, "What does he know?"

Jessica appeared in the doorway, carrying a tray of teas and coffees. "Have I missed something?" she asked, immediately picking up on the tension inside the room.

Phoebe helped herself to a hot drink on her way past. "Nothing important, mummy," she said.

Reg Parker strolled into Tyler's office waving three flimsy sheets of paper in the air. "The call and cell site data from Spencer's phone has just come in," he announced cheerfully.

Tyler merely grunted. He hated going through phone data. "Pull up a pew," he said, pointing to a chair.

Parker did as he was told, then passed the documents across to Tyler. "There's nothing to get too excited about," he warned as Tyler ran his eyes over them. "The first page just contains the subscriber details. As you can see, it's an unregistered Pay-As-You-Go that only came online yesterday morning. The second sheet shows that it's only made two calls so far, the first being a brief call to the probation service, yesterday morning, and the second being a longer call to an unidentified mobile ending in 137, yesterday evening."

"I'm guessing, from what Norfolk CID told me this morning, that the second call was to Spencer's cousin, Skippy?"

Parker nodded. "That's the most likely answer," he agreed. "I've got Dean running the number through the system to see if it's known to us, and I'll chuck in a subscriber check as soon as I finish here. In all likelihood, though, that'll probably come back as an unregistered PAYG as well."

Tyler absentmindedly tossed the three sheets of paper onto his desk. "Probably," he agreed, tapping the top sheet. "Now, tell me about this last document."

"Ah, yes. That's the cell site report. It shows that Spencer's phone, which ends in 654, was cell sited within the radius of the mast covering Shoreditch police station when he called the Probation Service yesterday morning. Later in the day, when it made the second call, the 654 number was cell sited within the radius of a mast covering quite an extensive area of Norfolk countryside. I've no doubt the barn that Spencer was holding her in will be in there somewhere."

Tyler stared at him intently. "And you're sure there's been no activity on the phone since then?"

"There doesn't appear to have been," Parker told him. "I'm waiting for Mr Dillon to get back so that we can discuss the possibility of pinging the phone with him." There were several ways that this could be done, but each carried a risk of alerting the user, who might then become suspicious and dispose of the handset.

Tyler took a moment to digest this and then nodded thoughtfully. "Okay, but tell him to run it by me first."

"Will do," Parker promised.

14

THAT CHOCOLATE BROWNIE'S GOT MY NAME ON IT

They arrived in Diss town centre at a quarter to one. By the time they had a little drive around to orientate themselves, and then sought out the car park that Phoebe Cunningham had been abducted from, it was just past the hour. "What time did you say we're meeting up with the SIO?" Gurjit asked.

Dillon checked his watch. "We're meeting him at the local nick at one-forty-five," he said, rubbing his arms animatedly. He stopped abruptly when he caught Gurjit giving him a strange look. "What? It's bloody cold in here."

Gurjit cranked the fan down a couple of notches. "Honestly, it's like being out with my mother."

Stepping into the sun was like suddenly being exposed to the heat from a blast furnace and, before long, Dillon found himself yearning for the Arctic temperatures of the air-conditioned BMW, although he decided against sharing that thought with Gurjit.

"See that footpath over there," Gurjit said, seeming totally at ease in the searing heat, "I think that's the route Miss Cunningham must have approached from when she returned to the car park."

Squinting against the sun, which was dazzlingly bright even with his shades on, Dillon scanned the car park's perimeter for CCTV cameras, but couldn't see any. Conceding defeat, he checked his watch again. "Come on, Gurjit, let's go and grab a quick bite to eat before we meet up with DCI Carrot Cruncher."

As they set off for the High Street, Gurjit's little legs struggled to keep pace with Dillon's giant strides. "Not so fast," he whined.

Dillon grinned at his discomfort. "It's good for you, and you could do with burning a few extra calories, especially as you're about to chuck a load more down your throat."

"I hate you sometimes, you know that?" Gurjit panted.

The little place that they chose to eat in was filled with the wonderful aroma of freshly baked cakes and buns, and a chocolate brownie in the display above the counter immediately caught Gurjit's eye. "That's got my name on it," he said, staring at it longingly.

After ordering hot drinks, baguettes, and the biggest brownie in the café for Gurjit, the two detectives took a seat over by the window.

"I know the abduction isn't our problem," Dillon said, as he tore a bite out of his cheese and ham baguette, "but I would be a lot happier if it had been caught on camera."

"Why?" Gurjit asked, also tucking into his food.

"Because it would corroborate everything the Cunningham girl's said."

Gurjit paused, mid-bite. "Don't you think she's telling the truth, then?"

"It's not that," Dillon said, dismissively. "It's just that, at the moment, it's her word against his, which means that Spencer's barrister will give her a really hard time over what happened when the case eventually goes to court, which he wouldn't be able to do if the incident had been captured on film."

"I suppose," Gurjit conceded, "but if Spencer's convicted of the murder, which he will be, he might just put his hands up to the abduction, and spare her the pain of having to give evidence."

Dillon shook his head. "That's not the vibe I'm getting from this arsehole. I reckon he'll put up a fight, and claim that she went with him willingly."

"Why would he do that?" Gurjit asked, perplexed.

"Think about it. He's just been released on licence after serving eight years for abducting and raping that poor girl, and yet within a day of getting out, he abducted her again. He's obviously totally obsessed with her, which means that he'll never admit to having harmed her. In his warped mind, he might not even think that he has."

Gurjit thought this through as he polished off the last of his baguette. "I see what you mean," he said, dabbing his lips with a serviette. A little smile of anticipation lit his face up as he reached for his chocolate brownie. "Come to daddy," he said, opening his mouth wide.

———

George Holland welcomed Tyler into his office with a warm smile. "Come in and sit down, Jack, and tell me how the latest job is coming along."

"Thank you, sir," Tyler said as he lowered himself into one of the chairs opposite Holland's large desk.

Instead of joining him, Holland moved to the windowsill, where a coffee percolator was burbling away. "I can never remember, do you take milk and sugar?" he asked, glancing back over his shoulder at Tyler.

"White with two sugars, please," Tyler said with a grateful smile. He liked the ambience in Holland's office. It had, much like the man himself, an air of authoritative efficiency to it. A neat row of grey filing cabinets lined the back wall, each one secured by a strong lock to protect the confidential documents they contained from prying eyes. Four large whiteboards had been screwed into the wall above them, and the first three of these contained an assortment of photos, graphs and charts correlating to the various

Cat A jobs the command was currently running. The latest was Operation Jackman, the recent murder of PC Alan Dawkins, which had been taken on by DCI Andy Quinlan. Despite the resources being thrown at it, the identity of the three suspects remained unknown.

A portrait of Queen Elizabeth II took pride of place on the wall behind Holland's desk and, unless he was much mistaken, it was an identical print to the one hanging up in his office, except that Holland's version hadn't been defaced by some disrespectful sod adding a curly moustache and a pair of round spectacles.

The remaining wall space was taken up by numerous commendations and a host of framed photos depicting Holland shaking hands with various high-ranking officers and dignitaries, including the current Commissioners, several of his predecessors, and the incumbent Home Secretary. There was even one of him being introduced to the queen when he received the Queen's Police Medal. The nice thing about George Holland was that nothing on display in his office was staged or pretentious. He didn't consider the commendations or photographs trophies; they were just happy memories of him doing a job he loved.

Holland placed a mug of Columbian coffee in front of Tyler and settled down behind his desk. "How's the manhunt coming along?"

"Slowly. The last confirmed sighting of our suspect was yesterday evening, in Diss, Norfolk."

Holland raised an enquiring eyebrow. "Has he got family or friends up that way?"

"No, sir. He was released on licence from Strangeways on Tuesday morning, having served eight years of a twelve stretch for abducting and raping a fourteen year old girl called Phoebe Cunningham. She's in her twenties now, and hasn't had any contact with him since he was imprisoned. Yesterday evening, he abducted her again from a car park in Diss town centre."

Holland's face darkened. "That's most disconcerting," he said, sitting forward and reaching for a pen.

"It is," Tyler agreed. "We have no idea how he knew where to find her, and that's something we'll need to look at in due course, but for now, the priority is arresting him."

"I would like to think that rescuing the girl is your top priority," Holland said, fixing Tyler with a piercing stare. "Why wasn't I informed of the kidnapping sooner?" He was jotting down notes on a pad as he spoke.

Tyler spread his hands placatingly. "I only found out about it this morning, and by that time the girl had already managed to escape from his clutches." He proceeded to give Holland a full rundown of events, concluding with her walking into Diss police station during the early hours.

Holland's relief was palpable. "Well, the fact that she's safe does put a different perspective on things," he allowed, lowering his pen and relaxing back into his chair.

"She had a lucky escape," Tyler said.

Holland nodded his agreement. "I take it that Norfolk Constabulary are pulling out all the stops to find him?"

"They are, sir. Dillon's visiting their SIO as we speak, to see if they have any information that might help us at our end."

Holland tented his fingers, and stared over the top of them at Tyler. "What about the reactive side of the investigation, how's that coming along?"

Tyler smiled. "In terms of evidence, we've got oodles of it. The CCTV from the bus, which shows Spencer committing the murder, is top notch. On top of that, we have some excellent statements from passengers who witnessed the event. We've recovered Spencer's blood-stained fingerprint at the scene. We've also recovered the murder weapon, Spencer's bloodstained coat, and the victim's wallet, which Spencer grabbed before having it on his toes."

Holland frowned. "So, this was a robbery gone wrong, was it?"

Tyler shook his head. "No, stealing the wallet was an afterthought."

"I see. So, what else needs to be done?"

"From a reactive point of view, there's not too much to do until he's nicked, and then it'll just be a case of conducting interviews and arranging ID parades for the witnesses. After all that, he'll be charged and remanded in custody."

"That's good to hear," Holland said, "but let's go back to the girl again for a moment. Have you carried out a risk assessment?"

"No, not yet," Tyler admitted, groaning inwardly. The Job seemed to have developed an unhealthy obsession with completing risk assessments. Pretty much everything required one these days and, if the rollout carried on at its present rate, it wouldn't be too long before officers were ordered to fill one out before visiting the loo.

Holland frowned. "Do you think that she's still in any danger? Is it possible that Spencer might have another go at abducting her?"

Tyler shrugged. "Honestly, I don't think so, but who knows. He's besotted with her, so I can't rule out any further attempts to snatch her."

"Not the answer I was hoping for," Holland said, tetchily.

"From an arse covering perspective, the good news is that the girl remained in Diss, so we haven't got to worry about managing that particular risk."

Holland grunted. "Let's hope you're right about that, and that those words don't come back to bite us."

Tony Dillon and Gurjit Singh were shown into DCI Craddock's office by a young constable who didn't look old enough to shave yet. It was a big room, light and airy with a nice high celling. Apart from an ancient mahogany desk, the only other furniture consisted of a couple of dented filing cabinets, an oval conference table, and six hard-backed chairs. There was an open door at the rear of the room, through which Dillon could see a small annex, informally furnished with a glass coffee table and some soft chairs.

Craddock greeted them enthusiastically, pumping their arms up and down with great vigour, as though they were long lost friends. After the introductions were made, Craddock told the constable to bring them some light refreshments and invited them to join him in the annex.

"Not often we get colleagues visiting us from the Big Smoke," he said, with a smile of genuine warmth. He indicated for them to take a seat around the coffee table and virtually threw himself into the nearest chair, which creaked and groaned under his weight.

Dillon's first impression of the Norfolk SIO was that he was highly intelligent, very resourceful, as stubborn as a mule, and about a subtle as a brick through a window. He figured that they would either get on like a house on fire or completely rub each other up the wrong way. "It makes a pleasant change for us to be able to get away from the city for a short while," he confessed. "I've never been to Diss before. It's really quite lovely."

Craddock seemed pleased to hear that. "We like it," he said, linking his fingers and resting them across his chest.

They made small talk until the youthful constable returned with a tray of hot drinks and some assorted biscuits. "We're not big on formalities around here," Craddock said, noticing the way that Gurjit was eyeing up the biscuits, "so feel free to help yourself."

"Thank you, sir," Gurjit said, making straight for a Jammie Dodger.

Dillon declined the offer. "Mr Craddock–"

"Call me Barty."

"Thank you. Barty, I know you've spoken to DCI Tyler over the phone, but would you mind giving me a quick rundown on where you are with the case?"

"Of course," Craddock replied, spreading his arms magnanimously. "Be glad to. What we know, so far, is that Miss Cunningham was abducted from a car park in Diss town centre about eight-fifteen p.m. last night. Her attacker, John Spencer, hit her over the noggin from behind, rendering her unconscious, and then bundled her into the back of a car."

"What do we know about the car?" Dillon interrupted.

"She thinks it was a light coloured BMW, but we don't have an index. There's no sign of a struggle at the scene; no blood or anything like that. We've had the car park photographed, and the first responders performed a walkthrough, searching for trace evidence. Nothing was found. The Duty Officer decided against preserving the scene for a full forensic sweep and, I must say, under the circumstances I fully support that decision."

Dillon took a moment to digest that, wondering just how thorough the search had been. He imagined a couple of PCs aimlessly wandering around, staring at the floor without having a clue what they were looking for. "Fair enough. Are there any CCTV cameras in the vicinity of the car park?"

Craddock's enormous eyebrows, which resembled a couple of unkempt hedgerows, knitted together. "I'm afraid not."

"Barty, I'm assuming that the local authority footage covering the town centre has already been seized, along with anything along the route Spencer would have taken to the barn?"

Craddock flashed him a sympathetic smile. "This isn't London," he said apologetically. "We don't have cameras on every junction like you lot do. There isn't a great deal of coverage in the town centre, but we've requested what little there is. As for the route that Spencer would have taken to the barn, well, that's all country lanes, not A Roads or motorways, so there's nothing there for us to seize, I'm afraid."

Dillon was silent for a moment as he considered this. So far, they weren't having much luck. "Were there any witnesses to the abduction?"

Craddock's eyebrows ran riot as he considered this. "If there were, they haven't come forward yet. I've got officers canvassing all the nearby shops as we speak but, realistically, all the buildings are too far away for anyone to have been seen anything."

Dillon sighed. "I agree. We had a little mosey around the car park ourselves before coming here, and we reached the same conclusion."

"We're not overly hopeful that local enquiries will turn up anything significant," Craddock admitted, "but we're doing them anyway. Oh, and I've arranged for a couple of uniforms to go back tonight for an anniversary visit. Who knows, maybe we'll be lucky and find someone who saw something."

Dillon hoped so, but he wasn't holding his breath. "Let's move onto the barn," he suggested. "What's happening with that?"

Craddock shovelled a chocolate biscuit into his mouth, chomped on it for a couple of seconds, and then swallowed. He washed it down with a large mouthful of strong tea. "Are you sure you don't want one?" he asked, holding the plate out towards Dillon.

"I'm fine, thank you," Dillon replied, eager to crack on.

"I'll have another one if that's all right?" Gurjit said, making his only contribution to date.

"The barn?" Dillon encouraged.

"Scenes of crime have already concluded their examination," Craddock said, snapping up the last Jammie Dodger before Gurjit could reach it. "The only things they found were a few strips of discarded gaffer tape and a flimsy white hat. No doubt, the gaffer tape was used to bind the girl's hands and feet. Not sure if the hat has anything to do with the kidnap or if it was left there by someone else. We'll get them submitted for forensic examination in due course. Other than that, the place was empty. There was no sign of any blood, which we thought there might be, considering she hit him over the head with a lump of metal. There was no clothing, either. The barn has been photographed, and there's a PC standing on guard, but I'll probably release it as a scene fairly soon."

"I'd like to see the barn before that happens, if it's possible?" Dillon told him.

Craddock smiled obligingly. "Of course. I'll get someone to take you there as soon as we're finished."

"You say she clouted Spencer with a metal pipe? Has that been recovered?"

Craddock shook his head. "No, afraid not. Miss Cunningham states she took it with her when she ran away, just in case he came after her and she needed to hit him again. She eventually threw it into a ditch, but she hasn't got a clue where she was at the time."

"Have you got anyone out searching for it?" Dillon asked.

Please tell me you have!

Craddock chortled good naturedly. "And where would they search? You're potentially talking about several square miles of rugged countryside. It would be completely different if we were talking about a murder weapon, of course, but we're not, and I can't justify sending out search parties and sniffer dogs just to get my hands on a bit of piping."

"If it has his blood on it, that pipe would give you the suspect's DNA, and put him at the scene," Dillon pointed out.

"If," Craddock countered. "And that's a very big if. Besides, the gaffer tape we recovered might do that for us and, even if it doesn't, Miss Cunningham's witness statement certainly will."

Dillon cleared his throat. "So, in summary, the only evidence you have at this stage is the girl's testimony and some discarded gaffer tape?"

"That's about the size of it," Craddock confirmed. "Both scenes have been photographed, searched, and examined forensically. We've requested all the local authority CCTV but, as I said, coverage is patchy, and there are no cameras close to either location. Unless the door-to-door enquiries in the vicinity of the car park, or tonight's anniversary visit, turn up any witnesses, that's all the evidence there is."

"What about Spencer?" Dillon asked next. "What's your plan for arresting him?"

Craddock shifted uncomfortably in his seat, which creaked and groaned in protest. "He's shown as wanted missing on the PNC, and we've circulated his description to all local officers. Other than that, there's not realistically a lot we can do at the moment," Craddock said. "My guess is that he's buggered off back to London, but we don't know the registration of the car he's using, so we can't circulate it or run it through ANPR."

"We think the car's likely to be stolen," Dillon informed him.

Craddock nodded his agreement. "I'd bet a month's wages on it."

"We're checking to see how many Beamers were reported stolen from Hackney during the period between Spencer's release and the girl's abduction. We hope to be able to identify the car he's using before too long. As soon as we do, we'll let you have the details, and we'll get it flagged up on the PNC and run it through ANPR."

An ever growing network of Automatic Number Plate Recognition cameras was cropping up around the country. While the initial roll out had mainly focused on motorways and main arterial roads, their use was now being extended into city centres and other urban areas. The way the system worked was that, whenever a vehicle passed beneath an ANPR camera, its details were run through the national database to see if there were any interest reports on it. If there were, for instance because it was stolen or concerned in crime, the vehicle was immediately circulated to local units in the hope that they could intercept it and detain the occupants.

"Once we've identified the car's registration number, we'll also commission a retrospective search with NADAC–" that was the National ANPR data centre "–to see if they can shed any light on Spencer's movements between the time that the car was stolen and now."

"Well then," Craddock said with a smile of satisfaction, "it seems to me that, between us, we've got all the bases covered. All we've got to do now is wait for someone to nick him, and then we can charge him and throw away the key."

Dillon wished it were that easy. Craddock was clearly content to bide his time until Spencer got himself arrested, which might be an acceptable tactic for the bodged abduction, but wouldn't do at all for the murder. "Is there any chance that he could be holed up somewhere local?"

"Why would he want to do that?" Craddock asked. From his tone, he clearly thought this was a ludicrous idea.

"I don't know," Dillon admitted. "In order to have another go at getting his hands on the girl, maybe?"

"Well, the area where he held her is very rural, and there are plenty of other old buildings that he could probably hide up in," Craddock conceded, "but you have to ask yourself, why would he want to? As for going after Miss Cunningham again, I really don't think he'd be that stupid, do you? He had the element of surprise on his side yesterday, but not anymore. Besides, this is a tight-knit community, and strangers tend to stick out." He allowed himself a devilish grin. "You can't even take a dump in these parts without someone gossiping about it. Trust me, if he's still out there, I'll hear about it soon enough."

It was a sound argument, Dillon had to admit. "You may be right," he acknowledged reluctantly.

"Contrary to what my good wife might tell you," Craddock said, levering his enormous frame out of the soft chair, "I usually am. Now, why don't I get someone to drive you out to the barn so you can see it for yourself?"

15

DISCOVERING THE BETRAYAL

Although Phoebe had only managed three hours of slumber, it had been the sleep of the dead, and she had woken up feeling surprisingly refreshed. The back of her head still ached, but nowhere near as much as it had previously. After getting dressed, popping to the loo and taking some paracetamols, she descended the stairs, steeling herself for another onslaught from her father, who she knew would be chomping at the bit to get back to London. She decided that the best way to handle him was to let him blow off some steam without interruption, and then politely decline. Regardless of what he wanted, Phoebe wasn't ready to return to the hustle and bustle of London yet, not while she still had unfinished business in Norfolk.

Muffled voices drifted up from below, and it took her a second to register that there were actually two separate conversations going on. The first was coming from the kitchen and, as she paused to listen, she instantly recognised the distinctive tones of her parents, who appeared to be arguing over what to do for the best regarding her future. As usual, dad was overreacting, while mum was trying to take a more balanced approach.

It was the second pair of voices that intrigued her, and these were coming from the direction of the lounge. As the door was closed, she couldn't decipher any of the words being said, but there were definitely two people speaking: one male; the other female.

Phoebe's curiosity was piqued. There had only been three other people in the cottage when she retired, but now there were four. She tiptoed down the remaining stairs, being careful to avoid the one at the bottom, which always creaked loudly, and padded her way along the hallway until she reached the lounge door.

The voices suddenly stopped, and she wondered if their owners had heard her approaching. She carefully placed her ear against the door, holding her breath as she listened. Nothing. Not a sound. Perhaps they had gone into the garden? Moving with exaggerated slowness, she pushed the door open and cautiously peered inside.

Phoebe didn't know what she had been expecting to see, but it certainly wasn't the sight that met her eyes. To her horror, Martin and Anna were standing in the middle of the room, locked in a passionate embrace. Eyes closed, the intensity of their kiss was such that neither of them noticed her arrival. For a moment, Phoebe just stood there, rooted to the spot in disbelief. Then, moving very slowly, she withdrew from the room.

Back in the hall, she leaned against the wall and raised a hand to her mouth to stifle a sob. The voices from the kitchen were intensifying, as her parent's debate deteriorated into an argument. Phoebe closed her eyes but, as soon as she did, the painful image of her fiancé and best friend's deception flashed into her mind.

How could they do that to her?

How could they betray her like that?

Phoebe took a deep breath and stilled herself. Although she was hurt, she wasn't terribly surprised by the discovery. In fact, if she was being completely honest with herself, she had suspected that something was going on between the two of them for some time now. Dabbing her eyes, Phoebe returned to the stairs, creeping up the first few. Then, she turned around and began descending loudly. She purposefully stood on the bottom step, which creaked loudly under her weight. "Where is everyone?" she called. Without waiting for a response, she barged into the lounge, to find Martin sitting on the sofa, looking as guilty as sin, and Anna Manson standing by the patio doors.

Quick to smile, Anna had an easy going way about her. She was in her early twenties, with green eyes, a slender nose, and a heart-shaped mouth. The black framed Gucci glasses that she habitually wore gave her an air of intelligence and refinement. Her long brown hair was styled into waves and, while she didn't possess the breath-taking beauty and model like figure that Phoebe had been blessed with, she was still a very pretty girl in her own right.

"Phoebe!" Anna exclaimed as her best friend entered the room. Breaking into a huge smile, she rushed forward, arms outstretched. "I'm so glad that you're safe. I've been really worried about you."

Phoebe didn't return the embrace. "I can see that," she said, letting her arms hang limply by her sides.

Oblivious to the fact that Phoebe was making no effort to reciprocate her affection, Anna continued to crush her friend to her chest, clinging to her with the steely determination of someone who never intended to let go.

Phoebe's parents came dashing into the room.

"You're awake!" her father declared, just in case the others hadn't noticed.

"How are you feeling?" her mother asked, placing a hand on her shoulder and stroking it tenderly.

"Crushed," Phoebe mumbled from deep within Anna's embrace.

Anna took the hint and released her. "Sorry," she said, taking a little step backwards. "I think I might've gotten a little carried away with myself there."

Phoebe stared at her for a long moment. *Not as carried away as you were when you were snogging Martin, you back-stabbing bitch.*

"Anna's driven all the way here from Leytonstone, just to be with you," her father told her, making Phoebe wonder if he planned to continue stating the obvious all day?

"Your parents told me you wanted to stay here for a few days, instead of returning to London with them," Anna said brightly, "so I quickly packed a bag and came up to keep you company." She beamed at Phoebe as she said this, and Phoebe half expected her to start clapping her hands in excitement at any moment.

"Isn't that great news?" Jessica said.

"Wonderful," Phoebe replied without a trace of enthusiasm.

"It was your mum's idea," her father added. "She thought you might prefer having Anna here to me hiring a couple of minders."

Everyone but Phoebe laughed. To her, their feeble attempts at gaiety sounded strained and unnatural.

Martin stood up and came over, his face plastered with concern. "How are you feeling?" he asked, wrapping an arm around her shoulder.

Phoebe bristled at the touch, not wanting him to come anywhere near her after what she had just seen. "I'm fine," she said, moving away from him and taking a seat on the sofa, where she absentmindedly picked at a patch of dry skin on the palm of her hand, gouging out the dead cells with bright red fingernails.

Jessica stared at her with growing concern. "While you were asleep, Dad drove Martin into Diss, and they brought your little Tesoro back for you, didn't you, boys?"

"That's right," Martin said, smiling down at her. "It's parked outside, in the driveway."

"We checked it out to make sure there was no damage," her father chipped in, eager not to be outdone, "and you'll be pleased to know there's not so much as a scratch on it."

There was an awkward silence, and Phoebe became conscious that everyone was staring at her intently. "What?" she demanded, glaring at them accusingly.

"Don't be like that, darling," Jessica soothed. She sat down beside her daughter and took her hand. "I know you don't like us making a big fuss, but we're all really worried about you. You've been through such a terrible ordeal, and we all just want to make sure that you're properly supported."

Phoebe's face softened. After a moment's hesitation, she leaned forward and gave her mum a big hug. "I know that," she said. "And I'm more grateful than you can ever imagine, but what happened last night has changed me, and I need a little space to process that."

Jessica leaned in and kissed her gently on the forehead. "We all appreciate that, darling, but please don't push us away. If you don't feel ready to come home yet, that's fine, but if you insist on staying here for a few days, at least let Anna stay and keep you company. She loves you like a sister, and your father and I will feel so much better knowing that you're not alone."

Martin coughed to get her attention. "I could stay as well if you like? I'm sure Ben won't mind me taking a few days off work to be with you while–"

"No!" Phoebe said, fiercely.

Martin blinked at her, shocked by the unexpected ferocity of the rebuff.

Ben huffed loudly. "Well, if anyone's interested in my opinion, I still think the most sensible thing to do is hire a couple of minders to look after you," he blurted out. "Honestly, Phoebe, you wouldn't even know they were here."

She glared at him, eyes smouldering. "No!"

"But–"

"I said *NO*, dad," Phoebe snapped. She barked out a mirthless laugh when she saw how hurt he looked. "Trust me, dad, I'm not at risk from Spencer anymore. In fact, *you're* probably in more danger than I am."

"Me?" Ben spluttered, pointing a finger at his chest.

"All of you," Phoebe said, with an all-encompassing sweep of her arm. "Now that Spencer knows how much I hate him, and that I would never be with him willingly, he won't come after me again. But, when we were in the barn last night, he kept obsessing about how the only person I needed was him, and that he wouldn't let my family or friends have anything more to do with me. Maybe, the warped bastard will come after you lot, thinking that I'll change my mind and return to him if I don't have anyone else."

Jessica gasped at the suggestion. "Phoebe, that's not funny. You shouldn't even joke about such things."

Phoebe stood up and looked at each of them in turn. "What makes you think I'm joking?" she asked, and there was something sinister about the way in which she said it.

"Did you tell the police what he said?" Jessica asked, clutching a hand to her chest in horror.

"Of course I did," Phoebe replied cattily, "but they didn't seem to think you were in any danger, so maybe I'm wrong."

Jessica let out a long sigh of relief. "I certainly hope so," she said, sounding thoroughly miserable.

Ben was still performing sentry duty, wearing out the carpet in front of the sofa. "Well, I'm not afraid of that little ballbag," he told them. "In fact, I'd love it if he came after me. It would give me the perfect excuse to knock his block off."

"Perhaps you should be afraid of him," Phoebe replied, coolly. "DC Stebbins told me that he's wanted for a murder in London. Apparently, he got into an argument with a man on a bus on Tuesday evening, and ended up stabbing him to death."

That wiped the cocksure sneer from her father's face.

The trip to the barn hadn't revealed anything of interest, and Gurjit was now driving Dillon along the A11 on their way back to London. "What do you reckon?" he asked.

Dillon was brooding because nothing constructive had come out of executing the search warrant at Spencer's room, and the visit to Diss had been a waste of his time. He folded his massive arms across his chest and let out a weary sigh. "Dunno. Evidentially, all they've got is the girl's statement and some gaffer tape. Granted, there's a good chance the lab will recover the girl's DNA from the sticky side, and Spencer's fingerprints from the shiny side, but I'd be happier if there had been a couple of witnesses and some CCTV to corroborate her account."

"I meant, what do you reckon the chances are that Spencer's still lurking in the area?"

"Oh, I see." Dillon glanced sideways, screwed his face up. "Can't see it myself," he said, dismissively. "I think Barty Craddock's probably right to assume that he's gone back to London. When you think about it, what else is he going to do? He doesn't know the area or anyone in it and, if he books into a little B&B, word will get out."

"True, but he could be living rough. Craddock said there are loads of old barns and the like dotted around the countryside."

"But what would be the point?" Dillon argued. "Now that the girl's shattered his dreams, there's nothing to keep him in that neck of the woods any longer, and why would anyone in their right mind choose to live rough if they didn't have to? Nah, I reckon Barty's right, and he's back in London, dossing down with a mate."

Gurjit grunted. "I suppose you're right," he accepted.

Dillon closed his eyes and wriggled around until he had made himself comfortable. "I'm going to have a power nap," he said. "Wake me up when we get back to the factory."

There was a light rap on his office door and, as Tyler looked up, Dean Fletcher strolled in, waving a printout in his hand.

"I think I've identified the car that Spencer stole for his trip to Diss," the researcher told him.

Tyler waved him to take a seat.

"You okay, boss?" Dean asked as he lowered himself into the chair. "You look troubled."

Tyler forced a smile. "I'm fine," he said. "Just juggling a lot of balls at the moment, that's all." At Holland's insistence, he had just finished documenting a lengthy risk assessment relating to Phoebe Cunningham, and how the Met would manage the situation if and when she returned to London.

Dean made a swatting gesture with his hand. "Don't worry about it," he said. "We'll have Spencer nicked in no time at all."

"I'm sure we will," Tyler agreed. "Now, tell me all about this stolen car."

Dean slid a printout across the desk. "Take a gander at that," he instructed. "It's a silver three series BMW taken from outside Moorfield's Eye Hospital yesterday morning, while the owner was inside having treatment. What makes this car a dead cert for me is that the theft coincides perfectly with the time that Spencer was at Shoreditch, registering with the Public Protection Unit."

Tyler waved the printout at him. "Can I keep this? he asked.

"Of course."

"Dean, can you put a warning flag on the PNC in relation to this car. If seen, the occupant is to be arrested, and the car is to be preserved for a full forensic search."

"Consider it done," Dean, said, treating Tyler to a rare smile.

"Have you got wind?" Tyler asked.

Fletcher self-consciously sniffed the air around him. "If you think you can smell something funny, I can assure you it's not coming from me," he said, indignantly.

Tyler broke into a wide grin. "It's just that I noticed a strange expression on your face a moment ago, and thought you might be in pain."

The penny dropped. "Oh, ha-ha," Dean said, his voice as expressionless as his face.

Tyler chuckled, grateful for a moment's levity in an otherwise shitty day. "Sorry Deano, I didn't mean to make fun of you, but it's not that often that I get to see you smiling."

"I'm always smiling," Dean insisted.

Tyler raised an eyebrow in challenge, but said nothing.

"Well, I'd better be getting back," Dean said, standing up and heading for the door. "I'll get the car flagged on ANPR, and then request a retrospective search to see if it's passed beneath any ANPR cameras since it was stolen."

"Thank you," Tyler said. "While you do that, I'll phone DCI Craddock and let him know about the car."

Dean paused by the door. "Just for the record, guv, I'd like to point out that I happen to have a very happy disposition, and I'm always smiling. Everyone knows that."

"Yes, of course," Tyler said, wishing that he'd never said anything. "Now that you mention it, I do seem to recall that your nickname on the team is 'Mr Happy'."

Before Dean could respond, he picked up the phone and began dialling Barty Craddock's number.

16

NO FURTHER USE FOR EITHER OF THEM

Just as she had known they would, Martin and her parents had callously brushed Phoebe's objections aside. Even Anna had poo-pooed them. It had been decided by group consensus – well by everyone in the group except for the one person whose opinion really mattered – that Anna would remain at the cottage with her until she was ready to return to London, later in the week.

After much hugging and kissing from her mother, and an equivalent amount of huffing and puffing from her father, who was still sulking over her refusal to let him hire her a team of bodyguards to protect her, she finally managed to persuade her parents to go home.

As she walked them to the door, Martin repeated his earlier offer to stay with her, but there was no mistaking his relief when she declined. Phoebe suspected this was down to the fact that the unfaithful git felt acutely uncomfortable at the idea of being trapped in the same house with both of them. She couldn't blame him for that; she wasn't overly enthralled by the idea herself.

"Promise you'll phone me if you need me," her mother called as she slid into the front passenger seat of the BMW X5.

"I will," Phoebe told her, having no intention of doing so.

"And make sure you lock all the doors and windows before you go to bed," her mother insisted.

"Really?" Phoebe responded sarcastically, "because I was thinking about leaving them wide open." She wondered if her mother's next little pearl of wisdom would involve telling her to make sure that she wore clean underwear every day, just in case she had an accident and ended up in hospital.

"Lock the bloody doors and windows when you go back inside," her dad barked, "not just at night." He glowered at Jessica, as though he thought her stupid for not having stipulated that in the first place.

Phoebe was starting to lose patience with them. "Stop worrying, dad. I'm a big girl, and I can take care of myself." Hadn't she just proved that?

Her father harrumphed loudly, clearly not buying into that at all.

"Don't worry, Ben," Anna assured him, like the little goody-two-shoes she liked them all to think she was. "I'm here, and I'll take care of her."

"Thank you, sweetie," Jessica fawned, blowing her a huge kiss. "I don't know what we'd do without you."

Phoebe gritted her teeth but said nothing.

Eventually, the others left and she found herself alone with Anna. As they walked back into the cottage, she reflected that there had been a time, not so long ago, when she would have enjoyed nothing more than spending a few nights alone with her bestie.

Not anymore, though.

That boat had well and truly sailed.

Growing up, Phoebe and Anna had spent virtually all their free time together. They had been inseparable, behaving more like sisters than friends, everyone had said so. And three years ago, when Anna's parents were tragically killed in a motorway pile-up that also claimed six other lives, Phoebe and her parents had brought her into their family, treating her like one of their own and promising that they would always be there for her.

She had trusted Anna implicitly, confiding all her hopes, dreams and fears in her. She had also trusted Anna with Martin, which she now realised had been a terrible mistake, because Anna had repaid her faith by committing the worst form of treachery; stealing her man and destroying all the wonderful plans she had for their future. Well, Anna could have him for all Phoebe cared because, after the betrayal, she had no further use for him.

In fact, she had no further use for either of them.

In their own deceitful way, they had hurt her every bit as much as Spencer had.

Anna was making a big effort to be bright and bubbly. "What shall we do for the rest of the day?" she asked as they walked back to the cottage.

"I'm going up to my room," Phoebe replied, coldly. "Make sure you do what daddy said, and lock all the doors and windows."

It was getting on for eight o'clock, and Tyler was enjoying a quiet fish and chips supper in his office with Dillon and Susie while they reviewed the case's progress. He had doused his cod and chips with so much vinegar that it had soaked through the paper wrapping and was now making a small puddle on his desk. Biting a chunk out of his pickled onion, he smiled contentedly. "Whoever thought of combining pickled onions with fish and chips deserves a bloody medal, if you ask me," he said as he chomped away happily.

Susie smiled. "You're very easily pleased, you know that?"

"That's what Kelly tells me," Dillon chortled, his mouth half full.

Tyler responded with a crass smile. "Ha-bloody-ha! That was so funny I almost cracked a rib laughing."

Ramming more chips into his mouth, Dillon noisily sucked each of his fingers in turn. "I've got some sachets of tomato sauce if you're interested," he said, waving them tantalisingly in the air.

Tyler snatched them out of his hand. "Don't mind if I do," he said, tearing the corner off the first one.

There was a polite rap on the door, and Tyler glanced up to see Dean and Reg standing there.

"Uh-oh! Trouble's here," Dillon announced.

"Sorry to interrupt your food, but can you spare us a few minutes when you're finished?" Reg asked.

Tyler waved them into the room. "If you don't mind talking while we eat, we can do it now." He gestured for them to take a seat. "I would offer you a chip," he said in a tone that made it clear he had no intention of actually doing so, "but I haven't eaten since lunchtime, and I'm starving."

"No worries," Dean said, "we've already eaten."

"So, what can I do for you?" Tyler asked, shoving a lump of cod into his gob.

"I'll let Deano have the floor, first," Reg said, leaning back to escape the vinegar fumes.

Dean coughed, then blinked his eyes. "Sorry, but Reg is right, that vinegar's a bit strong."

Tyler grinned indulgently. "I know, but it's the only way to eat fish and chips."

Dean's expression said otherwise. "I've identified Skippy," he said, getting straight to the point. "His given name's Tommy Skipton, he's Spencer's maternal cousin, and he resides in Adworth Road, Stratford. Needless to say, he's just as much of a toe-rag as his cousin, with form for everything from shoplifting and nicking cars to burglary and going equipped to steal. His PNC file name's Tommy Marsh, which is why he wasn't showing up on any of the searches I ran earlier. Marsh is his father's surname, by the way, and whenever he's been nicked over the years, he's always given that."

"Well done," Tyler said. "How did you find him in the end?"

Dean responded with a self-deprecating shrug. "I found his name and address hidden amongst the paperwork the Police Liaison Officer from Strangeways sent me," he told them. "Turns out Skipton was Spencer's only approved visitor and, because it's a high-security prison, all visitors have to produce government issued photo ID before being allowed in, which is probably why he gave them his real name, and not the Marsh alias he normally uses."

"Right, my turn now," Reggie said, still leaning back to avoid the vinegar fumes. "If you recall, Spencer purchased a PAYG phone yesterday morning. The number ends in 654, and we know it's only made two calls to date. The first was to his probation officer, and the other one was to a number ending in 137. That's an unregistered PAYG as well. So far today, the 137 number's rung Spencer's phone eight times. The calls didn't get through because Spencer's phone's still switched off, but the 137 number left five voicemails."

"Someone's obviously very keen to speak to him," Dillon observed.

"And I'm guessing you think that's Skipton?" Tyler added.

Reg nodded. "Although there's no intelligence to link the 137 number to Skipton, I'm convinced it's his phone. Who's going to ask me why?"

Tyler rolled his eyes. Reg had an annoying habit of grandstanding whenever he had a big reveal for them.

"Why?" Susie asked, sparing Tyler from having to do so.

A big grin broke out on Reggie's cherubic face. "I checked the cell site co-ordinates, and the calls were made from within the azimuth that covers his current address."

"Remind me what that means," Susie asked, staring at him blankly.

"Simple." Reg opened his daybook and turned to a blank page. On this, he drew a structure that looked a little like a mini Eiffel Tower. "Imagine this is a telephone mast," he told Susie. "Every telephone mast is split into three sectors, with each having its own antenna." He drew a crude circle around the Eiffel Tower and divided it into three distinct areas. In one of them, he drew a little house. "The antennas are erected at 120-degree intervals to ensure that the mast gets the best all-round coverage, and each 120-degree arc is known as an azimuth. As you can see from my drawing, Skipton's flat is in this azimuth, and that's the one that the signal was strongest in."

It was a very interesting update, Tyler conceded. "Is there any way we can get copies of the voice mail messages from the service provider?" he asked, wiping the grease from his hands with a napkin.

Reg extended his left hand and, keeping it palm down, wobbled it from side to side. "Maybe," he said. "The service providers only retain voicemail messages for five days so, if we can get a wriggle on, there's a slim chance we can retrieve them before they drop off."

"Do your best," Tyler instructed him.

"What do you want to do about Skipton?" Dillon asked.

Tyler considered this. "Let's send a couple of officers over to speak to him first thing in the morning, to see what he's got to say for himself. We won't let on that we know about the calls he's made, or that we're aware he regularly visited Spencer in prison. If he's got nothing to hide, he'll have no reason to hold those things back from us. If he does, then we know he's up to something."

Dillon gave his chin a thoughtful stroke. "We should probably send someone who'll get in his face."

Susie grinned. "It sounds like a job for Kevin Murray. That man could push His Holiness, the Pope over the edge." She crossed herself as she spoke.

Tyler smiled. "Agreed. And let's send Charlie with him. If anyone can wind him up, it's those two."

Phoebe lay in her bed, tossing and turning restlessly. It didn't help that it was so humid again. Even with the window wide open, there was no air circulating in the room, and the large electric fan standing by the side of her bed didn't seem to be making any difference as it whined away in the darkness.

It was getting on for ten o'clock, but she could still hear Anna moving around downstairs, tidying up before she went to bed.

After Martin and her parents departed for home, Phoebe had spent the remainder of the afternoon in her room, brooding about the affair. She hadn't emerged until it was time for dinner. Neither of them had been in the mood to cook, so Anna had suggested they order a takeaway from a nearby Indian restaurant.

They had managed to get through two bottles of wine with their meal. Well, to be precise, Phoebe had enjoyed a large glass with her lamb biryani, while Anna guzzled down the rest.

After finishing their food and loading the dishwasher, Phoebe had been hoping that Anna would bugger off to bed and leave her in peace, but she hadn't. Instead, she had insisted that they curl up on the sofa together, just like old times, and watch a rom-com to cheer themselves up. Like Anna had anything to be miserable about in the first place!

In the end, feigning a headache, Phoebe had excused herself halfway through the film, on the pretext of needing an early night.

Her smiling parents stared back at her from within the frame on her bedside table, and she reached out and turned it away so that she wouldn't have to see their smug faces every time she glanced at the clock. With a sigh of frustration, Phoebe rolled onto her side, fidgeted for a while, and then rolled onto her other side and repeated the process. Then she tried plumping up the pillows and rearranging them, but that didn't make the slightest difference. Plumping quickly turned to bashing, but that didn't help either.

In the end, she gave up trying and reached for a book. The trouble was, she just couldn't concentrate on the story within, and she found herself reading the same page over and over, unable to process the words that were printed on it.

Turning the light off, she settled down for a second attempt at sleeping, but every time she closed her eyes, a revolting image of Martin and Anna, kissing passionately, popped into her mind, making her stomach churn.

Phoebe had spent much of the afternoon and evening wondering how long their sordid little relationship had been going on, who had instigated it, and whether it was serious. She doubted that it was, at least not for Martin. He was a self-serving bastard who knew which side his bread was buttered on. No, the chances were that this was just a meaningless fling to him; another notch to carve onto his bedpost before he settled down into married life with Phoebe. The thought made her blood boil. It wasn't bloody meaningless to her! He had hurt her, and he would be made to pay for doing so. They both would.

Phoebe was as angry with herself for having allowed their torrid affair to happen right under her nose as she was with them for betraying her. She had first noticed a subtle change in Martin and Anna's behaviour around Easter time, but she had wilfully closed her eyes to the possibility that they were having an illicit relationship. Well, she certainly wouldn't be turning a blind eye any longer, that was for sure. The days of her burying her head in the sand like her mum, and hiding away from problems instead of facing them head-on, were over.

Angrily kicking the top sheet away from her, Phoebe decided that, if she could get the better of a raping scumbag like Spencer, she was more than capable of dealing with the likes of Martin and Anna. She would punish them for hurting her when the time came. First though, she had other, more pressing, matters to take care of.

"Goodnight, Phoebe," Anna's muffled voice called from the hallway. "Sweet dreams."

Phoebe didn't bother to respond.

17

Friday 27th July 2001
RUFFLING FEATHERS

As there were no major developments to discuss with the team, Tyler decided to keep the office meeting short and sweet. "Let's kick off with a quick update on forensics," he announced, nodding to Jarvis.

Jarvis opened his green exhibits book and ran a finger down the page. "Exhibits wise, everything we have is now at the lab. As you know, we already have the result back for the suspect's fingerprint, which was found in the victim's blood on the bus. The lab reckons we should get the DNA results from the discarded jacket and knife back by end of play today, and the victim's wallet sometime tomorrow."

Tyler jotted this down in his daybook so that he could update the Decision Log later. When he'd finished, he looked up at Susie Sergeant, who was sitting to his left. It struck him that she seemed unusually tired, and he wondered whether this was simply a case of her working long hours on the new job, or if it had anything to do with all the stress she was under from being estranged from her shitbag of a husband. He made a mental note to speak to her in private when they got a moment, just to make sure that she was okay.

"What about the preparations for the interviews and ID parades, for when Spencer's eventually arrested?"

"All in hand," Susie confirmed. "I've already picked the interview team, drafted out the staged disclosure documents, and collated the first descriptions that were provide by the four witnesses we're going to use on the ID parades."

Tyler made another quick note. "Excellent. Now, I want to talk to you about a man called Thomas Skipton. He's Spencer's cousin and the closest thing that he has to a friend. We know that Skipton regularly visited Spencer while he was in Strangeways. When was the last time, Deano?"

Dean checked his notes. "According to the prison records, the last visit took place three weeks before Spencer's release."

Tyler nodded his thanks. "What's interesting," he continued, "is that Spencer purchased a Pay-As-You-Go mobile phone the day after he was released. He's only been in contact with two people since then. The first was his probation officer, but we believe the second person was Skipton. Dean's research shows him living at an address in West Ham. Charlie, you and Kevin are going to pay Skipton a little visit this morning, and I want you to make a point of ruffling his feathers."

The two men shared a knowing look. "We can certainly do that," Charlie promised, allowing himself a malevolent grin.

"Since speaking to you last night, I've also identified one other associate," Dean told them. "He's a bloke called Honest Steve Higgins, and he lives in James Riley Point, on the Carpenters Estate in Stratford. Higgins was Spencer's next door neighbour when they were kids, and they've been nicked together a few times over the years. If Spencer's looking for somewhere to doss down, this bloke is about the only other person he could turn to."

"Why's he called Honest Steve?" Steve Bull asked.

Dean spread his arms. "No idea. From what I can see, the bloke's as crooked as a corkscrew."

An apt description, Tyler thought. "In that case, we should send a couple of people to see him as well," he said, making a quick note. He looked around the office until he spotted Reg Parker. "Any more activity on either Spencer or Skipton's phones?"

Reg shook his head "Nothing since my last update. I'll let you know as soon as anything happens."

Tyler turned to Dillon. "Anything you can add as far as the manhunt goes?"

"Well," Dillon said, slowly. "Spencer's been banged up for eight years, so we've not got a lot of background material to work with. There hasn't been any financial activity. He's got two bank accounts. The first one has sod all in it, and the second one has even less. As Reg just said, his phone is still switched off. It's being live-monitored by the TIU, so if there's any activity, we'll be told about it straight away. We only have two associates to check out. If Whitey's going to see Skippy, I'm quite happy to visit this Honest Steve character. Dean, if you can have a quick look at him for me before I go, just to see if anything flashes up from an officer safety perspective, that would be very helpful."

"What about pinging Spencer's phone?" Tyler asked. "I know that Reg was going to discuss that with you. What did you decide in the end?"

Dillon turned his nose up. "As the phone's dormant at the moment, there's no point in doing that, but we'll bear it in mind for later, if it ever goes live again."

―――

Anna Manson awoke with a skull-splitting headache. Sitting up slowly, she clutched her head and cursed her stupidity for having consumed so much wine the previous evening. She was certainly paying a hefty price for her overindulgence this morning. As she gingerly put on her glasses, it felt as though someone was running amok inside her head with a pneumatic drill.

After Martin and her parents had set off back to London yesterday afternoon, Phoebe had been in a very fractious mood, and she had remained that way for the rest of the day.

Phoebe had made a string of catty comments over dinner, and Anna had soaked them all up without retaliation, partly because her friend had just been through a terrible ordeal and therefore deserved some leeway, but mainly out of guilt. Although it probably sounded cliché, neither she nor Martin had planned the relationship that had developed between them and, deep down, she had come to believe she was a truly terrible person for betraying her best friend by falling in love with him.

The affair had begun in early May, after Martin confided that his relationship with Phoebe wasn't working out. He had confessed that he was desperate to end it but, with Phoebe being so needy, he was finding it impossible to do so. From the outset, they had agreed not to see each other romantically until he was officially a single man again, and they had largely kept to that, apart from a couple of drunken incidents where they had ended up in bed together.

But how long did he expect her to wait? Things had been dragging on for months now, and Anna had reached the point where she'd had enough, which is why she had recently started putting pressure on Martin to leave Phoebe. That had made her feel guilty, too. The poor dear already had more than enough on his plate, coping with Phoebe's mood swings, without her adding more pressure to the mix.

As Anna stood up, she caught an unwelcome glimpse of her reflection in the full-length mirror adorning the far wall. "Christ! What a mess," she groaned, running a hand through her bird's nest of brown hair. It was sticking up in random places and badly matted, making her look as though she had just been dragged through a hedge backwards. And her face! It was pasty white, with ugly black splodges underneath her eyes from where she had gone to bed without removing her makeup. She suppressed a shudder, grateful that Martin couldn't see her in this sorry state.

The guest room she was staying in overlooked the front of the cottage. As she started brushing her tangled hair, she heard the sound of a car door opening down below. Rushing over to the window, Anna looked out to see Phoebe loading a large blue cool bag into the boot of her Alfa. Alarmed, she pulled the net curtains aside and stuck her head out of the window. "Phoebe, what are you doing? Where do you think you're going?" she called out.

On the drive below, Phoebe glanced up at her but said nothing.

"Shit!" Anna cursed, throwing her brush onto the bed. She grabbed her dressing gown from the peg on the back of the door, wrapped it around herself and ran down the stairs, feeling terribly remiss in her duties. She was supposed to be looking after Phoebe, and yet she had almost slept through her leaving the house. Ben and Jessica would go spare if she let Phoebe give her the slip after having promised to take care of her.

Running down the stairs, Anna jerked open the street door and ran onto the drive, ignoring the sharp pain of gravel digging into the soles of her bare feet. "Phoebe, Stop! Where are you going?"

"I'm going to do some painting," Phoebe told her, pointing towards the easel resting on her back seat. "I want to finish my latest watercolour before returning to London."

"What?" Anna stared at her as though she were crazy. "But Phoebe, the madman who kidnapped you is still out there, running free," she objected. "You can't just go off gallivanting around the countryside on your own. It's far too dangerous."

Phoebe's mouth compressed into an angry thin line. "Can't I?" she bristled. "Just watch me." She opened the driver's door and made to get inside.

"Wait!" Anna exclaimed, putting a hand on the door to prevent her from getting in. "Let me get dressed. I'll come with you."

"I don't need babysitting," Phoebe told her.

"But what if he–"

Phoebe reached into the driver's footwell and withdrew an old hatchet that the family used to chop up wood. It was normally kept in the woodshed at the back of the garden. She hoisted it above her head like some kind of warrior princess. "So help me, if Spencer comes anywhere near me again, I'll cut his bloody balls off."

Anna's hands flew to her mouth. "Jesus, Phoebe! If the police stop you with *that* in the car, they'll arrest you for carrying a weapon."

Phoebe sighed, then lowered the hatchet until it was hanging by her leg. "No, Anna, they won't," she said with a mirthless laugh. "If the police stop me, I'll tell them who I am and what happened to me on Wednesday, and they'll probably give me an escort home and search the house for me, in case he's hiding inside."

Anna's shoulders slumped. "Maybe you're right," she said, keen not to rile her friend any further, "but it won't hurt to let me come along for the ride and keep you company. Just give me five minutes to throw some clothes on."

Phoebe stared at her for a long moment, saying nothing. "Go on, then," she eventually conceded. "Five minutes, but I'm not waiting a second longer."

Anna smiled her relief. "Wait there," she said, and began jogging back towards the house.

She was panting by the time she reached her bedroom, and her stomach was doing little flips from where she needed to eat, but that would have to wait. She barely had time to get dressed and pop to the loo before–

The sound of the car starting up made her jump. Running to the window, she looked out just in time to see the red Alfa Romeo Spider pull out of the driveway. "Phoebe, wait," she called, but it was too late.

Her friend had gone.

———

"I'm just popping down to the canteen," Susie said when Tyler called a short break in the case management meeting they were holding. "Do either of you want anything while I'm down there?"

Tyler looked up from the strategy document he was engrossed in. "Would you mind grabbing me a cheese and tomato sandwich, a can of diet 7-Up, and a bag of cheese and onion crisps, please?" As he spoke, he reached into his pocket for some cash.

Susie held up a hand. "That's alright, you can pay me when I get back," she told him with a smile. Then, turning to Dillon: "What about you, Tony? Do you want anything?"

Dillon stood up and stretched. "Actually, I think I'll take a stroll down to the canteen with you, if you don't mind the company?"

"You're more than welcome," she said, smiling earnestly.

As they walked along the empty corridor, heading for the main set of stairs in the centre of the building, he impulsively wrapped a bear-like arm around her shoulders and drew her into him. "I'm worried about you," he confessed, giving her a big hug. "I know it's none of my business, but are you doing okay? You know, since Dan walked out on you?"

"I'm not feeling great," she admitted as they descended the stairs, "but I'm coping. I'm not the first woman whose husband left her for another woman, and I'm sure I won't be the last."

"I just wanted you to know that, if you ever need anyone to talk to, I'm here for you," he said, blushing. This sort of thing wasn't his forte, and he felt awkward raising the subject.

"Thank you," she said, smiling gratefully.

"He's an arsehole," Dillon suddenly said.

Susie stared at him, raised an eyebrow. "Who is?"

"Dan. He's an arsehole for leaving you."

Susie smiled. "I know."

"Over the years, I've come to the unfortunate conclusion that most people are, in fact, arseholes," Dillon announced, philosophically.

"Of course they're not," Susie admonished him.

"They are," Dillon insisted. "If you don't believe me, when we walk into the canteen, shout out: 'Oi, arsehole,' and see how many people look up."

Susie laughed. "I might just do that," she promised.

Charlie White pulled the pool car up outside a row of terraced houses in Adworth Road. "That's the place," he said, pointing to the one they wanted.

Murray ran his eyes over the property and then wrinkled his nose in disgust, "What a dump."

White grunted in agreement. "So, who do you want to be? Bad cop or very bad cop?"

Murray sniggered, nastily. "Let's both be very bad cop, shall we?"

White's eyes twinkled with mischief. "Aye, that sounds good to me."

They alighted the car and passed through the gate into the small front garden. Music was blaring out from inside the premises. "We want the door on the left," Murray said.

While White banged on the wooden door, Murray cupped his hands against the bay window and peered in. "Someone's moving about inside," he said. "It looks like Skipton." Dean had printed them off some stills of Spencer and Skipton from the custody imaging system, just in case Spencer opened the door and pretended to be his cousin.

A few moments later, they heard the latch being slid off, and the door opened a couple of inches. "Yes?" a timid voice enquired from inside.

Charlie White pushed the door wide open, and it cannoned into Skippy, who was standing directly behind it, knocking him back a step. "Thomas Skipton?" he demanded, holding his warrant card out for inspection.

Skippy licked his lips nervously. "Y-yes, that's me." As he spoke, his eyes nervously darted over White's shoulder, as if calculating his chances of getting away.

White picked up on this, and he shifted sideways so that he was completely blocking the doorway.

Murray appeared at White's shoulder. "Mind if we come inside, Mr Skipton?" he asked, and then stepped through the door without waiting for a reply.

As the two detectives advanced, Skippy clumsily backtracked along the narrow hall, trying to maintain the gap between them. "What's this about?" he asked, and there was more than a hint of panic in his voice.

"Let's go into your living room to chat, shall we?" White said, pointing towards the open door.

"Sure, if you want," Skippy said, reluctantly stepping into the lounge.

White followed him in, but Murray continued along the corridor.

"Oi, where's your mate think he's going?" Skippy demanded.

"He'll be back in a minute," White told him, leaning against the doorframe to prevent Skippy from leaving.

"But he can't just wander around my gaff without my permission," Skippy protested.

White stared at him, his eyes cold and accusing. "What's the matter Mr Skipton? You dinnae have anything to hide, do you?"

Skippy paled at the implication and averted his eyes. "No," he said, a little too quickly. "Of course not."

Murray reappeared, shook his head. "There's no one else here," he declared as White moved aside to let him in.

"Who were you expecting to find?" Skippy demanded, looking from one to the other in confusion.

"You tell me?" White responded, his voice thick with suspicion.

Skippy was starting to get angry. "I dunno, do I? For all I know, you were expecting to find the queen hiding in me wardrobe."

A short burst of mock laughter escaped from White's lips. "Very funny. Fancy yourself as a bit of a comedian, do you, Mr Skipton?"

Skippy wasn't sure how to respond, so he remained silent.

Murray glowered at him. "I wasn't looking for the queen," he said. "Her Majesty wouldn't be seen dead in a shithole like this. In fact, I very much doubt that any self-respecting rat would want to live in this cesspit, but as for a cockroach like John Spencer, I reckon he'd be right at home here."

Skippy was becoming agitated. "Spence? I haven't seen him in years," he insisted. "Last I heard, he was doing bird in Strangeways."

"Aye, he was," Charlie White confirmed, "but the wee shite was released on Tuesday morning, and we thought he might've popped round to see you, what with you two being kin an' all."

Skipton was quick to shake his head. "Nah, we ain't that close, mate. I didn't even know he was out."

Charlie White folded his arms with a belligerent huff. "Do you seriously expect us to believe you havenae seen him?" he scoffed, studying Skipton's face carefully for a reaction.

"N-no, I haven't," Skipton said, but the warble in his voice gave the lie away.

"You must have at least spoken to him on the phone, surely?"

Staring at his feet, Skipton shook his head. "No, I told you, I didn't even know he was out."

"Don't suppose you know if he's got a mobile phone we could contact him on, do you?" Murray asked.

Skippy had started to perspire.

"You alright there, pal?" Charlie White asked. "Do you need a piss or something?"

"I'm fine," Skippy insisted. His face said otherwise.

"Then answer my colleague's question," Murray ordered.

Skippy swallowed, hard. "I ain't got a phone number for him," he bleated. "How could I when I ain't even spoken to him since he got out?"

"How indeed?" Murray sneered. "When was the last time you visited him in prison?"

"I didn't visit him in prison," Skipton lied. "Told you, I ain't seen him in years."

"Okay," Murray said. "We'll take your word for that, for now at least, but if we find out you've been lying to us, it won't end well for you."

"I ain't lying," Skippy assured them. "Now, if we're finished, I'm a very busy man."

"What's your mobile phone number, Mr Skipton?" Murray asked. "Just in case we need to speak to you again."

Skippy shook his head. "Sorry, officer. I ain't got a phone. Got no need for one."

"Is that right?" Murray asked, cynically tossing the mobile

handset he'd found in the bedroom onto the coffee table. "So, whose is this, then?"

"Maybe it's stolen," Charlie White suggested before Skippy could respond. "Maybe we should nick him and let him stew in a cell for a few hours while we make some enquiries. What do you think?"

"Sounds like a plan to me," Murray agreed, removing a set of handcuffs from his belt.

"No! Wait!" Skippy blurted out. "Okay, so it's my phone. I don't use it a lot and I forgot I had it."

The two detectives exchanged knowing glances. "Anything *else* you've 'forgotten' to tell us about?" Murray asked.

Skippy shook his head, sulkily. "No," he mumbled.

"So, what's the number for your mobile?" White asked, opening his notebook in readiness to jot it down.

With a sigh of defeat, Skippy reeled off his mobile number.

White pulled out his Job mobile. "It's not that I don't trust you," he said, smiling affably, "but, well, I don't trust you!" He dialled the eleven digits and waited for the phone on the coffee table to ring. When it did, he killed the call and pocketed his phone. "I bet you dinnae remember the last time you did that, do you?"

Skippy screwed his face up in confusion. "Did what?"

"Told a police officer the truth," White said, caustically.

18

HONEST STEVE HIGGINS

Entering the slip road to the Carpenters Estate in Stratford, the unmarked silver BMW drove past the low rise housing in Dorian Walk and glided to a halt at the base of James Riley Point, one of three tower blocks on the estate that dated back to the late sixties.

Closing the driver's door behind him, Dillon squinted up at the twenty third floor, some 215 feet above. They were there to speak to Honest Steve Higgins, Spencer's only other known associate. "Of course, he couldn't just live on the first floor, could he?" the big man groused.

Emerging from the passenger side, Tyler smiled at his friend. "Stop whinging. We'll take the lift. It'll be fine."

Dillon had never liked using the lifts in high-rises, and he pulled a sour face at the suggestion. "You watch. It'll either be out of order or smell like an overflowing toilet," he complained. As they set off towards the grim looking block, he cast a backwards glance at the BMW. "Let's just hope the car's still here when we get back," he said miserably, pressing the fob to activate the central locking.

"You're in a very negative mood today," Tyler pointed out as they strode into the entrance foyer, which was marginally cooler than an oven. With his Decision Log up to date, and everything else seemingly under control, he had jumped at the chance to get out of the office for a change and do some actual leg work, instead of being chained to his desk and filling out endless reams of paperwork.

They caught the lift, which not only smelled like a blocked toilet, but was as hot as a blast furnace. As it slowly transported them upwards, Tyler made a point of ignoring Dillon's disquieted rumblings, focusing instead on the floor counter above the door and wishing that the rickety old contraption would go a bit faster. By the time they reached their destination, both men were sweltering hot and couldn't get out quickly enough.

"Well, that was deeply unpleasant," Dillon complained, peeling his cotton shirt away from his sweating body.

The view across the East End of London from the top floor was impressive, if not exactly pretty, and Tyler spent a few moments taking it in while he cooled down. Leaning over the balcony to let the weak breeze wash over him, he looked down through the shimmering heat haze at the twisting canals of the River Lea, the meandering train tracks of the Great Eastern Railway, and the rows of Victorian terraces that lined the surrounding streets. Truth be told, here in the arse end of Stratford, you were more likely to be blown away by machine gun toting gangsters than you were by the stunning scenery, but he still found the spectacle mesmerising.

"I'd hate to be stuck in one of these places if there was ever a fire," Dillon remarked, joining him.

Tyler shuddered. One of his favourite films was *The Towering Inferno*. "It doesn't even bear thinking about," he said.

"Shall we get this over with?" Dillon asked, removing his sunglasses and tucking them into the top pocket of his shirt.

They crossed the balcony and Tyler rapped on the door to Higgins' flat. "What do you reckon?" he asked.

Dillon grinned, evilly. "From the way Dean described him, I reckon that Higgins will have webbed feet and six fingers on each hand from where mummy married uncle daddy."

Tyler laughed. "I meant, do you think we'll get anything out of talking to him?"

Dillon shook his head. "Nope. Nothing, unless you include the entertainment value of seeing him squirm. There's no current intel to link him to Spencer, so this is probably going to be a complete waste of time."

Tyler responded with a stoic smile. "Yeah, well, we've got nothing to lose, and if we shake enough trees, something's bound to fall out of one of them, sooner or later."

The door opened a crack to reveal a skinny white man in his early thirties, with unkempt brown hair and dishevelled clothing. He looked like he hadn't shaved in a week, and he smelled like he hadn't washed in a month. "Can I help you?" he enquired, meekly.

They recognised him at once from the custody imaging shot that Dean had printed off for them earlier. Both detectives produced their warrant cards. "Mr Higgins, I'm DCI Tyler, and this is my colleague, DI Dillon. We're from the Homicide Command, and we'd like to ask you a few questions if that's okay?"

As though someone had just opened a stopcock, the colour flooded from Higgins' face. "W-why would you want to talk to me?" he asked, his shifty hazel eyes darting nervously from one to the other.

The two detectives exchanged knowing glances. Like sharks smelling blood in the water, they moved towards him, hunting instincts on full alert. Something was definitely wrong. Of course, it was probably something trivial, like he had a little stash of ganja in his flat and he was worried they would find it if he invited them in. But, what if it was something more baleful than that? What if he was behaving skittishly because Spencer was hiding in one of his rooms?

Dillon placed a hand on the street door and pushed it wide open. "You don't mind if we step inside for a minute, do you?" he asked with a sanguine smile.

Higgins opened his mouth to protest, but it was too late, the big man had already crossed the threshold.

The hallway was long and narrow, with five doors branching off it: two on the right, two on the left, and one at the back. As he took in his surroundings, Tyler noticed that all of the doors were open, apart from the rear one.

Dillon had obviously spotted this, too. "Is that the lounge, at the end?" he asked, walking straight past Higgins.

A look of fear flashed across Higgins' face. "No, that's my bedroom," he said, hurriedly nipping in front of Dillon to block his path. "The lounge is in there," he said, pointing towards the second door on their right, from where the sound of a TV could be heard. "Honest."

Dillon stared at him for a long moment, his expression neutral, and then he stepped inside.

At Higgins' behest, Tyler did likewise.

Following them in, Higgins closed the door and leaned back against it, giving Tyler the distinct impression that he didn't want them snooping around the rest of his flat.

"A bit hot to be closing doors, isn't it?" Tyler asked, fixing him with a penetrating stare.

Higgins shifted uncomfortably. "Sorry. Force of habit. Honest."

Deciding not to pursue the matter, Tyler took a moment to survey the room. It was a decent size, square in shape, with two good sized windows letting in lots of light. To the right of the windows, a glazed door led out onto a small balcony area, from which an assortment of men's clothing could be seen hanging on a makeshift washing line.

Even with the balcony door wide open, the room reeked of stale smoke and body odour.

Tyler wondered if it had been decorated by someone who was colour blind, because the garish pink of the faded wallpaper clashed violently with the casino-style multicoloured carpet, creating an almost psychedelic effect. An old sofa and two battered armchairs rested against the wall to Tyler's right, with a glass-topped, rectangular coffee table sitting between them. A large TV occupied pride of place in the far corner. It was the only thing in the room that looked remotely new, and Tyler hazarded a guess that it was rented.

"Have a seat, if you want," Higgins said, indicating the sofa. The beige fabric was worn and faded, with numerous cigarette burns and a variety of unpleasant stains.

"No, thank you," Tyler said, wrinkling his nose. "We'll be fine standing."

"Suit yourself," Higgins replied with a lacklustre shrug.

The coffee table was littered with newspapers, but there was also an overflowing ashtray and two half-finished mugs of tea.

Two cups, not one. That was interesting.

Higgins nervously snatched up a plastic remote control from the arm of the sofa. Pointing it at the TV, he pressed the mute button.

"So, what can I do for you?" he asked with a forced smile

"Does anyone else live here with you?" Tyler asked, watching for a reaction.

Higgins squirmed uncomfortably. "No. It's just me, honest."

"Is anyone else here now?" Tyler enquired, glancing at the two cups on the coffee table.

Following his eye, Higgins swallowed hard. "N-no, just me, honest."

"When was the last time you saw John Spencer?" Dillon asked, joining in the conversation.

The question threw Higgins. "Spence? I ain't seen him in years," he told them. "Honest."

Tyler's eyes narrowed. "So, you haven't seen or heard from him since he was released from prison on Tuesday?"

"No, guv. Honest. I didn't even know he was out. The only person Spence is tight with these days is his cousin, Skippy. Have you tried speaking to him?"

"We've got officers doing that right now," Dillon assured him.

Tyler folded his arms. "If you haven't heard from him, you won't mind us having a quick gander at your mobile phone's call history to verify that, will you?" His inflection made it clear that this wasn't a request.

Higgins forced another smile. "Course not," he said, but he made no effort to hand it over. Staring down at the floor, he started folding and unfolding his arms as if he didn't quite know what to do with them.

Dillon quickly lost patience with him. "Your phone," he demanded, holding out his hand.

"In my bedroom," Higgins replied without looking up.

Dillon rolled his eyes, theatrically. "Well sod off and get it, then," he snapped, shooing Higgins away with his hands. "Hurry up. We haven't got all day."

"Okay, okay. Give me a bleeding chance," Higgins whinged, pulling open the door. "I'll be back in a jiffy, honest."

Skulking out of the room, he pulled the door shut behind him.

"The little shit's lying through his teeth," Dillon said as soon as they were alone. "I reckon there's someone in his bedroom he doesn't want us to know about."

Tyler was too preoccupied with the coffee table to reply.

Two cups, not one.

He reached out and touched them; they were both still warm. "Dill, these drinks aren't even cold yet."

Dillon looked at the cups and then at him. "So, either the person who used the second cup left just before we arrived or they're still here?"

Tyler nodded, deep in thought. "Did you notice how uncomfortable he was, leaving us in here on our own?"

"I did. In fact, I got the distinct impression that the slimy little git was having a bit of a dilemma. He didn't want us to follow him into his bedroom, but he didn't want to leave us to our own devices in here, either."

Tyler ran his eyes over the pile of newspapers and was immediately struck by the fact that they were all opened on pages featuring the same story. "Dill, come and have a look at this," he said, picking one up and holding it out for his friend to take.

"What is it?" Dillon asked, accepting the offering.

Tyler scooped up two more red tops, skim-reading the headlines.

"Why are all these newspapers opened on pages containing articles about the poor PC from Leyton who was murdered last week?"

Dillon's brow's knitted. "It is a bit odd," he admitted, tossing the paper back on the coffee table and dusting his hands together.

Tyler had seen the briefing note that had been disseminated across the command, and he knew that the, as yet, unidentified shooter was reputed to be a great brute of a man with a military buzz-cut, not a skinny rake with messy hair like Higgins. He returned the papers from whence they came. "I think we need to search this place properly," he said, glancing around the room to see if there was anything else that might be of interest. On an impulse, he took a peek behind the sofa. "Dill, come here, quickly."

"What is it?" Dillon asked, striding over to join him.

Tyler manhandled the sofa away from the wall until it was sticking out at a forty-five degree angle. Kneeling down in the gap he'd just created, he gazed at the two tamper-proof cash-in-transit bags that had been hidden there. Both bags had been forced open, releasing the purple security dye they contained, and this had stained all of the cash within, rendering it completely useless to the robbers.

"Well, what have we got here?" Dillon asked, bending over Tyler's shoulder to get a better look.

Tyler refrained from touching the cash bags, but he could clearly see the bundles of dye covered banknotes within. "Dill, let's get that little shit back in here and see what he has to say about this," he said through gritted teeth.

As they turned towards the door, it swung open and Higgins entered, clutching a small black object in his right hand. Closing it behind him, he said: "Here's my phone. Sorry I was so long but–"

"I think you've got some explaining to do," Tyler interrupted, jerking his thumb over his shoulder towards the sofa.

Higgins glanced at the pulled out sofa. Stuttering, his mouth opened, closed, opened again. Then, without warning, he threw the phone at Tyler's head and made a dash for the door.

Tyler instinctively ducked, and the handset shattered harmlessly against the wall behind him. With a snarl of anger, he rushed forwards and grabbed Higgins by the shoulder, yanking him backwards before he could open the door.

Higgins must have been anticipating this because he went with it, spinning around and throwing a wild punch at Tyler's chin. Unfortunately for him, the detective had been a very good amateur boxer during his younger days, and he effortlessly avoided the clumsy swing, countering with a beautifully timed short hook to the other man's ribs that stopped him dead in his tracks.

As Higgins doubled over, struggling for breath, Tyler grabbed him by the shoulders and face-planted him into the nearest wall. Taking control of Higgins' left wrist, he twisted it up behind his back. "You are well and truly nicked," he growled.

As Tyler cautioned Higgins, Dillon appeared by his side, smiling. "See, this is much more fun than being stuck in the office," he said, producing a set of handcuffs, which he dangled over his index finger for Tyler to take. Leaning against the wall with his massive arms folded, Dillon seemed quite content to watch as Tyler applied the first cuff to Higgins' left wrist.

"You could help if you wanted to," Tyler complained as he tried to secure Higgins' free arm, which was still flailing around.

Dillon shook his head. "That's okay. You need the practice."

At that moment, the door slammed open, crashing into Dillon, who was standing directly behind it. A snarling monster filled the doorway, brandishing a sawn-off shotgun. "Let him go," Micky Harrington raged, pointing the gun directly at Tyler's head.

Tyler reacted quickly by spinning Higgins around in front of him and using him as a human shield. "Don't be silly," he said, managing to sound a lot calmer that he actually felt. "Put the gun down."

Harrington strode into the room, exuding menace from every pore. "I said, let him go," he snarled. As he advanced towards Tyler, Dillon emerged from behind the door and grabbed the barrel in both hands, ramming it upwards, towards the ceiling. There was a deafening explosion as the weapon discharged, and the distinctive aroma of cordite filled the air as plaster rained down upon them from above.

Still holding the barrel in both hands, Dillon let out a roar as he pushed the gunman backwards, slamming him against the wall with a bone-jarring thud.

Harrington grunted in pain. Then, issuing a blood-curdling battle cry, he lowered his head and shunted Dillon backwards until the detective crashed into the door, which rattled on its hinges. Harrington's massive shoulders rippled beneath his T-shirt as he tried to wrench the gun from Dillon's grip.

Evenly matched in size and strength, the two men rocked and swayed, pushing and pulling each other in their battle for ascendancy. Suddenly, the gun barked for a second time, and the snazzy TV disintegrated as buckshot tore into it.

"Help me, Micky," Higgins screamed, renewing his efforts to break free of Tyler's grip.

"Shut up," Tyler snapped, sweeping the struggling man's feet from underneath him, and taking him down to the floor. Higgins landed facedown with a satisfyingly heavy thud that knocked all the air out of him, and Tyler followed him to the floor, planting his knee in the small of his back and pinning his head to the floor with his left hand. He quickly regained control of the prisoner's cuffed left wrist, and then dragged his right wrist across his back to join it. Applying the loose handcuff, he squeezed the ratchet tightly, until it bit into Higgins' flesh. With Higgins finally under control, Tyler pulled his mobile from his trouser pocket, keyed in 999, and pressed the green button. They needed assistance, and they needed it fast.

In the middle of the room, the fight between the two big men gathered momentum. Snapping his head forward, Harrington tried to butt Dillon's nose, but the detective saw it coming and thrust his shoulder into the way. While not doing the damage that Harrington had hoped for, the impact was powerful enough to make Dillon's arm go numb. As his right hand involuntarily spasmed open, Harrington gained the leverage that he needed to wrench the shotgun away from him. With a malevolent grin, he took a quick step back, pointed the shotgun at Dillon's midsection, and pulled the trigger.

Anna Manson was having a truly awful day. After Phoebe had driven off without her in an act of deceit that she was finding hard to forgive, she had dressed hurriedly, and then set off for Diss in the hope that she would find her friend set up somewhere around the Mere.

Wilting under the unbearable heat, and suffering from the hangover from hell, all she yearned to do as she finished the Diss Circular Walk was return to the cottage, collapse into bed, and sleep the damn thing off.

Feeling like death warmed up, Anna sought refuge at a quaint little café at the edge of the lake, intending to spend a few minutes sitting in the shade while she gathered her thoughts.

The attentive waiter fetched her a cold bottle of mineral water, which she knocked back all in one go, and a delicious latte that she took her time consuming. She was tempted to order a large glass of wine as well, as a hair of the dog, but decided against it. As she sat there, Anna found herself guiltily thinking that Martin might have been right after all when he'd told her that Phoebe was a spoiled little bitch who was playing them all. In all probability, Phoebe had set up her easel in one of the area's many beauty spots and was, at this very moment, painting away to her selfish little heart's content. It really grated on Anna that her so-called best friend had blatantly lied to her, and then driven off and abandoned her.

Taking another sip of her coffee, Anna mulled over what to do next. Should she ring Ben and Jessica and confess to losing Phoebe? Should she call the police and report her missing? But Phoebe wasn't missing, was she? Not in any sense that the police would be interested in. No, she had simply taken herself off because she didn't want to be with Anna.

Before driving into Diss to look for Phoebe, Anna had flipped through a stack of touristy type leaflets she'd found scattered around the cottage, hoping to compile a detailed list of local beauty spots. There had been too many to choose from and, to her dismay, it had quickly become apparent that she wouldn't be able to cover them all in a week, let alone in a single morning.

With a sigh of defeat, Anna pushed her coffee cup aside and reached for her mobile. Perhaps Martin would have some idea where Phoebe had gone. If she had a favourite place, he might know of it and be able to give her directions. The phone rang for ages, and she was on the verge of hanging up when his dulcet tones came on the line.

"*Hello gorgeous, how are you?*"

"You took your bloody time answering," she snapped, and instantly felt guilty for venting her frustration on him. Taking a deep breath, she massaged the bridge of her nose, wishing she had some paracetamol to ease the dull ache behind her eyes. "Sorry, didn't mean to bite your head off. It's just that Phoebe's given me the slip, and I'm in a bit of a panic because I don't know where she is."

A moment's hesitation. "*What do you mean, given you the slip?*"

"I mean, she went out this morning without me, and now I'm worried shitless that something terrible might have happened to her."

Martin tutted. "*Why did you let her do that?*" he demanded, and she could hear the irritation in his voice.

The insinuation that this was her fault stung, and Anna ground her teeth together in anger. "I didn't bloody well let her," she replied, frostily. "The cunning little cow tricked me. She said she was going out to do some painting, but I've checked the Mere, and I've completed the Diss Circular Walk, and all I've got to show for my troubles are a pounding headache and blisters. I was hoping you might have some idea where she is. Are there any little out of the way beauty spots that she's particularly fond of?"

"*There are loads of places,*" he said, unhelpfully, "*but I never bother going with her when she wants to paint. It's too bloody boring. Have you told Ben and Jess, yet?*"

Anna recoiled at the thought. "No, I haven't! And don't you dare say a bloody word to them. I don't want them worrying unnecessarily."

"*Look, Anna, you need to stop worrying,*" Martin advised her. He sounded like he was getting bored with the conversation. "*I've told you before, this is what Phoebe does to get attention. She's just playing mind games with you to mess you up, so don't give her the satisfaction. When she comes back, and she will, just blank her and act like nothing's happened.*"

He was probably right, but that didn't make her feel any better. Anna glanced at her watch. It was getting on for two. "Look, I've got to go. I'll call you when she turns up."

―――――

There was a dull click, but nothing happened when Harrington pulled the trigger. He stared down at the weapon in disbelief, thumbed back the hammer and tried again, with the same result.

"You've already fired your two rounds," Dillon said, rubbing his injured shoulder.

Harrington reacted by spinning the gun around so that he was holding the barrel in both hands. Raising it above his head like a baseball bat, he took a swing at Dillon's head, intent on caving it in.

Instead of retreating, as Harrington had expected him to do, Dillon stepped inside the downwards arc and grabbed the gun by its stock. Then, he thrust his hip into the other man's groin, allowing Harrington's own momentum to do all the hard work for him as he performed a perfectly executed hip throw that sent the gunman tumbling over his shoulder.

Harrington crashed down on top of the coffee table, which was completely obliterated by his weight, sending shards of wood, and splinters of glass, flying everywhere.

Harrington lay flat on his back, moaning in pain.

Trying to avoid stepping on broken glass, Dillon relieved him of the shotgun and casually tossed it aside. As he bent down to grab Harrington's arm, the robber lashed out with his right foot, catching Dillon in the midsection and catapulting him backwards into the wall.

Harrington stumbled to his feet, shaking himself like a dog

emerging from water. His mouth curled upwards in a nasty smile. His face was covered with numerous cuts from where shards of glass had embedded themselves in his skin, and two red lines trickled down his cheeks as though he were crying tears of blood.

Breathing heavily, the two giants squared off against each other.

"I'm gonna rip your fucking head off," Harrington promised.

Dillon kicked the remains of the coffee table aside to create more room to manoeuvre in. "You're welcome to try," he said, calmly.

Elbows bent, Harrington's massive arms hung out from the side of his body, forced there by the bulging latissimus dorsi muscles that gave his back such a distinctive V shape. Crouching like a Sumo wrestler, he circled Dillon, flexing his fingers as he looked for an opening.

Harrington suddenly rushed forward, drawing his right fist back to deliver a haymaker, but Dillon was prepared for this, and he kicked out, catching the oncoming man squarely in the midsection. With a surprised grunt, Harrington staggered backwards, clutching his stomach. Then, baring his teeth in anger, he lowered his head as though he was going to use it as a battering ram, and charged Dillon again.

For such a big man, Dillon was very fleet of foot, and he nimbly sidestepped the attack, leaving his adversary to crash headfirst into the wall.

As Harrington straightened up, Dillon hit him hard in the kidneys, a swift right followed by a left. He followed the punches up by driving his right elbow into the base of the other man's skull, sending him face first into the wall. Harrington's nose splattered with a dull thunk, staining the wall red. Stepping back, Dillon raised his right foot and stamped down on the rear of the man's knee. There was a sickening crunch as something inside the joint snapped, and Harrington screamed out in agony. Dillon wasn't finished yet. Wrapping his arm around the other man's neck, he applied pressure, cutting off his oxygen supply until the struggling man went limp and fell to the floor.

Breathing heavily from his exertions, Dillon placed the unconscious man in the recovery position and made sure that his airway was clear. Then he sat down beside his prisoner and smiled wanly at Tyler.

"Maybe I was wrong," he panted. "Maybe this wasn't a wasted trip after all."

19

DON'T BE SUCH A DRAMA QUEEN

The urine scented lift had broken down, so they were forced to take the urine scented stairs instead. In addition to reeking of piss, the stairwell was hotter than a greenhouse, and Tyler found himself taking a moment to sympathise with the poor uniformed officers who had recently run up twenty-three floors to come to their aid. The poor sods had all looked fit to drop when they'd burst through the door of Higgins' flat, a half-hour earlier. No wonder they had been red faced, covered in sweat and panting for breath when they arrived.

Tyler had ordered that the flat be preserved as a crime scene, and there was now a uniformed constable stationed outside the door with a Scene Log on the go.

Higgins and Harrington had been carted off to separate police stations, and the escorting officers had been given strict instructions that Harrington was not to be left unattended until gunshot residue swabs had been taken from his hands and face. It had become common knowledge amongst criminals who used firearms that urine was a very effective means of removing GSR, and the first thing that most of them did when they arrived at the station nowadays was ask to be allowed to use the loo, so that they could piss over their hands and wash it off.

He and Dillon had conducted a cursory search of Higgins' bedroom, which had revealed another blue cash-in-transit bag sitting beside the unmade bed. Unlike the two in the lounge, no attempt had been made to open this one, and Tyler guessed that, having already spoiled the cash in the first two, the robbers had decided to hold fire on trying to open the third.

During the search, Tyler had spotted two spent shotgun cartridges lying on the bedside table, no doubt dumped there when Mad Micky Harrington replaced them with fresh shells before bursting into the lounge.

Tyler had only just come off the phone from speaking to Andy Quinlan, who had been overjoyed to hear that his murder suspects were in custody. He had promised to drum up an exhibits officer and a CSM and dispatch them straight down to the scene.

During the call, Quinlan had informed him that two spent shotgun cartridge cases had been recovered at the scene of PC Dawkins' murder. The lab hadn't managed to extract fingerprint or DNA evidence from either of them, so he was incredibly excited that a shotgun had been recovered in Harrington's possession. If ballistic testing confirmed the gun's firing pin matched the indents found on the cartridges from Dawkins' shooting, that would conclusively prove that Harrington's firearm was the murder weapon.

"Well, it's good to know that we've solved Andy's case for him, even if we're no nearer to finding Spencer," Dillon said, as if reading his mind.

"Yep," Tyler agreed. "As they say, every cloud has a silver lining."

"It bloody pongs in here, doesn't it?" the big man complained as they descended the stairs.

Tyler glanced over his shoulder. "I just assumed that was your manky aftershave," he said with a wry grin.

"Well, I'm wearing the cheap stuff you bought me for Christmas, so it's your fault if it is," Dillon fired back.

As the detectives emerged from the tower block, Tyler shut his eyes to protect them from the glaring light while he fumbled around for his sunglasses. Breathing a little sigh of relief as he slipped them on, he gingerly opened his eyes and blinked away the lingering sunspots. Turning to his friend, he was surprised to see that Dillon hadn't donned his yet. "Not putting your shades on, Dill?" he enquired.

Dillon responded by holding up a mangled mix of metal and glass, the remains of his broken sunglasses, which had been crushed during his battle with Harrington.

"Oh," Tyler said, trying not to smile.

On a positive note, at least the Job BMW was where they had left it, and it was still in one piece, with all its wheels and everything.

It was getting on for five o'clock when the red Alfa Romeo pulled into the driveway.

Sitting in the lounge, Anna sprang out of her seat as soon as she heard the sound of an approaching engine. She rushed to the front door and yanked it open. When she saw that it was Phoebe's car, she sagged against the doorframe in relief.

"Where the hell have you been?" she shouted at Phoebe the moment the driver's door opened.

"I've been painting," Phoebe replied, removing her easel from the back seat.

Anna strode angrily across the gravel to confront her. Her initial relief at seeing Phoebe return safe and well had quickly evaporated, to be replaced by an overwhelming sense of anger and resentment at the unnecessary stress her selfish friend had put her through. She stomped to a furious halt by the front bumper and put her hands on her hips. "That was a nasty thing that you did to me, this morning," she seethed. "I've been worried out of my mind about you all day.

That's *not* how you treat friends." Her voice had risen with each word and, by the time she finished her rant, she was shouting.

Phoebe eyed her coolly. "Don't be such a drama queen," she said. "I'm fine. Nothing bad happened to me. I've just been sitting in the countryside, enjoying the peace and quiet, and finishing off my painting."

Anna reacted angrily. "A drama queen?" she spluttered. "You were kidnapped a couple of days ago, for Christ's sake, and the man who abducted you is still at large. Can't you get it through that thick skull of yours that, until the police catch him, you'll always be in danger? You stupid, stupid girl." A tear ran down her cheek and she swatted it away savagely. "I dropped everything to come here and support you, and this is how you repay me."

Phoebe stared at her, dispassionately. "You didn't have to come here," she said, flatly. "I don't need you or anyone else babysitting me. I thought I made that clear yesterday." She picked up her easel and started walking towards the house.

Anna watched her go, thinking that she no longer knew her friend. "If that's how you feel, I might as well return to London," she called after her.

Phoebe glanced back over her shoulder. "Do what you want," she said. "I'm heading back myself in the morning, anyway."

Skippy was warming up a ready meal in the microwave when his phone pinged. He didn't get many messages, and he wondered if it might be from Spencer, who still hadn't called him back, despite the many voicemails that he'd left. Sure enough, it was a text from his cousin. It read:

Sorry I haven't called you. Been hiding up in Norfolk with my phone off to save battery power. Will be returning to London tomorrow. Things didn't go as planned here.

Skippy read the message a second time. Things didn't go as planned. No fucking kidding! He angrily tapped out a response:

U R a fucking idiot. I've had the pigs round here today looking for U. Didn't tell them anything. Call me when U can.

After pressing send, he tossed the phone onto the kitchen counter.

The earlier visit from the police had unsettled him, but he knew it had just been a fishing trip, and he was satisfied they had left none the wiser. One thing was now crystal clear to him: the sooner Spencer was arrested, the sooner all the fuss would die down, leaving him free to carry out the kidnap on his own.

Carrying his microwave meal through to the lounge, he switched on the TV and sat down. The early evening news was playing, and he was about to switch channels when he saw Honest Steve Higgins' photo appear on the screen, alongside a mugshot of Mad Micky Harrington. The female news anchor was speaking over the images, and he turned up the volume to listen.

"*...Earlier today, two men were arrested in connection with the brutal murder of police constable Alan Dawkins, who was gunned down last Wednesday by armed robbers fleeing the scene of the crime in Wanstead. The men, named as Steven Higgins and Michael Harrington, are currently being held at separate police stations in East London...*"

Skippy shook his head in regret. It seemed that everyone he knew was either being actively sought by the police or had already gotten themselves arrested. Mad Micky was no loss to anyone, but Honest Steve was a good lad, and Skippy would miss him. A frown creased his brow. With Spencer and Honest Steve indisposed for the foreseeable future, the only other person he could trust to help him with the kidnap was G-Man. Perhaps he should give him a quick call and sound him out?

The phone pinged again.

It was another message from Spencer.

When I get back to London, I'm gonna take care of unfinished business.

Skippy frowned again. What the hell was that supposed to mean? Presumably, he was talking about having a second go at kidnapping the girl, but that would be disastrous. Why couldn't Spencer behave like a normal person, and either fuck off to the other side of the country to lay low for a while, or turn himself into the police? Cursing under his breath, Skippy lowered his fork and began tapping away.

Don't be daft. It's too hot for you to try and grab the girl again. You need to keep your head down for a while.

To his surprise, Spencer replied almost immediately.

Don't worry. I'm not going after her again. Got something better in mind. When I'm finished P will be begging me to take her back.

Tyler and Dillon were sitting at a quiet table at the rear of the canteen in Forest Gate police station, where they had come to write up their arrest notes. "Tell you what, I'll get these time-stamped if you get the coffees in," Tyler offered, scooping up the Incident Report Book that his friend had just completed.

"How about I get them stamped and you get the coffees in," Dillon countered.

Tyler stood up. "Nice try, tight arse, but I paid for the last round." As he turned to leave, the canteen doors opened and Andy Quinlan breezed into the room. On seeing them, he smiled and waved at the two detectives. "Would either of you like a cup of tea?" he enquired, heading towards the serving counter.

"I'll have a coffee," Tyler replied, sitting down again.

"Same for me," Dillon shouted.

A few minutes later, Quinlan joined them. "There you are," he said, placing their drinks in front of them. "It's the least I can do, considering that you've just solved my job for me."

Sitting down opposite them, Andy Quinlan removed his Joe 90 spectacles and began polishing the lenses with a tissue. With them on, he had a professorial look about him but, without them, he more closely resembled the cartoon character, Morocco Mole, as he squinted across the table short-sightedly. "I must say," he said, replacing his glasses and running a hand through his jet black mop of hair, "you two really do seem to have all the luck."

Tyler raised an eyebrow at that. "Luck! I'd hardly call us lucky, Andy. That nutter with the sawn-off tried to kill us."

Quinlan swatted his objection aside. "Tried and failed. You got the bugger in the end, and that's all that matters. I wouldn't be surprised if George puts the pair of you up for another commendation." He chuckled at the thought, and then became serious again. "I've just sent the family liaison officer over to see PC Dawkins' parents and give them the good news that we've caught their son's killer."

Tyler understood just how important that was to Quinlan. Having been charged with solving a murder, it was always an incredibly satisfying moment when an SIO informed the next of kin that the person responsible for their loved one's death had been caught. The trouble was, at least in Tyler's experience, it was always a hollow victory. Catching the killer wouldn't bring the victim back and, once the initial euphoria of seeing justice done wore off, the family would still be left grieving.

"So, do you think all the money from the robbery has been recovered?" Dillon asked.

Quinlan shook his head. "Alas, no. Four cash bags were stolen, and there were only three at Higgins' flat, which means we're still one adrift. That's probably with the third suspect, wherever he is."

Tyler stared at him. "There was a third suspect? I didn't know that."

Quinlan nodded. "It was in the bulletin I sent out. Still, to be completely honest with you, Jack, I'm not overly fussed if we never find him, or recover the outstanding money. All I care about is that the man who shot PC Dawkins is in custody."

Tyler grunted. He appreciated that charging the person responsible for pulling the trigger was Andy's primary concern, but it still went against the grain to let anyone who was connected with the post office blagging off the hook.

As he took a sip of his coffee, Tyler's phone started ringing. It was Reggie, calling from Hertford House. "*Boss, there's been some activity between Spencer and Skipton's phones.*"

"What sort of activity?"

"*A series of text messages. Basically, Spencer text Skipton that he's still in Norfolk, but he's returning to London tomorrow.*"

"We need to get back to the office," Tyler informed Quinlan as soon as he'd terminated the call. "Thanks for the brew, Andy. Let me know what they say in interview." Standing up, he patted his friend on the shoulder.

"Will do," Quinlan promised.

———

"*So, she's definitely coming home tomorrow?*" Martin asked.

"That's what she said when she got back from going walkabout, but she hasn't spoken a word to me since," Anna said, miserably. "It's like she hates me."

"*At least she's talking to you,*" Martin complained. "*She hasn't answered any of my calls, or replied to any of my messages since I left the cottage.*"

"Are you sure you're not ringing her old number by mistake?" Anna asked. Before returning to London, Phoebe's parents had popped into Diss and purchased her a new phone to replace the one that Spencer had taken from her.

"*Positive. I double checked with Jess, and I've definitely been calling the new number. She's just ignoring me for some reason.*"

A chill ran down Anna's spine. "Perhaps she knows about us?" she said. "That would certainly explain her frostiness towards me." As she spoke, she wandered over to the bedroom door and placed her ear against it, suddenly paranoid that Phoebe was lingering outside, eavesdropping on their conversation.

Martin snorted. "*It would, but there's no way that she could have discovered we were seeing each other, unless you've been careless and let it slip.*"

Anna baulked at the accusatory note in his voice. "I haven't been careless," she retorted. "We agreed that you would be the one to tell her when the time came, and I've honoured that, even though it's killing me not to be able to tell her."

Anna heard a noise outside. Walking over to the window, she saw Phoebe down by her car, removing the large blue cool bag from the boot. "Look, we'll talk more when I get back," she said. "Unless she was winding me up about leaving, I'll see you at some point tomorrow."

After hanging up, Anna went downstairs in search of Phoebe. She found her outside, returning the hatchet she had taken with her for protection to the woodshed. "What do you want to do about food?" she asked, leaning against the wall. It was almost seven, and she was getting hungry.

"I don't know," Phoebe said with a little shrug. "Maybe we could order a pizza?"

Anna nodded. That suited her. "I'll phone the order in. Do you want your usual?" Phoebe was boringly predictable when it came to pizza, and she always ordered a thick crust pepperoni."

"Sure, why not?"

Anna turned to go.

"Anna…"

Anna looked around and was surprised to find Phoebe wringing her hands together and looking terribly repentant.

"Look, I'm sorry I was so bitchy earlier," Phoebe said, staring down at her shoes as she spoke. "I've been a little stressed since I escaped, but that doesn't excuse me for being so horrible to you."

Anna's heart melted. In an instant, all was forgiven. "That's okay," she said, rushing forward to grasp Phoebe's hands in hers. "After what you've been through, you're entitled to be a little off."

They hugged, awkwardly at first, and then with more feeling. Kissing Phoebe on the forehead, Anna returned to the house with a smile on her face.

Phoebe watched her go, eyes cold, heart even colder. What was the old saying? 'Keep your friends close and your enemies even closer.'

They had just pulled out of the back yard at Forest Gate police station when Tyler's phone rang again. It was Dean, calling from the office with an update.

"*Boss, we've had some retrospective ANPR hits come back on the Beamer that Spencer stole from outside Moorfields.*"

Tyler reached into his man bag for a pen and his daybook. "Anything that might help us to figure out where he is now?"

"*Afraid not,*" Dean said. "*The only thing this data confirms is that the stolen Beamer joined the M11 near the Waterworks roundabout in Walthamstow on Wednesday morning, then took the A11 towards Norwich, before branching off onto the A1066, which would have taken it into Diss. There are no further hits to suggest that it's come back to London. If it had, the ANPR cameras dotted along the A11 and M11 would have detected it.*"

Tyler considered this. "So, you think it's still up in Norfolk?"

"*I do,*" Dean confirmed. "*Either abandoned or burnt out.*"

Tyler thanked him, hung up, and turned to Dillon. "Okay, this is starting to get interesting. From the text messages he sent to Skipton, we know that Spencer's still in Norfolk and that he's planning to return to London tomorrow. The ANPR data confirms that the stolen car was driven there on Wednesday morning, but there haven't been any activations since then, and there would have been if it had come back to London. The question is, will Spencer drive the Beamer back tomorrow? If we think he will, we'll need to have a couple of interceptors on standby, ready to deploy the moment that it activates an ANPR camera."

Dillon nodded, thoughtfully. "He definitely won't come back by public transport. That's just not his style, so he'll either use the Beamer or dump it and nick another motor. Either way, we should have a couple of cars on standby."

Tyler ran his hand across the stubble on his chin. "He's bound to come back via the A11 and M11. It's the most direct route, so we should look to place interceptors somewhere along the M11 to stop him once he's London bound."

"Agreed. We could plot up one car at the weighbridge on the Harlow roundabout, that's at junction seven, and another at

Motorway One-One." Motorway One-One was the Met's M11 traffic base, located between the M25 and A406 exits.

Tyler's phone rang again. "DCI Tyler," he said, annoyed at the interruption.

"Ah, good afternoon, Jack. It's Barty Craddock calling from Diss. I'm just ringing to let you know that the stolen BMW Spencer travelled up to Norfolk in has just been found abandoned."

Tyler sat forward. "Where?" he demanded.

"It was hidden in an old barn about a mile or so away from the Cunningham's cottage," Craddock informed him. "Some kids found it earlier this afternoon, but the little scallywags didn't bother telling anyone about it until they got home for tea this evening. I've got officers en route as we speak, and I'll let you know if they find anything of interest in it."

Tyler thanked him and then hung up. Turning to Dillon, he was unable to hide his disappointment. "The local plod in Norfolk just found the stolen Beamer, so Spencer won't be coming back in that."

Dillon sighed, despondently. "That's a pity," he said, "but I still think we should have a couple of interceptors on standby. He's bound to nick another car to come back in. As long as it's reported stolen, it'll activate the ANPR cameras once he's on the motorway."

"You're right, of course," Tyler agreed, but he struggled to show any enthusiasm. The Beamer that Spencer had stolen for the journey up to Diss hadn't been entered onto the ANPR system until several hours afterwards, and he suspected that the same issue would crop up again. He brooded in silence, wondering how they were ever going to catch Spencer if he managed to reach London undetected. The only good thing to come out of any of this was that he now had a genuine excuse for not attending Jenny and Eddie's dinner party tomorrow evening. He would have to call them later to explain, but at least he could do it in good conscience, and not feel like a total heel for lying to them.

It was time to set off for his evening shift at the pizzeria. Before leaving, Skippy nervously poked his head out of the street door, glanced up and down the road in case any of Jonas Willard's cronies were lying in wait for him, and then breathed a little sigh of relief when he saw that the coast was clear. The three grand he owed the loan shark was due to be repaid in full by the end of the day, and he still didn't have it. Truth be told, he didn't have 300 quid let alone 3K. He had planned to visit Willard earlier in the week to request an extension but, because of all the shit that had gone down with Spencer, he had completely forgotten. Now he had to choose between begging the old man for a last-minute reprieve, or going to ground and hoping that he could avoid falling into the bastard's hands until he scraped the money together. Mulling his limited options over in his head, Skippy closed the door behind him, crossed the road, and jogged the twenty yards to where his car was parked up. As he was unlocking the driver's door, he became aware of a hostile presence behind him. Spinning around, he came face to face – well, face to barrel-sized chest – with Casper Wright. Casper wasn't the man's real first name of course. That was Patrick, but everyone called the albino man-mountain Casper because his pale skin and white hair resembled that of the famous ghost.

Unlike the cartoon character, Casper Wright was anything but friendly. He was the sort of person who derived pleasure from ripping the wings off little birds, drowning puppies, and breaking people's legs. Staring at Skippy with his beady eyes, Casper seized his right shoulder in one of his massive hands and squeezed until Skippy cried out in pain.

Casper smiled at that. He enjoyed the sound of suffering.

"That'll do, Casper," the gravelly voice of his associate, Fred Wiggins warned. "Mr Willard don't want him injured, at least not yet." Wiggins was the antithesis of Casper; short and slim, he was well dressed, well-educated, and he had an air of refinement about him. Having been in Willard's employ since leaving school, twenty years earlier, he had steadily worked his way up through the ranks until he had become Jonas Willard's right-hand man.

"Hello, Mr Wiggins," Skippy said, nodding his head deferentially. "To what do I owe the pleasure?"

Wiggins smiled, like a vulture evaluating its next meal. "Mr Willard asked me to pay you a little visit, to remind you that you owe him a considerable amount of money, and to point out that the debt is due to be paid by the end of the day. You haven't forgotten about that by any chance, have you?" He glanced up from examining his fingernails and smiled disarmingly.

"N-no, of course not," Skippy said, quickly, "but I was going to pop in and have a word with Mr Willard this evening, to see if there was any chance of him seeing his way to giving me another week. Obviously, I'd make it worth his while."

Wiggins shook his head regretfully. "Oh dear, oh dear, oh dear," he said, adopting a woeful expression. "I had a feeling you were going to say something like that." A nod to Casper, who punched Skippy so hard in the gut that his hand almost passed clean through the smaller man's body.

Skippy doubled over, fell to his knees, coughing and puking.

Wiggins stared on, unimpressed. Another nod to Casper, who grabbed hold of Skippy's hair and yanked him to his feet.

"P-p-please," Skippy begged, his chin covered in drool.

"Now," Wiggins asked with a polite smile, "did I imagine it, or did you just have the audacity to ask for an extension on your credit?"

Gasping for breath, Skippy's face was contorted in pain. "Just one week. That's all I–"

Wiggins nodded, and Casper smashed Skippy's forehead into the roof of the car.

It connected with a dull thunk, and Casper allowed himself a little smile of satisfaction as Skippy bounced off and fell to the floor.

The two loan sharks watched on in silence as Skippy writhed around in agony, clutching his face and making strange mewling noises.

"I'm sorry?" Wiggins said, cupping a hand to his ear, "I must have misheard you. Are you really sure you want to ask Mr Willard for more time to pay your debt?"

Skippy was still holding his face, and he mumbled something incoherent from within his hands.

Wiggins nodded again, and this time Casper put the boot in, connecting squarely with Skippy's ribs. There was a maniacal glint in his little piggy eyes as he drew back his foot in readiness for a second kick, but Wiggins stayed him with a raised hand.

Wiggins knelt down beside the fallen man. "What makes you think that you'll be able to pay Mr Willard back next week when you can't do so now?" he casually enquired.

"I-I've got a big job coming off next week," Skippy sobbed. "By next Friday I'll have more than enough dough to pay off my debt. All I'm asking for is one week. If I don't make good, you know where to find me, and I know exactly what'll happen, so I won't let you down."

Wiggins stood up, adjusted his suit jacket. "I'll put in a call," he said, removing his mobile

phone, "but I wouldn't hold your breath if I were you."

While Wiggins spoke to his boss, Skippy dragged himself to his feet. His stomach was on fire, and his head was throbbing; he could already feel a lump the size of a small Christmas pudding coming up.

Pocketing his phone, Wiggins returned to the car, which Skippy was leaning against for support. "I have some good news and some bad news," he said.

Skippy groaned, afraid that this meant he was about to find himself on the wrong end of a shoeing from Casper, who was grinning in gleeful anticipation.

"Mr Willard has agreed to grant you an extra week, but it will cost you a thousand quid more. Can you afford that?"

The smile faded from Casper's face, instantly replaced by a hateful scowl.

Ignoring him, Skippy nodded vigorously. "Yes... I swear I can."

"Very well," Wiggins said. He turned to go, beckoning Casper to follow him with a snap of his fingers, summoning the man as though he was a dog. "That was the good news. The bad news is that, if you don't have the wonga by then, instead of breaking a few bones, there's a cement mixer waiting to turn you into a support pillar for a motorway bridge."

Skippy swallowed hard. "I'll have it," he promised. With a shaking hand, he reached for his mobile. He needed to set up an urgent meeting with G-Man. It was going to take a bit of doing, but with his knowledge of her movements, there was no reason why they couldn't kidnap Phoebe Cunningham the following week.

20

Saturday 28th July 2001
THERE'S A STRANGE MAN LURKING OUTSIDE

It was coming up to seven thirty and Tyler was sitting alone in his office, feeling uncharacteristically downcast. There was no valid reason for him to remain at work any longer, but the truth was, he just didn't feel like going home. Since he and Jenny had divorced, seven years earlier, he had been perfectly content living on his own and not having anyone else to worry about, but Kelly had changed his entire outlook on life, and now the house felt unbearably empty without her.

When she had called him the previous evening, to confirm that she wasn't going to be able to make it back that weekend, her voice had sounded like music to his ears, and he had been startled to realise just how much he'd missed hearing it. They had talked for twenty minutes, catching up and just generally enjoying each other's company. Expressing concern over how tired he sounded, Kelly had proceeded to rattle her way through a long list of questions in order to satisfy herself that he was taking proper care of himself while she was away. He had told her not to make a fuss, secretly enjoying every second of it and not wanting her to stop.

Although he had described the difficulties that the team were having in finding Bannister's murderer in great detail, he had purposely avoided mentioning anything about the dramatic arrests at James Riley Point for fear of alarming her. She would, no doubt, find out about his involvement in the incident when she returned the following weekend, and she wouldn't be happy with him for keeping her in the dark, but he would deal with that when the time came. In the meantime, he was determined that she should enjoy the remainder of her course without worrying unduly about him.

Kelly had made his day by declaring that she was missing him unbearably, and that she couldn't wait for the course to end so that she could get back to him. He was rather looking forward to that, too, he had assured her with a contented smile. When it was time to say goodnight, neither one had wanted to be the first to hang up, so they had agreed to count down from three, like a pair of teenaged lovebirds, and then hang up at the same time.

When Tyler had rung Eddie Maitland, to break the news that they wouldn't be able to make Saturday's dinner party, he had expected Eddie's reaction to be one of bored indifference but, to Tyler's great surprise, the man had sounded genuinely disappointed. It would have been quite touching, had Eddie not run off with his wife a few years earlier.

Putting his feet up on his desk, Tyler reflected that the day had been a complete washout. Despite having a couple of police interceptors on standby, with their crews twiddling their thumbs in boredom, there had been no ANPR activations along the A11 or M11. If Spencer had come back to London, he had managed to do it under the radar.

Because Skipton had lied to Charlie White and Kevin Murray, a decision had been made to put his flat under covert surveillance. After busting a gut to get the relevant authority in place this morning,

Dillon had arranged for a battered nondescript van to be parked outside the man's address. The Technical Support Unit had equipped it with a covert video camera, and a live feed from this was being microwaved to Hertford House, allowing the team to monitor any comings and goings at the address in real time. If Spencer showed up, as they were all hoping he would, an arrest team would to be sent straight to the venue to detain him.

Checking his watch, Tyler was disappointed to see that only five minutes had elapsed since the last time that he'd looked. He leaned back in his chair and ran a weary hand through his short hair. Maybe he should call it a day and go home after all? If he left now, he could grab a curry on the way and curl up on the sofa to watch a Bond film. Goldfinger would go down a treat. As he contemplated this, Dillon appeared in the doorway.

"Why don't we knock it on the head and pop over the road for a quick one?" the big man suggested.

Tyler grimaced. "There's no way I'm going to any of the pubs around here."

Dillon thought about that for all of two seconds. "Not a problem. Let's go to Wanstead High Street. It's only five minutes away, it's on the way home, and it's full of lovely places to stop off for a quick pint."

Tyler tried to think of a reason to say no, but failed miserably. "Okay," he said, tossing his biro onto his desk. "Let's do it."

To celebrate Phoebe and Anna's return from Diss earlier in the day, Ben had insisted on reserving a table for all five of them at his favourite restaurant in Wanstead High Street. Phoebe had been set against it, preferring to spend a quiet night in but, in his usual bullish style, he had overruled her, declaring that life had to go on and that they should all go out together to show solidarity.

The table had been booked for seven thirty and, to keep Ben happy, they had all dressed up for the occasion.

The meal had been consumed in stony silence. Great food; terrible atmosphere. Realising that they had made a mistake, and that the occasion had fallen flat, they left without even bothering to order dessert.

"Are you coming back to my place tonight, or staying with your parents?" Martin asked from the X5's rear seat, where he was sandwiched between Phoebe and Anna.

"I don't know," Phoebe replied, staring listlessly out of the tinted window.

Martin felt a sharp dig in his ribs and, when he turned to investigate, Anna was giving him daggers. Did that mean she was annoyed with him for asking Phoebe, because she wanted to go back with him herself? After making sure that Ben wasn't watching them in his rearview mirror, he raised a questioning eyebrow at her. She responded with an almost imperceptible shake of her head.

Great!

What was that supposed to mean? With no idea, Martin folded his arms huffily, and settled into a confused sulk.

A few minutes later, the car drew up outside the gates of the Cunningham's lavish house in Hollybush Hill. Cursing under his breath, Ben started patting his pockets for the remote control that would open the security gates.

Jessica struggled to contain her annoyance. "I don't know why you don't just leave the clicker thing in the cupholder like I do," she complained.

Ignoring the bickering that her comment triggered, Martin looked out of the window, desperately wishing that Ben would just shut up and get a move on. The evening had been a total nightmare from his perspective and, sitting between two girls who were both giving off hostile vibes for completely different reasons, was a bit like being stuck in purgatory. All he wanted to do was say goodnight to everyone, and then jump in his car and head off home for some peace and quiet. If Phoebe wanted to spend the night with her parents, instead of accompanying him back to his place, that was fine by him. It would save him from having to put up with her self-pitying whining. As for Anna, he really didn't give a toss one way or the other what she did anymore.

Suddenly, Martin stiffened. "Look, over there," he said, pointing across Anna into the darkness beyond. "I thought I just saw someone hiding in the bushes."

Everyone but Phoebe looked.

"I can't see anyone," Jessica said, cupping her hands to the glass.

"Neither can I," Anna said, doing likewise.

"I bet it's that swine, Spencer," Ben growled, undoing his seatbelt.

"Ben, what are you doing?" Jessica spluttered, staring at him in horror. "Don't go out there, you might get hurt."

"I told you before," he snapped, "I'm not scared of that little runt." With that, he threw open the door and stepped out into the warm evening air. "Come out and show yourself," he bellowed. Clenching his fists in anger, he set off toward the tall hedgerow that spanned the house's perimeter.

"Ben come back," Jessica called, frantically reaching for her phone.

"Anna, let me out," Martin said, urgently. "I can't let him go wandering off on his own."

As he unclipped his seatbelt and slid past Anna, he could hear Jessica talking into her phone.

"Yes, operator, I need the police, someone's trying to break into our house…"

By the time Martin emerged from the car, Ben was already a good ten yards ahead of him. "Ben!" he yelled, breaking into a trot. "Wait for me!"

Martin was beginning to think that he might have imagined seeing someone lurking in the shadows, and that he had created a big fuss over nothing, when a hooded figure in dark clothing broke away from the shrubbery and dashed across the road. For a moment, all Martin could do was stand and gawp, but then the initial shock wore off and he took off after the unknown intruder, quickly overtaking Ben and then leaving him for dust.

The hooded man cut into the dense woodland adjacent to the house and disappeared from view.

"Stop!" Martin yelled, ducking beneath a low-hanging branch. As he straightened up, his foot snagged on a protruding root and he stumbled into some nearby bramble. Untangling himself from its painful embrace, he awkwardly set off in pursuit of the absconding man, who was now a fair way ahead of him. Martin was furious with himself for having taken a tumble. "I know it's you, Spencer," he screamed, his voice vibrating off the elm and oak trees around him, "and when I get my hands on you, I'm going to beat the living shit out of you."

As he ran, a stitch began to set in, and he clutched at his side, wishing that he hadn't eaten quite so much. He risked a quick glance over his shoulder, but Ben was nowhere to be seen. Struggling to breathe because of the worsening stitch, Martin skirted a vicious looking thorn bush, ducked under another branch, and clambered over a large log that was blocking his path. Up ahead, through a gap in the trees, he caught sight of a road, and spotted Spencer running across it.

As Martin emerged from the forest's interior, ten seconds later, he ran straight into the path of an approaching police car, which screeched to a halt beside him with the blue lights on its roof bar blazing brightly. Two uniformed men immediately sprang out and rushed towards him.

Gasping for breath, he pointed in the direction that he had last seen Spencer running. "He went that way," he said, doubling over with his stitch.

To Martin's irritation, instead of setting off in pursuit of Spencer, the two idiot policemen grabbed hold of him. "What the fuck are you doing?" he protested, trying to pull his arms free. "I'm not the criminal here, you useless pair of muppets. The man you want is John Spencer, and you're letting him get away."

The pub they had chosen was called The Cuckfield, and it was located in Wanstead High Street, opposite the Memorial Green. It was already busy by the time they arrived but, after queuing at the bar for ages to get served, Tyler and Dillon managed to find a nice little spot at the rear of the beer garden to sit in.

Tyler was just starting to relax when the call came in. With a disgruntled groan, he dragged his phone from his pocket. "DCI Tyler speaking," he said, taking a sip of his drink.

"*Boss, Charlie here, thought you'd wanna know, there's been a sighting of our suspect at the Cunningham's house in Wanstead.*"

Tyler sat up straight. "When was this?" he asked, lowering his glass.

"*I've got Ilford's control room on the other line as we speak,*" Charlie said. "*They've got local units there now, and India 99 and a dog unit have been scrambled to search the area for the wee shite.*"

"Give me the address," Tyler ordered, pulling a pen from his pocket and making a scribbling motion towards Dillon, who promptly passed him a tissue to write on.

"What's going on?" Dillon asked, as soon the call ended.

Tyler was already on his feet. "Hollybush Hill, that's only around the corner from here, isn't it?"

Dillon nodded. "It's up by Snaresbrook Crown Court, less than five minutes away. Why?"

"Spencer's just been sighted near there."

Dillon knocked back the last of his drink. "He must be thinking about having another go at snatching the girl," he said, digging the car keys from his pocket.

"That's what I'm afraid of," Tyler admitted. "Hopefully, she's still up in Diss, which will make her Barty Craddock's problem, not ours."

It was easy enough to work out which house belonged to the Cunningham family as there was a police car parked directly outside the open security gates. Just inside, a small gathering of people stood on the driveway, talking animatedly.

A harried looking constable was unsuccessfully trying to placate a smartly dressed man in his mid-twenties, who was ranting on about bringing lawsuits for unlawful arrest and false imprisonment. Behind them, another officer was talking to a bearded man in his early fifties, from whose arm a stunning woman of similar years hung. As Tyler approached them, he recognised the bearded man's voice from their telephone conversation on Wednesday evening.

"Of course it was Spencer," Cunningham was insisting. "We all saw him, didn't we, Jess?"

The woman nodded, dutifully. "We did, officer," she confirmed.

The harangued looking constable hurriedly scribbled this information down into his notebook.

Tyler's eye was drawn to the two women standing just behind the Cunninghams. Both in their twenties, they were watching the exchange in stony silence. The nearest girl wore a white, tie-back crepe summer dress with a striking floral design. He groaned inwardly as he noticed the striking resemblance between her and Mrs Cunningham.

Could this be Phoebe?

He sincerely hoped that it wasn't.

The second girl, also pretty but in a more homely way, possessed a fuller figure and wore designer gasses. She seemed ill at ease, as though she couldn't wait to get away. Her eyes kept darting towards the younger man, who was still giving one of the constables a hard time over the way he'd been treated. There was a certain intimacy in the look that they shared when their eyes met briefly, and Tyler got the distinct impression that they were romantically involved.

As he and Dillon approached the group, all eyes turned on them.

"Can I help you?" Ben Cunningham demanded, staring at them with open hostility.

Tyler flashed his warrant card. "Mr Cunningham, I presume?" he asked with a polite smile.

"Yes," Cunningham replied, immediately suspicious.

"I'm DCI Jack Tyler. We spoke earlier in the week. This is my colleague, DI Dillon."

Cunningham frowned in thought as he searched his memory, and then a flicker of recognition passed across his face. "Tyler. Yes, I remember you." He came forward to offer his hand.

Tyler accepted it, noting that Cunningham's handshake was that of a Freemason. Tyler wasn't on The Square himself, but he had an uncle who was, and he was familiar with the various grips, which were based on one's rank within the organisation. "I understand that John Spencer was recently sighted outside your house?"

Cunningham pointed back out into the street, and his face darkened into an angry scowl. "The scumbag was hiding in the bushes when we got back from our meal. Luckily, Martin spotted him, and we chased him off."

"Martin...?" Tyler enquired.

"Yes, Martin Whitling, Phoebe's fiancé. He would have caught the little shit too, if those two dim-witted idiots –" he jerked his chin at each of the policemen in turn "– hadn't mistaken him for an intruder and collared the wrong man. Thanks to their incompetence, Spencer got clean away."

Keeping his face studiously neutral, Tyler glanced at the two officers, who were staring back sheepishly.

You couldn't make it up.

Tyler indicated the pretty girl in the floral dress. "Is that your daughter, Phoebe, by any chance?"

Please say no!

Cunningham's eyes lit up with pride. "It most certainly is. She got back from Diss this afternoon. I hope your mob's going to provide her with better protection than those bumbling fools in Norfolk did. As an absolute minimum, I'm expecting you to park a patrol car outside the house at all times."

Tyler smiled, diplomatically. "Mr Cunningham, it doesn't quite work like that in real life, I'm afraid. Before we go, my colleague and I will check the premises for you to make sure they're secure, and we'll arrange for uniform patrols to pay regular visits during the night, but we can't station someone outside permanently. We just don't have the resources. Do you have a private security system installed here?" In his experience, a lot of these high-end homes had alarms and CCTV systems fitted. Combined with the high walls and thick shrubbery surrounding the perimeter, and the electrically operated gates, Tyler suspected that the place was pretty much impregnable once all the doors were closed.

Before Cunningham could reply, they were joined by Phoebe and Martin, neither of whom bothered to acknowledge Tyler's presence. "I've decided that I'm going to stay at Martin's place tonight," Phoebe informed her father. "Spencer doesn't know where he lives, so I think I'll feel more relaxed over there."

"Nonsense!" Cunningham sputtered, stamping his foot in anger like a petulant child. "You can't do that! You'll be *much* safer here, you know you will. Martin's flat doesn't even have an alarm fitted."

"It'll be fine," Phoebe insisted. Before he could object, she kissed each of her parents on the cheek and set off towards the house. "You go ahead," she called over her shoulder to Martin. "I need to throw a few things into an overnight bag, so I'll follow you over in a little while."

Martin seemed quite taken aback by this. "But Phoebe, wouldn't it make more sense for me to wait for you so that we could both go in my car?"

Phoebe shook her head. "You and daddy are playing golf in the morning, and I don't want to be stuck at yours till you get back."

Forgetting all about Tyler, Ben Cunningham hurried after his daughter, shouting objections as he went.

Offering Tyler a polite wave goodbye, Jessica followed suit, but at a much slower pace.

Tyler ambled over to join Dillon, who had made himself busy debriefing the local officers out in the street.

"Apparently, there was no sign of Spencer by the time that the helicopter and dog unit arrived to search the surrounding area," Dillon said, ushering his friend to one side as Martin Whitling's sleek BMW Coupe drove out of the gates.

Tyler watched it go, then turned to the two PCs. "Do either of you honestly think that Spencer tried to break into the premises?"

"No, sir," the elder one replied, shaking his head emphatically. "In fact, when you dig into their story, all they actually saw was a man wearing a hoodie loitering in the street outside their house. He might've been up to no good, but he might just as easily have been passing by." He cast a cautious glance over his shoulder at the house, then leaned in and lowered his voice conspiratorially. "With all due respect guv, Mr Whitling and Mr Cunningham are both a little highly strung if you ask me. I reckon the bloke they saw might have just run off because he thought they were going to give him a kicking."

His colleague was quick to nod in agreement. "If the way they behaved towards us is anything to go by, you can bet that they were pretty aggressive when they challenged the suspect. We checked all the doors and windows in the house, and we did a walk around the perimeter, checking for breaches. There's a gate at the back of the property, leading into the rear garden, but it's made of solid wood and very secure. Plus, there's razor wire running along the top of the walls surrounding the garden, and anyone daft enough to attempt climbing over that would probably end up giving themselves a DIY vasectomy."

Tyler smiled at the image this conjured up. "So, you think they made a mistake do you?"

The officers nodded in unison.

"Interesting," Tyler said, stroking his chin. "Speaking of mistakes, what's all this about you two grabbing the girl's boyfriend instead of going after Spencer?"

Both constables blushed, and the junior one took a sudden interest in his shoes. The older man shifted uncomfortably. "Well, er, the call described a suspect wearing dark clothing who had run into the forest after being disturbed from an attempted break-in. We were on our way to the house when Mr Whitling ran out in front of us. He was wearing dark clothing, and he had just run out of the forest, so what were we meant to do? We detained him, checked him out, and then, once we'd verified his story, we dusted him down and drove him home. It was an honest mistake."

Tyler grinned at them, said nothing. Words were superfluous.

"Right, we won't detain you any longer," Dillon said, waving for the cringing constables to return to their car.

21

AN UNWELCOME TEXT MESSAGE

Phoebe arrived at the third floor flat in Redbridge Lane West about twenty minutes after Martin. By that time, he had changed into a baggy tracksuit and was curled up on the couch, working his way through his second glass of Glenfiddich. The lights had been dimmed, the TV was on, and the opening titles of *Four Weddings and a Funeral* were showing on the screen.

It was fortuitous that she hadn't arrived a few seconds earlier because, had she done so, she would have walked in on him and Anna having a real humdinger of an argument over the phone.

The call had ended so badly that he was beginning to regret ever having become involved with her. Licking his wounds from the totally undeserved telling off that she had just given him, he was half tempted to end their relationship and give things with Phoebe another go, just to spite her.

"I put this film on especially for you," he called as she walked through the door carrying a holdall and her blue cool bag. It was her favourite film, and he had chosen it purely to assuage his guilt. "It's literally only just started."

"Pause it," she called from the master bedroom, where she had disappeared to get changed.

Martin grabbed the remote from the coffee table and clicked the pause button, transforming an image of Hugh Grant's smiling face into a flickering blur.

As he made himself comfortable, he listened to her clunking about in the bedroom, wondering why it always took her five times longer to do anything than it did him? "Hurry up," he called, swishing the remainder of his single malt around the bottom of the glass. At this rate, he would be on his third before she even sat down.

"I'm coming," she said, appearing in the doorway. She had changed into a pair of silk pyjamas and tied her hair back into a ponytail.

Martin smiled up at her and patted the cushion beside him, indicating for her to join him there. "I bet your dad had the major hump with you for not staying there tonight."

She shrugged, indifferently. "You know what he's like, all bark and no bite. He'll have forgotten all about it by the morning."

Martin laughed. "He does sometimes get himself into an unnecessary state about the most trivial of things," he said, levering himself off the sofa.

"Where are you going?" she asked. "You've just been whinging about me taking too long, and as soon as I get here, you bugger off."

He smiled at her on his way to the kitchen. "Don't worry. I'm just going to get myself another drink before we watch the film. Do you want anything?"

"I'm fine," she called after him. Flopping down on the couch, she set about stealing the cushions that he had been laying on, rearranging them to prop herself up. As she was trying to make herself comfortable, Martin's phone pinged. Wondering who was messaging him at this late hour, she leaned forward and picked it up from the coffee table, where he had left it. As she studied the message on the screen, her mood darkened, and she gripped the Nokia so tightly that the plastic casing creaked in her hand.

Martin. I know the timing is bad, but I've decided that if you don't tell Phoebe about us, I will. Anna xx

Full of anger, she deleted the message and then replaced the phone where she had found it.

Martin returned, carrying a drink in one hand and a bag of popcorn in the other. "Thought we could treat ourselves to a little snack while we watched the film," he said, offering her the popcorn.

"No thanks," Phoebe replied, coldly. "I'm not hungry."

22

Sunday 29th July 2001
AN UNTIDY MESS ON THE FLOOR

Ben Cunningham was surprised to see Phoebe's car sitting in the drive when he went out to load his golf clubs into the back of the X5. "Jess," he called, walking quickly back into the house. "Phoebe's car's outside. When did she get home?"

Jessica emerged from the kitchen, wiping her hands on a towel. She shrugged, looking as bewildered as he felt. "I didn't know she was," she told him. "I didn't hear her come in, and I've been up since half seven, so it must have been before that."

Cunningham checked his chunky Breitling, which told him it was getting on for nine. His brow crinkled into a worried frown. "Do you think we should go up and check on her, to make sure that she's alright?" he asked, looking up at the ceiling.

Jessica shook her head. "No, dear, I don't. If you wake her up just to ask her that, she really won't thank you. Let her sleep in, and I'll speak to her when she surfaces. If anything's wrong, if they've had an argument or something, you'll probably find out from Martin long before she crawls out of her pit."

Cunningham grunted. "True. If I find anything out, I'll give you a call." Kissing Jessica on the cheek, he donned his sunglasses and set off.

"Drive safely and make sure you wear lots of sunblock," she called after him.

After starting the car, he cranked the air-con up to full. There wasn't a cloud in the sky, and it promised to be another glorious summer's day. He wondered how the course at Theydon was fairing in the unrelenting heat. If the green became too distressed, the grass could become thin and frail, in some cases dying off completely, which would make playing it less enjoyable. Hopefully, the groundsmen were on top of the situation and were keeping it well watered.

He would have to remember to drink lots; hydration was all-important in the heat. Before they set off, he would be sure to grab a couple of those fancy sports-type drinks that were always on sale in the golf shop, the ones with electrolytes. That should do the trick. At least he was wearing the right kit: loose fitting, lightweight material that was quick drying and didn't absorb sweat, and breathable golf shoes. He had also packed sun cream, a hat and his golfing umbrella.

During the six minute drive to Martin's flat, he tried to focus on the coming day, which he had been looking forward to for ages, but his mind kept drifting back to Phoebe's kidnapping. It was nothing short of a miracle that she had escaped unharmed, and he was so proud of her for having done so. Nonetheless, he couldn't shake the nagging fear that she would crash and burn at some point during the next few days, and he wondered if he ought to give her counsellor a discreet call in the morning, just to see what he advised.

Pulling up outside the entrance to Martin's block, Cunningham rang his future son-in-law to let him know that he was outside. They were already running slightly late, and he wanted to make the most of the day. There was no reply, so he gave it thirty seconds and redialled.

After the third unsuccessful attempt, he decided to go up and knock for him. Knowing Martin, he had his phone on silent and hadn't heard it ring. Either that, or he was in the loo.

Cunningham was out of breath by the time he reached the third floor. Fanning his face, he strode along the carpeted corridor until he reached Martin's flat. He rapped loudly on the door, which he noticed was slightly ajar. He assumed that Martin had deliberately left it like that because he'd seen the missed calls, looked out the window at the empty X5, and realised that Ben was on his way up. "Come on," he shouted, pushing the door open wide. "I haven't got all bloody day, and I don't want to be late teeing off."

There was no response from within.

Cunningham was an impatient man, and he could feel himself getting annoyed. Martin loved the game as much as he did, and he was usually ready and waiting for him when they went golfing together, so why was he dragging his heels today? Perhaps it had something to do with why Phoebe had come home during the night. They must have argued, he decided, and Martin was running late because he had hit the bottle and overslept.

Silly sod!

Cunningham walked into the entrance hall. "Martin, where the hell are you?" he shouted.

He poked his head around the kitchen door, but the room was empty. With a sigh of impatience, Cunningham crossed the hall and entered the lounge. "Earth calling Martin, where the hell–"

The remaining words choked in his throat.

Lying on the floor, his throat slit from ear to ear, Martin Whitling stared up at the ceiling through sightless eyes. A handful of candy coated chocolates had been scattered on the floor around his head, and a few of them had landed in the gaping wound below his jawline. In addition to having had his throat cut, Martin's body looked like it had been used as a pincushion.

It was just after eleven when Tyler and Dillon arrived at the crime scene. The call had originally been fielded by the on-call HAT car from Hendon in West London but, once the connection to Tyler's ongoing investigation had been established, the DCI from West had called him and requested his attendance.

After signing in with the cordon officer stationed outside the flat, the two detectives, now clad in full barrier clothing, entered. They were met in the hallway by DCI Kim Daily and Juliet Kennedy, both of whom were wearing white Tyvek suits and face masks.

"Nice to see you again, Kim," Tyler said, accepting the nitrile gloved hand that had been offered in greeting.

In her early forties, Daily was a short, slim woman, with piercing blue eyes. Her voice, when she spoke, was warm and friendly and full of humour. "Good to see you, too," she said, her words slightly muffled by the Victoria mask.

"So, what have we got?" he asked, looking around the tastefully decorated hallway and thinking that Whitling was doing pretty well for himself, or at least he had been, until someone had prematurely ended his life.

"We think this might be the work of the same bloke you're looking for," Daily said, getting straight to the point. "The victim's name is Martin Whitling, and he's the fiancé of Phoebe Cunningham. As you'll see for yourself in a minute, he's been stabbed to death in what can only be called a frenzied attack." She paused, allowing him a moment to digest this. "Oh, and just for good measure, his throat's been cut," she added as an afterthought.

Tyler grimaced. "What makes you so sure that Spencer did this?" he asked, although his gut told him that it couldn't be anyone else.

Daily glanced at Kennedy, inviting her to explain.

The CSM stepped forward, adjusted her mask and let out a bored sigh. "As you know, the incident on the bus started with Spencer throwing candy coated chocolates at the two shop workers who were sitting opposite him."

Tyler raised an enquiring eyebrow. "So...?"

"So," she said patiently, "whoever topped Whitling deliberately scattered a whole bag of them over his corpse. I'll have the sweets compared with those seized from the bus in due course, but I'm almost certain they're the same brand."

"You think he deliberately left the sweets as a calling card?" Dillon asked.

Juliet turned to look at him, shrugged. "Can't think of any other reason, can you?"

Dillon's paper suit rustled as he shook his massive head. "Not really."

"Is it possible that someone else could have killed Whitling, and then scattered the sweets over the body to divert attention away from themselves?" Tyler asked.

Kennedy's harsh laugh told him that he was grasping at straws with that one. "Not a chance, Jack," she said, dismissively. "The clustering of the stab wounds in the victim's torso mirror the pattern of attack we saw used on David Bannister."

"You say that," he objected, "but Bannister's throat wasn't cut."

"That's very true," Juliet allowed, "but he *was* stabbed in the neck. Also, you need to take into account the fact that Bannister was murdered in a public place, with lots of people watching. Maybe, here inside the flat, without witnesses to worry about, Spencer felt that he could take the time he needed to express himself more freely."

The thought left a nasty taste in Tyler's mouth, but he had to admit that the behaviour Juliet had just described was totally consistent with the way that serial killers generally evolved, committing increasingly violent crimes just to maintain the same thrill level.

"Let's go and have a look at the body, shall we?" Kennedy suggested. Without waiting for an answer, she led the way through to the lounge.

It was a really nice room; light and airy, and tastefully decorated. The furniture was expensive, if understated, and the place had an undeniable touch of class to it.

There were no obvious signs of a struggle: no damaged or overturned furniture, no smashed glasses or dented walls. Everything was neat and tidy. Well, everything apart from the blood-soaked corpse making an untidy mess on the expensive wooden flooring.

Arms and legs akimbo, and surrounded by a pool of blood, Whitling's body lay on its back, directly in front of the sofa. His grey tracksuit top was stained a deep, ugly red, and there were so many holes in it that it could easily have been mistaken for a string vest.

Bending over him, Tyler counted twelve separate stab wounds, although there could easily have been more. His eyes were drawn to the ragged tear across Whitling's throat. Like a second mouth, it gaped open in a cruel parody of a smile. The wound had exposed the vertebrae, and Tyler knew it would have taken considerable force to achieve that. "I see what you mean about a frenzy," he said, glancing unhappily at Daily, who was standing passively by his shoulder.

Straightening himself up, Tyler looked around the room, trying to fathom out exactly how Whitling had met his end. Had he been sitting on the sofa when Spencer attacked him, Tyler would have expected to see clear evidence of blood staining, not just on the cream coloured leather, but also on the cushions. As there was none, it seemed logical to conclude that both men had been standing.

In his mind's eye, he pictured Spencer rushing into the room and angrily confronting Whitling over Phoebe. The attack, when it came, would have been sudden and brutal, with Spencer repeatedly stabbing Whitling until he fell to his knees, weakened by a catastrophic loss of blood. He imagined Spencer leering down at him in triumph, telling Whitling that Phoebe was his and his alone, before callously shoving the wounded man backwards onto the floor. After that, it would have been a simple matter of kneeling down behind him and finishing the job off. The blood spatter around the body certainly seemed to support his theory.

Tyler looked up at Juliet Kennedy, who was watching him impassively. "The attack demonstrates a real display of rage on the killer's part," he told her, which fit perfectly with Phoebe Cunningham's description of Spencer as an insanely jealous man. "Juliet, in your professional opinion, was Whitling's throat cut first, or left until the end?"

"Definitely the latter," she said, moving forward to join him. "If you look at the arterial bleed, you can tell that he was lying flat on his back when the incision was made. Had he been standing up, the blood spatter would have started higher and spread further afield as he moved around." As she spoke, she used her arms to pantomime blood gushing from her own throat, waving them in the direction that it would have travelled to help him visualise what she was saying. "As you can see, it's relatively low and it's contained to one specific area. From that, I'm confident that Whitling was lying on the floor when it happened. Also, the blood leakage around the body is consistent with him already having been stabbed multiple times by that point. I'm guessing that the killer knelt behind him, placed one hand on his forehead to keep his head still, and then calmly leaned forward and sliced open his throat." She helpfully mimed doing this, too.

"Can we call out a BPA expert?" Tyler asked. "I think it might be helpful to see if they can recreate the attack from the angle and trajectory of the blood spatter."

"Already in hand," Kennedy assured him. "A Blood Pattern Analyst's en route from Lambeth as we speak."

Tyler stood up, moved away from the body. "Who found him?"

"Ben Cunningham," Daily said. "He called around to pick the victim up for a round of golf just after nine, and found him brown bread on the floor."

"Where's Cunningham now?" Tyler asked.

"We shipped him off to the local nick to seize his clothing and get a key witness statement from him. He wasn't a happy bunny, I can tell you."

Tyler could imagine. "What was he most annoyed about?" he asked, cynically. "Martin's death, missing out on his round of golf, or having his clothing seized?"

"Not sure, to be honest," Daily replied, and Tyler could hear the smile in her voice. "I didn't warm to the opinionated twat, so I got one of my DCs to whisk him away before I lost my temper with him."

Kim didn't have a lot of time for fools. Tyler liked that about her. "Any signs of a forced entry?" he asked.

"None," Daily confirmed. "So, either the suspect had a key, or the victim answered the door and then let him in. Oh, and there's no sign of a struggle or a search in any of the rooms, and nothing seems to be missing."

"I don't suppose there's any CCTV coverage in or around the building?" Dillon asked. He had remained by the door, doing his best to avoid getting too close to the body.

Beneath her mask, Daily's face scrunched up in disappointment. "Afraid not, Tony. Considering that this is an upmarket block, with lots of wealthy residents residing here, security is piss poor. There isn't even an entry buzzer system on the door, so anyone can just walk in."

"What about the murder weapon?" Tyler asked.

"We've only carried out a flash search, so far," Kennedy informed him, "but that hasn't turned up anything obvious."

Tyler grunted. "Why am I not surprised?"

"There is some good news though," Kennedy said, picking up on the disconsolate tone of his voice. She made a come hither gesture and walked over to the door, which was currently open.

Tyler followed obediently, stopping when she held her hand up.

"Ta-da!" Kennedy said, pushing the door too.

On the back, Tyler was surprised to see a clear red handprint.

"As you can see, our killer wasn't wearing gloves," Kennedy announced, "and he rather considerately left us a lovely little handprint to remember him by."

"Very thoughtful of him," Tyler agreed, grinning beneath his Victoria mask.

"I've been doing this job a long time now," Kennedy told him, "but I don't think I've ever seen a print with such clear swirls and ridges. We'll get it photographed, swabbed, and sent off for urgent analysis."

Tyler contemplated the gruesome hand mark for a few seconds. "The prints are going to belong to Spencer," he predicted.

"Which is why I called you," Daily said. "If this *is* his work, then Whitling's murder becomes part of a series you're already investigating, and it seems only right that your team should take the job on."

"I'll have to speak to George Holland first," Tyler said, "but I suspect you may be right."

"Looking at this from a practical point, how long will it take to get the prints compared?" Dillon asked.

Juliet considered this. "Well, as we're initially only asking The Yard to check the handprint against Spencer's record, and not run it through the entire system, we should get an answer back pretty quickly."

"Best you crack on with getting that organised," Tyler told her. "In the meantime, I'll give George Holland a ring. Kim, your team will have to hold the job until we get the fingerprint results, and I'd appreciate it if you can get some people started on the house-to-house enquiries. If Spencer's responsible for Whitling's murder, as seems likely, I'll obviously take the job on, and we can do a formal handover later this afternoon."

When Skippy awoke, he found that Spencer had sent him another text message overnight. This one read:

I've taken care of the opposition. She'll soon come running back to me now that he's out of the way.

Reading it a second time, he frowned at the screen. What was that supposed to mean?

The message was timed at 02:06 hours.

He tried ringing Spencer back but, as usual, the mobile was switched off. With no other option, he angrily tapped out a text message.

WTF does that mean? Ring me U muppet.

An ear piercing scream echoed through the flat, and everyone inside the crime scene paused for a moment, looking back towards the street door. The anguished howl had come from the corridor outside.

"What the hell was that?" Kim Daily asked.

"From the sound of it," Tyler said, "I would hazard a guess that Ben Cunningham's passed on the news of Whitling's death to his family, and his daughter's rushed over to see if it's true."

Beneath her Victoria mask, Daily's face crinkled in annoyance. "Well, I'm sure the cordon officer can deal with it."

"We're finished here now, anyway," Tyler informed her. "I'll have a quick word with her on my way out."

Dillon cast him a 'do we have to?' look but said nothing.

Waving goodbye to Daily and Kennedy, Tyler beckoned to his friend to follow and then set off to investigate the source of the screaming. As he emerged from the flat, removing his face mask and pulling the hood of his Tyvek coveralls down, he was surprised to see that it wasn't Phoebe Cunningham standing there, but rather Anna Manson, and her tear-stained face was distorted in unspeakable pain.

"I'm sorry, miss," the cordon officer was saying as sympathetically as he could, "but this is a crime scene, and I can't let you inside."

Anna was close to hysteria. "But it can't be true," she sobbed. "He *can't* be dead. Ben must have made a dreadful mistake."

Tyler walked over. "It's Miss Manson, isn't it?" he enquired, much to the relief of the cordon officer, who promptly took a backward step, leaving Tyler to deal with her.

Anna nodded, staring up at him forlornly. "Didn't I see you at the house last night?" she asked between sobs.

Tyler smiled, doing his best to put her at ease. "That's right. I'm DCI Tyler, and this is DI Dillon."

Acknowledging Dillon with a tearful nod, she sniffled into a soggy tissue.

"May I ask what you're doing here?" Tyler enquired, gently.

"Ben... Ben called me a little while ago," she informed him in a quivering voice. "He told... he told me that..." She shook her head, unable to continue.

Tyler leaned in and gave her arm a gentle squeeze. "It's okay," he said, knowing that it was anything but. "Take your time."

Anna nodded gratefully, blew her nose like a trumpet, and tried again. "Ben said... Ben said that he found Martin dead in his flat this morning, murdered in the most horrible way. Please tell me he's wrong."

Her eyes were imploring him to tell her it was all a big mistake, and the sheer desperation in her trembling voice brought a lump to Tyler's throat. There was no doubting that she was deeply in love with Whitling, and there was no easy way to break the news to her. He took a deep breath. "I'm so sorry to have to tell you this, but I'm afraid that Mr Whitling was murdered in his flat during the night."

Anna stared at him in disbelief for a moment, and then she let out a tortured howl and fell to her knees.

Taking an arm each, the detectives helped her back to her feet. "I'm so sorry for your loss," Tyler said, guiding her along the corridor and away from the crime scene.

She had made so much noise that several residents had opened their doors to check on the commotion. "Go back inside, please," Dillon instructed them. "There's nothing to see here."

Outside, in the fresh air, they gave her a few moments to compose herself before speaking to her again. "Did you have any further contact with Mr Whitling, after he drove away from the Cunningham's place last night?" Tyler asked when she had finally pulled herself together.

Anna nodded. "Yes. We had a brief telephone conversation about ten minutes after he left, and then I went home to bed. I was having breakfast when Ben called me, and I couldn't believe it, so I got dressed and rushed straight over."

"I see," Tyler said, studying her face intently. "I don't suppose you happen to know if anyone else had any contact with Martin between his leaving the Cunningham's house and his body being discovered this morning, do you?"

Anna stared up at him blankly for a moment, before nodding.

"You should speak to Phoebe," she said. "She spent the night with him as far as I know."

The two detectives shared a look, and Dillon slipped away to check with the cordon officer, to see if Phoebe had been present when the first responders arrived. Somehow, Tyler doubted it; Kim Daily would have told him if that had been the case.

Dillon returned a few seconds later and shook his head. "The only person here when the locals arrived was Ben Cunningham," he whispered.

"Miss Manson, forgive me for being so direct, but this is a murder investigation so there's no time to tread lightly around the subject. Were you and Mr Whitling romantically involved?"

A look of guilt flashed across Anna's face, answering his question before she had even opened her mouth. "We... That's to say..."

"It's okay," Tyler said quickly. "I'm not here to judge you, but I do need to know, in case it's relevant to the enquiry."

Anna stared at him intently, searching for signs of insincerity. A tight smile briefly pulled at her cheeks when she didn't find any, and she let out a deflated sigh. "We were in love," she blurted out tearfully. "He was going to leave Phoebe. He was just waiting for the right moment to tell her."

That was interesting. "Does Phoebe know about the relationship?" Tyler asked.

Anna was struggling to open a new tissue, which was badly needed to replace the waterlogged one in her other hand. "Not as far as I'm aware," she lamented. "When I called him last night, we had a terrible argument about it. Afterwards, I messaged him to say that, if he didn't hurry up and tell her, I would." Sucking in air, she stared up at the ceiling and blinked away the falling tears. "I can't believe that he's gone," she sobbed, "and that the last words we ever exchanged were angry ones, full of bitterness and recrimination."

23

AWKWARD CONVERSATIONS

"Are you ready to begin?" Evans asked with an encouraging smile.

Phoebe started, as though having been woken from a dream, but she recovered quickly. "What? Oh, yes, sorry."

Because the taking of her key witness statement needed to be recorded, they were having to use one of the interview rooms in the custody suite at Leyton police station. Taking her statement under such stringent conditions was necessary, he had explained when he'd collected her from her parent's house, because she was the last known person – apart from the killer – to have seen Martin Whitling alive.

The interview room was windowless and stuffy, and it reeked of body odour and guilt. The padding in the chairs they were sitting on was almost non-existent, leaving him in no doubt that they would both have numb bums before too long. "I'm sorry I've had to bring you in here," he told her, "but this is the only place in the station that's equipped with recording equipment."

"That's okay," she said, looking around the depressingly drab room. "It could use a lick of paint, though."

It could use several licks, Evans thought as he smiled at her. A can of air freshener wouldn't go amiss, either. "Do you need to use the loo before we start?"

Phoebe shook her head. "No, thank you," she said, slouching down in her chair and trying to get comfortable.

Good luck with that!

"If you can try and avoid leaning on that," Evans said, hurriedly pointing to a thin strip of dark rubber that protruded from the wall at the exact point where she was about to lean on it, "I would be very grateful. Only it's a panic alarm, and if you accidentally set it off, a load of burly coppers will come rushing in and tell me off."

Phoebe carefully repositioned herself. "Of course," she said, offering him a polite smile. "I really hope that this isn't going to take too long, only I'm keen to get back to my family so that we can mourn Martin's passing together."

"I completely understand," Evans assured her. "I'll be as quick as I can."

There was no 'one size fits all' method to conducting an interview. Sometimes, you had to go in hard. On other occasions, you had to proceed as though you were treading on eggshells. Sometimes, all you had to do was ask them what they knew, and then sit there quietly while they spilled their guts and told you everything. There were also times where just getting a person to confirm their name and date of birth was like trying to draw blood from a stone.

Evans had a real knack for reading micro expressions and, from what he had seen of her so far, he suspected that Phoebe Cunningham was the type who would instantly clam up if he put her under too much pressure, so he decided to take things slowly until he gained her trust. "Are you sure you don't want a cup of tea or coffee?" he asked.

An economic shake of her head. "I'm fine, thank you."

"Then let's begin," he said, pressing the red button that set the tape recording. He waited until the long beep that told him the machine was working properly had finished, and then went through the tedious introduction process, explaining what they were doing and what would happen with the end product when they were finished. "So, as I said before, you're here as a witness, not a suspect, and as such you're free to leave at any time. Now, Phoebe, can you please tell me a little about your relationship to Martin Whitling."

"Why is that relevant to his murder?" she asked, folding her arms obstructively.

It was a subconscious act of resentment, signalling her reluctance to discuss intimate or sensitive issues with him. Evans knew he would have to tread carefully if he was going to coax the information he needed from her. "I know it's hard," he said, "and it may seem totally irrelevant to you, but we really need to get a picture of your relationship if we're to understand whether that had any impact on the killer's motivation for murdering Martin."

"Of course it bloody well did," she snapped, her face flushing with anger. "We both know that John Spencer killed Martin to hit back at me. I warned DCI Craddock that he would do this, but he didn't listen to me. No one *ever* listens to me, and I'm sick of it." Phoebe slammed the table with the palm of her hand. "I'm so, so sick of it."

Evans had picked up on the inflection in the word 'ever' and he made a mental note to revisit the comment later in the interview. "Okay," he said with a smile of encouragement, "let's park that topic for the moment and switch to what happened last night. Tell me everything, from the moment you arrived at Martin's flat."

Phoebe fidgeted uncomfortably in her seat, sighed impatiently. "I arrived about twenty minutes after Martin did. He'd already changed into a tracksuit and was lounging on the sofa, waiting for me. He'd had a couple of drinks by then, but he wasn't squiffy. When I sat down with him to watch *Four Weddings and a Funeral*, he decided to pop into the kitchen for a refill, and while he was out of the room a message came through on his phone." She shrugged. "As he wasn't there, I opened it for him."

Evans raised an eyebrow. "Do you normally do that?" he asked.

Phoebe crossed her legs. "Not normally, but it was right in front of me on the coffee table, and I could see from the caller ID that the message was from Anna, so I was curious. After all, there was no reason that she should be texting him at that time of night."

Her voice had become defensive, he noticed. "I see, and can you tell me what the message said?"

Phoebe's eyes clouded, became guarded, and her mouth compressed into a thin line. "It's personal," she said.

"I'm sorry, Phoebe, but it can't be. We need to know, and we'll find out anyway when we look at his phone, so you might as well save us some time and tell me now."

"I deleted the message," she said, staring at him defiantly.

Evans found that strange, but didn't challenge her about it. If any challenges were necessary, they would come later, after he had given her a chance to say everything that she wanted to. "Not a problem," he told her. "Even if it's deleted from the phone, we can obtain it from the service provider."

That seemed to shock her. "Fine," she said, with a huff. "It basically said that, if he didn't tell me about their affair, she would."

Ouch! Now Evans understood why she hadn't wanted to talk about this. It would have been extremely painful for her. "I'm sorry to hear that," he said gently. "Was that the first that you knew of the matter, or did you already suspect?"

Phoebe barked out a mirthless laugh. "No, I already knew. I'd suspected that something was going on between them for a while, but I'd only known for sure since Wednesday, when I walked in on them kissing at the cottage in Diss."

Double ouch! "What did they say when that happened?" he asked.

She shook her head, wearily. "Nothing. They were so engrossed in each other that they didn't even notice me. I slipped out of the room straight away, and I haven't said anything about it to either of them since, as I wanted some time to decide what to do for the best."

"So, what happened last night, after you deleted the message?" Evans asked.

"When he came back from fetching his drink, we watched the

film. I didn't say anything at first but, in the end, it was just festering inside me, so I confronted him about it. He confessed all, broke down in tears and said that he'd made a terrible mistake and that he wanted to give us another go. He promised he would call Anna in the morning and break things off with her."

"How did you react to that?"

"Angrily. I told him I wasn't sure if I wanted him anymore, not after his betrayal. In the end, I got dressed and drove home. I told him I needed a few days to think things over, and that I'd contact him when I was ready to talk."

"What time did you leave?" Evans enquired.

A sluggish shrug. "I don't know for sure. Midnight, maybe. Possibly half past."

"And when you left, did you see anyone loitering around outside, or anything to make you think that he might be in any danger?"

She snorted at that. "I'd just had a blistering argument with him about his infidelity. I wasn't thinking about his safety when I left. I was too busy trying to hold my shit together to give a damn about him or anyone else."

The result of the fingerprint comparisons came back from The Yard within a couple of hours of being submitted. Sure enough, the bloodied hand mark that Kennedy had found on the inside of Whitling's lounge door belonged to John Anthony Spencer. There was no longer any doubt that he was their murderer, and the motive for the attack seemed glaringly obvious: He had been getting rid of the opposition. The question was, now that Whitling was out of the way, would he target anyone else?

"We'll need to carry out a detailed risk assessment on Phoebe's parents," Tyler told Susie, who was sitting in his office along with Dillon and Steve Bull. "And we'll need to get someone around there straight away to warn them that they might be in danger."

"Cunningham won't be pleased," Dillon predicted. "He'll demand around the clock protection, you know that?"

Tyler nodded, pensively. "I'm fully expecting him to," he admitted, "and I think we're going to have to agree to that, under the circumstances. Or at least to posting an officer at the front of the address for a few days, until we catch the deranged bastard."

Steve Bull let out a long, disgruntled sigh. "I suppose, as Case Officer, it's only fair that I prepare the risk assessment," he said without enthusiasm. The forms were a complete nightmare, and they required a language all of their own to complete.

"Good man," Tyler said. "For now, limit it to her parents and their home in Wanstead. From what I can gather, apart from Whitling, they're the only people that Spencer specifically referred to when he made his veiled threats to Phoebe at the barn."

"Do you want me to go and pay the Cunninghams a visit?" Susie offered. "To discuss safety issues and such."

Tyler paused for a moment before answering. "I'll tell you what," he said. "Why don't we go together?" That would give him the opportunity he had been looking for to have a quiet chat with her, so that he could satisfy himself that she was coping okay following the separation from her husband.

"If you like," she replied, shooting him a quizzical look.

"Let me make a couple of calls first, to let George Holland and Kim Daily know about the fingerprint ident, and confirm that we'll be taking the job, and then we can be on our way."

"While you do that I'll put in a call to the local Duty Officer and arrange for a uniform presence to be posted outside the Cunningham's address until further notice," Dillon offered.

———

"So, how are you enjoying life as a DI?" Tyler asked. They were on their way to visit the Cunninghams in Wanstead.

Susie glanced sideways at him. "I'm enjoying it very much," she told him, truthfully.

"Good," he said with a warm smile. He cleared his throat, wondering how best to broach the awkward topic of her separation. Having been through this himself, he knew how thorny a subject it was, and the last thing he wanted to do was poke his nose in where it wasn't wanted. That said, Susie had been a bit subdued lately, which was totally unlike her, and he wanted to make sure she was okay.

"Is there something you want to say to me?" she asked him abruptly, and he could feel her green eyes boring into him suspiciously. "Only, if there is, stop beating about the bush and come out with it."

Tyler grinned, sheepishly. Not much got past Susie. "I just wanted to make sure that you were okay," he told her, feeling clumsy and a little embarrassed. "You know, after splitting up from Dan."

Susie leaned back against the headrest, closed her eyes, and let out a long sigh. "To be honest, Jack, I don't know what to tell you. I'm functioning fine if that's what you mean, but I just feel numb inside. I still can't believe he did the dirty deed on me. A part of me wants to cut his balls off with a rusty knife, but another part of me really wants him to come back. You have no idea how angry I am with myself for being so pathetically weak that I would even contemplate allowing him to do that."

She was wrong. Tyler understood her feelings all too well. "I've been there," he said. "Well, except in my case I wanted to cut Eddie's balls off, not Jenny's," he added with a wry smile.

"What's making it worse is that he's not answering any of my calls or text messages, and I really need to talk to him, so that we can sort out what's going to happen to the house and our joint finances."

Tyler considered this. "Perhaps, that's exactly why he's putting off speaking to you, because he knows that, when he eventually does, it's going to be a conversation that makes the split final. Maybe, on some subliminal level, he doesn't really want things to end, and he's trying to work out what to do for the best before he reaches the point of no return."

Susie's eyes blazed, and a hard edge crept into her voice, making her sound quite scary. "Are you seriously suggesting that the cheating little swine's avoiding me so that he can come back and resume playing happy families once his fling's over?"

Tyler said nothing, but that was exactly what he secretly thought. He didn't know Dan Sergeant particularly well. They had never worked together, and had only spoken to each other in passing at work related functions. Truth be told, he had never warmed to the man and had only ever tolerated his company out of respect for Susie.

"Well, once he's finished fucking her, he can go and fuck himself," she said angrily. "I just want to make a clean break and start anew."

"Well then, maybe the time has come to instruct a solicitor?" he suggested.

Susie folded her arms and stared out of the window. "Maybe," she said, miserably.

―――――

They met at a rundown pub in Stratford. It was a rough place, well frequented by the local criminal classes and avoided by pretty much everyone else. Inside, the windows were shuttered and the lighting was subdued. The threadbare carpet was tacky underfoot, and the mawkish smell of warm beer filled the air.

A middle-aged stripper with sagging breasts and stretch marks was gyrating around a dancing pole on the stage, illuminated by a solitary spotlight, and both men leered at her while they waited to be served. After purchasing their beers, they waited for the stripper to finish her act and then retreated to a table in a quiet corner at the rear of the premises before she could come around with her collection jar and accost them for tips.

"Nice to see you again," Skippy said, clinking his glass against G-Man's.

"You too, mate," G-Man responded, gruffly. His shifty eyes traversed the room as he spoke, making sure that no one was close enough to overhear their conversation. Seemingly satisfied, he took a deep glug of his drink, and then wiped away the frothy moustache that had formed on his top lip with the back of his hand.

Even in the darkness, Skippy noticed how sallow his drinking companion's complexion had become. G-Man had obviously started hitting the gear pretty hard since his release from prison.

"You're looking well," G-Man said.

"You too," Skippy lied.

G-Man suffered from benign essential blepharospasm and hemifacial spasm, which meant that his left eye and the muscles surrounding it would suddenly begin twitching wildly for no apparent reason. When they had first met in prison, Skippy had found it most disconcerting, until he'd realised that the sudden bouts of winking were down to a medical condition and not a case of G-Man coming on to him.

"What happened to your noggin?" G-Man asked, tapping his own forehead as he spoke.

"I walked into a door," Skippy said, self-consciously touching the huge bump that protruded from the centre of his head like the beginnings of a unicorn's horn.

G-Man smirked. "Course you did."

Skippy retreated further into the shadows to make his injured head less conspicuous. "Pity about Honest Steve," he said, changing the subject.

G-Man grunted. "Yeah, I know. Still, life goes on, eh?"

"It does, mate."

G-Man studied his drink for a few moments. "So, to what do I owe the pleasure of your company?" he eventually asked.

Skippy leaned forward, lowered his voice. "I wanted to talk to you about a tasty little job that I'm about to pull off. It'll be worth a shed lot of money, but I can't do it on my own. I was planning to work with my cousin, Spencer, but the wanker's got the Old Bill breathing down his neck at the moment–"

"So I've heard."

"–so I was wondering if you wanted in?"

After another furtive glance around the room, G-Man leaned across the table. "Sounds very interesting," he said as his left eye started twitching, "but I need your help with a little job of my own, first."

Skippy tensed. "Nah, you don't understand," he said, shaking his head fiercely. "My job's *really* important, and it's got to be done this week or it'll be too late."

"My job's important, too," G-Man countered.

"But–"

Cutting him off with a raised hand. "Listen, Skip, you know that armed robbery Honest Steve and Mad Micky just got done for?" he whispered. "Well, I was in on it with them. It was my mate who put up the information. Anyway, he called me again on Friday with news of an even better job. Trouble is, it's a one off and it needs to be done on Tuesday morning. I'm gonna need a good wheelman and, with Honest Steve out of action, you're the next best getaway driver that I know."

Skippy glared at him, unimpressed. "Cheeky git! What do you mean, the *next* best getaway driver you know? I'm every bit as good as Honest Steve."

"Listen Skip, I ain't talking peanuts. This blagging's worth a hundred grand to us, and the best part is that the money won't be in those poxy booby-trapped cash-in-transit bags like the last job. This time, it'll be loaded in old fashioned money sacks, which means we won't have to worry about damaging the cash when we open them."

Skippy's eyes lit up with avarice. "A hundred grand? How much would my cut be?"

G-Man shrugged. "Dunno for sure. There'll be three of us doing the robbery, and my mate gets an equal share for putting the job up. We'll split the takings four ways so, as long as my mate's information is solid, you're looking at twenty five grand."

Twenty five grand! That was more than enough to pay off his debts to Jonas Willard. "Where's the job?" he asked, suddenly eager to know more.

G-Man shook his head. "No more details until I know you're in."

It was a no-brainer, but Skippy pretended to think it over for a few seconds so that G-Man wouldn't realise just how desperate he was. "Alright," he eventually said. "I'm in. I'll put my job on the back burner until we've pulled this one. If our little partnership pans out, we can come back to my job in a couple of weeks' time."

"I'll drink to that," G-Man said, extending his glass so that they could toast the agreement.

———

"How did you get on with interviewing Phoebe Cunningham?" Dillon asked.

Paul Evans was sitting at his desk in the main office. With a contemplative sigh, he leaned back in his seat and opened his daybook to review the extensive notes he had made. "To be honest, guv, I didn't warm to her at all," he admitted.

Dillon perched himself on the end of Evans' desk. That was unlike Paul. He normally only saw the best in people. "Really? Why's that?"

Evans considered his reply carefully. "Hard to put my finger on it, but I've interviewed a lot of people over the years; suspects, victims and witnesses alike, and there was definitely something off-kilter about her. She said all the right things, but there was a coldness to her, a remoteness, that made me feel uncomfortable."

"It's hardly surprising that she's become a bit detached, not after everything she's been through."

Evans shrugged. "Maybe," he allowed, but he didn't sound overly convinced.

"Try putting yourself in her position," Dillon suggested. "When she was only fourteen, she was abducted, held captive, and repeatedly raped. I dread to imagine how much psychological damage that must have caused her. Then, eight years later, the same man kidnaps her again. As if that's not enough, her fiancé and best friend were having it off behind her back and, the day after confronting him about it, he's found dead, murdered by the man who abducted her. That's got to have screwed her up a little, so maybe we should cut her some slack."

Evans still wasn't sold. "I get all that," he said, "but I'm telling you, there is something not right about that girl."

Dillon had tremendous respect for Evans. The man was one of the best interviewers he had ever met. He was intuitive, and he rarely misread anyone, but Phoebe Cunningham's circumstances were so out of the ordinary that Dillon doubted the normal rules of engagement applied to her. "Was she able to shed any light on Whitling's killing?" he asked.

Evans shook his head. "No, I'm afraid not. To be fair to her, after confronting him about Manson's text message, she stormed off back to her parents. She told me her last words to him were, 'I hate you and I wish you were dead.'"

Dillon winced. "Well, she certainly got her wish. God! Can you imagine how fucked up her head must be after that? It's no wonder that she was a bit cold when you interviewed her, is it?"

Evans sighed. "Not when you put it like that," he relented.

Anna Manson lived in a small terraced house in Leytonstone. She had lived there for almost a year now and, while the place still needed a lot of work doing to it, she loved it. Being an only child, she had inherited her parents' entire estate, which consisted of a four bedroom detached house in Cornwall and thirty thousand pounds, following their untimely death. She hadn't felt able to sell the house, which her parents had adored, so she had rented it out instead, and was using the income to pay for the mortgage on her London home.

There were only two bedrooms, a good sized double and a single that barely had enough space for a bed and a wardrobe to coexist in. Downstairs, there was a large lounge, a small dining room, and a reasonably sized kitchen. The garden, all eighty feet of it, was an overgrown mess that badly needed to be cut back, but that was right at the bottom of her list of things to do.

Anna had returned straight home after leaving the crime scene earlier in the day. In a state of shock, she had sat on her bed and cried until there were no tears left to fall.

Jessica had been calling her all afternoon, and she had invited her to come over and be with them so that they could all mourn Martin's passing together. Phoebe was devastated by her loss, Jessica had explained, and she needed Anna's support, as well as their own, during this most difficult of times. Feeling truly awful for lying, Anna had claimed to be unwell, but she had promised to come over the following day as long as she was feeling better.

The doorbell suddenly rang, and its sharp, intrusive melody startled Anna. She wasn't expecting anyone, and she really wasn't in the mood for visitors. Pulling the net curtain aside, she glanced out of the large bay window in the lounge and was gobsmacked to see Phoebe standing there, arms folded, foot tapping impatiently. Releasing the curtain, she quickly ducked behind the nearest wall before her friend saw her.

Anna closed her eyes, conscious that her pounding heart was beating faster by the second. She really didn't want to see Phoebe. Although she knew she was being selfish, she wanted to spend a few hours grieving for her lover in private, not putting on a brave face to comfort her friend. Her secret grief was every bit as painful as Phoebe's, but the girl at the door was her best friend, her surrogate sister, and she was obviously in dire need of Anna's support.

With a resigned sigh, Anna sluggishly moved away from the wall just as Phoebe rang the doorbell a second time. "Coming," she called, her voice reduced to timid squeak.

She paused in the hall to examine her reflection in the mirror. Her eyes were red-rimmed, and her face was all puffy from crying. "God, what a mess," she moaned, hurriedly running her hands through her hair to make it look a bit more presentable.

The bell rang for a third time, a sustained trill of impatience.

"I said I was coming," she called out.

Taking a deep breath, Anna opened the door and stood aside to allow Phoebe in. "How are you?" she asked as her friend walked through to the kitchen, which was at the rear of the property, backing onto her jungle of a garden.

"How do you think?" Phoebe replied, listlessly.

Anna was struck by how serene Phoebe was, until it occurred to her that Whitling's death probably hadn't hit home yet. When it did, Phoebe would implode, and she would need all the support that she could get. Putting her own needs aside, Anna walked over to Phoebe and gave her an awkward hug. "I'm so sorry about Martin," she said in a wobbly voice. "After everything else that you've been through, this must feel like such a terrible blow." Releasing her friend, she crossed to the fridge. "Would you like a cup of coffee, or would you prefer something a little stronger?" As she spoke, she reached inside and removed a bottle of white wine.

Phoebe pointed at the bottle. "Wine. Make it a large one."

Anna removed a couple of glasses from a cupboard above the worktop and poured them both a liberal amount. A weak smile. "Shall we go through to the lounge?"

They made themselves comfortable on the faux leather sofa, and Anna turned the volume down on the stereo so that they could talk without having to raise their voices.

She had been listening to her favourite R.E.M album and, very poignantly, *Everybody Hurts* had just begun to play. Just hearing the opening words was enough to make her well up. Martin had once told her that the song was about someone who was contemplating suicide, and without him in her life, that was exactly what she felt like doing. Anna blinked the tears away. "Phoebe, I know there's nothing I can say to lessen your pain, but I really want you to know that–"

"I know all about you and Martin," Phoebe said, cutting her off.

Anna blanched, and her stomach did a little somersault. "What? I don't know what you mean. I–"

"Cut the bullshit," Phoebe said, angrily. "I know you two were having an affair."

Anna sat there in stunned silence, staring down at the glass in her hand. She knew she ought to deny the allegation, for Phoebe's sake, but she just didn't have the energy. "When did you find out?" she asked.

Phoebe's voice was brittle. "On the day that I escaped from the barn. I walked in on the pair of you when you were kissing at the cottage."

Anna's face flushed with shame. "I'm so sorry," she whispered, almost choking on the words.

Phoebe regarded her with unconcealed loathing. "Sorry for being caught, you mean." The bitterness in her words stung far worse than any slap ever could.

A tear ran down Anna's cheek and she quickly brushed it away. "I swear we didn't mean for it to happen," she sobbed. "Neither of us ever wanted to hurt you, but we fell in love and couldn't help ourselves."

Phoebe's laugh was harsh. "He wasn't in love with you, you stupid girl," she said with a contemptuous sneer. "He was going to dump you."

Anna gasped. "You're wrong," she said, shaking her head fiercely. The tears were flowing freely now. "He was going to leave you as soon as he found the right moment to tell you. He promised me."

Phoebe stared back at her with contempt. "I saw the message you sent him last night," she said. "We spoke, and he told me that you meant nothing to him, and that he was going to end it with you today." A cold smile of triumph flickered across her face. "So, you see, in the end, he was mine, not yours."

"That's a lie," Anna snapped, becoming angry. Martin would *never* have said that. She appreciated that Phoebe was hurting badly, but was there really any need for her to be that nasty? Her grip on her wine glass tightened until there was a little clink, and the stem broke in two, spilling what was left of her wine all over her lap.

"It's not a lie," Phoebe gloated, standing up and placing her glass on the little table next to the sofa. "Deep down, you know that every word I'm telling you is the truth. You were never more than a notch on his bedpost, a meaningless fling, and everything he promised you was hollow, a pack of lies to get you to open your cellulite-ridden legs for him."

"Stop it!" Anna yelled, springing to her feet. "Get out." She pointed towards the door. "Get out of my house, right now!"

24

TOO MANY LOOSE ENDS

Tyler hated press conferences, and he was glad that George Holland had offered to do all the talking. Good old George was far more diplomatic about these things than he was.

They were in the media briefing room at NSY, and the press had turned out in impressive numbers. "Not the way I envisaged spending my Sunday evening," he whispered to Susie Sergeant, who was sitting next to him.

"Me neither," she admitted with a wry grin.

George Holland was escorted into the room by the Press Liaison Officer, a pencil-thin man in his mid-twenties who exuded nervous energy from every pore. His name was Archie, and Tyler had first encountered him a couple of years back, while investigating the Whitechapel murders. In those days, Archie had been a fresh-faced newbie, straight out of university, and he had been full of enthusiasm and drive, determined to change the world for the better. Since then, however, he had become as jaded as everyone else in the Press

Bureau, and he looked distinctly pissed off at having been called into The Yard on a Sunday evening to organise a last-minute press conference for the Homicide Command.

"Evening," Holland said brusquely, as he took his seat beside Tyler.

Tyler was just about to respond when he saw Imogen Askew slip into the room and sidle up to Archie. His face darkened. What was she doing there?

"Right, leave all the talking to me, but be prepared to answer questions at the end," Holland instructed, shuffling his notes on the desk in front of him.

"How come that TV researcher's here?" Tyler asked, nodding at Askew.

Holland cast him a sideways glance. "Imogen asked me to call her if anything happened over the weekend," he replied, stiffly. "She wants to get a feeling for what we do on the Homicide Command prior to commencing filming."

Tyler raised a worried eyebrow. "Filming? What filming?"

Holland tutted. "I told you, her company's making a documentary about one of my old cases," he said, tetchily. "They're also considering commissioning a fly-on-the-wall type show about murder investigations in general, and their producer asked me if there's any possibility of them sending a film crew out to shadow the HAT car one week, you know, to show the world what happens during the initial stages of an investigation."

Tyler was appalled. "You've turned them down, right?"

"Actually, I'm giving the idea serious consideration," Holland replied in a clipped tone that suggested it would be extremely unwise of Tyler to question his judgement. "After all, it wouldn't do us any harm to get some positive publicity for once."

Not trusting himself to say anything constructive, Tyler merely grunted.

Susie elbowed him and, when he looked in her direction, she fixed him with a disparaging scowl. "Play nice," she mouthed, nodding towards Holland.

Gritting his teeth, he said, "No, sir, we could do with all the good publicity we can get."

"Indeed," Holland replied, skimming through his briefing notes.

Beside him, Susie smiled approvingly.

Moving to the middle of the room, Archie clapped his hands to get everyone's attention. "Right, if everyone's ready, I think it's time to get started," he announced.

As everyone took their allotted seats, the room fell into expectant silence.

On either side of the table they were sitting at, the lights that had been rigged up for the cameras exploded into life like mini supernovas. Caught off guard, Tyler squinted against the sudden, painful glare and it took several seconds for his eyes to adjust.

Clearing his throat, Holland ran his eyes over the assembled reporters and film crews. "Good evening ladies and gentlemen," he began, addressing them in a suitably solemn voice.

The journalists shifted in their plastic seats, leaning forward and hoping for something disturbingly graphic. The gorier the better as far as they were concerned. Gore was good; it sold newspapers and raised ratings. What they didn't want was a recapitulation of the same bland rhetoric that had been spouted at every other murder related press conference they'd attended.

"I'm Detective Chief Superintendent George Holland from the Met's Homicide Command, and I'm here this evening to appeal for the public's help in finding a man who is wanted in connection with the murder of two men here in London, and the abduction of a young woman in Norfolk. His name is John Anthony Spencer, and he was last sighted yesterday evening in the Wanstead area of East London. Spencer is considered extremely dangerous, and should not be approached by the public. Anyone with information about his current whereabouts is urged to contact the incident room directly. Alternatively, they can provide information via Crimestoppers. All calls will be treated in the strictest of confidence and..."

Blah, blah, blah!

As Holland continued, cameras clicked and whirled, and there was an endless succession of flashes. Tyler sat there in silence, hating every second of it. Finally, the time came for the press to have their question and answer session. As a flurry of hands went up, Archie glanced around the room and then pointed at a distinguished looking woman in the front row.

"Anthea Barrington. Independent News. Detective Chief Superintendent, can you tell us why you haven't been able to find The Candy Killer when you've known his identity for several days now?" she asked, bathing him in a saccharine smile.

Predictably, Holland deflected this in Tyler's direction.

Tyler took a deep breath, determined not to react to the woman's provocative use of Spencer's nom de guerre. "Firstly, can I reiterate my colleague's comments by saying that any calls received will be treated in the strictest confidence, and urge anyone with any information to come forward immediately. Secondly, let me assure you that every effort is being made to locate and arrest John Spencer and that considerable resources have been allocated to this investigation."

"Yes, but are those resources enough?" Barrington shot back. "The fact that he's killed twice within the space of a week suggests otherwise."

"I'm afraid that we only have time for one question each," Archie admonished her, clearly annoyed that she had breached protocol.

"That's okay," Tyler said with a strained smile. "I want to assure the public that everything that can be done is being done."

Still tutting at Barrington, Archie pointed at another reporter, indicating that it was his turn to ask a question.

"Bradley Oaks. The London Echo. What happens if The Candy Killer strikes again?" Oaks was a middle-aged man with a shiny bald patch and curly moustache, and he spoke with a smarmy voice. "What precautions should the general public be taking to safeguard themselves against attack?"

Tyler took an instant dislike to the man, who was deliberately scaremongering. He glanced at Holland to see if he wanted to field this one, but his boss signalled for him to handle it.

Great!

"While I can't discuss the specifics of the investigation, let me be clear that we don't believe the abduction or the second murder were random attacks. We think that Mr Spencer had a grudge against specific individuals, and that the risk to the general public is minimal." As soon as the words left his mouth, he regretted saying them. If Spencer killed again, the press would immediately regurgitate his comment and use it against him.

Archie allowed several more questions before calling the conference to a halt, and Tyler did his best to answer them without actually saying anything that he might later regret.

"Well, that wasn't too bad," Holland said when it was all over.

Tyler snorted. "I think I might have dropped the ball when the bloke who looked like a walrus started going on about what happens if Spencer kills again."

"Don't worry about it," Holland told him. "As long as you catch him before he does, it won't be a problem."

Skippy pulled up outside the little post office in Lea Bridge Road. It was getting on for ten o'clock, but he was too hyped up to relax. Besides, he wanted to scope the place out properly, so that he could work out the best escape route to take after committing the robbery.

The nearest police station was a good couple of miles away so, unless a patrol car just happened to be passing by when G-Man and his buddy pulled the robbery, they should have plenty of time to make good their escape.

The post office itself was a small establishment, one of those places that doubled as a corner shop, so security wouldn't be anywhere near as tight as it was in some of the bigger branches, and that should work in their favour.

Skippy was hugely excited about the robbery. It couldn't have come along at a more opportune time for him and, if G-Man's contact was right about how much cash would be on the premises when they pulled the job, he would be able to pay off his debt to Jonas Willard that same night. Once the loan shark was out of his hair, he would be able to take his time fine tuning the kidnapping plan. As he pulled away, Skippy felt happier than he had in a long time. Things were definitely starting to look up and, as long as Spencer didn't suddenly show up and throw a spanner in the works, everything should slot nicely into place for him.

Phoebe felt utterly drained as she climbed into bed. It was hard to believe that Martin really was gone for good, and that he would never walk through that door or share her bed ever again. For a moment, the rawness of her pain was unbearable; the knowledge that she would never see him again, never hold him close, left her feeling bereft. But then she pictured him kissing Anna, and her sadness morphed into anger and resentment. She would never forgive him for doing that to her; she would never forgive either of them.

Martin's bathrobe was hanging from the hook next to hers on the back of her door, and she looked away when she saw it. They had allocated each other wardrobe space at their respective homes. Martin even had a dedicated drawer for his underwear. She decided that she would bag up all of his belongings the following morning and drop them off at one of the many charity shops that had cropped up in the area at some point over the next couple of days. Maybe she would just leave them in the doorway one night; that way, she would be spared from having to explain why she was getting rid of them to some nosey shop assistant.

Phoebe had taken a sleeping pill before going to bed, but it didn't seem to be having any effect on her. After a while, she got up and wandered over to the window. Her bedroom overlooked their tree-lined rear garden, with its perfectly mowed lawns and abundance of colourful plants. It was a tranquil sight, and she stood there for several minutes, just watching the trees sway in the breeze. Eventually, she began to feel sleepy, so she returned to her bed and closed her eyes. Thankfully, this time around, no images of Martin and Anna kissing were waiting to torture her.

As she tossed and turned beneath the cotton sheets, the interview with DC Evans weighed heavily on her mind. Something about the way that the friendly Welshman looked at her had unsettled her. He had been perfectly pleasant throughout, but she sensed he harboured reservations about her story. Why he should do so was beyond her, but the fact that he did made her feel uneasy.

And then there was the police car parked out front. Her parents were delighted to have it stationed there, but it bothered her immensely. She appreciated that its purpose was to protect them, but it made her feel trapped, like she was now a prisoner in her own home.

Phoebe found herself wishing that she had somewhere she could go and stay for a few nights, just until all the excitement died down and the police left them in peace. She briefly contemplated returning to the family cottage in Diss, but she knew her parents would never agree to that. Ironically, if she hadn't fallen out with Anna, she could have stayed there.

Susie Sergeant was sitting in her car, which was parked up in Morley Road, not far from the back entrance to Leyton police station. It was half-past ten, which was changeover time for the division's pursuit car. Dan was an advanced driver, and he had been driving Juliet One for the late shift, so he should be coming out any minute now. She felt incredibly silly, lying in wait to ambush him like this, but what choice did she have? He wasn't answering her calls or text messages, and she needed to know what his long-term plans were. Did he want her to put the house on the market? Was he happy for her to contact the bank and dissolve their joint accounts? All she was asking for was five minutes of his time so that she could start moving on with her life.

Her heart skipped a beat as a man emerged from the rear yard, but then she realised it wasn't him. A few seconds later, another figure appeared. Tall, slim, short brown hair, good looks.

It was Dan!

As she opened the door, intending to get out and intercept him, a pretty young woman in half-blues jogged out of the yard and looped her arm through Dan's. His face broke into a big grin, and he wrapped his arms around her shoulders and pulled her into him.

The sound of their giggling cut through the stillness of the night.

Susie looked away, cringing at the painful sight of her husband embracing another woman.

Looking up a few seconds later, she watched in stony silence as Dan led his new love interest along Morley Road towards his parked car. They were all smiles and laughter, ambling along as though they had all the time in the world while she sat there like a loser, feeling sorry for herself. With a heavy heart, Susie closed the driver's door and started the engine. This had obviously been a bad idea. Disastrous was the word that sprang to mind. Maybe, as Jack had suggested earlier, it was time to instruct a solicitor and leave it all to them?

Susie felt physically sick as she pulled away. There could no longer be any doubt in her mind that the marriage was over. Not that she had ever realistically thought otherwise, but having it confirmed like this made it seem very final.

Neither Dan nor the woman in his arms looked up as Susie drove past them. They were far too absorbed in staring into each other's eyes to care about anyone else.

Phoebe's eyes shot open. What was that she had just heard? She lay still in her bed, straining her ears. Maybe the sound that had awoken her was nothing, but that wasn't what her instincts were telling her. There it was again; a rustling from just outside her window. At least she thought it was outside. What if it wasn't? What if the noise had actually come from within her room?

She cautiously pushed her duvet aside and slid her feet onto the floor. Standing up, she padded into the centre of the room. With the blackout curtains drawn, the room was pitch black and she could barely make out the shape of her hand in front of her face. Standing perfectly still in the gloom, she began to feel a little silly, and she was on the verge of returning to bed when she heard it again. "Hello...?" she whispered. "Is anybody there?"

"Hello, Pheebs, did you miss me?"

The disembodied voice that came out of the darkness was unmistakably Spencer's. But how could that be? She opened her mouth to scream for help but, before she could make a sound, his calloused hand clamped over her face, cutting off her air supply.

Grabbing her hair with his other hand, Spencer frogmarched her back to the bed and pushed her down onto it. "Did you think you could ever escape me?" he hissed, leaning over her prone form so that their faces were only inches apart. "That was a nasty little trick you pulled on me back at the barn, but it's my turn now."

She tried to break free but he was far too strong. In desperation, Phoebe tried to bite his hand, but he just laughed at the feeble attempt and squeezed her jaw until she thought it would snap.

"Now, now," he giggled. "Play nice."

Her mind was reeling. How had he managed to get into her room? Through the window, obviously, but how had he slipped past the police guard stationed at the front of the house?

"I came in through the gate at the back of the garden," he gloated, as though reading her mind. "There ain't no rozzers there."

Phoebe's blood ran cold as she gazed up at the menacing figure pinning her to the bed. She instinctively knew that this was the end of the line for her. Spencer had hunted her down, and now he was going to kill her. Suddenly, she felt the blade of his knife pressing against the soft flesh of her throat. In the darkness, her eyes bulged, imploring him to spare her. She attempted to speak, but all that came out was a muffled whimper.

"Relax," Spencer cooed, applying more weight to the blade. "It'll all be over in a minute."

With that, the knife tore across her throat, leaving a deep, wide gash in its wake. The nerve receptors in her skin barely had time to register pain as the lifeblood spurted from her severed jugular.

Phoebe suddenly realised that he was no longer holding her down, that he had stepped back from the bed to avoid being drenched in her blood. She instinctively reached up to try and stem the bleeding but the blood gushed out from between her fingers at an alarming rate.

Phoebe tried calling for help, but she was drowning in her own blood, and the only sound to escape her lips was a whimpering gurgle.

In the darkness, Spencer was laughing merrily. "I always told you, Pheebs," he announced happily, "if I can't have you, nobody can."

Inside her head, Phoebe let out a long, tortured scream.

NOOO!

She jerked into a sitting position, hands desperately groping her neck for the terrible wound that Spencer's knife had just inflicted but, to her astonishment, it was no longer there. In fact, her throat was completely intact. For a moment, she struggled to make any sense of what was happening.

How could that be?

And where was Spencer? He had been there a moment ago.

Relief flooded through her as she realised the truth: It had all been a dream; a terrible nightmare.

Utterly exhausted, Phoebe flopped back against the headrest, gasping in the warm night air. She was covered with sweat and her whole body was shaking, but the life-affirming thud of her racing heart confirmed that she was definitely very much alive.

"Oh my God," she breathed, running a trembling hand through her hair.

She glanced sideways, at the glowing face of her digital clock. It wasn't even midnight yet.

25

Monday 30th July 2001
THE JOB'S OFF

Skippy opened the street door cautiously, afraid that Wiggins and his pet enforcer, Casper, might be paying him another visit. He was relieved, if a little surprised, to see G-Man standing there, looking sorry for himself. "What do you want?" he demanded, suspiciously. "I was just getting ready to go out and boost a car for tomorrow's job."

"Forget it," G-Man said as he pushed by him and walked into Skippy's flat. "The job's off."

"What?" Skippy spluttered, rushing after him. "You can't be serious? I'm relying on that money to pay off a bloody debt to Jonas Willard."

G-Man shrugged, indifferently. "Yeah, well, I was relying on it too, but my contact has just called me to say that the delivery isn't happening now, so we're both fucked, ain't we?"

On hearing this, Skippy began walking in agitated circles, holding his head in his hands. "Fuck, fuck, fuck!" He finally came to a stop in front of G-Man. "Are you sure? Are you absolutely fucking sure?"

"Don't be a prat. Of course, I'm bloody well sure."

Skippy slumped down in an old armchair, feeling utterly deflated. He ran his hands through his short hair, then sagged forward, almost folding himself in half as he dry washed his unshaven face. "Christ! What a disaster," he mumbled through his fingers.

Closing his eyes, Skippy was immediately confronted by an image of Casper, grinning as he pinned him down inside a cement mixer while cold, wet concrete was poured over him. Suppressing a shudder, he wondered how much suffering would be involved before he drowned.

G-Man appeared by his shoulder, nudged him. "What about that job you were telling me about?" he asked. "Can't we pull that instead?"

Skippy stared up at him vacantly. "What? Oh, I don't know," he mumbled. Sitting up straight, he forced himself to focus. "Maybe..."

G-Man folded his arms, impatiently. "Can we or not?"

Skippy held up a hand to silence him. "Give me a minute," he said, distractedly.

Phoebe Cunningham had returned to the family home in Wanstead, and there was no way that he was going to risk snatching her from there. As he'd told Spencer, the place was a fortress. He couldn't wait until she returned to the cottage, because that was unlikely to happen until the weekend, which was too late. The only alternative was to snatch her from the street in broad daylight. It would be fraught with risk, but it was definitely doable.

"Maybe," he said again, trying to remember her routine.

"Let's do it then," G-Man said enthusiastically, then frowned. "What exactly is the job, anyway?"

The supervisor's meeting began at three o'clock sharp. With him, the two DIs and all three skippers crammed into Tyler's office, it felt a bit cramped, but there was nothing he could do about that.

"How did the SPM go?" Tyler asked Susie.

"It went pretty much as expected," she replied with a non-committal shrug. "Claxton found fifteen stab wounds in the victim's torso, and Whitling would definitely have died from those injuries, but Spencer speeded the process up by slitting his throat."

"What did Claxton say about the murder weapon?" Dillon asked. It hadn't been recovered, so the killer had obviously taken it with him when he'd fled the scene.

"He thinks it was probably a large kitchen knife, of similar dimensions to the one that was used on David Bannister."

That surprised no one.

"I'm worried that Spencer's going to attack her parents next," Tyler told them, and they could all hear the tension in his voice. "We need to catch him before he does. Trouble is, he seems to have dropped off the face of the earth."

"Do you think he'll definitely go after them?" Steve Bull asked.

Tyler responded with a disheartened shrug. "I'm finding it hard to second guess him, but I have to proceed on the basis that he will, or we risk being caught with our pants down."

Charlie White looked up from the document he had been reading, and his brow puckered into a thoughtful frown. "What do we think Spencer meant in his last text to Skipton, the one when he went on about P begging him to take her back?"

The response was a room full of blank looks.

"P obviously means Phoebe," Tyler said, retrieving his copy of the TIU report from his desk. Clearing his throat, he read the text that Charlie had referred to aloud for the benefit of the others. "'Don't worry. I'm not going after her. Got something better in mind. When I'm finished P will be begging me to take her back.'" He lowered the document with a frustrated sigh. "Honestly, Charlie, I have no idea what that means, but he's definitely planning something, and that really worries me."

Dillon nodded his agreement. "I'll tell you what worries me," he said, glancing at each of the others in turn. "Why has Spencer been switching his phone off when he's not using it? Has he worked out that we can track him from its signal?"

"I was discussing that with Reg earlier," Steve Bull chipped in. "As he rightly pointed out, mobile phones are a completely new form of technology to him, so there's no way he could possibly be that savvy about how they work."

"Maybe, Skipton warned him?" White suggested.

"It's more likely that he's just trying to conserve battery power, and he's only turning the phone on when he needs to use it," Bull said. "At least that's what Reg thinks, and he knows more about this stuff than all of us put together."

Dillon considered this. "Actually, that makes a lot of sense," he conceded, looking somewhat relieved.

"Speaking of Skipton," Susie interjected. "Has anything useful come out of the covert surveillance on his flat?"

Dillon shook his head. "Alas, no. According to the viewing log, he hasn't received any visitors and he rarely goes out."

"In that case, is it even worth continuing the observations?" Susie asked. "At the moment, we've got people watching the live feed around the clock, and I don't need to tell you how resource-intensive that is. If it isn't proving useful, maybe we should knock it on the head now?"

"No, we keep it going," Tyler said, making it clear the subject wasn't up for debate. "I'm convinced that, at some point in the near future, Spencer's going to show up at Skipton's place and, when he does, I want us to be in a position to act quickly."

"How did the Cunninghams react when you informed them that we'd found Spencer's handprint at Whitling's place?" Deakin enquired.

Tyler shuddered at the memory. From his limited exposure to the man, he had come to understand that drastic overreaction was Ben Cunningham's default setting. "Not well," he said, and left it at that. "We've agreed to keep a uniform presence at the house until

Spencer's caught, and we've given the family the standard advice about personal safety and risk management, but there's a limit to what we can do for them, and it falls well short of Cunningham's demands, which are that we assign each member of his family an armed personal protection officer."

"So, where do we go from here?" Susie asked, spreading her arms questioningly. "We've got Spencer's cousin under surveillance. Higgins is his only other known associate and he's been arrested. We're live monitoring Spencer's phone. He's circulated as wanted. There's been no financial activity on his banking or saving accounts. We don't know if he's got access to a car, so ANPR can't help us. What options do we have left?"

"I've authorised the Dedicated Source Unit to start showing his photograph to all the snouts on their books," Dillon said. "We'll see if that yields anything."

Susie blew out her cheeks, vexed by their lack of progress. "There must be something else we can do?" she insisted.

"We're working on it," Tyler promised but, secretly, he shared her frustration.

"Has anything interesting come out of last night's TV appeal?" White asked.

Deakin pulled a face like he'd been sucking lemons. "We've had about a dozen sightings of him reported so far," he gloomily informed the room. "He's been spotted working for an oil company in Aberdeen, on a sewerage farm just outside Cardiff, as a sailor on a cross channel ferry sailing out of Dover, and as a dustman in Ealing, to name but a few."

Tyler smothered a grin, knowing that all the sightings would have to be followed up, no matter how bizarre or unlikely they sounded, and it was creating a mountain of unnecessary work for Deakin and the MIR. "So, nothing terribly promising?"

"Not a sausage," Deakin said, with a disappointed shake of his head.

Leaning back in his chair, Tyler stared at the others over his steepled fingers. Something was niggling him, but he couldn't quite put his finger on it. And then it came to him. "Why is it that nothing of value was taken from Martin Whitling's flat?"

"I don't understand the question," Bull admitted, staring at him in bewilderment. "We know that Spencer acted out of jealousy, not greed, so wouldn't it be more disconcerting if something had been taken?"

"You're missing the point," Tyler said, irritably. "Spencer's penniless. His bank and savings accounts are both virtually empty, and all he left prison with was a forty six pound discharge grant, which won't get him very far."

"You say that, boss, but don't forget he stole Bannister's wallet," Deakin pointed out. "From checking Bannister's bank statement, we now know that he withdrew two hundred pounds on the day that he was murdered, and we have to assume that Spencer has that money in his possession."

"I fully appreciate that," Tyler acknowledged, "but, if anything, what you just said emphasises the point that I'm trying to make. Spencer's a thief by nature; it's wired into this DNA. There's no way he would have passed over an opportunity to line his pockets while he was at Whitling's flat. He would have ransacked the place and helped himself to anything that wasn't nailed down. Yet, nothing's missing. Not a penny, and it just doesn't make sense to me."

The room fell silent as the others processed this. Leaving them to their thoughts, Tyler reached for his phone and asked Dick Jarvis to pop in. A few seconds later, there was a tentative knock on the door, and Jarvis poked his head around it.

"You wanted me?" he asked.

"Come in," Tyler said, and waited until Jarvis had closed the door behind him. "Tell me, Dick, was there any loose cash lying around at Whitling's flat, or any other valuables that a thief might easily convert to cash via the services of a fence?"

"Well, yes, of course," Jarvis said.

"Like what?" Dillon demanded.

"Well, for starters, I found several hundred pounds in cash sitting in the top drawer of his bedside table," Jarvis said. "Then there was his Nokia phone, a fair bit of jewellery, including a Rolex watch, and every burglar's favourite item these days: a top of the range DVD player."

Tyler looked around the room. "See what I mean? It just doesn't add up that a career criminal like Spencer would leave any of that stuff behind."

He had a point, they all agreed.

―――

Skippy swivelled his head to give G-Man a prolonged death stare. His newfound partner was slouched in the front passenger seat, snoring his head off. It was a nasty grating sound, like a saw cutting through timber, and it was driving Skippy crazy.

Oblivious to the scathing look he was receiving, G-Man smacked his lips together like he was puckering up to deliver a wet kiss, then mumbled something incoherent in his sleep. A string of drool trickled down his stubbled chin and his left eye suddenly started twitching madly.

It was late afternoon, and they had found a shady spot in a little side road off Hollybush Hill to park up in. From their vantage point, they could just about see the gates to Cunningham's mansion. A police panda car with its jam sandwich stripes running along the side was parked outside, containing a solitary constable who was flicking through a newspaper instead of watching the house.

Although G-Man had offered to help, all he'd done so far was get on Skippy's nerves, and the incessant drone of his adenoidal snoring was fast becoming unbearable. Desperate to escape the dreadful racket, if only for a few seconds, Skippy stepped out of the car and set off towards the Cunningham's residence in order to take a closer look.

Skippy hadn't been sure that G-Man would still want to go ahead with the job once he'd revealed what it entailed, but he needn't have worried. G-Man hadn't been remotely fazed by the risks involved with snatching Phoebe Cunningham from the street. In fact, he had been dismissive of them, boasting that they were no greater than those he had taken during the armed robbery in which the cop had died.

Skippy had sweetened the deal by telling him that they would each get an equal share of the half-million that he intended to demand as a ransom for the girl's release. Had G-Man known that Skippy actually intended to demand a cool million for her release, he might not have been so happy with what was on offer, but Skippy figured what G-Man didn't know wouldn't hurt him.

As he'd hoped, the gates to Cunningham's house were wide open, and Phoebe's red Alfa Romeo was clearly visible parked in the centre of the gravelled driveway, right next to Ben Cunningham's X5. On a whim, Skippy stopped beside the police car. Jamming his hands into his pockets to make himself appear less threatening, he stared in at the bored driver through the open window. "What's going on in there, then?" he asked, jutting his chin towards the house.

The officer lowered his paper, lazily ran his eyes over Skippy, and pulled a disapproving face. A desultorily sigh made the point that he was getting fed up with all the nosey parkers who kept stopping to ask him this. "Nothing happening here, mate," he said, waving Skippy on.

Skippy was just about to ask another question, when the street door opened and Phoebe Cunningham emerged. Her pink dress was festooned with bright yellow sunflowers, and she had a straw bonnet on her head to protect her from the sun. Closing the door behind her, she set off towards her car, fiddling with the keys as she walked.

Realising that the constable was still staring up at him, clearly peeved that he hadn't taken the hint and buggered off, Skippy self-consciously cleared his throat. "Right, well, I'd better be on my way," he said with a friendly smile. "I'll leave you to read your paper in peace." With an ironic bow of his head, he made his way back to the car and G-Man's rhonchial snoring.

Slamming the door hard to arouse his passenger from his stupor, he allowed himself a self-satisfied smirk as G-Man sat bolt up, blinking his eyes in confusion. "I must have dozed off for a moment," he yawned, stretching like a bear emerging from hibernation.

"The girl's on the move," Skippy announced, starting the car.

G-Man checked his watch. "About bloody time," he said, moodily.

The Alfa turned left out of the gate and set off towards the Green Man roundabout.

Skippy waited for a gap in the traffic and then pulled out after her but, by the time he did, Phoebe had already put a healthy distance between them

"Put your bloody foot down," G-Man complained. "I won't be happy if you lose her after we've spent all this time watching the house."

Skippy could quite happily have strangled him for saying that. *We! The only thing you've been watching is the inside of your eyelids!*

Luckily, the Alfa was held up at the roundabout, so they were able to catch it up and slot into its slipstream as it pulled out. They followed Phoebe along Leytonstone High Road, keeping another car between them wherever possible.

"Wonder where she's going?" G-Man grumbled, and Skippy noticed that his left eye was twitching again.

"Looks like she's heading for her mate's house," he said. "This is the route she usually takes to get there." As she turned off the High Road and started cutting through the quieter back streets, Skippy became increasingly confident that Phoebe was making her way to Anna Manson's house. When the Alfa pulled up outside Anna's address, he drove straight past it, found a space further along the road, and parked up.

"Now what?" G-Man asked, irritably. "It's all very well and good following her around all day, but how is that actually helping us?"

Skippy rolled his eyes. "I've already told you, we can't snatch her from the family address because there's too much security there, even without PC plod parked outside, so we need to follow her until an opportunity to grab her crops up."

G-Man expelled a short, sharp grunt of dissatisfaction. "That could take days. Why don't we just jump her when she comes out of her mate's house? It's pretty quiet around here, and we've got masks." He jerked his thumb over his shoulder, to the carrier bag resting on the back seat, which contained two sets of balaclavas and gloves.

Skippy stared at him in disbelief. *Are you really that stupid?* "Listen, G-Man, the street might be empty, but it's daylight and we don't know who's looking out of their windows. We either grab her somewhere remote, where we won't be seen, or wait until darkness falls."

Skippy had taken the precaution of fitting a set of false plates to the car so, even if someone clocked the registration number when they snatched her, the Old Bill would never be able to link it to him. Unfortunately, the previous owner of the 1990 Ford Sierra Sapphire he was driving had resprayed it bright yellow and added a big tail fin to make it look like the RS Cosworth version of the car. Not a problem when you were cruising the streets trying to impress the chicks, but a bit of a bummer when you were planning to commit a kidnapping and didn't want to be seen in a car that stood out from the crowd.

"So, what do we do, now?" G-Man wanted to know.

"We wait and we watch, and we bide our time until the right moment presents itself," Skippy replied, speaking slowly so that the words would sink in.

Anna was startled to see Phoebe standing there when she opened the door, and her eyes narrowed suspiciously. After their last acrimonious meeting, she hadn't expected to see Phoebe so soon.

"Hello, Anna."

Anna stared back without answering. While Phoebe's tone hadn't sounded remotely confrontational, the scornful expression on her face didn't inspire confidence, so she decided to wait and see how things unfolded before responding.

Phoebe picked up on her reticence. "Relax, I haven't come here to fight," she said, spreading her arms in a peace offering. "I know I said some pretty hurtful things the last time we spoke, but can you really blame me? You cheated on me with my fiancé, for Christ's sake."

Anna cringed when the word, 'cheated,' was uttered, and her face instantly flushed with shame. "No, I suppose not."

Phoebe looked over Anna's shoulder, into the narrow hallway. "Can I come in?" she asked.

Anna reluctantly stood aside, and Phoebe walked past her, going straight through to the kitchen.

Taking a deep breath, Anna closed the door, praying that this wasn't going to deteriorate into another slanging match. The schism that had developed between them was almost as painful to her as Martin's death. She was really struggling to cope with the stress of the situation and, as she followed Phoebe through to the kitchen she felt like a ticking time bomb, ready to explode at the slightest provocation. Although she had desperately tried to convince herself that Phoebe's boast about Martin planning to dump her had been a spiteful pack of lies, devoid of any substance, she secretly suspected that every hurtful word had been true. "Would you like a drink?" she heard herself ask.

Phoebe nodded. "Coffee, please," she replied, forcing a smile.

Anna was struck by how stunning Phoebe looked. She had obviously made a real effort over her appearance, because her makeup had been applied faultlessly, her hair was glistening, and she smelled absolutely divine.

Anna, on the other hand, knew that she looked a complete mess. It had taken a supreme act of willpower just to drag herself out of bed this morning. She hadn't showered, done her hair or bothered with makeup, and she had thrown on the same shorts and a T-shirt she had worn the previous day. Just to add to her overall state of distress, Anna's eyes were red raw and gritty from all the crying that she'd done over the past twenty-four hours.

Martin's untimely death had sucked the life out of Anna. It had left a huge void in her life, a dark, empty space that had once been filled with love and hope. Without him by her side, she wasn't sure that she wanted to continue living. She felt empty; she felt lost, and she would never be whole again because her broken heart would never heal.

All these thoughts passed through her mind as she filled the kettle.

He had only been gone a day, but it felt more like a year. Anna knew that life had to go on, and that she had to put these depressing thoughts out of her mind and find a way to continue functioning, but she was struggling badly, and she suspected that her pain would get a whole lot worse before it got any better.

Phoebe, on the other hand, appeared to be coping admirably. Anna understood that everyone handled grief differently, and maybe this was just her way of dealing with it? Perhaps the air of indifference she was giving off was just a front; a barrier she had erected to keep her emotions at bay?

"Why have you come here?" Anna asked, her voice as dead as Martin.

"I want to make peace," Phoebe told her. "Martin's gone, and we'll never get him back, but if we don't sort this out, then I'll lose your friendship as well."

Anna was taken aback by Phoebe's change of heart, especially after the scathing comments she'd made the previous day. "But how can you possibly forgive me for... for having a relationship with Martin?"

"I don't know that I can," Phoebe admitted candidly, "but I feel like I ought to try."

Anna considered this as she poured their coffee. "I would like that," she said, handing a cup to her friend.

They lapsed into an awkward silence, which neither of them knew how to fill.

Phoebe blew on the steaming liquid and then took a sip. "How are you coping?" she asked. "Dad told me you went to the flat, yesterday. Did you see Martin's body?"

Anna shuddered, recalling the police tape, and the serious faced detectives she had spoken to. "No, they didn't allow me inside."

"Did they say anything about his injuries?" Phoebe asked.

Anna shook her head. "No, but while I was talking to a detective outside, it kept running through my mind that poor Martin was lying in there, cold and alone."

Phoebe sipped her coffee, frowned in thought as though considering her next question. "Have you heard the latest update?" she asked. "They found a bloodied handprint in the flat, and the forensic people have confirmed that it belongs to Spencer."

Anna blanched. "A bloodied handprint!" Feeling a little faint, she leaned on the counter to steady herself. "Your mum called me this morning, and told me that Spencer's fingerprints had been found inside the flat, but she didn't say anything about blood."

Phoebe stared at her for a moment. "My dad probably didn't tell her," she said. "You know how squeamish she is."

Anna nodded. Jessica was renowned for being a complete wuss, and something like that would have totally freaked her out. Anna felt her eyes welling up. "How much blood was there?"

Phoebe shrugged. "How would I know that?" She asked, rolling her eyes. "Honestly, Anna, they just said a bloodied hand mark, they didn't say how much blood. It could have been a pinprick or a gallon for all I know."

Anna dabbed at her eyes with a sheet of kitchen roll, then blew her nose. "Sorry," she said, voice trembling.

"Are you going to come over today?" Phoebe enquired, casually.

Anna shook her head. "I'm sorry, I know I should be there for you all, but I'm in a bit of a state, so I thought I'd stay in and grab an early night."

Phoebe placed her empty cup on the work surface and stood up. "Probably wise," she said. "You look like shit."

Anna smiled. "I do, don't I!"

Phoebe placed a hand on her shoulder. "Get some rest," she said. "We'll talk again tomorrow." Waving goodbye, she set off towards the street door. "I'll show myself out," she called over her shoulder.

For a long moment, Anna stood there, chewing her bottom lip and wondering if she ought to ask the question that was playing on her mind. "Phoebe," she called out, just as her friend was about to exit the house.

"What?"

When she spoke next, Anna's voice was riddled with shame and guilt. "You... you haven't told your family about me and Martin, have you?"

Phoebe shook her head. "Don't worry, I haven't said a word to them."

26

WE'VE LOST HER

Dillon's presence had been requested in the ground floor viewing room where the Technical Support Unit had set up the equipment needed to receive the video signal that was being beamed from the van parked outside Skippy's address. "What have you got?" he asked as he closed the door behind him.

Jim Stone looked up from the screen, blinked several times, then yawned.

"Keeping you awake, are we?" Dillon chided, playfully.

Stone stifled another yawn. "Sorry. Staring at this bloody screen for hours on end is sending me to sleep," he complained. There were two monitors on the table in front of him. The first was for the live feed, while the second allowed another person to review older footage. The recordings were all stored electronically on a hard drive, and Stone was busily tapping instructions into a keyboard to retrieve the section of footage he wanted to show Dillon.

"Take a look at this," he said when he found it. Pressing play, he leaned back so that Dillon could get a better view of the screen. "The clip's only a few seconds long, and it shows a grungy looking white male turning up at Skippy's house this morning. It's obviously not Spencer, but I thought you'd want to take a gander anyway."

Dillon stared at the screen as a slender man of medium height appeared. He had lank brown hair that fell to his shoulders. There was something tantalisingly familiar about him but, as he kept his back to the camera, Dillon was deprived of a clear view of his face. A moment later, the street door opened and Skipton appeared, staring at his visitor in confusion. Something was said, and they both disappeared inside.

"I'll also play you the footage of the him and Skipton leaving, not that you get a clearer view of his face."

Dillon sat in silence while Stone found the relevant segment, wondering why he thought the male had seemed familiar.

"Here we go," Stone said a few moments later. "This is them leaving the address together, about an hour later."

The street door opened, Skipton stuck his head out, looked up and down the road, and then stepped out.

"Skipton's well on edge," Dillon observed.

"He does that every time he leaves," Stone told him. "Don't know why, but he's always really nervous, and acts like someone might be lying in wait for him."

The long haired visitor emerged next, and Dillon leaned in to get a better look. Annoyingly, his face was shielded by Skipton, who was taller, as they walked out of the gate into the street.

"See," Stone said. "You don't get a good look at him when he leaves, either."

Dillon sat back, crossed his legs, and placed his hands behind his head. "Has he ever shown up before?" he asked.

Stone shook his head. "Nope. I've double checked the viewing log, and this is definitely the first visitor that Skipton's had since we began monitoring."

Dillon shrugged. "Let me know if he turns up again. There's

something vaguely familiar about him, so I'd be very interested to see his face."

———

About an hour after she had arrived, Phoebe Cunningham left Anna Manson's house and climbed into her car.

Watching her in his rearview mirror, Skippy nudged G-Man, who had fallen asleep again. Thankfully, his snoring had been a little less intense this time around, and he had managed to blot it out by turning the radio up.

G-Man opened his eyes, blinked in confusion. "Uh? What is it?" he demanded in a surly tone.

Skippy started the engine. "Oh, I'm sorry for interrupting your slumber," he retorted angrily. "But the girl's on the move.

With a sluggish yawn, G-Man pulled his seat belt on. "Alright," he said, defensively. "Don't get all premenstrual on me. I told you, I'll keep watch later and you can have a kip then."

Skippy bit his lip, not trusting himself to respond without saying something that would antagonise his new partner, who was clearly as allergic to criticism as he was to using deodorant.

They trailed Phoebe in silence as she took a reciprocal route back to her home in Hollybush Hill. To their surprise, instead of turning into the drive, she drove straight past it, pulling into the side road that they had used while keeping watch on the house earlier in the day. Skippy followed her in, being careful not to get too close. When Phoebe found a parking space on the left, he drove straight by. "Don't look," he warned G-Man out of the corner of his mouth.

"I wasn't going to," his passenger bristled. "I'm not a fucking amateur."

Skippy ignored the outburst. "Now, why would she choose not to park on her drive?" he pondered aloud.

Beside him, G-Man shrugged. "There was a police car parked across the gates," he offered. "Maybe she's planning to go out again later, and doesn't want all the palaver of having to get plod to move."

That seemed feasible.

Skippy pulled into the kerb about fifty yards further along the road. He watched her alight, but waited until she had disappeared into the main road before turning the car around. "We need to find somewhere we can keep watch on the car and still see the gates," he said.

"Why?" G-Man challenged. "Surely, as long as we're watching the car, we'll see her when she returns to it?"

Skippy closed his eyes and pinched his nose. "We'll see her *if* she gets in her car, you plonker, but what about if she goes out on foot or someone else drives?"

"Fair point," G-Man allowed, pulling his greasy hair into a ponytail and tying it off with an elastic band. "In that case, what about parking up in that little layby on the main road? We'd be able to see the house and the car from there."

Skippy knew the place he was referring to, and he agreed that it would be the perfect spot. The only downer was that it would leave them exposed to the police officer guarding Cunningham's house. He took great pleasure in pointing this little oversight out to G-Man.

G-Man shrugged it off. "So what? We ain't breaking no laws, and the car can't be traced back to either of us if they run a check on it."

Skippy considered this. The officer he had spoken to earlier certainly hadn't been overly attentive. They could have been parked on the drive next to him, with their bumpers touching, and he wouldn't have noticed. Maybe G-Man was right.

With two murders to investigate, Tyler's team should have been stretched to breaking point but, for some reason, that wasn't proving to be the case. Against all expectations, they actually found themselves in the highly unusual position of having everything under control. All the important witness statements had been taken. All the relevant CCTV had been gathered and viewed. The preliminary forensic results relating to Bannister's murder had come in, and they had yielded such a treasure trove of fingerprint and DNA evidence that Tyler was literally spoilt for choice.

There was still a lot of work to do regarding Whitling's murder, of course, but this was all slow-time stuff that would gradually come together over a period of weeks.

Paul Evans had taken witness statements from Ben, Jessica and Phoebe Cunningham. That only left Anna Manson, but she had been unwell when he'd contacted her earlier in the day, so new arrangements had been made for Evans to visit her at home the following morning.

There was no CCTV in the immediate vicinity of Whitling's block and, although Tyler had ordered the local authority footage seized, he doubted it would contain anything that would be of use to them.

The good news was that the bloodied hand print Juliet Kennedy had discovered on the inside of Whitling's lounge door definitely belonged to Spencer, and Tyler was confident that the DNA profile from the blood would match the victim's.

Both SPMs had been carried out. A second would be organised for each body in due course, either requested by Spencer's legal team following his arrest, or ordered by HM Coroner before the bodies were released, if no arrest had been made by that time.

Reg had recently provided him with an interesting report, showing the dates and times of all the text messages that Spencer had sent to Skipton, along with any replies that had been made. It also contained cell site information, revealing the locations of the handsets when each of the messages were sent.

Sitting alone in his office, Tyler skimmed through the various text messages, starting with those sent on Friday 27th July.

Spencer to Skippy: *Sorry I haven't called you. Been hiding up in Norfolk. Will be returning to London tomorrow. Things didn't go as planned here.*

Skippy to Spencer: *U R a fucking idiot. I've had the pigs round here today looking for U. Didn't tell them anything. Call me when U can.*

These were more relevant to Barty Craddock's abduction case than the murders he was investigating. The exchange that occurred later in the day was of more interest to him, as this demonstrated Spencer's intent to go after Whitling, making the attack premeditated.

Spencer to Skippy: *When I get back to London, I'm gonna take care of unfinished business.*

Skippy to Spencer: *Don't be daft. It's too hot for you to try and grab the girl again. You need to keep your head down for a while.*

Spencer to Skippy: *Don't worry. I'm not going after her. Got something better in mind. When I'm finished P will be begging me to take her back.*

The final message that Spencer had sent Skippy was timed at 02:06 hours on Sunday 29th July.

Spencer to Skippy: *I've taken care of the opposition. She'll soon come running back to me now that he's out of the way.*

The timing was consistent with the estimated time of death that Creepy Claxton had come up with for Whitling's murder, and the cell site data put Spencer's phone within the radius of the mast covering Whitling's address.

Skippy had replied the following morning: *WTF does that mean? Ring me U muppet.*

The text messages were pretty damning, especially when viewed in context with all the other evidence that the team had accrued.

From Tyler's perspective, the case against Spencer for both murders was pretty airtight. All they needed to do now was locate and arrest him, and therein lay the problem. Spencer had done a better job of disappearing than Harry Houdini!

Dillon wandered into the office, eating a banana. Munching away, he said something unintelligible.

Tyler smothered a grin, somehow resisting the urge to draw a comparison between his oversized friend and a gorilla. "Try that again when your mouth isn't quite so full of food," he suggested.

Dillon swallowed. "I said that I was thinking about letting the troops head off home." He promptly shoved the last bite into his mouth and tossed the skin into Tyler's bin.

Tyler checked his watch. Nodded. "Go for it," he said, smothering a yawn. "I doubt anything interesting is going to happen overnight."

In that respect, he could not have been more wrong.

It was almost eleven when Skippy spotted her approaching the car. He had been dozing in the front passenger seat while G-Man kept watch, but he had been woken up by the sound of someone revving a motorbike engine.

To his astonishment, Skippy discovered that the throaty roar of the motorbike was actually G-Man snoring. His imbecilic partner had reclined his seat to make himself more comfortable, and he was using his tented hands as a makeshift pillow.

Skippy was speechless. For a moment, all he could do was stare at the man in amazement. Then, as his anger boiled over, he leaned over and roughly elbowed him in the ribs. "Wake up you idiot," he hissed.

Unbelievably, G-Man just rolled over and carried on snoring.

Skippy grabbed him by the shoulders and shook him violently. "Wake up, damn it!"

"Argh! Wasamatter?" G-Man spluttered, forcing his eyes open.

Releasing him, Skippy turned to check on the girl, and saw that she was loading a couple of bags into the boot of her car.

"What's going on?" G-Man asked, still staring at him gormlessly.

"You fell asleep, you useless twat," Skippy fumed.

The Alfa's lights came on and, a second later, the engine started.

"Hurry up and start the bloody motor," Skippy growled.

"Alright, alright! Keep your hair on," G-Man said, turning the key.

Nothing happened.

"It won't start," G-Man told him, trying again.

Phoebe's car was now driving slowly towards them.

"Keep bloody trying," Skippy ordered. His car could be a bit temperamental at times. The starter motor was on its way out, but he didn't have the money to replace it.

Every time that G-Man turned the key, there was a clackety-clack sound, but the engine stubbornly refused to catch. The noise grew noticeably weaker as the battery drained down.

For some reason, G-Man started pumping the gas pedal as he turned the key.

"Don't do that!" Skippy shouted. "You'll bloody well flood it."

G-Man was arguing back now, swearing at him and banging the steering wheel in frustration. "If you think you can do better, why don't–"

There was no time to swap drivers, so Skippy ignored him.

Phoebe's car slowed on the approach to the junction with Hollybush Hill but, as there was no traffic on the main road, she was able to turn left without stopping.

Powerless to do anything, Skippy watched as the Alfa set off towards the Green Man roundabout. "START THE BLOODY CAR!" he screamed at the top of his voice.

"I'm trying, but it won't–"

The engine finally caught, and G-Man frantically slipped the gear lever into first. There was a loud clunk as the transmission jumped out of gear, and G-Man cursed as he battled to get it back into first. "This is like trying to stir a bucket of bricks," he complained as he finally pulled out after the disappearing Alfa.

Skippy wiped the sweat from his brow. "Fucking useless idiot," he cursed under his breath.

By the time they reached the roundabout, Phoebe Cunningham's little red car had completely disappeared. "Now what?" G-Man demanded. "She could have gone anywhere."

"I don't know," Skippy said, shrugging miserably.

"I can't believe we've been at this all day and now we've lost her," G-Man complained.

"*We* haven't lost her," Skippy snarled. "This is all *your* fault. If you hadn't fallen asleep, you useless prick, we would have seen her in plenty of time to follow her."

"It's not my fault your car's a crock of shit," G-Man bit back.

"No, but it's your fault you're such a twat."

A car waiting behind them honked its horn.

"FUCK OFF!" they both shouted in unison.

Still honking his horn, the driver pulled around them, pausing long enough to shout some abuse and make a 'wanker' gesture with his hand.

When he'd gone, G-Man turned to Skippy. "Where do you want me to go?" he asked.

Skippy didn't have a clue. "Shut up, and let me think."

27

STRANGE NOISES IN THE NIGHT

Anna awoke with a start. The sudden noise that had aroused her from her fitful slumber had sounded like someone treading on one of the loose floorboards in her bedroom. Laying perfectly still, she strained her ears, barely daring to breathe, but the only sound she heard was that of her beating heart. She remained motionless for several tense seconds, too afraid to even open her eyes. To her relief, there were no more strange noises, and she eventually began to wonder if it had all been a dream. She had been having such vivid ones, which she thought was probably down to the pills she had taken to help her relax.

Cautiously raising her head off the pillow, Anna ran her eyes over every inch of the room. Even with the curtains drawn, there was enough ambient light for her to see that it was empty.

Lying down again, she chided herself for being silly and settled down to sleep.

Anna was just starting to drift off, entering that warm fuzzy place between wakefulness and sleep, when she sensed a dark presence, malignant and dangerous, looming over her. Her eyes sprang open, and she could feel her entire body shaking with fear as she scanned the darkness for an intruder.

There was no one there.

Anna's head flopped back down on the pillow, and she breathed a sigh of relief.

Stop it, you stupid girl! It's all in your bloody mind!

Feeling restless, she glanced at the glowing red display of her digital clock, trying to work out the time. Without her glasses on, the numbers were meaningless blurs but, by squinting until her eyes felt like they were going to pop out of her head, she could just about make out that it was eleven-fifteen.

Even with the window wide open, the room felt hot and sticky. Sitting up, Anna reached for the glass of water on her bedside table, downing half of it in one go. While she was awake, she decided that she might as well pop to the loo. Pushing the covers aside, Anna scoffed at her overactive imagination, embarrassed that she had let it run riot.

She shuffled across the floorboards, which creaked underfoot, until she reached the door, then trudged along the corridor towards the bathroom. Closing the door behind her, she pulled the hang-cord to turn on the light. As she crossed to the toilet, she paused to examine her reflection in the bathroom mirror. It wasn't a pretty sight. Her face was pale and gaunt, and her hair was sticking up all over the place. She looked like a cross between *Stig of the Dump* and one of the zombies from *Night of the Living Dead*. Anna self-consciously ran a hand through her tangled hair, thinking that she really ought to book an appointment with her hairdresser. Martin wouldn't want to be seen out with her looking like...

She remembered that Martin was dead, and that he would never see her looking like that or like anything else ever again. Her eyes suddenly felt hot and moist, and she felt her heart shatter all over again.

Her grieving was interrupted by the sound of a creaking floorboard. Stiffening at the noise, Anna quickly walked into the hall and turned the light on. "Hello...?" she asked, hurriedly looking right and left, and wondering what direction the unwelcome sound had come from.

Silence.

Moving warily, she crept back to her bedroom, where she kept a baseball bat in the wardrobe, a precaution she had taken just in case she was ever invaded by burglars. She had left her mobile on the bedside table, and she decided that she would lock herself in her room and call the police to come and check the place out, just to be on the safe side.

"Is anybody there?" she asked as she crossed the threshold.

From the darkness within, a masked figure suddenly lunged forward, grabbed her by the wrist and pulled her into the room. Anna screamed as she was thrown against the far wall with considerable force. Gasping as the air was expelled from her lungs, she bounced off the wall and toppled to the floor. She looked up to see her attacker standing in the doorway, silhouetted by the light spilling in from the hall. "Please," she begged, raising an arm to protect herself.

Saying nothing, her attacker stared down at her through the slits in his balaclava, head cocked to one side as though evaluating her. And then he took a slow, menacing step towards her, raising what appeared to be an iron bar above his head.

Anna's eyes widened in fear, and she frantically scuttled backwards, only stopping when she clattered into the base of her bed and could go no further. She opened her mouth to scream, but her attacker had anticipated this and, before she could make a sound, he lunged forward and delivered a hefty blow to her skull. The impact sent a jarring blast of lightning into Anna's brain. As she toppled over, the world dissolved into darkness.

Susie Sergeant was just starting to drift off when the phone rang. It was the house phone, not her Job mobile, which was extraordinarily rare. Sitting up in bed, she checked her watch.

23:20

Her stomach flipped. It obviously wasn't work related, and calls made at that time of night only ever heralded bad news. She sat up hurriedly, feeling her heart rate go through the roof. After switching the bedside table lamp on, she snatched the receiver out of its cradle. "Hello?"

Please God, don't let anything bad have happened to any of my family...

At the other end of the line someone was breathing heavily, sounding very distressed. Susie's heart lurched. "Mum, is that you?"

There was a long pause, and everything went silent, as though the caller was holding their breath.

"Mum...?"

"Susie..."

She immediately recognised her husband's voice, but he sounded like he had been crying, and she wondered if something awful had happened at work. "Dan...? What's wrong?"

A heavy sigh. *"We had a big argument and she kicked me out,"* he sobbed. *"She said it was all a dreadful mistake and she doesn't want to know me anymore."*

Susie pulled the receiver away from her ear and stared at it for a long moment, struggling to believe that her estranged turd of a husband really had disturbed her rest just to inform her that his mistress had kicked him out. Was he for real? Her jaw tightened in anger. "And what do you expect me to do about that?" she demanded. If he was expecting her to let him come back, he could think again.

"I've got nowhere to go," he said, obviously feeling very sorry for himself.

Her voice was devoid of emotion. "And why would I care about that?"

There followed several seconds of intense sobbing, during which time Dan made himself sound increasingly pathetic. "*Susie, I was so wrong to leave you for her. I can see that now. Please... Can I come home?*"

So, he *was* angling to come back! "No! You bloody well can't!" she snapped, aware that her entire body was shaking with rage. "Now, grow a pair and start acting like a man, you useless shite. Oh, by the way, if you don't call me back tomorrow so that we can sort out the finances, I'll set a bloody solicitor loose on you, so help me." She slammed the phone back down in its cradle so hard that she feared she might have cracked the casing.

Anna's eyes flickered open. Her head was sagging down on her chest, and it was throbbing like hell. As soon as she looked up, the world started spinning uncontrollably. She closed her eyes again quickly, before the nausea became so bad that she threw up.

She felt disorientated, as though her world had been turned all topsy-turvy.

Thankfully, the motion sickness passed after a few seconds, and she tentatively opened her eyes a second time. Her vision was blurry, even more so than it normally was without her glasses on, and she wondered if the blow to her head had resulted in a mild concussion.

Sitting up straight, she blinked several times, but the room kept swimming in and out of focus. Taking a moment to survey her surroundings, Anna realised that she was still in her bedroom, but she was sitting in one of her dining room chairs, and her wrists were tied to the arms.

How had that happened?

The intruder could only be Spencer, and she guessed that he had carried the chair upstairs while she was unconscious. On closer inspection, she saw that thick tape had been used to secure her wrists and ankles to the arms and legs of the chair, and it had been applied so tightly that she could barely feel her fingers or toes. She struggled to pull her wrists free from their bindings, but there was no give in the tape, and all she did was chaff the skin until it was red raw.

A sudden noise from behind made her jump.

She wondered how long she had been unconscious. Long enough for Spencer to tie her up and search her house, it seemed. Was he going to kill her the same way that he had Martin? It seemed inevitable, and she consoled herself with the thought that they would at least be reunited in death.

Try as she might, Anna couldn't understand what Spencer stood to gain by killing her. Was he so insanely jealous that he wanted to rid the world of everyone Phoebe loved? Who would be next? Presumably, Ben and Jessica? Anna needed to make him understand that this was pure madness. Killing the three of them wouldn't bring Phoebe running back to him. How could he be so warped that he would even think that?

She heard the floorboards creak behind her, and a chill ran down her spine as she realised that he had just entered the room. She sensed him standing by her shoulder, just beyond the range of her peripheral vision. "You're making a terrible mistake," she croaked, throat dry, voice thin and raspy. "Killing me won't make Phoebe take you back. It'll just make her hate you more. Surely you can understand that?"

He said nothing, but she could hear him just behind her, his breathing eerily calm. And then he started laughing. It was a tortured sound, made by someone whose mind had lost touch with reality.

She flinched as she felt his hand on her left shoulder. His touch was surprisingly light, almost a caress. Suddenly, he grabbed her hair, yanking her head back so that her throat was exposed. A kitchen knife appeared in front of Anna's face, held in a gloved hand. Its gleaming blade reflected the light that was shining in from the hallway.

Anna froze as the blade touched her flesh. It felt cold and hard. She gasped as it was pressed into her, breaking the outer layer of skin.

"Stop struggling or I'll cut your throat," he hissed.

Anna was too afraid to even breathe. Any second now, he would drag the blade across her throat, severing her jugular. To her astonishment, the pressure suddenly eased and the blade was removed.

Spencer's masked figure walked into view, coming to a halt directly in front of her. He was just a blur without her glasses on, but he was shorter than she had imagined from the way that Phoebe had described him. Tears streamed down her face. "Please," she begged, sobbing uncontrollably. "Please let me live."

Spencer tilted his head to one side, as though considering the request. But then the laughter started again.

"You evil bastard!" she screamed as a surge of red hot anger momentarily overcame her fear. "I hope you rot in hell for this."

Still laughing, Spencer reached up and pulled the balaclava from his face.

Anna gasped. "No! This can't be?"

There were no words to describe her shock.

"Oh, but it can be," the man standing in front of her assured her. Only he wasn't a man at all. He was a woman.

"Well, this is fun, isn't it?" Phoebe Cunningham said with a sadistic smile.

28

Tuesday 31st July 2001
THE KIDNAP

By the time they reached Anna Manson's terraced house, it was just after midnight. The red Alfa Romeo was parked directly outside. G-Man slotted the Sierra into an empty space a little further along the road. Killing the engine, which juddered and coughed before eventually dying, he turned to berate Skippy. "You should have thought of checking here sooner," he complained.

Skippy made a point of ignoring him. All the man ever did was moan. Well, that and fall asleep. Switching the internal light off, he quietly alighted the car.

"Where are you going?" G-Man objected, all red faced and angry.

Skippy shook his head at the sheer stupidity of the question. "Just wait there," he whispered with forced patience. Shutting the door softly, so that it wouldn't make a horrible clunking noise, he set off towards Manson's house, the front of which was in total darkness.

Fortunately, there were no streetlights in the immediate vicinity, so he was confident that no one would notice him prowling around. Pausing by the gate, he checked for twitching curtains in the adjoining houses, then slipped into the front garden.

Lifting the letterbox, he strained his ears for sounds of activity inside. Nothing. No talking, no TV playing. It was as quiet as the grave. He placed his eyes against the slit, hoping to see if there were lights on at the rear of the property, but a metal box had been fitted inside to catch the post, so there was no way of telling. Having spied on Phoebe for a number of months, he knew that Manson's kitchen was located at the rear of the house, so the chances were, they were sitting back there, having a coffee and chatting.

Moving away from the letterbox, Skippy crept over to the bay window, cupped his hands against the glass, and tried to peer into the lounge. The curtains were drawn, so he couldn't see a thing.

He walked back to the car, feeling intensely frustrated. Should they call it a night, and get some rest while they could, or hold tight and gamble that Phoebe would come out again?

"Well?" G-Man demanded as soon as he sat down in the car.

"We wait," Skippy told him, hoping that he had made the right choice.

Phoebe sat on the edge of Anna's bed, holding the carving knife in her right hand and tapping the point with her gloved left forefinger, as though testing its sharpness.

Sitting directly opposite, unable to move, Anna squirmed uncomfortably in her chair. "Please, Phoebe, I don't understand what's happening," she sobbed. "Why are you doing this to me?"

Looking up from the knife, Phoebe cocked her head to one side, genuinely surprised that Anna should ask such a ridiculous question. "Isn't it obvious?"

Anna shook her head, and immediately regretted doing so as it triggered another bout of motion sickness. "I thought you were Spencer," she snivelled, trying and failing to understand what Phoebe was playing at. "I thought you'd come here to kill me." Her eyes, full of terror and confusion, pleaded for answers.

Phoebe tittered at that. "I have," she admitted, gaily.

"That's ridiculous," Anna spluttered, unable to believe what she was hearing. "Why would you want to do that?"

Phoebe shifted forward until their faces were only inches apart. As the light from the hall played across her features, they seemed to twist and distort until they took on a demonic appearance. "You betrayed me," she hissed, covering Anna in a spray of spittle. "You were supposed to be my best friend, but instead you stole the love of my life from me. *That's* why."

Despite her fear, Anna suddenly found herself overwhelmed by the shame of her transgression. "I'm so sorry," she wept, unable to meet the other woman's gaze. "I swear to you that I never meant to hurt you."

Phoebe snorted, derisively. "Of course you did." Her voice became flat and hard. "Martin was weak, like most men, and he thought with his dick, but you should have known better, especially after all we've been through together over the years. What you did was unforgivable."

"Don't you think I know that?" Anna snivelled, almost choking on her own guilt. "Do you honestly think that I was ever comfortable with any of this? You have no idea how difficult it's been for me to keep the truth from you."

Phoebe considered this dispassionately. "Yes, well, sometimes we have to make decisions in life that make us uncomfortable. I mean, can you imagine how difficult it was for me, when I decided that I'd have to kill my back stabbing best friend?"

"Oh, please don't say that," Anna begged her between sobs.

Phoebe shrugged, callously. "What do you expect me to say? I hate you for what you did to me."

"I don't blame you for that," Anna cried. "I hate myself, but I don't want you to do something that you'll live to regret. Think about what it would do to your parents."

Phoebe's lips parted in a cruel sneer. "Oh, I'm not going to do anything that I'll regret, I can promise you that."

Anna was lost for words. This wasn't her life-long friend speaking; this was a total stranger. The only possible explanation was that Phoebe had suffered a catastrophic mental breakdown in the wake of her kidnap. "Phoebe, you're not thinking straight," she said, staring at her friend imploringly. "You need help. Untie me and let me call your parents. They'll know what to do." Ben and Jessica could book her into a private clinic, just like they'd done when she'd gone off the rails as a teenager. "No one else needs to know about this, and I promise you won't get into trouble."

"Ummm." Phoebe pretended to consider this, even going as far as to stroke her chin thoughtfully.

Tears were streaming down Anna's cheeks now. "Why are you doing this to me?" she beseeched her friend between sobs. "You know I love you."

Leaning forward, Phoebe gently stroked Anna's hair. "I love you too," she said, smiling tenderly. The smile vanished in an instant, replaced by a chilling hardness. "Or, at least, I used to." With that, Phoebe lunged forward and clamped her hand tightly over Anna's mouth. "No more talk," she said.

Anna's left shoulder exploded with pain as the carving knife was plunged deep into it. The blade must have nicked a nerve on the way in, because a burning jolt of pain flew along her arm, all the way down to her wrist. She screamed in agony, but the noise was muffled by Phoebe's hand.

"Shhh!" Phoebe soothed, slowly removing the blade from the gaping wound.

Anna's sweat soaked face was contorted with pain. "Please don't do this," she begged, breathing heavily.

Phoebe returned to the bed.

Ignoring Anna's whimpering, she calmly studied the streak of crimson running down the blade's edge. "I suppose, as I'm going to kill you, that you're entitled to an explanation of sorts," she said, as though she were doing Anna a big favour, "but you need to understand that, if you make the slightest noise, I won't hesitate to slit your throat. Do you understand?" As she spoke, she sliced the blade through the air directly in front of Anna's face to emphasise her point.

"Y-yes," Anna replied through gritted teeth. "I understand perfectly." Blood was running freely from her injury, but the pain was easing off and, as long as she didn't try to move her arm, it was just about bearable.

Lying in the unfamiliar bed, unable to sleep, Dan Sergeant still couldn't believe that Janet had ended their relationship simply because he'd answered her question truthfully and replied that Susie was great in bed. Why had she been so offended by that? It wasn't as if he had been implying that she was shit by comparison! He had immediately tried to salvage the situation, pointing out that no matter how good his wife was in the sack, he had still chosen to leave her for Janet. He had expected his words to appease her, but they had only added fuel to the flames, transforming her anger from what could politely be called a simmering rage into a full blown nuclear meltdown.

Why did women have to be so complicated?

Janet was the one who had raised the subject, and because he hadn't immediately said that Susie was a rubbish shag, she had got the right hump, twisting his words into something that he had never intended them to be. What had started off as a minor squabble had quickly deteriorated into a full blown argument, during which she had taken it upon herself to dissect every aspect of their fledgling relationship. She had stood there, citing every annoying trait that he had, and every habit that she didn't approve of, ticking them off on her fingers, one by one.

To his dismay, it turned out that there were rather a lot of them.

Any sane woman would have reacted by banishing him to the spare room for the night, but Janet had flown completely off the rails, terminating their relationship on the spot and booting him out of her house. He had tried calling Susie, in the hope that she would let him come home, but his appeal had fallen on deaf ears. With nowhere else to go, he had been forced to take a room at the nearest hotel, a little two-star place in Lea Bridge Road. It was fairly basic but quite comfortable, and at least it was close to work.

In hindsight, he now bitterly regretted calling Susie. It could hardly be considered his finest moment. She already held him in low esteem, and now he had given her more ammunition to use against him. Worryingly, she had sounded deadly serious about getting a solicitor involved, and he decided that he would call her first thing in the morning to apologise for behaving like such an arse.

With any luck, Janet would have cooled off by then. He certainly hoped so, because they were rostered to work together as the early shift crew of Juliet One, and he really didn't fancy being trapped in a car with her for eight hours while she sulked.

―――

Anna was afraid on so many levels. She was afraid of Phoebe, and of what she had become; she was afraid of dying; she was afraid of being made to suffer before she died. It terrified her that her life was in the hands of a woman who seemed completely unhinged and who had clearly lost all sense of perspective.

"I've worked out what you're doing," she told Phoebe.

Phoebe raised an enquiring eyebrow. "Have you now? Well, don't leave me in suspense. What do *you* think I'm doing?"

Her mocking tone angered Anna. "You think that, because Spencer killed Martin, you can kill me and frame him for the murder, but you won't get away with it."

Phoebe laughed, low and nasty. "What makes you think that I won't?"

"Because there won't be any evidence here to connect Spencer to the crime."

Phoebe smiled, knowingly. "What, like the bloodied handprint that Spencer left at Martin's flat? Yes, I do see what you mean."

It worried Anna that she didn't seem remotely bothered by this.

When Phoebe stood up and moved towards her, Anna cowered, and the sudden movement sent a searing wave of pain through her arm, making her gasp.

"Relax," Phoebe reassured her as she walked out the room. "I'm not going to hurt you... At least, not yet."

Closing her eyes, Anna let out a low, pitiful moan. "I don't want to die," she sobbed.

"No one does," Phoebe said, appearing behind her and making her jump. "I doubt Martin wanted to die," she said casually, "or Spencer."

Anna stiffened. "What are you talking about? Spencer's on the run. He isn't dead."

"Oh, I think you'll find he is," Phoebe said with absolute certainty.

"He can't be," Anna argued. "He only killed Martin two days ago."

Phoebe giggled mischievously, and Anna thought that she sounded totally insane.

"That's right, so he did, and we know this because of the handprint that the police found in his flat."

Something heavy landed in Anna's lap. Looking down, she was horrified to see that it was a human hand, severed at the wrist.

"Just between you and me, they're going to find a bloody handprint here as well," Phoebe said, firing a conspiratorial wink at Anna.

Anna was too busy screaming to notice.

———

"How much longer are we going to give it?" G-Man's argumentative tone implied they were wasting their time. "We've been at this all day now, and we've got bugger all to show for it. I don't know about you, but I'm dog tired and I've had a bloody belly full. Let's knock it on the head and get some kip."

Skippy did a double take. "Tired? How can you possibly be tired? All you've done all day is sleep."

G-Man pouted. "I suffer from Narcolepsy," he said defensively. "I can't help it."

Skippy didn't have a clue what that was, but he wasn't in the mood for feeble excuses. "Let's get something straight," he said, deciding it was time to lay down the law. "This is my job, and I'll decide when we call it a day, not you. If she hasn't shown her face by one o'clock, we'll pop back to mine and grab some shut eye, but we'll have to be back first thing in the morning, in case we get a chance to snatch her as she leaves."

G-Man glanced down at his watch, groaned miserably, then folded his arms. "I'm beginning to think you're yanking my chain, old son, and that this so-called job of yours is nothing more than a pipe dream."

Skippy reacted angrily. "Maybe I should've said that when your post office job blew out?"

"That wasn't my–"

Skippy steamrollered over his objection. "Just shut up and think about the half million quid we're gonna get paid when her old man coughs up the ransom for getting her back."

"If we ever manage to snatch her."

"I don't know why you're whinging so much, I've done all the hard graft, following her around for months on end to learn her routine. All you've got to do is provide a bit of extra muscle, so maybe you should be bloody grateful instead of complaining all the time."

"That's not strictly true though, is it, mate?" G-Man said, jutting his chin forward indignantly. "You seem to have conveniently forgotten that it was *me* who came up with a safe place to hide her for a few days, because *you* couldn't think of one."

That stung. Skippy *had* come up with a safe place, a very safe place as a matter of fact, but his dim-witted cousin had burned it by taking the girl there on Wednesday evening.

"Yeah, well, I've already said I'm grateful for that," Skippy grudgingly allowed.

As luck would have it, G-Man's father was the caretaker at a local primary school, which was currently closed for the summer holidays. Apparently, there was an old store room at the back of the building where no one, not even his father, ever went. If they locked her in there, no one would ever know.

G-Man smirked at him, as though the acknowledgement was a major victory, and this incensed Skippy so much that he had to look away.

A muffled ping from his pocket alerted Skippy that a message had just come through on his phone. Digging it out, he saw that it was another text from Spencer. He groaned inwardly, wondering what his idiot cousin wanted now.

I've done it. I've taken care of the last obstacle. I'm heading out of London till the heat dies down so don't worry if you don't hear from me for a while.

The message made no sense at all, and he was too tired to bother replying. Tucking the phone back in his pocket, he returned to the business of sulking.

G-Man nudged his elbow.

"Sod off," Skippy responded, angrily. He wasn't going to give the irritating wanker the satisfaction of goading him any further.

G-Man nudged him again, with more urgency this time. "Look, there's movement by the door."

Skippy cast a dubious eye in the direction that his irksome partner was pointing in. Sure enough, the street door to Manson's house had just opened and, as they watched, a darkly dressed figure emerged, carrying what looked like a large cool box and a smaller holdall.

"Is that her?" G-Man asked, excitedly.

Skippy nodded. He was almost too hyped to breathe, let alone speak.

This was it!

This was the chance they had been waiting for.

There might never be another.

As Skippy hurriedly pulled on his gloves and balaclava, he

noticed that his palms were damp, and his hands were visibly shaking. Luckily, it was too dark inside the car for G-Man to have noticed this. "Quick! Get ready," he hissed, voice brimming with tension.

Reaching for his own balaclava, G-Man was grinning at him like an idiot, no doubt seeing pound signs in front of his eyes, and thinking about how he was going to spend his share of the ransom.

Skippy's lips curled downwards in disgust. "I need you to stay focused," he snapped.

G-Man dismissed the agitated warning with a contemptuous wave of his hand. "Relax. This isn't my first rodeo."

Closing the street door behind her, Phoebe carried the bags to her car and opened the boot. There was no sign of Manson, which was a relief. With Phoebe's head buried in the Alfa's boot, Skippy grabbed the leather cosh from the footwell, finding its weight surprisingly comforting.

"Give me a couple of seconds to sneak up on her, and then bring the car over," he instructed, before slipping out of the vehicle and setting off as stealthily as he could.

As he reached the Alfa, Skippy heard G-Man starting the Ford's engine behind him. Thankfully, the temperamental heap sparked into life at the first attempt.

Aiming for the top of her skull, Skippy raised the cosh high above his head and brought it down quickly. However, just before impact, Phoebe turned her head to the left, and the blow merely glanced off the side of her skull before crashing into her shoulder. Skippy hit her again, much harder. This time, the blow connected squarely, and she dropped like a stone. For one awful moment, he feared that he might have hit her too hard, because she seemed terribly still, and he couldn't hear her breathing. Then she let out a small moan, and a wave of relief flooded over him. As he stood over her, he became conscious of G-Man pulling the Ford up beside him. Thankfully, he'd had the good sense not to turn his headlights on. "Help me get her into the boot," Skippy whispered, urgently beckoning him over.

G-Man clambered out and rushed to his side. "I'll take the legs," he said, bending down and grabbing Phoebe's ankles. Between them, they unceremoniously lifted her up, carried her to the Sierra's boot, and lowered her in.

As Skippy made to close the boot, G-Man placed a restraining hand on his arm. "Shouldn't we tie her up and gag her first?" he asked. "What if she wakes up and kicks off?"

Skippy shook his head, emphatically. "Let's drive to one of the car parks off Hollow Ponds and do it there," he whispered. "She's out cold, and it'll only take us a couple of minutes to get there."

"But what if she wakes up?".

"She won't wake up," Skippy said firmly. Holding G-Man's eye until the other man looked away, he gave a little grunt of satisfaction and closed the squeaking boot.

Skippy jogged back to the Alfa, retrieving the keys that Phoebe had dropped when he'd hit her. As he opened the driver's door, G-Man came rushing over. "What the fuck are you doing?" he demanded, pugnaciously.

Skippy tutted impatiently. It really was like working with a dim witted child. "We can't leave her car here, can we?" *You retarded knobhead.* "We need to dump it somewhere quiet, where it won't be found for a few days."

G-Man looked like he was going to argue.

"Let's not do this here," Skippy seethed. "Just get back in the poxy car and follow me, and we'll sort it all out when we stop." Cursing under his breath, he started the engine, slipped the clutch, and pushed the gear lever into first.

29

SYSTEM SHUT DOWN

Kevin Murray and Jim Stone had drawn the short straw. As a result, they were covering the night shift monitoring of the live-time feed that was being beamed in from the van parked outside Skippy's flat.

Sitting in the little viewing room that had been set up at Hertford House, they were taking it in turns to watch, each doing an hour on and an hour off. Their shift had started at eleven p.m., and it was now almost one. Only another six hours until they were relieved.

Murray had just returned from a trip to the petrol station on the other side of the Barking Roundabout, where he'd gone to stock up on coffee and snacks to relieve the boredom. He had also purchased some scratch cards. Pulling a pound coin from his pocket, Murray leaned against a wall and worried away at each of the scratch cards in turn. "Crap. Rubbish. More rubbish," he complained as he discarded them, one after another. He finished with a sigh. "Well, that was a complete waste of a fiver," he whinged as he pushed himself away from the wall and wandered over to peer down at the screen. "Anything happening?" he asked.

Stone shook his head. "Dead as the grave."

Murray returned to his chair, sat down, fidgeted for a while, and then got up again. "What do all these buttons do?" he asked, examining the machine sitting on the desk next to the monitor.

"Don't touch them," Stone told him without taking his eyes off the screen.

Murray seemed to interpret that as a challenge. "Why?" he demanded, attempting to press the nearest one, just for the sake of it.

Jim Stone angrily swatted his hand away. "I said, don't touch anything. The wizards from the Technical Support Unit took ages to configure all this stuff, and they said not to touch any of the settings as the system can be a bit temperamental."

Murray laughed. "They always say that. What does this one do?" He pressed a square red button in the centre of the control panel. There was a click, a whir, and then a panel of lights at the top of the console started blinking. The TV screen flickered and then went blank, and the computer started shutting down. "Shit!" Murray said, instinctively taking a backwards step.

Stone glared at him in anger. "You useless wanker! You've just rebooted the system. God knows how long that will take, and we won't have sight on the target address for the duration."

Murray paled. "How was I supposed to know that?" he said, instantly becoming defensive. "It's not like there's a bloody great sign there, telling me not to touch it, is there?"

Stone stood up and cuffed him around the top of the head. "I told you not to touch it," he snapped. "Twice!"

"What do we do now?" Murray asked. Rubbing his head, he was staring at Stone for guidance.

Stone shrugged, stoically. "We wait for it to reboot, and hope that we don't miss anything important during the time it's down. I'll put an entry in the log, so that someone can review the footage in the morning, when everything's back on line."

Murray gave him puppy eyes. "Make sure you emphasise that the system failed on its own, not because I accidentally touched a button."

Accidentally!

Stone shook his head. "You're a complete moron. You know that, right?"

The little clearing by Hollow Ponds was darkly foreboding, surrounded by tall, whispering trees from which thick branches extended like grotesque claws, waiting to snatch the unwary traveller and whisk them away into the night.

Thankfully, the moon was high and the sky was clear, so there was plenty of ambient light for them to work in. Although the clearing was currently deserted, they both knew that could change in an instant; the car parks around the ponds were notorious meeting places for people seeking illicit sexual thrills, and someone could cruise by at any moment, either looking for a willing partner or hoping to watch a couple of doggers going at it.

Glancing nervously over his shoulder, to make sure that no one was going to emerge from one of the winding footpaths that disappeared into the thick undergrowth and surprise them, G-Man opened the Sierra's boot and looked in on Phoebe. He gave a little grunt of satisfaction when he saw that she was still unconscious.

Skippy appeared by his side. "See, I told you she wouldn't wake up."

Between them, they secured her wrists and ankles with the gaffer tape they had found in the boot of her car, stuffed an oily rag in her mouth, and put a strip of tape across her mouth to keep her from spitting it out.

"Make sure she can still breathe properly," Skippy warned. She would be no good to them dead.

With a petulant sigh, G-Man leaned over the girl, peeled back the tape from her face, and stuck two gloved fingers into her mouth to ensure that she couldn't accidentally swallow the gag and choke.

When he was happy that her airway was unobstructed, he replaced the gaffer tape and stood up. "She's fine," he said, grumpily.

Skippy slammed the boot shut. "Right, I'll follow you to your dad's school. Once we've got her safely locked in the store room, we'll give her old man a nasty little wakeup call and tell him to sort our money out." Giving G-Man a 'well done' pat on the back, he set off towards Phoebe's Alfa.

"Whoa!" G-Man called after him.

Skippy stopped, spun around, irritated. "Now what?"

G-Man's neck seemed to retract into his shoulders, like a turtle tucking his head into his shell. "We can't, we can't take her to the school tonight," he stammered.

"Why not?"

G-Man looked down at the floor. "I, er, I haven't got the keys," he mumbled.

Skippy was dumbfounded. "What? WHAT!"

"I can't get the keys until the morning," G-Man said, becoming flustered. "Didn't I mention that before?"

Skippy was in his face in an instant. "No, you fucking well didn't!" Running his hands through his hair, he started pacing up and down the car park, swearing under his breath.

G-Man remained by the boot, saying nothing.

"Christ! I thought Spencer was fucking useless, but you take the meaning of the word to a whole new level," Skippy ranted. Taking a deep breath, he checked his watch. "Okay, we'll just have to take her back to my place for tonight. Follow me, but keep your eyes peeled when we get there, because if anyone sees us and calls the filth, we're both fucked."

"I'm sorry, mate," G-Man said, smiling sheepishly. "I promise I'll get the keys first thing in the morning, and then we can whisk her straight over to the school."

———

The system hadn't rebooted of its own accord, as Stone had been hoping it would, and he was now on the phone to the out of hours TSU engineer, who was trying to talk him through a manual restart.

"*And how did you say it went dead on you?*" the engineer asked, sounding half asleep.

Stone glared at Murray before answering. "It was all working fine one moment, then there was a strange whirring noise and it just started shutting down," he lied.

Murray smiled, patted him on the back.

Stone shrugged his hand away and covered the mouthpiece so that the engineer wouldn't be able to hear him. "You owe me big time for this," he growled.

Murray nodded, enthusiastically. "I'll make it up to you," he promised, relieved that the former paratrooper hadn't dropped him in the brown smelly stuff.

"*That's most odd,*" the engineer said. "*If we can't get it going tonight, I'll get someone out first thing in the morning to run a full diagnostic.*"

"Let's hope it doesn't come to that," Stone told him, "because my boss will throw a major strop if we have to wait until then."

Behind him, Murray swallowed hard. He could deal with Tyler getting the hump; he was more worried about how Dillon would react if he ever discovered that this was his fault.

There were several empty spaces outside Skippy's flat, so he pulled the Alfa into the first and indicated for G-Man to park the Ford behind him. "Wait there," he whispered as he jogged past G-Man on his way to his flat.

Opening the street door, he went straight through to the little bedroom at the back, made sure that there was nothing in it that might identify him, and grabbed a sheet from the bed. An old carpet would have been better, but beggars couldn't be choosers. He paused at the street door for long enough to satisfy himself that the coast was clear, and then signalled for G-Man to open the boot.

Peering inside, he was relieved to see that the girl was still unconscious. With G-Man's help, he quickly wrapped her in the sheet, securing it by wrapping strips of gaffer tape around the top, middle and bottom. That ought to prevent it from slipping off as they carried her into the flat. "Right, let's be as quick as we can be," he whispered, looking around nervously.

Taking an end each, they scooped the girl up and set off towards the front garden at double quick time. Almost immediately, their load sagged in the middle and G-Man nearly dropped his end. "Wait! I'm losing my grip," he hissed, scrabbling for a better purchase. "Okay," he said a moment later, nodding for Skippy to carry on.

Shaking his head in despair, Skippy said nothing.

They carried Phoebe along the narrow hallway to the bedroom at the rear of the flat and dumped her, face down, on the mattress. Breathing heavily from his exertions, Skippy set about unwrapping her. He searched her pockets, but the only thing she had in her possession was a cheap mobile phone, which he powered off and jammed into his pocket. When he was done, Skippy pulled an old draw string fabric shoe bag he'd had since his school days over her head, and waved for G-man to follow him into the kitchen.

"Okay, so far, so good," he said, removing his gloves and wiping the sweat from his brow. "We'll have to take turns watching her for the rest of the night, just in case she gets any ideas about making a break for it when she wakes up. We'll get her out of here the moment you get your hands on those poxy keys."

"Why do we need to watch her?" G-Man asked. "Her hands and feet are tied, she's gagged and hooded, so it's not like she can do anything."

"I ain't arguing with you," Skippy told him, firmly. "I'll put a chair in the doorway, and one of us will have to stay with her at all times." The clever little bitch had already demonstrated her resourcefulness by escaping from Spencer, and he had no intention of underestimating her the way his cousin had. "I'll take the first watch," he offered, grabbing a hard back chair and dragging it into the hall. "We'll swap over in a couple of hours."

"If you say so," G-Man said with a weary sigh. Grabbing a can of Coke from the fridge, he set off towards the lounge. "In the meantime, I'm gonna get some much needed kip."

"Like you haven't had enough of that already," Skippy muttered under his breath.

Nooooo!

This couldn't be happening.

Not again!

Panic mushroomed inside her chest.

She couldn't see; she couldn't move; she could barely breathe, and the revolting cloth in her mouth was making her retch.

Keep calm, control your breathing. Remember, you're strong. You've moved on. You're getting your life back.

The top of her skull felt as though it had been cleaved in two, and the pain was so intense that it was making her feel sick. Even though she was lying completely still, the world around her was spinning violently, and all she could do was hang on and wait for the damn thing to stop. Only it didn't; it started spinning faster and faster, until she could no longer tell the difference between up and down.

She was flying, or falling, or being carried.

And then she blacked out.

When she came to a few moments – or minutes – later, she heard distorted voices in the background. They were snapping at each other, and the tension between them was palpable.

She tried to focus on what they were saying, hoping it would reveal something about where she was being kept, but every word uttered seemed to echo, as though they were shouting up at her from the bottom of a deep ravine.

"... I'm-I'm-I'm gonna-gonna-gonna get-get-get some-some-some much-much-much needed-needed-needed kip-kip-kip," one of them was saying.

Phoebe passed out again.

She didn't know how long she was out for but, when she came to, her head felt a little clearer, although it was no less painful. She was lying face down on what she assumed was a bed, because it was soft and giving, unlike the hard concrete floor she had found herself on the last time she'd come around after being abducted.

The last time! Like it was a regular occurrence!

Thankfully, the world was no longer spinning out of control, but Phoebe's brain still felt addled. Her thoughts were in complete disarray, and the harder she tried to focus her mind, the more it made her head hurt.

It seemed obvious that Spencer had somehow found her again, and this time he'd had help.

But who?

As her mind became sharper, she recalled that Spencer was dead. She had caved his head in with an iron bar, back at the barn.

But what if he wasn't dead?

What if he had somehow survived the attack?

She dismissed that thought at once. Spencer was definitely dead; she had battered his skull until most of his brains had been splattered over the floor.

He had still been dead when she'd returned to the crime scene the following day, to chop off his right hand before dumping his body where no one would ever find it.

So, if this wasn't Spencer, then who the hell was it?

She heard a noise nearby as someone fidgeted in a chair, cleared their throat and then yawned. Phoebe stiffened. Was someone watching her? If so, had they realised that she was awake?

When no one came over to check on her, she concluded that her guard hadn't noticed, and she decided that the safest thing to do for the time being was to continue playing dead. If they thought she was still out cold, they might relax their guard around her and say something that she could later use to her advantage.

Using her tongue, she tried to push the rag out of her mouth, but there was something blocking its exit. To her surprise, instead of sending her into a frenzied panic, the knowledge that she had been gagged merely stoked her anger, making her even more determined to escape. She would find a way out of this, just as she had the last time and, when she did, she would make them pay for what they had done to her.

Tyler pulled into the car park at Hertford House just after seven-thirty. He was tired, grumpy, and in desperate need of coffee. He parked next to Dillon, who was just getting out of his car. "Morning, Dill," he said as he pressed the fob to activate the central locking.

Dillon, looking as fresh as a daisy, gestured at the cloudless azure sky above them and sighed contentedly. "Morning, Jack. Lovely day, isn't it?"

Tyler looked up, unimpressed, and squinted as the sun burned his eyes. "Ask me that again later," he grouched, "after I've had time to wake up."

Dillon wagged an admonishing finger at him. "Stop being such a sourpuss, you know that the morning is the best time of the–"

Tyler cut him off with a raised hand. "Don't you dare say it," he warned.

" –day," Dillon said, completing the sentence with a triumphant grin.

Tyler scowled at him, and strode off without saying a word.

When they reached the office, a few minutes later, Tyler was surprised to see Jim Stone sitting there, talking to Dean Fletcher and Reg Parker. "I thought you and Kevin were monitoring the live feed overnight, so shouldn't you have gone home by now?"

Stone grimaced. "The feed broke down just after midnight," he said, apologetically. "We tried to get the on-call engineer to talk us through a system reboot, but nothing worked, so we're waiting for someone to come out this morning and get it back up and running."

Tyler's mood darkened, and he turned to glare at Dillon. "What were you saying about this being a lovely day?"

Dillon raised his hand in a calming gesture. "Leave it to me," he said, soothingly. "I'll give the TSU a call and see if I can chivvy them along."

"I've already done that," Stone told them. "They've promised an engineer will be here before eight."

Tyler glanced at his watch, tutted bad temperedly. "I suppose these things happen," he grudgingly conceded, "but there's no need for you to stay on, Jim. Why don't you go home and get some rest?"

Stone shook his head. "As there was nothing we could do last night, me and Kevin slept on the camp beds that Chris Deakin keeps in the MIR, so we're both fully rested and raring to go."

At that moment, the door swung open and Kevin Murray staggered in, his arms so full of exhibits that he could barely see over the top. "Morning tossers," he declared loudly. Dropping the exhibits on his desk, he did a double take when he saw Tyler and Dillon standing there. "Oh, beg your pardon," he said, blushing. "I didn't realise that you two were here. Obviously, I wasn't including you in that." With a polite nod, he turned around and walked out of the office as quickly as he could.

"Wanker," Stone muttered under his breath.

"Has there been any activity on Spencer's phone, Reggie?" Tyler asked, hoping that someone would have some good news for him.

Reg logged on to his computer and checked his e-mails. "Looks like another text was sent to Skipton overnight," he said, looking up from the screen. "It's timed at 00:40 hours and it was sent from within the radius of a cell covering Leytonstone. It reads: 'I've done it. I've taken care of the last obstacle. I'm heading out of London till the heat dies down so don't worry if you don't hear from me for a while.'"

"I wonder what he meant by that?" Dillon said, glancing uncertainly at Tyler.

Tyler could only shrug. "I don't know, but I don't like the sound of it."

"Me neither," Dillon confessed. "Did Skipton reply?"

Parker shook his head. "Nothing as yet, but he was probably asleep. I'll let you know as soon as he does."

Tyler grunted. "I'll be in my office if anyone needs me," he said. "Dill, unless I'm much mistaken, it's your turn to make the coffee."

―――――

As soon as they realised she was awake, one of her kidnappers raised the smelly bag until it was clear of her mouth, and then clumsily removed the gag. Phoebe dry heaved as his fingers touched the back of her throat, triggering her gag reflex. Sucking in air, and trying not to throw up, she listened to the bastards laughing at her discomfort.

They initially refused her request to visit the loo, but soon changed their minds when she screamed that she was going to soil herself if she didn't get to a toilet quickly. Like a couple of squabbling kids, her captors stood there for what seemed like ages, arguing over who should take her. In the end, still bickering, they pulled the hood back down below her chin and carried her into the nearby toilet between them. Yanking her tracksuit bottoms and knickers down, they plonked her on the loo so that she could relieve herself. Urinating with the toilet door wide open, knowing that they were watching her, probably sniggering to themselves like a couple of smutty perverts, proved to be an indescribably humiliating experience.

When they dumped her back on the bed, she begged them to untie her hands, but they refused. They did, however, agree that the gag could stay out as long as she behaved herself. Before leaving the room, the man who was clearly in charge gave her a couple of paracetamols for her headache, and some water to wash them down with. Holding the glass to her lips, he assured her that no harm would befall her as long as she did precisely what they told her to do.

As she lay there, bound and hooded, she was struck by the sublime irony of the situation. She had managed to commit three perfect murders, and she had almost gotten away with it, but now her brilliant scheme was in danger of being blown out of the water by the ineptitude and bad timing of her kidnappers. Why couldn't they have waited another day before abducting her? By then, she would have disposed of all the incriminating evidence in the boot of her car, and it wouldn't have mattered. Despite the seriousness of her predicament, she just had to laugh. It seemed to her that everything now hinged on her father paying the ransom quickly. If he did that, and they released her straight away, there might still be a way for her to salvage the situation. All she could do in the meantime was stay strong, bide her time, and pray that luck would be on her side.

Jim Stone was back in the viewing room with the TSU engineer, a slender man in his late forties with thinning brown hair. He wore tortoiseshell glasses with thick lenses, and his rather large forehead was permanently marred by an intense frown of concentration. As he beavered away at the control panel, running a series of diagnostic checks, his tongue incessantly clucked away inside his mouth, making him sound like an out of control Geiger counter.

Eccentric was the word that came to Stone's mind.

Kevin Murray popped his head around the door. "Everything alright?" he enquired, glancing nervously from one to the other. It was almost eight o'clock, and the office meeting was due to start any minute now.

Tyler had made a point of coming down to speak to the engineer as soon as he arrived. He had made his displeasure over the loss of 'product', and the amount of time that it had taken for someone to come out and fix the equipment, brutally clear. Before leaving, Tyler had insisted that the engineer report back to him with a detailed explanation of what had gone wrong before leaving.

"Oh, hello," the engineer said, looking up and smiling. Behind his lenses, which looked like they could have doubled as bullet proof glass, his pale blue eyes were magnified to at least twice their normal size, making him resemble an owl. "My name's Norman."

Murray nodded an acknowledgement. "Have you worked out what went wrong yet?" he asked, "only it was most inconvenient, losing sight of the target address like that."

To Stone's embarrassment, Murray had the cheek to tut disapprovingly.

"I really don't know what to tell you," Norman said, sounding mortified that his beloved equipment had let them down so badly. "It doesn't usually do this. According to all the checks I've run, and I've run them twice to confirm my findings, everything's working properly. The only possible explanation for it behaving the way it did was for someone to have pressed the reset button without closing the programme down first, but I know that no one would ever do that."

"Most definitely not," Murray assured him in a tone that implied it was an affront that Norman should even consider such a thing.

Stone glared at him, then buried his head in his hands to hide his embarrassment.

Norman was too busy pressing buttons to notice. "I'll have it back online in a minute or two," he promised, "and then one of you can review the footage for the time period that the monitor was down."

"That'll be down to the early turn shift to do," Murray said, checking his watch. He turned to Stone. "Look, I need to run a load of exhibits up to the lab for Dick Jarvis, so would you mind letting the boss know that I won't be able to make the morning meeting."

Stone opened his mouth to object, but Murray cut him off before he could utter a word. "Great, that's settled, then. Oh, don't worry, I haven't forgotten that I owe you one for sorting *that*–" he nodded towards the monitor "–out for me." Then, without waiting for an answer, he made for the door as though his life depended on getting out of the room within the next ten seconds.

"Here goes," Norman said as he fired up the system. There was a loud whirring noise, and the monitor's screen burst into life, displaying a clear view of Skippy's front door and the stretch of pavement immediately outside his flat. "There we are," Norman announced proudly. "Everything's back online, and working perfectly."

30

THE RANSOM

G-Man returned to the flat at seven-fifty. As he closed the door behind him, he was looking particularly pleased with himself. His dodgy left eye seemed to have found an extra gear this morning, and it was twitching faster than ever. "I've got them," he called triumphantly. "I've got my dad's keys." To prove this, he held them up and jangled them for Skippy to see.

"Good," Skippy replied from his chair in the hallway. "Where did you park her car? Not outside my place, I hope?"

G-Man huffed, resentfully. "Give me some bloody credit," he said. "I've parked it a street over to the left, in a little car park behind some flats. We can take it out to Epping Forest and torch it later, once we've got the little princess sorted out."

Skippy levered himself out of the uncomfortable chair, placing one hand in the small of his back to support his aching lower vertebrae. "Good," he said with a grimace of pain. "Now listen, I'm gonna call her dad and let him know that we've taken her, so I need you to keep an eye on her while I get the burner from the kitchen."

G-Man frowned. "I thought you wanted to move her first?"

"I did," Skippy confirmed, "but that was when I thought we could do it before the rush hour started. There are too many people out and about now, and we can't risk someone seeing us, so we'll have to give it a couple of hours."

Leaving G-Man to watch over the girl, he walked into the kitchen and grabbed a cheap Pay-As-You-Go phone from the counter. He had purchased it from the Stratford Centre the day before, charged the handset overnight, and pre-programmed it with Ben Cunningham's number. Powering it on, he strolled back into the bedroom.

"Now listen carefully," he told Phoebe. "In a minute, I'm going to ring your dad and tell him that we've got you. Naturally, he'll wanna talk to you, and I'll let him but, when I do, you'd better just tell him that you're alive and well, and nothing else. Do you understand me, girly?"

Phoebe hesitated, then nodded timidly.

Her apathetic response annoyed Skippy. Grabbing Phoebe's right arm, he gave it a hard squeeze, smiling in satisfaction when she yelped in pain. "I asked you a fucking question," he snarled. "Do you understand me?"

"Y-yes," she stammered, her voice quivering with fear.

Skippy leaned in close. "You need to understand something," he told her, jerking her arm as he spoke. "We can either do this the easy way or the hard way. It makes no difference to me, but it'll be much better for you if you cooperate and do exactly as I say. Now, do you understand?"

"Yes," she responded quickly, eager to appease him.

He shook her again, harder this time. "Do you fucking understand?"

"Yes!" she cried. "Yes, yes, yes."

He stared at her for a long moment, then released her arm and sat down beside her. "When you speak to him, the loud speaker will be on, so I'll be able to hear everything you both say," he warned. "Don't try to be clever, little girl, and don't say anything about where we are or where we snatched you from. Got it?"

"Yes," she said, nodding to emphasise her understanding.

Skippy glanced at G-Man, who was watching him expectantly. "Okay," he said, licking his lips and taking a deep breath. "Here we go." His hands were shaking as he pressed the green button to make the call. "Let's earn ourselves some money."

―――――

"Ben! Your phone's ringing," Jessica called. Annoyingly, he had left it on the kitchen work surface when he'd popped out to visit the loo a few moments ago. He was always doing that, and it really got on her nerves. What was the point in having a mobile phone if you never took it with you?

A quick glance at the caller ID told Jessica that the call was being made from a withheld number, and she wondered if it could possibly be the police, ringing with news that Spencer had finally been arrested. She hadn't slept properly since his release and, after everything that he had put Phoebe through, she wouldn't be able to rest until he was back in a cell, where he belonged.

Out in the hallway, she heard the sound of a toilet flushing. "Ben," she called again, but there was no answer. Biting her bottom lip, Jessica stared at the phone indecisively. Should she answer the call or not? In the end, she snatched up the Blackberry and pressed the green button. "Ben Cunningham's phone," she said, continuing to unload the dishwasher as she spoke.

Silence.

"Hello..?"

"*Who's this?*" a coarse male voice demanded.

Jessica didn't take kindly to his tone. It was rude and disrespectful. "This is his wife speaking," she replied prissily. "Who's calling?"

"*Put your old man on the phone, and be quick about it.*"

Jessica felt her hackles go up. "Don't you talk like that to me, you cheeky git," she snapped. "Didn't your mother teach you any manners?"

A sigh of exasperation. *"Look, I ain't got time for this. Put your old man on the phone, now."*

Jessica pressed the red button, cutting him off, and tossed the phone back onto the worktop. "Up yours," she told it, just as Ben walked into the room.

"Who are you talking to?" he asked.

Before she could answer, the phone rang again.

Ben scooped it up. "Hello."

Jessica watched with interest, wondering if the caller was the same obnoxious man that she had just hung up on. If it was, Ben would soon put the little upstart in his place.

"Yes, this is Ben Cunningham," he said, smiling at her. "Who's this?" He listened for a moment, and then his brow creased into a worried frown. "What? Say that again," he demanded, sounding nonplussed. He listened for a few seconds longer, growing increasingly agitated. "Is this a bloody wind up?" he suddenly shouted.

Jessica was used to him shouting at people over the phone, but his rantings were usually driven by anger, not fear, and she began to feel a little uneasy.

Ben covered the mouthpiece. "Where's Phoebe?" he demanded, anxiously.

Jessica shrugged. "Upstairs in bed, as far as I know. Why?"

"Go and check," Ben snapped at her. "Hurry."

Something about the way that he said this made her blood run cold. Jessica ran into the hall, up the stairs and along the landing until she came to Phoebe's door. She gave a brisk knock and opened it without waiting for a reply.

"Phoebe, darling, are you okay?"

The room was empty, the bed unslept in.

Feeling her knees go weak, Jessica ran back downstairs. "She's not in her room," she said, breathlessly.

"What about her car? Is it outside?" Ben asked, and there was no mistaking the urgency in his voice.

Jessica shook her head. She didn't need to check; she already knew the answer to that one. "She told me that she dropped it off at the garage yesterday afternoon. It's booked in for a service and MOT this morning, and she didn't want to have to get up early to take it in."

Ben groaned, removed his hand from the phone's speaker. "Okay, I'm listening," he said, and she could hear the defeat in his voice.

Jessica couldn't make out what the man at the other end of the line said next but, whatever it was, Ben reacted as though he had just been struck. He gasped, staggered backwards, and had to lean on the kitchen counter for support. When he spoke, his voice was quivering with rage and fear. "I swear, if you've so much as harmed a hair on her head, I will hunt you down and–"

Jessica felt her stomach constrict into a tight ball of ice. "Ben? What's wrong?" she said, instinctively taking a step towards him.

He held up a hand to silence her. "How do I know you're not making this up?" he asked the unknown caller. Then, after pausing to listen to the man's response, "I want to speak to her."

Jessica's hands flew to her mouth. "Ben, what the hell's going on?" she demanded, fearfully.

As he pressed the button to activate the phone's loud speaker, Jessica noticed that her husband's hands were shaking. She had never seen him so traumatised, and it was deeply unsettling. "What's wrong?" she asked, grabbing his arm. "You're really frightening me."

Eyes moist, he raised a finger to his lips, shushing her.

"*Right, I'm putting her on,*" a crackly voice announced over the loudspeaker, and she immediately recognised it as belonging to the uncouth man who had spoken to her previously.

"Daddy...?" It was Phoebe's voice, and it sounded so small and vulnerable, so full of fear.

Jessica let out a little cry. "Ben! What's going on?"

Ben ignored her. "Phoebe, darling, are you okay?" he asked in a voice that was fraught with worry.

"*I'm scared, daddy,*" she cried. "*Please do as they say so I can come home.*"

Ben's face was ashen, and he looked like he was going to keel over.

"Don't panic, my angel," he told Phoebe in a voice that seemed to have aged ten years since taking the call. "I'll get you back home, safe and sound. I promise you I will."

The male voice was back on line. "*You will, but only if you do as you're told.*"

"What exactly is it that you want from us?" Ben Cunningham demanded through gritted teeth.

The caller laughed. "*I want money,*" he said, as though that should have been blatantly obvious.

Closing his eyes, Ben Cunningham sucked in air. "How much money?"

"*I'll call you again in an hour's time with my demands. In the meantime, I've got people watching you, Cunningham, so no funny business. If you go to the police, if you bring them in on this, you'll never hear from me again, and we'll chop your little princess into a thousand pieces and post them to you one at a time. Do you understand?*"

"I'm warning you," Ben snarled, regaining some of his usual bluster. "I'll kill you with my bare–"

The line went dead.

"NO! WAIT!" Ben screamed. "Hello...? Are you there?" He looked up at Jessica, his face gaunt from the stress of the situation. "He hung up on me," he told her in disbelief.

"Ring him back," she pleaded.

Breathing heavily, Ben quickly pressed the redial button but nothing happened. He turned to Jessica, crestfallen. "I can't ring him back," he said miserably. "He was calling from a withheld number."

Jessica threw herself in his arms, sobbing uncontrollably. "Oh, Ben, that animal's kidnapped her again. What are we going to do?"

As he rubbed his wife's back to comfort her, Ben Cunningham's jaw was set in grim determination. "Whatever it takes to get her back," he promised.

―――

Tyler was impatient to crack on. The meeting was already late starting, and he wanted to get it over with as quickly as possible because he had so much to do. What should have been a straightforward job had turned into a case that was anything but, and in the week since Spencer had stabbed David Bannister to death, he had gone on to abduct Phoebe Cunningham and murder Martin Whitling. Not only was he still on the loose, but there was a real risk that he would target Phoebe's parents next.

Looking around the room, Tyler saw that everyone was present apart from Kevin Murray. He held his hands up to shush them. "Right, settle down everyone," he said, raising his voice above theirs. "Before we start, does anyone know where Kevin is?"

Jim Stone raised a hand. "Sorry, boss, I forgot to tell you, he's had to make an urgent trip up to the lab for Dick Jarvis, so he asked me to send you his apologies."

Tyler glowered at Jarvis. "Is that right, Dick?"

Jarvis looked like a bunny caught in the headlights. "Er...." He began, but was saved from any further embarrassment by the sound of Tyler's phone going off.

Tyler glanced down at the handset, annoyed at the unwanted interruption. He recognised Ben Cunningham's number and killed the call, making a mental note to ring him back once the meeting had concluded. "Sorry, Dick, you were saying?"

The phone started trilling again. With an exasperated sigh, Tyler was forced to look at his handset for the second time in less than a minute. To his great displeasure, it was Cunningham again. The man was nothing if not persistent, he would give him that. He killed the call and switched his mobile to silent.

"Right, third time lucky," he told Jarvis with an apologetic smile.

"Well, sir, Kevin did offer to take the latest batch of exhibits up to the lab for me this morning, but I–"

Tyler held up a hand to cut him off. "Sorry, Dick," he said, looking down at the vibrating phone dancing across his lap. It was Cunningham again. The man clearly wasn't going to give up and, if Tyler turned his phone off, he would just start ringing the incident room instead. "I'm really sorry," he said, looking around the room, "but I need to take this. Susie, can you take over until I get back."

"Of course," she said, with an obliging smile.

Tyler stood up and wandered over to his office. "DCI Tyler speaking," he said, closing the door behind him.

"*You took your bloody time answering,*" Cunningham exploded. "*I had to call you three bloody times because the stupid phone of yours kept cutting me off.*"

Tyler took a deep breath, released it slowly. He really wasn't in the mood to indulge Cunningham's over inflated sense of self-importance this morning. "I was in a meeting," he explained, forcing himself to be polite. "Now, unless this is vitally important, Mr Cunningham, I'll call you back when I've fin–"

"*Of course it is vitally bloody important!*" Cunningham shouted so loudly that Tyler snatched the phone away from his head to prevent his eardrum from being perforated. "*It's that maniac, Spencer. He's kidnapped my Phoebe.*"

Tyler stopped dead in his tracks. "Say that again," he instructed, wondering if he had misheard.

"*Are you deaf, man? I just told you, Spencer's kidnapped Phoebe. If anything happens to her, I'll be holding you personally responsible for not having caught him by now. I mean, what the hell are you lot playing at? If I ran my company this badly, I'd bloody well be bankrupt by now. It's a bloody shambles and I–*"

Tyler's back went up. He appreciated the stress that Cunningham was under, but that was no excuse for him to shoot his mouth off like this, not when the officers on Tyler's team had been working themselves into the ground trying find Spencer. "Hold on a minute, please, Mr Cunningham," he snapped. "Let's save the vitriol for later. Right now, all I'm interested in is finding your daughter. Now, why do you think Spencer's kidnapped her?"

"*I don't think. I bloody well know. He's holding her prisoner, and he's going to call me back in about forty-five minutes to give me his demands.*"

Tyler was starting to lose his temper with the man. "Mr Cunningham, I need you to take a deep breath, and then tell me exactly what happened. Start off by explaining how you know that Spencer's kidnapped Phoebe."

"I bloody well know because he phoned me and told me so," Cunningham spluttered. "That's how. How else would I know? I'm not psychic, am I?"

"Calm down, Mr Cunningham," Tyler soothed. "Did he provide any proof to verify his claim?"

Cunningham was breathing heavily. "Yes. He put her on the phone. She..." His voice cracked and he struggled to go on. "She sounded absolutely terrified."

Tyler was making frantic notes. This was unbelievable. "Mr Cunningham, I'd like you to check your phone's call log and tell me the exact time the call was made, and the number that it was made from."

"The calls were made from a withheld number," Cunningham said.

"Sorry, did you say calls?" Tyler queried, picking up on the plural.

"Yes, calls," Cunningham snapped. "He rang us twice. The first time I was in the loo, so my wife answered, but the nasty little shit was so rude to her that she hung up on him. He rang back a minute later and, that time, I answered. That was when he told me that he'd kidnapped Phoebe. He warned me that they had someone watching us at all times, and that if we involved the police they would chop her up into tiny bits and post them back to us, one at a time."

They? That implied that Spencer had help.

"And the times of the calls?"

"Er, hang on." There was a pause while Cunningham checked his phone. "*The first was made at 07:55 hours, the second a minute later.*"

Tyler scribbled the information down. "Mr Cunningham, kidnappers often say things like that to deter the victim's family from involving the authorities, but it's rarely true. Nonetheless, I promise you that we'll take the warning seriously, and be very circumspect in all our contact with you from here on in. Let me ask you what might sound like a silly question: how do you know that it was Spencer? Did he identify himself to you?"

There was a long pause. "Well, no, but who else could it be?"

It was a fair assumption to make, but Tyler worked on evidence, not assumptions. "Did you recognise his voice, perhaps?"

"*No, of course not,*" There was exasperation in the man's voice. "*I've only ever heard the little shit speak once, and that was when he gave evidence at his trial, years ago.*"

"So, humour me. Why do you think it's Spencer?"

"*Why do you think it isn't?*" Cunningham countered. "*He's already done it twice before. Mark my words, Chief Inspector, I'll be suing everyone who played a part in having that scumbag released from prison. I warned them that the man was a total menace, and that this would bloody well happen, but did anyone listen? Like hell they did. All those condescending lefty do-gooders did was laugh at me. Well, let's see who's laughing by the time my solicitors get through with–*"

"Mr Cunningham," Tyler interrupted, "I understand how you must feel, really I do, but at the moment time is of the essence and I need you to focus on helping us to get your daughter back."

There was a sharp intake of breath. "*Yes, of course,*" Cunningham said, suddenly sounding tired. "*But how are we going to make that happen?*"

How indeed? It wasn't going to be easy. "Do you know where she was abducted from?" Tyler asked, deflecting the question by asking one of his own.

"*No,*" Cunningham said, miserably. "*Phoebe went to bed at the same time as us last night, and until the call came in, we thought she was still asleep in her room.*"

"Did either of you hear anything unusual during the night?" Tyler asked. "Anything that, in hindsight, could be construed as the sounds of a struggle?"

"*Nothing,*" Cunningham replied immediately, "*and I'm a very light sleeper.*"

"I take it there are no signs of a break in?"

"*Not that we can see,*" Cunningham told him.

"What about your alarm, was that on last night?"

"*Yes, I set it before we went to bed. Jess, was the alarm still on when you* got up this morning?" The last was directed towards his wife. "What...? Are you sure...?"

Tyler realised that Cunningham must have covered the handset, because whatever was being said became muffled. When he came back on line, several seconds later, Cunningham sounded flustered.

"*Apparently, the alarm had already been switched off when Jessica got up this morning, so it looks like Phoebe must have left the house early for some reason.*"

Tyler wondered if the officer stationed outside could give them a time of departure. "Okay, here's what's going to happen," he said. "Once you hang up, I don't want you to use your phone anymore. I want you to keep the line free for when Phoebe's abductor calls you back with further instructions. Do you have a back entrance to your property?"

"*Yes. There's a gate in the rear garden that leads out into a little alley that runs straight through to a side road. Why?*"

"I'm going to be sending some people over to you," Tyler explained, "and I want them to avoid using the front door if at all possible, just in case someone's watching the house. Can you make sure the garden gate is unlocked, so that they can get in?"

"*Of course,*" Cunningham said. "*I'll go and unlock it at once.*"

"Good. Now, listen. If the kidnapper calls back, I don't want you to get drawn into a slanging match with him, no matter what he says. If he demands money, stall for time, but don't refuse or say anything negative to antagonise him."

"*What exactly do you suggest I tell him?*"

"Tell him that you'll get straight onto it, but that it'll take you a day or two to get it together. Don't mention that you've spoken to us. Lastly, I know it's easy for me to say, but try not to worry. I promise you that we're going to be doing everything possible to get your daughter back to you." Tyler glanced at his watch, aware that time was against him. "I'm going to go now, because I've got an awful lot to organise and not much time to do it in. We've already got your wife's number so, if we need to speak to you, we'll call you on that." Lowering the phone, Tyler sat back in his chair, ran his hand through his hair and let out a long, stressful sigh. "Just when I thought this bloody job couldn't get any worse," he said.

The morning meeting was still in full flow when Tyler returned. "Right, can I have your attention," he said, interrupting Jim Stone, who was just explaining about the outage they had suffered during the live monitoring of Skipton's flat.

All eyes turned on him and, from the grim expression on his face, it was clear that there had been a serious development. The office quickly descended into a tense silence and they all stared at him in uneasy expectation.

"I've just spoken to Ben Cunningham, who informed me that his daughter, Phoebe, has been kidnapped," he informed them.

Surprised gasps echoed around the room, and several pockets of conversation broke out, which Tyler silenced with an impatient glare. "Mr Cunningham received two calls from an unknown male this morning," he continued. "The first was at 07:55 and this was answered by his wife, who hung up on the caller because he was rude to her. The same male rang back a minute later and, this time, he spoke to Ben Cunningham. During this call, Cunningham was allowed to converse with his daughter briefly, to confirm that she was okay. The kidnapper ended the call by stating that he would ring back in an hour to make his demands."

"I take it the kidnapper's after money?" Dillon asked, his face grim.

"It looks that way," Tyler confirmed.

"Is this Spencer's handiwork?" Susie asked.

Tyler shrugged. "Cunningham certainly thinks so and, as he rightly pointed out, Spencer's already done it twice before, which does rather make him the obvious candidate."

"But you're not sold on that being the case, are you?" Dillon said.

Tyler shook his head. "Dill, I accept that, in theory, it makes perfect sense, but it just feels completely wrong to me."

"Why?" Susie asked, her brow puckering into a tight frown.

Tyler considered his response carefully, searching for the right words to articulate his concern. "As I see it, Spencer's totally besotted with the girl, and I don't think he would dream of swapping her for money. I might be totally wrong, of course, but it makes absolutely no sense to me."

"Surely it has to be him?" Steve Bull insisted. "It would be a too much of a coincidence for anyone else to have abducted her, don't you think?"

"If it was someone else, that poor wee lass must be the unluckiest girl in the world," Charlie White said, shaking his head in sympathy.

All at once, little pockets of discussion broke out as his team debated the likelihood of Spencer being behind the abduction. Tyler didn't want them getting bogged down by senseless speculation, so he held a hand up to kill the conversation. "At this point in time, it doesn't matter who kidnapped her," he said, firmly. "Our overriding priority has to be to get her back in one piece, and to do so as quickly as possible."

There were ripples of agreement all around the room.

"The caller warned Cunningham not to contact the police, claimed he was being watched and that they would know if he did. As I see it, the only person that Spencer could possibly have drafted in to help him with that is his cousin, Skippy. Jim, as a matter of urgency, I want you to start reviewing the unseen footage from last night. Gurjit, go with him to start monitoring the live feed. I want to be told immediately if there are any signs of movement at Skipton's address."

Without a word, the two detectives stood up and headed for the door.

"Charlie, I want you to hotfoot it over to Cunningham's address and take charge there, but don't enter the property via the front door. Apparently, there's a hidden gate in the back garden wall, which can be reached from a side road near the house. If you call Mrs Cunningham when you get near, she'll tell you how to find it. You can get her number from the MIR. The Cunninghams didn't hear their daughter leave the house this morning, so they think she went out very early, before they got up. I need to know where she was going and if she was planning to meet anyone, so search her room and see if you can find anything that'll steer us in the right direction." Waving the Glaswegian off, he turned to Debbie Brown. "Debs, I need you to track down and debrief the PC who was watching the front of the house when Phoebe left. I want to know what time she went, and if anyone picked her up."

Debbie Brown nodded vigorously. "Leave it to me," she said, standing up.

Next, Tyler sought out Steve Bull. "Stevie, get onto the Technical Support Unit and let them know what we're dealing with. I need them to send someone straight over to Cunningham's house and set up equipment to record and monitor all incoming calls." His head swivelled towards Reg Parker. "Reg, ring the TIU for me. Let them know we're dealing with a kidnap, so we're going to need live time monitoring on Ben Cunningham's phone. I want them to go through his call data and establish the number that the kidnappers called him from earlier." Although it had shown up as withheld on Cunningham's phone, a check with the service provider would quickly reveal the number. "I want to know everything there is to know about the phone the kidnappers used. It's bound to be a PAYG, but I want to know when and where it was purchased and how much credit's been put on it. If it was bought using a credit card, I want to know who the card belongs to, and I want to know if there's any CCTV at the shop it was obtained from. I need to know how many calls that phone has made and received since going live, and I'll want subscriber, call data and cell site applications submitted on every number that it's been in contact with."

Poor Reg was hunched over his daybook, writing so fast that Tyler half expected his pen to start smoking.

"Dean, as soon as we get the phone data back, I need you to research all the people identified from it and see if we can link any of them to Spencer or his cousin, Skipton." Tyler paused to draw breath, then continued, this time singling out Paul Evans. "Paul, what time are you meant to be going around to Anna Manson's house this morning to take her statement?"

"I'm due there at ten," Evans replied, "but I can push the meeting back if you need me to do something else instead."

Tyler shook his head. "No. I want you to get yourself over there right now. She's Phoebe's best friend and closest confidant. I need to know if she has any idea where Phoebe was going or who she planned to meet today."

Tyler steadily worked his way through the rest of the team, assigning each of them a wide variety of tasks. "Don't worry about the various authorities needed for all the actions I've given you," he concluded. "As soon as we finish here, I'll be going straight down to see Mr Holland to brief him and obtain the necessary urgent oral authorities we need."

Chairs scraped against the floor as the team all rose, their faces set in grim resolve. Tyler watched them bustle out of the room in silence, dispersing into the corridor to crack on with the various assignments they had been given. A young girl's life hung in the balance, and none of them wanted to let her down.

31

FROM BAD TO WORSE

Skippy made the second call from his lounge. Closing the door behind him so that G-Man wouldn't be able to hear, he pressed the green button and waited anxiously for Ben Cunningham to pick up. The call was answered almost immediately, as if the girl's father had been sitting by the phone, waiting for it to ring. Skippy smiled. That was good. It meant the Cunninghams were taking the abduction seriously, as well they should.

"*Hello...?*" There was a delicious note of desperation in Cunningham's voice.

Skippy allowed the silence to drag on for a few seconds, just to make the man sweat.

"*Hello...? Are you there?*"

"If you want your daughter returned, it'll cost you one million pounds."

There was a gasp, followed by some indignant spluttering. "*One* million pounds? Are you out of your head? I don't have access to that kind of money!"

Skippy had expected this. "Don't lie to me," he said, giving short shrift to the argument. "I ain't no mug. I know you're minted, and I want a million quid."

"But I can't get hold of—"

"Tell you what," Skippy said, cutting him off mid-sentence, "I'll chop her right ear off and then you won't have to pay quite so much."

"*No! Wait!*" Heavy breathing down the line, followed by a sigh of capitulation. "*I – I can get you the money, but it'll take me a couple of days to organise it.*"

"You don't have a couple of days," Skippy told him. "I want that money today."

"*But that's impossible. Surely you realise that? I don't have that kind of money sitting in the bank. I'll have to sell off a load of stocks and shares to raise the cash, and that takes time.*"

Skippy didn't have the slightest idea what selling stocks and shares involved, and he didn't want to make himself sound stupid by asking. "Tomorrow then," he compromised, "but no later or I start cutting bits off and posting them to you."

"*I'll try,*" Cunningham promised, "*but these things take time. I'll get onto my broker as soon as we finish speaking, but he has to find buyers for the shares, and then the money has to be transferred. Give me till Thursday evening. Surely that's not unreasonable?*"

It probably wasn't, but Skippy wanted to keep the man under pressure. "I'll give you till ten o'clock on Thursday morning," he relented, "but if my money's not ready for me by then, I swear you'll never see your little princess again."

There was a sharp intake of breath. "*It'll be ready,*" Cunningham assured him. "*Just don't hurt my daughter.*"

"I want it in non-sequential notes," Skippy informed him. He had no idea what that actually meant, but he had heard it said in a heist film once and it had sounded good.

"*How do I get the money to you?*" Cunningham asked. "*And how do I know you'll keep your word and release Phoebe once I do?*"

Skippy laughed. He had anticipated this question. "I'll call you back with instructions tomorrow," he said. There was no way he was going to divulge that kind of information in advance. "As for me releasing her, you'll just have to take my word for it."

Cunningham huffed and puffed. *"That won't do at all,"* he protested, angrily. *"I demand that you give–"*

"You're not in a position to *demand* anything," Skippy yelled, momentarily losing his cool. "You'll do exactly what I tell you, when I tell you. Do as I say and you'll get your little girl back safe and sound. Cross me and she'll end up floating face down in the river. Now, stop yapping, and get my fucking money sorted. I'll call you back with further instructions tomorrow."

Terminating the call, Skippy sagged back in the armchair and smiled contentedly. He was confident that Cunningham would do exactly as he'd been told, he was far too worried about his daughter to even consider disobeying the instructions he'd been given.

―――

Paul Evans parked the pool car outside Anna Manson's house, checked his battered blue clipboard to make sure that he had enough statement continuation forms with him, and then stepped into the glorious sunshine.

With everything else that was now going on, Evans couldn't help but feel that he was missing out, being tasked to take a mundane statement instead of being allowed to get stuck into the juicier work of trying to find the kidnapped girl. Still, Anna was Phoebe's best friend and, if anyone might have an inkling as to where she was heading when she sneaked out of her house overnight, he would lay money on it being her.

He opened the garden gate and strode along the small concrete path to the front door. The lawn was neatly trimmed and there were hanging baskets on either side of the door, each containing a vibrant mix of colourful Surfinia. Evans banged loudly on a brass knocker mounted in the centre of the door, knocking three times in quick succession. He waited for a minute but no one answered, so he tried again, pounding it even louder this time.

Still no one came to the door. Frowning, he cupped his hands and peered through one of the frosted glass panels. As he leaned against it, the door sprang open with a little click.

Evans realised that the latch to the Yale lock hadn't engaged properly when it had been closed. That sometimes happened with old doors; the wood became slightly bowed over time and had to be closed firmly. He pushed the door open and took a tentative step into the hallway. "Hello...?" he called out. "Anna, are you there? It's DC Evans. I'm here to take a statement from you."

There was no response.

As he was an hour early for their appointment, he could hardly complain that she wasn't there. With any luck, she had just popped down to the shops and would be back shortly. He was about to close the door and return to his car, when a mark on the wall caught his eye. It was an ugly red smear about six inches deep and a foot wide, and it looked like it had been caused by something wet being dragged along paintwork.

Checking his daybook for her number, Evans tried calling Anna again. To his surprise, a phone began ringing upstairs. That was odd. He killed the call and the ringing stopped. He redialled and it started again. Had Anna forgotten to take her phone with her when she had gone out?

Looking up the stairs, he noticed more red stains on the magnolia paintwork, and one of them looked decidedly like a handprint. "Shit," Evans said as the hackles at the back of his neck stood up.

What if Anna hadn't forgotten her phone when she went out?

What if she hadn't gone out at all?

Tyler was engaged in an animated discussion with Susie Sergeant and Steve Bull, trying to formulate an effective kidnap strategy, when the telephone on his desk barked into life. He was expecting a call from George Holland, who had agreed to speak to the Technical Support Unit and the Telephone Intelligence Unit on his behalf, and he snatched it up before the first ring had even finished.

"Boss, it's Gurjit here. You need to come down to the monitoring room straight away. We've just found some suspicious activity on the overnight footage of Skipton's place, and I think it might be connected to the kidnap."

Tyler tensed at the news. "What makes you think that?" he enquired, signalling for the others to be quiet.

"It'll be quicker to just show you," Gurjit said.

"Okay, we'll be right down," Tyler told him. Standing up, he indicated for Susie and Steve to follow him. "That was Gurjit," he explained as they descended the back stairs to the ground floor. "He reckons he's found something important on the footage from Skipton's flat."

Two minutes later, they were in the monitoring room, bunched around the viewing screens. "Okay, what have you got?" Tyler asked.

Gurjit indicated the screen on the left. "That's the live feed," he informed them, before turning to its companion. "This screen is purely for viewing pre-recorded footage." There was nothing playing on it at the moment. He picked up the viewing log and flicked through it until he reached the overnight entries. "Okay, so the outage happened at 00:58 hours. Twelve minutes later, at 01:10 hours, there was some important activity at the address." He pressed a button on the control console and the screen burst into life. "The van with the covert camera is parked outside a house a couple of doors along from Skipton's place," Gurjit was saying. "As you can see, it gives us a really good view of his street door–" he tapped the centre of the screen to highlight the particular door he was referring to "–and the parking spaces directly outside his premises. Unfortunately, the camera angle doesn't stretch to the other side of the road, which is where Skipton normally parks his car."

Tyler studied the footage that had started to play. Skipton's flat was in darkness, as were the properties either side of it. A stretch of road directly in front of the van was empty, leaving a gap that was probably large enough to accommodate several cars. The little timer in the top right hand side of the screen showed the time and date as: 01:09 hours - 31/07/01.

"At 01:10 hours, two cars are going to arrive in convoy," Gurjit said, pre-empting the footage they were about to watch. "The first is an Alfa Romeo Spider. The second is Skipton's old Sierra. For some reason, Skipton's driving the Alfa, not his own car. That's being driven by someone we haven't yet identified."

Tyler leaned in to get a better look, and he was conscious of Susie and Steve doing the same, until they all ended up shoulder to shoulder, eyes glued to the monitor.

As the timer changed to 01:10 hours, the Alfa that Gurjit had just told them about pulled into the gap in front of the unmarked van, its brake lights dazzlingly bright in the darkness. A Ford Sierra Sapphire tucked in behind it. Skipton alighted the Alfa and went into his flat. He was clearly in a hurry and he was unmistakably nervous.

"Look how eyes about he is," Steve Bull observed, referring to the way that Skipton's eyes were pinballing all over the place. "They're definitely up to no good."

That in itself didn't mean much; people like Skipton were always up to no good.

Moments later, Skipton re-emerged. Pausing at the door to have a good look around, he then rushed over to the boot of the Sierra, carrying what looked like a scrunched up bedsheet in one hand. The other man had, by now, opened the boot. Both men leaned in and began fumbling around clumsily. As they worked, they were repeatedly glancing over their shoulders, making sure that no one was watching them.

"Have you ever seen two more dodgy looking characters in your whole life?" Susie asked.

"Is that gaffer tape he's using?" Tyler asked as Skipton tore a thin strip from a roll he was holding in his left hand.

Gurjit nodded. "Looks like it to me."

"What are they doing?" Bull asked, as the two men on screen stood with their backs to the camera, scrabbling around inside the Sierra's boot.

"You'll see in a minute," Gurjit promised.

Sure enough, a few moments later, both men stood up, and it was clear they were carrying a long, bulky object between them.

"Oh my giddy aunt," Susie exclaimed as they turned side on, struggling with what looked like a body wrapped in a sheet. "Tell me that's not what I think it is!"

As they started making their way towards the flat, the unidentified man almost dropped his end.

"Bloody hell!" Bull gasped as the man quickly readjusted his grip. "This is like watching a comedy sketch by the Chuckle Brothers."

As soon as the suspects disappeared into the flat with their dodgy cargo, Gurjit pressed the stop button and looked at Tyler expectantly. "Well, what do you think?" he asked.

Tyler was still staring thoughtfully at the screen, even though the footage had ended. "It's got to be her," he said.

Gurjit's phone rang. He answered it, listened for several seconds and then smiled gratefully. After hanging up, he turned to Tyler. "That was Dean, up in the Intel cell. I rang him while you were on your way down and asked him to run a PNC check on the Alfa's registration number. He just called back to confirm that it's Phoebe Cunningham's car."

Tyler nodded, decisively. "That clinches it," he said. "I'm satisfied we've found our kidnappers. Is there any way that the unidentified male with Skipton could be Spencer?"

"He doesn't look anything like the suspect we saw on the bus CCTV during Bannister's murder," Susie pointed out. "Yes, he's of similar height and build, but his hair's much longer and his gait looks perfectly normal. If you remember, Spencer had an odd stoop, and his head bobbed up and down whenever he walked."

Tyler considered this. "Maybe he's wearing a wig as a disguise, and people tend to walk differently to how they normally do when they're carrying heavy objects."

"I can show you some footage of him walking normally," Gurjit offered. "We've got him leaving the premises just after seven a.m., so it's lighter too. That might help."

Tyler nodded. "Play it for me."

Gurjit immediately set about finding the relevant footage.

"How many people do we think are inside the premises right now?" Tyler asked.

"The unidentified suspect returned at seven-fifty," Gurjit informed him, "so all three are there." He quickly played the two segments of footage for Tyler; one of the suspect leaving the flat, and another of him returning a while later. Neither provided a clear shot of the man's face, but they all agreed his gait seemed perfectly normal.

"I really don't think that's Spencer," Susie said.

Tyler merely grunted. He was busy thinking about something else. "When he left," he said after a moment's reflection, "the unidentified suspect drove off in Phoebe's car. Why didn't he come back in it?"

Gurjit rewound the tape to the moment that the suspect appeared, walking along the pavement with his back towards the covert camera. "He might have done," he said. "He might just have parked it out of view."

Tyler shook his head. "But there are two perfectly good spaces right outside Skipton's flat. Why didn't he park in one of those if he still had her car?"

No one could answer that question for him.

―――――

Evans found Anna Manson's body sitting on a hard backed chair in the main bedroom. The wrists and ankles had been secured to the arms and legs of the chair with what looked like gaffer tape.

Manson's head was slumped forward onto her chest, which was covered in blood. Evans counted a number of ugly stab wounds in her torso, and it was clear from the girl's tortured expression that she hadn't died well.

After donning a pair of nitrile gloves, he knelt down and felt for a pulse in her neck. There was none, and her waxen coloured skin was cold to the touch, telling him that she had already been dead for a number of hours.

Standing up, he looked around the room. A mobile phone, presumably hers, was visible on the bedside table. To make sure, he rang it again, killing the call the moment that her handset came to life.

A large amount of already congealing blood had pooled in her lap, and there was some visible blood spatter on the floor around the body, which he was careful to avoid stepping in. All the internal doors in the house were made of varnished oak, so the bloodied handprint he could see on the rear of Manson's bedroom door was unlikely to yield fingerprints. However, there had been two similar prints on the magnolia painted wall directly outside her room, and these were so clear as to be perfect, and he doubted that the killer could have left more defined marks for them if he had deliberately set out to do so.

Returning to the street, Evans put in a call to Tyler, but the number was engaged. He tried Susie Sergeant instead, and was immediately rewarded by a ring tone.

"DI Sergeant," Susie said, answering the call. The two of them were back in Tyler's office, while Steve Bull had been sent off to drum up a TSG rapid entry team to storm Skipton's flat.

"Susie, it's Paul. Listen, I've just arrived at Anna Manson's house to take a statement from her. When I got here, the street door was open, and I've just found her body upstairs, tied to a chair. It looks like she's been stabbed multiple times."

Susie's eyes flew to Tyler, but he was still locked in a heated telephone conversation with Holland and she didn't want to interrupt. "Jesus, Mary and Joseph," she said, standing up and walking out of the room.

This day has just gone from bad to worse.

She crossed to her own office and closed the door behind her.

"Any sign of a forced entry?" she asked, opening her daybook and reaching for a pen.

"*None,*" Evans confirmed.

"What about the murder weapon?"

"*No sign of it, but I'm not wearing barrier clothing so I haven't searched, for fear of contaminating the scene.*"

A worrying thought occurred to her. "Do you think that Spencer did this to her?"

There was a long pause, followed by a meaty sigh. "*It has to be him, doesn't it?*"

"Probably," she agreed, wondering how Tyler would react to the news. "Okay, stay where you are. I'll get units running to support you. The boss is talking to the DCS at the minute, but I'll get him to call you back as soon as he's free."

32

PANIC

When Phoebe first heard snoring, she thought she must be imagining it but, as the sonorous, grumbling grew steadily louder, it dawned upon her that the man who was supposed to be watching over her had dozed off. For a while, she lay perfectly still, listening to the gargling and snorting noises, and the long gaps in between, until it became clear that he had fallen into a deep sleep.

Feeling her pulse accelerate, she arched her back and worked her hands down underneath her buttocks. It was a tight squeeze and, at one point, red faced from straining, she thought that one of her shoulder joints was going to pop out of its socket, but then her hands were clear of her rump and she slid them down the back of her thighs and calves, all the way down to her ankles.

Thankfully, her kidnappers hadn't secured her wrists as tightly as Spencer had back at the barn, otherwise she would never have been able to do what she just had. As soon as her bound wrists cleared her ankles, she sat up straight and nervously eased the smelly hood off of her head, blinking at the sudden influx of light.

Apart from the single bed she was sitting on, the room contained a tatty wardrobe and a small chest of drawers. Several posters adorned the walls. There was one of a Harley-Davidson motorbike, another of West Ham United football team, and the third was of a female tennis player whose skirt had risen in the wind, exposing her tanned buttock.

A tall, skinny man was slouched on a hard backed chair in the doorway, blocking her only way out of the room. He looked like a nasty piece of work, with lank, greasy hair and an unshaven face. His creepy left eye was twitching uncontrollably in his sleep, like it was repeatedly winking at her even though it was closed.

Phoebe knew she didn't have much time. She craned her neck to peer out of the small window behind the bed, and was elated to see that she was on the ground floor, overlooking a small unkept rear garden. If she could somehow get free of her bindings and open the window, she would have a half decent chance of getting away.

Her eyes scanned the room for a weapon, but found nothing remotely suitable. She did, however, spot a small red pocket knife on top of the chest of drawers. It was only a couple of inches long, so it would be pretty useless to her in a fight, but it would certainly cut through her bindings. Standing up, and being ultra-careful not to make any noise, she unsteadily hopped the short distance over to the drawers and scooped it up.

Returning to the bed, she paused to check that her guard was still asleep, and then set about trying to pull the blade out. The locking mechanism had rusted stiff from lack of use, and she cracked several nails trying to prise it open.

When it finally moved, she saw that the blade was badly corroded. Phoebe gingerly ran her finger along the edge, and was disappointed to find that it was also totally blunt, and therefore quite useless as a cutting tool. Refusing to accept defeat, she tried poking the dull tip through the tape. If she could make a big enough hole to insert a finger, she might be able rip her bindings off that way.

Working quickly, she began twisting the tip backwards and forwards, forcing it into the surprisingly resilient material. Eventually, she succeeded in making a small hole, which she worried away at until it became big enough for her thumb to fit into. Encouraged by her painfully slow progress, Phoebe tugged until the gap began to widen.

Suddenly, without warning, the tape gave way and her hands were free. She turned to check on her guard, worried that the loud ripping noise had alerted him, but he slept on, blissfully unaware. Watching him carefully, she began massaging her wrists, working the blood back into her hands.

Next she set to work upon her ankle bindings. They proved much easier. Using her chipped nails, she was able to find the end of the gaffer tape and peel it off.

Dropping the tape on the floor, she straightened up and stared at the sleeping man. His head was sagging to one side, exposing his jugular. She looked at the two inch blade in her right hand and wondered if she would be able to drive it deep enough into this throat to kill him before he could overpower her.

Probably not, she decided.

The street door beckoned to her from the far end of the narrow hall, and it seemed tantalisingly close, but she thought there was little chance of her being able to slip by her guard without waking him. Even if she succeeded in doing so, the other kidnapper was bound to be in one of the rooms, and if he came out to investigate, she would be trapped. Besides, if they had any brains, they would have locked the street door from the inside. That's what she would have done in their place. Taking all things into consideration, she decided that trying to reach the door was probably a very bad idea.

That left the window. It was ancient, one of those old metal things that was fitted with single glazing and rattled every time the wind blew. She could see its rusted frame beneath the flaking paint. It was a narrow side opener, and getting through would be a tight squeeze, even for her. Nonetheless, she had to try. Taking a deep breath, she wiped her sweaty palm against her leg.

Here goes!

Phoebe took a firm grip and pulled downwards, but nothing happened.

NO!

Her heart was in her mouth as she tried again, twisting even harder this time. With a fierce creak of protest, the handle moved an inch. She cringed at the harsh noise it made, but she was committed now, and she just had to go for it. Throwing caution to the wind, Phoebe gritted her teeth and yanked the handle again, putting all her weight behind the movement. Suddenly, the latch snapped and the window sprung open. Stepping onto the bed to gain a little more height, Phoebe quickly thrust her right leg through the gap.

A lovely warm breeze buffeted her, and the fresh air had never tasted so good!

I can do this! I'm strong. I've moved on and I'm getting my life back.

Behind her, the sound of a chair being overturned made her jump.

"Skippy! She's doing a runner!"

Glancing over her shoulder, Phoebe saw that the startled guard was on his feet and rushing towards her. With no time to lose, she thrust her head and torso through the gap, ignoring the sharp pain as her shoulder collided with the frame.

A calloused hand wrapped itself around her ankle, crushing it in a vice like grip. "Come 'ere you little slag," its owner snarled as his other hand reached through the window and took a firm grip of her hair.

Phoebe gasped in pain as he started yanking her back through the window. "Help!" she shrieked. "Somebody please help me!"

"Shut up," the twitchy eyed man growled at her.

A second man ran into the room and immediately started shouting instructions. He was a skinny guy with short hair and a badly pockmarked face. She immediately recognised his voice as belonging to the man who had telephoned her father.

The man with the twitchy eye was half hanging out of the window, trying to drag her back into the room, and he was gradually succeeding. Just as all seemed lost, Phoebe remembered that she still had the rusty pocket knife, and she drove it into the hand that was wrapped around her ankle.

With a howl of pain, Twitchy let go.

As soon as he did, she whipped her leg through the window and turned to run, but he still had hold of her hair, and she came to a jarring halt with enough force to give her whiplash. "Let go, you bastard," she yelled, taking a wild swing at him with the pocket knife. The tip of the blade caught him on the underside of his wrist, drawing blood.

With a surprised yelp, he let go.

Finally free of his grasp, Phoebe jumped back out of reach.

"Fucking slag," Twitchy yelled, trying to climb through the window after her.

Looking left and right, Phoebe's heart sank as she realised that the property was terraced, and that there was no side access from which she could reach the street. That meant she would have to go over the garden fences.

Her twitchy eyed pursuer was nearly out of the window, but his size was impeding his progress, making it slow and cumbersome.

Phoebe chose the lowest fence and jumped up, swinging her right leg over it in one fluid motion. As she heaved herself up, she felt hands grab her ankles and drag her backwards.

Nooo!

She tried to kick out, to dislodge the man holding onto her, only to experience pain like she had never known before as he hit her in the kidneys with a heavy punch. Her knees buckled, and if she hadn't been holding on to the fence, she would have fallen to the floor.

He hit her a second time, and then a third. "You fucking bitch," he hissed as the final punch landed. "I'll kill you if you ruin my plans."

Unable to cling on to the fence any longer, Phoebe fell to her knees, landing heavily. A powerful kick to the ribs sent her toppling sideways to land on her back. Gasping for air, she looked up to see the man with the pockmarked face looming above her, his ugly features twisted with hatred.

Phoebe opened her mouth to scream but, before she could, he

kicked her again, even harder than before. She felt a rib crack. Curling into a foetal position, she tucked her elbows into her body to protect it from the barrage of blows that followed.

The man with the pockmarked face seemed to have lost control, and he was shouting and swearing as the kicks reined in. On the verge of passing out, Phoebe suddenly realised that she was no longer being kicked. Looking up, her vision slipping in and out of focus, she saw the twitchy eyed man was holding his struggling compatriot back. With the coppery taste of fresh blood rich in her mouth, the world faded into blackness.

The briefing for the Territorial Support Group rapid entry team was carried out in the ground floor conference room at Hertford House. There were twenty one TSG officers present. They had arrived in three carriers, each containing one sergeant and six PCs.

"Not you lot again," PS Bobby Beach said when he saw Dillon walk into the room.

Dillon grinned and walked over to shake his hand. "I think this one might be a little more exciting than the last job you did for us," he confided as the smaller man pumped his hand up and down.

"I should bloody well hope so, too," Beach chortled. "That was a complete blowout."

Steve Bull and Gurjit Singh had accompanied Dillon and, while Bull walked around the room handing out copies of the briefing document, Singh made himself busy setting up the TV video combo.

"There aren't enough of these to go round," Bull said as he walked amongst them, "so you'll have to share one between every two of you."

"That's okay," Beach said with a mischievous grin. "Half of this lot can't read anyway."

Dillon walked to the front of the room. "Right, let's crack on," he said, waving them to silence. "Let me start by thanking you for coming to our rescue for the second time in a week. This time, you're here to conduct a rapid entrance into a downstairs flat in Adworth Road, Stratford." He walked over to a large white board that had been erected in the corner. The layout of a one bedroom flat had been crudely drawn on its surface in red felt tip. "This is a floor plan of the address," Dillon told them, tapping the board with his biro. "Two of our officers visited this address earlier in the enquiry, so we know this is an accurate depiction of the flat's layout. As you can see, once entry is made through the front door, you'll find yourselves in a narrow hallway, off which there are five doors. The lounge and kitchen will be on your left. The bedroom will be directly ahead, at the end of the corridor. On your right, there will be doors leading to the toilet and bathroom. The sole occupant is Tommy Skipton, a thirty-one year old white male with previous convictions for shoplifting, various car crimes, burglary and going equipped to steal. Surprisingly, he has no form for using violence or carrying weapons, but that doesn't mean he's a boy scout so don't feel obliged to go too easy on him. We know there's another white male currently inside the flat with Skipton but, as yet, we've been unable to identify him. We have good reason to believe that these two men are holding a twenty-two year old female called Phoebe Cunningham captive against her will. Her father, Ben Cunningham, received a ransom demand from an unregistered Pay-As-You-Go phone just before 08:00 hours today. The phone was cell sited within the radius of the mast covering Skipton's flat."

A hand went up. The owner was a tall PC with a balding head, a little pot belly and a Pancho Villa style moustache. "Sir, how much did they demand?" he asked.

"A million pounds," Dillon said.

The constable wriggled his moustache. "That's a lot of money," he said, clearly impressed.

"We're going to play you three bits of footage from a covert camera that's covering the address. The first is timed at 01:10 hours this morning, and it shows Skipton pulling up outside the flat in a red Alfa Romeo that's registered to Phoebe Cunningham. The second suspect pulls up immediately behind, and he's driving Skipton's Ford

Sierra Sapphire. You'll see them remove what looks like a mummified body from the Sierra's boot and carry it into the flat.

The moustache totting PC raised his hand again.

Dillon raised an eyebrow. "Yes, PC...?"

"PC Reeve, Sir. Does that mean we think she's already dead?"

"I bloody well hope not," Dillon said. "When Mr Cunningham received a call from the blackmailers at 08:00 hours this morning, they let him speak to her as proof of life. I see no reason for her condition to have changed since then."

"And do we think she's still inside the premises?" PC Reeve asked.

Dillon smiled politely. "If you'd let me get on with the briefing, instead of constantly asking questions, I'd be able to tell you."

PC Reeve's face turned the colour of beetroot.

"Yeah, shut up you old git," one of the TSG officers in the row behind said in a northern accent, and the rest of the crew laughed.

A burly, square-jawed constable sitting next to PC Reeve wrapped an arm around his shoulders. "You'll have to excuse poor old Reevo, guv," he said with a grin. "He doesn't get out much."

Shrugging the arm off, Reeve stared daggers at his traitorous friend, which only made the rest of the crew laugh harder.

Dillon allowed them a moment to settle down and then continued. "The second clip we're going to show you features the, as yet, unidentified suspect leaving the flat around 07:00 hours this morning. He drove away in Miss Cunningham's Alfa and returned about an hour later, on foot. We're working on the premise that he left the flat to get rid of the car, and came back after disposing of it." Dillon nodded to Gurjit, who killed the lights and played the footage.

The officers all leaned forward, watching in silence. There were a couple of gasps as Phoebe's shrouded body was removed from the boot of the Sierra, but no one spoke.

"Any questions?" Dillon asked when the viewing was over and the lights flickered back on. He looked directly at PC Reeve, who blushed and stared down at the floor.

"Just the usual things," Beach said. "What type of door? How many locks does it have? Does it open left to right or right to left? Any animals or kids inside? Any intelligence to suggest the presence of firearms?"

Dillon nodded. These were all important things for the entry team to know. "Okay, as you will have seen from the footage, the house is divided into two flats, one up and one down. The door we're interested in is the wooden one on the left, not the PVC one on the right. I'm reliably informed there's just one Yale type lock, and the door opens inwards, going from left to right. There are no kids or animals inside, and there's nothing in the system to suggest that either man has access to firearms."

"What about rear access?" PC Reeve asked.

Dillon grinned at him. At last, a relevant question from the man! "It's a mid-terraced house. The officers who attended the premises earlier in the enquiry didn't go into the back garden, but India 99 has flown over it for us this morning. If you turn to page five in your briefing packs, you'll see the aerial shot they sent us of the rear garden."

There was a concentrated flurry of page turning.

"Okay," Beach said, studying the photograph. "If the suspects take to the gardens, they'll have to go over a dozen fences before they reach a point where they get to a road. As long as we station people at either end, we should be able to head them off if they try to do a runner."

"Don't forget that you'll have the helicopter hovering overhead when you go in," Dillon pointed out, "so we'll have eyes on any runners."

"Would it be worth identifying the house directly behind the target address and getting a couple of our lads to go over the fence into the suspect's rear garden before we go through the front door?" the officer with the buzzcut, sitting beside PC Reeve, asked.

Beach nodded thoughtfully. "That's actually quite a good idea, Ron," he said.

"That's a first," Reeve said, glancing sideways at his mate.

Someone in the seat behind meowed

"Leave it with us," Beach told Dillon. "We'll get a couple of officers into the back garden before we make entry."

Dillon nodded gratefully. "Okay, I'll leave your unit supervisors to work out the specifics of who's doing what as far as the entry goes. Officers from the Homicide Command will be waiting outside to take control of the scene once it's been secured."

"Where are we taking the prisoners?" Beach asked.

"I don't want them having any chance to talk to each other while they're in the cells," Dillon said, "so they'll need to go to separate stations. I'm hoping to send one to Leyton and the other to Forest Gate, but we'll have to see what cell space is available once they're in custody."

Beach stood up and indicated for the other two TSG supervisors to join him. "Right, boss, I think we have all the info we need. Give us ten minutes to decide who's doing what, and we'll be ready to kit up and move out."

―――

"You fucking idiot," Skippy shouted as they carried Phoebe's unconscious form through the patio door into the lounge. "How did she get out of the room?"

"Well, it ain't my fault," G-Man yelled as they moved into the hall. "I turned my head for one second and she made a dash for it."

"Turned your head!" Skippy said as they dropped her on the bed. "More like you fell asleep again, you useless wanker."

Flinching at the rebuke, G-Man pulled the window shut, but said nothing.

Skippy ran back into the garden, checking to see if any of the neighbours had come out to investigate the commotion. It was a hot day, and most houses had their doors and windows wide open, so the noise of her screaming for help would have carried. For all he knew, a half dozen people had already rung the Old Bill to report a domestic disturbance. He bit his lip anxiously. What to do? What to do? Turning on his heel, he stormed back inside, feeling deeply troubled.

In the bedroom, the girl was still out cold, and G-Man was resecuring her wrists with the gaffer tape.

"I think you might've cracked a couple of her ribs," G-Man said as he started tying her ankles.

"Serves her fucking right," Skippy growled. He looked around the room, weighing up the likelihood of their getting a visit from the police. "It's no good," he eventually said. "We can't risk the fuzz turning up and finding her here, so we'll have to move her."

"We should've moved her as soon as I got back with the keys," G-Man pointed out, which only served to put Skippy in an even darker mood.

"What the fuck is wrong with you?" he snapped. "Why is it that every time I turn my back on you, you fall asleep?"

"Told you," G-Man said, defensively, "I've got Narcolepsy. I can't help it."

"You've got lazyitis, more like," Skippy said, shaking his head in disgust. "While you're at it, you'd better gag her. We'll wrap her in the sheet again and throw her straight in the boot, then we'll run her over to your dad's school."

The five vehicle convoy was underway, making a blue light run from Hertford House to Adworth Road. Two unmarked cars, containing detectives from Tyler's team, were sandwiched between the second and third TSG wagons.

"Exciting stuff," Dillon said, raising his voice to make himself heard above the wail of the sirens. Steve Bull and three DCs were travelling together in the Omega, while he and Tyler had the Beamer to themselves.

The forward staging point, where they would stop before making the final approach to the target address, was Forest Gate police station in West Ham Lane. A dog unit was meeting them there in ten minutes time. India 99 had been forced to return to Lippits Hill to refuel, but Tyler had been assured it would be ready to resume its station above the target venue in time for them to make entry.

"Wouldn't it be nice if we caught the kidnappers and they gave us Spencer's location?" Dillon said.

"It would," Tyler agreed, "but I'm still not convinced he's got anything to do with her abduction. I mean, the text messages he's been sending Skipton don't tend to support that theory, do they?"

Before Dillon could respond, Tyler's phone rang. "DCI Tyler," he said, sticking his forefinger in his ear so that he could hear the caller above the sirens.

"*Boss, it's Jim Stone here. How far away are you from the suspect's address?*" His voice was taut with tension, which was totally out of character for him, and therefore worrying.

"We're about five minutes out. Why?"

"*I think our suspects are on the move. The unidentified one just came out and opened the Sierra's boot, and now he's gone back inside the address.*"

Tyler felt his stomach tighten. "Okay, let me go so that I can speak to the TSG, but call me back immediately if there's any more movement." Hanging up, he turned to Dillon. "Forget about the staging post. We need to go straight to the address. I think they might be getting ready to leave."

"You'd better let the TSG know," Dillon said, taking his eyes off the road long enough to risk a quick sideways glance.

Tyler was already on the phone to PS Beach, who was in the lead carrier. "Bobby, it's Jack Tyler. Listen, the live monitoring room has just been on the phone to me. They think our suspects are getting ready to leave the target address, so we need to go straight there… That's right, don't stop at the forward staging post. Bob, they're trying to call me back. I'll have to go." He ended the conversation and tried to accept the incoming call from Jim Stone's mobile but, in his haste, he somehow managed to cut that one off too. Swearing under his breath, he redialled Stone's number, only to find it engaged.

"Oh for goodness sake," he said, rolling his eyes in exasperation. Terminating the call, he tried Gurjit Singh's number instead.

Next to him, Dillon's mobile started to trill. "That'll be them trying to reach you on my phone," he predicted, pulling it from his pocket and handing it over.

Tyler was starting to get stressed as he answered the call. "Tyler here. What's happening now?"

―――

Skippy was holding onto the girl's shoulders, with G-Man taking her legs. "Be quick," he said breathlessly. They were carrying her through the narrow hall towards the street door.

"I'm going as fast as I can," G-Man complained, "but she's a lot heavier than she looks." It didn't help that, being unconscious, she had gone all floppy and had sagged in the middle.

Pausing at the door, Skippy stuck his head out to make sure that the coast was clear. He immediately spotted a woman with a pushchair and young child walking along the pavement towards them. "Go back inside," he snapped, pushing his end of the girl back into the flat.

The sudden redistribution of her weight caught G-Man off guard and, as he took an involuntary step backwards, he dropped his end of the cargo. Phoebe's shoulders were yanked out of Skippy's hands, and she dropped to the floor with a heavy thud. "Shit!" he exclaimed. He tried to slam the door shut, but it clunked into the side of the unconscious girl's head and bounced open again. "Quick! Pull her back inside," he hissed at his partner.

G-Man's left eye was twitching madly as he grabbed her by the ankles and dragged her back until her head was clear of the door.

Skippy slammed it shut and sagged against it, panting for breath. He gave the woman and her kid a minute to go by, and then peeped out cautiously. To his relief, they had progressed well beyond the flat. "Okay," he said, bending down to grab Phoebe by her shoulders, "let's try again."

As they staggered out into the front garden, the sheet snagged on the doorframe, jolting them to an abrupt halt.

"Now what? Skippy demanded.

G-Man was too busy trying to unsnag the material to respond.

"For fuck sake, hurry up," Skippy wheezed, his pockmarked face red from the effort of having to bear most of the girl's weight.

A moment later, G-Man nodded and they resumed their cumbersome journey.

Pulling open the creaking gate, Skippy shuffled backwards, taking little penguin steps until he reached the rear of the Sierra. As soon as G-Man drew level, they dumped their heavy burden inside. Having run out of gaffer tape, they had simply wrapped the sheet around her unconscious body and hoped for the best. Reaching into the boot, Skippy tugged it away from her. Thankfully, they would be hidden from view once they got inside school grounds, so there would be no further need for secrecy there.

Slamming the boot shut, G-Man leaned against it, panting. "That was bloody hard work," he said, wiping his brow with his forearm. "I've got a dodgy back and I think lugging her about has tweaked it."

Skippy stared at him in disgust. How many ailments could one man have? First the twitchy eye, then the sleep disorder, and now a dodgy back! He began to wonder if there was any part of the man's body that functioned properly? "Get in the bloody car," he said impatiently. "We need to get going."

33

HEADLESS CHICKENS

"Guv, they're loading the body into the boot as we speak," Gurjit said as soon as Tyler answered the phone. Leaning over Stone's shoulder, he watched in morbid fascination as the two kidnappers clumsily bundled her sheet covered form into the car and closed the boot. Holding the sheet in his left hand, Skipton slumped against the car, panting for breath, while the taller one with the ponytail started massaging his lower back.

"*We're still several minutes away from the address,*" Tyler told him, unhappily. "*The only thing I can do is put it out over the local channel and see if any divisional units are close enough to intercept it before we get there.*"

On screen, the man with the ponytail turned to face the camera and, for the first time, Gurjit got a clear and unobstructed view of his face. "Fuck me," he exclaimed as the man's left eye suddenly started twitching like mad.

"I beg your pardon?" Tyler demanded, obviously thinking that the comment had been addressed to him.

Gurjit didn't answer at first. He was too busy studying the face on the screen. "Boss, tell Mr Dillon that the unidentified suspect's the same bloke who kicked off when we went to search Spencer's room at the halfway house in Hackney. His name's Gerry something or other."

At the other end of the line, Tyler relayed the message. *"He wants to know if you're sure,"* he said a few moments later.

"Oh, I'm sure, alright," Gurjit said with a huge grin. "It was his twitchy eye that gave him away."

"His what...?"

"Mr Dillon will explain," Gurjit promised, and then his voice turned serious again. "Hang on guv, they're both getting in the car. Yep, it's pulling away from the kerb and heading towards Tennyson Road. It's now lost from sight."

"I've got to go," Tyler said, and promptly hung up.

Gurjit turned to Jim Stone, shaking his head miserably. "These two twats are going to have us running around like headless chickens," he predicted.

———

Dan Sergeant was driving Juliet One along Crownfield Road towards Leytonstone High Road. Unfortunately, Janet's mood hadn't thawed overnight as he'd hoped it would, and she had been giving him the full Arctic freeze treatment since coming on duty. A transmission over the Main Set broke the strained silence that had existed between them all morning.

"All cars, all cars from MP, believed concerned in a kidnap, and last seen in Adworth Road, E15, driving towards Tennyson Road in the last two minutes, a yellow Ford Sierra Sapphire, registration number..."

Janet turned the volume up and started taking notes.

"...The car contains two IC1 males. If sighted, the vehicle is to be stopped immediately, and all occupants arrested..."

"I said I'm sorry, what more do you want?" Dan suddenly snapped. The question had been festering inside his head for hours.

She held up a hand to silence him. "Shush! I'm trying to listen to this circulation."

"But I–"

"Shush!" she shouted.

Dan sighed his frustration, before mumbling something under his breath.

"...India 99, are you available to make your way to the vicinity to assist ground units search for this vehicle?" the operator at Information Room was now asking.

"MP from India 99, we're just taking off from Lippits Hill and will be making our way straight there. Our ETA is three minutes..."

When they reached the junction, Dan signalled to turn left.

"What do you think you're doing?" Janet demanded. "Don't go left, go right."

Behind the darkened lenses of his sunglasses, Dan's eyes narrowed confrontationally. He was the senior PC; it was up to him to decide where they patrolled, not her. "What for? If we go that way, we'll be leaving our own ground and straying onto Forest Gate's patch."

"I know that." Janet's tone burned like acid. "But the car that was just circulated could be coming this way, and I don't want to miss out on the chance of nabbing a couple of kidnappers."

Dan rolled his eyes theatrically, and then realised that the gesture had probably been completely wasted on her as it was masked by his sunglasses.

Janet pursed her lips in what he had come to recognise as a sign of growing irritation. "It *could* be coming this way," she insisted, like the know it all probationer she was.

Like we're going to be that lucky!

Dan decided to keep his thoughts to himself. For the sake of an easy life, he changed the indicator signal to right and did as she'd asked. The self-satisfied smirk that appeared on her face, when she got her own way, made him wonder what he'd ever seen in her.

Most of the blokes at the nick had fancied Janet when she arrived at the station, and being the one to actually pull her had felt like a bit of a coup at the time, but the sobering truth was that they actually had absolutely nothing in common, and he now felt like a complete fool for having allowed himself to be seduced by the shameless way she had fawned over him. The adulation had made him feel clever and special, and he had become so addicted to it that he had been prepared to sacrifice the life he had worked so hard to build with Susie for the cheap thrill it had given him. Now that he was no longer thinking with his dick, Dan could see Janet clearly for what she was and, while she might look good on the end of his arm, she wasn't half the woman Susie was, and she never would be. As if a mist had cleared, he finally realised what a catastrophic error of judgement he had made, and how much he wanted his wife back. Gripping the wheel firmly, he promised himself that, if he could somehow find a way to salvage their relationship, he would never, ever, make such a stupid and costly mistake again.

With a heavy sigh, he set off towards Maryland Point, keeping his eyes peeled for a yellow Ford Sierra. It was a pretty pointless exercise, he knew, but at least it would keep his troubled mind from dwelling on the calamitous state of his personal life for a little while longer.

———

The convoy pulled up outside Skipton's place in Adworth Road. Leaving one carrier to force entry into the flat, the other two TSG wagons shot off to start combing the area for Skipton's vehicle.

"Remember," Tyler told PC Smith, the officer who lugged the 'big red key' out of the back of the carrier, "you'll all be on film when you go in, so be on your best behaviour."

Pausing long enough to arch his right eyebrow in a manner worthy of Roger Moore, Smith hoisted the Enforcer onto his shoulder. "We're always on our best behaviour, guv," he said, piously.

The door opened inwards with one blow, and Smith nimbly stepped aside to allow the rest of the carrier's crew to rush inside and secure the flat. As soon as that was done, they handed it over to the detectives and scrabbled aboard the carrier, which then zoomed off to join in the hunt for Skipton's Sierra.

As Dan Sergeant drove Juliet One around the roundabout opposite Maryland British Rail station, Janet jumped in her seat as though she had just sat on something sharp. "Look!" she yelled, excitedly extending her hand across his face and pointing towards a yellow car that was going around the roundabout in the opposite direction. It was the first time all shift that she had showed any emotion.

From the brief glimpse that Dan was afforded before it disappeared from view, he was able to make see that the yellow vehicle she had just drawn his attention to contained two scraggy looking white males in their early to mid-twenties.

Janet was already reaching for the mic on the dashboard.

"Easy, tiger!" he cautioned, raising a hand to stay her. "Let's wait a minute and make sure that we've got the right vehicle, otherwise we'll end up with egg all over our faces."

Janet's frown betrayed her frustration. "But if that *is* the kidnapper's car, they're gonna go for it as soon as they clock us."

Dan gave her a condescending look. "Oh puh-lease!" he said, aware that he was overdoing the smugness but unable to stop himself. "I'm a Hendon trained advanced driver in a high-powered pursuit vehicle. What chance is some little oik in a clapped out Ford Sierra going to have against me?"

By the time he circumnavigated the roundabout and set off after the yellow car, a half dozen vehicles had slotted into the gap between them. Janet was bobbing up and down in her seat, craning her neck left and right to get a clearer view of the Sierra's registration number.

"Will you please just sit still?" Dan snapped.

"We need to get nearer," she replied, fidgeting restlessly.

"Relax," Dan told her. "Any minute now, it'll catch a red traffic light and then we can have a proper look."

Janet's mouth formed a tight little moue. "Why don't you just stick the blue lights on and go down the outside?"

Dan glared at her. "Just be patient," he said in a tone that implied she should also shut up.

Phoebe groggily opened her eyes. She was lying in a dark, confined space, and she had no recollection of how she had got there. There was a thin carpet beneath her, and she could feel vibration coming up through it. As her eyes acclimatised, she noticed that there were little slithers of light bleeding in from cracks in the corners of her container. She tried to turn her head, but it collided with something solid. Craning her neck until it cricked, she was just about able to make out the shape of a tool box.

She sniffed the air, picking up a faint smell of petrol.

There were a lot of different noises for her to process. The first was the sound of an untuned engine clattering away. Then there was the distinctive sound of wheels travelling over tarmac.

I'm in the boot of a bloody car!

She felt a soft bump as the wheels went over a pothole, and the suspension groaned and creaked in protest, telling her it was an old car.

Her body ached all over, and drawing anything other than a shallow breath was agonisingly painful. That kidnapping bastard had worked her over good and proper. Moving gingerly, she tried to roll over, only to discover that her captors had retied her hands behind her back.

Not again!

She tried her ankles next, but they had also been secured.

She wondered where they were taking her.

Phoebe tried to spit out the vile tasting gag they had plugged her mouth with, but the tape across her face prevented this. It was only a small consolation, but at least they hadn't covered her head this time. Because she had now seen their faces, they probably figured that there was no point in bothering. A worrying thought occurred to her: Could they afford to let her go, knowing that she could identify them?

She suspected not.

By straining her ears, she could just about hear their muffled voices up front. There was a sudden outbreak of laughter, and this infuriated her. Those two scumbags were laughing and joking while she was trussed up in the back, terrified out of her wits and fighting for her life.

Phoebe's anger empowered her. *I'm strong. I've moved on and I'm getting my life back.*

She turned her mind to the tool box and what it might contain. If she could get free of her bindings before they arrived at their destination, she might be able to find a big hammer or a sharp screwdriver to use against them. Phoebe wriggled her hands and feet to test the tightness of the bindings, and was pleasantly surprised to find that the gaffer tape had been applied sloppily. Encouraged by this, she started working her hands backwards and forwards, ignoring the pain of the tape chafing her wrists. When she had worked the tape as loose as she possibly could, she tucked her thumb into her palm and started dragging her hand downwards. The pain was excruciating, but she did her best to ignore it. Eventually, grunting from the effort and drenched in sweat, she pulled one hand free.

Pheobe ripped off the tape that was covering her mouth and spat out the gag. Then, gratefully sucking in air, she set about untying her ankles. As she ripped the tape off, it occurred to her that her attempted escape must have really flustered her kidnappers because, in their desperation to get her away from the house, they had done a terrible job of tying her up.

They had made a big mistake by not taking more time and, as she started rummaging through the tool box in search of improvised weapons, she sincerely hoped that it was going to be a fatal one.

———

"You know what I'm saying makes sense," G-Man insisted.

It did make sense, but Skippy wasn't a murderer and, if the idiot sitting next to him hadn't fallen asleep and allowed the girl to escape, they wouldn't even be having this conversation.

"We can't just kill her," he argued. "If we're convicted of murder, we'll go away for life."

"Yeah, but how long do you think we'd get for a poxy kidnapping? Ten years? Twenty? If you're in for a penny, you might as well be in for a pound, that's what I say. The little slag's seen our faces now, and we can't take the chance of her picking us out of a line up if we get nicked."

Skippy thought about this for a moment. "What if she couldn't pick us out?" he said, as an idea occurred to him.

G-Man scratched his head. "What the fuck you talking about?"

Skippy gave him a snide, sideways glance. "We don't have to kill her, we just have to make sure that she can't see us."

A pause. A mystified frown as he tried to decipher Skippy's cryptic words, and then a slow smile spread across G-Man's face as the answer came to him. "Blind her, you mean?"

Skippy nodded. "If we're caught, better to do time for GBH than murder."

G-Man chuckled. "You sly old dog," he said, elbowing Skippy's arm playfully. "What a fucking good idea."

Skippy didn't share his amusement. If they released her unharmed, the investigation might just flounder and die but, if they mutilated her, the police would never stop looking for them. "You'll have to do it, though," he said. "It's your fault she saw our faces, so it's up to you to make things right."

G-Man seemed totally unfazed by the suggestion. "Whatever. Unlike you, me old son, I ain't bothered about getting me hands dirty."

"We'll have to drug her first," Skippy said. "Otherwise, she'll struggle like mad."

"Don't worry about it," G-Man said with a lopsided grin. "It'll all be over in the blink of an eye."

Skippy laughed, relieved that G-Man wasn't trying to wheedle his way out of putting things right. "Yeah," he said. "She won't even see you coming."

"She definitely won't see me going," G-Man replied, cracking up with laughter.

Up ahead, the traffic lights changed to red. Still giggling, Skippy pulled up behind a big white van.

"There we go," Dan said, triumphantly. "I told you they would have to stop at traffic lights before too long.

"Clever you," Janet responded, icily.

Dan bridled at the remark. Not so long ago, she would have been praising his foresight and telling him how wonderful he was for having anticipated this. The Sierra's onward path was blocked by a van, so it couldn't go anywhere until the lights changed. "Let's get a bit closer and have a proper look," he said as he guided the Rover along the outside line of the stationary traffic.

The road widened from one to two lanes on the approach to the junction, and the suspect car was sitting in the first lane, which made Dan think that it was going to turn left at the lights. The second lane was empty, so he slowly cruised along this until they got their first clear view of the Sierra's registration plate.

"You see!" Janet exclaimed, reaching for the mic. "I was right! It's the car from the kidnap!"

Dan was surprised. He genuinely hadn't expected the vehicle Janet put up to be the one that everyone was searching for. "Call it in," he said, breathing faster as adrenaline surged through his veins.

"You've driven straight past it!" Janet exclaimed, horrified that he hadn't stopped when they had drawn level.

"I had to," Dan told her. It would have looked far too suspicious if he had stopped next to the Sierra when the road ahead of him was completely clear. Besides, if possible, he wanted at least one other unit to join them before showing out. Using his nearside wing mirror, Dan kept a close watch on the Sierra's occupants. Both had visibly stiffened as he'd driven by, but now that the police car was ahead of them, and in a different lane, they seemed to have relaxed.

"Call it in," he repeated.

Taking a deep breath to calm her nerves, Janet toggled the PTT button. "MP, MP, active message from Juliet One. The yellow Ford Sierra circulated in CAD 1087 is now stationary at red ATS in Leytonstone Road at the junction with Crownfield Road, E15. The car contains two IC1 males, and we think it's going to do a left into Crownfield Road when the lights change to green. Can we have units to assist us in stopping it."

There was a crackle of static. *"Juliet One from MP, that's all received,"* a plummy female voice responded. *"Be advised, the latest information suggests that the kidnap victim is locked in the boot of the car."*

Dan and Janet exchanged glances. "Shit!" he said. He hadn't paid much attention to the original transmission, and it had come as a bit of a shock to hear that the victim was actually inside the car.

Numerous units were putting themselves up to assist, including several TSG units who were already in the vicinity. India 99 was also making its way and would be with them imminently. *"Juliet One from MP, keep the commentary going. Do not – repeat DO NOT – attempt to stop the vehicle until India 99 is above."*

"All received by Juliet One," Janet said. She glanced sideways at Dan, and the daunted expression on her face said: 'What have we got ourselves into?'

As soon as the lights changed, the white van beside them turned left. Dan remained where he was. The car immediately behind him gave a tentative honk on the horn, clearly not wanting to annoy the policeman in front, but not wanting to miss the lights either.

Dan watched as the Sierra moved off, signalling left. As it drew level with the Rover, the driver shot him a furtive glance. Was it his imagination, or had the colour just drained from the man's pockmarked face?

Turning left, the Sierra's engine roared unhealthily, and a huge cloud of smoke bellowed out of the exhaust as it accelerated, rapidly going up through the gears.

"Bollocks!" Dan said with a grimace. "They've made us." Flicking the blue lights and headlights on, he activated the siren and set off in pursuit.

"I thought we were supposed to wait for India 99!" Janet observed, tartly.

"I *know* that, and you *know* that, but the bastard driving the bandit car clearly doesn't," Dan replied in exasperation. "What do you want me to do, risk losing him?"

Scowling at him, Janet squeezed the PTT. "MP from Juliet One, the bandit's spotted us and he's going for it. We're in pursuit, heading west along Crownfield Road towards Leyton High Road. He's doing forty five MPH in a thirty limit." She glanced over at the speedometer. "Make that fifty-five," she added as an afterthought.

"*MP from India 99, we're almost directly overhead.*"

"*Received by MP. Keep it going, Juliet One.*"

Inside the Rover, Janet was having to shout to make herself heard above the noise of the siren. "MP from Juliet One, we're now approaching the junction with Leyton High Road. The traffic lights are red against us. Break lights showing on the bandit vehicle, stand by for a direction of travel."

34

THE CAR CHASE

"Jack!" Dillon called from the driver's seat of the BMW, where he had retreated out of the heat to wait for Tyler, who was currently briefing George Copeland prior to his commencing a flash search of Skipton's flat.

On hearing his name, Tyler looked up, frowning.

Dillon waved for him to come over to the car urgently. "It's just come over the Main Set that a unit's behind Skipton's Sierra in Leytonstone," he called out.

Tyler ran over, jumping into the front passenger seat as Dillon started the engine.

As Dillon pulled the selector into drive, an excited female voice erupted from the speaker, talking over the wail of a siren. "...*MP from Juliet One, the bandit's spotted us and he's going for it. We're in pursuit, heading west along Crownfield Road towards Leyton High Road. He's doing forty five MPH in a thirty limit...*"

"Do you know where that is?" Tyler asked.

Dillon nodded. "Of course."

"Let's make our way over there," Tyler said, pulling his seatbelt on. "I want to be in on the kill when they catch them."

"You'd better hang on to your hat, then," Dillon said, flicking the switches to activate the concealed blue lights in the BMW's front grill.

"What the fuck are you doing?" G-Man screamed. "Are you completely off your trolley?"

Weaving onto the wrong side of the road to get past a slow moving taxi, Skippy ignored him. He redlined the car until the engine sounded like it was going to explode before taking the next gear. Once past the taxi, he swerved back onto the right side of the road, avoiding a head on collision with an oncoming postal van by the smallest of margins.

G-Man glanced over his shoulder, peering through the dust covered rear window. Behind them, the police car had been forced to wait until the oncoming vehicle passed, but now it pulled out and accelerated effortlessly past the taxi. Within seconds, it was back on their tail. Twisting around to face the front, he bit his lip in worry. "You ain't ever gonna lose the Old Bill in this piece of shit," he said, miserably.

"Shut up and let me think," Skippy hissed through gritted teeth.

"You ain't got time to think," G-Man protested. "You need to do something, now!" Licking his lips nervously, he reached under his T-shirt and removed an old Luger P08 pistol from his waistband.

Skippy's eyes darted to the gun. "Where the fuck did you get that from?" he demanded, staring at it in horror.

"Mad Micky gave it to me for the robbery we did last week, but he never took it back," G-Man said, clumsily working the breach to chamber a 9mm round.

"Put it away," Skippy snapped.

G-Man shook his head in defiance. "I ain't going down quietly," he declared, stroking the gun's barrel ominously.

As the Sierra hurtled towards Leyton High Road, the traffic lights controlling the junction began to change, turning red against them. "Don't stop," G-Man ordered, fearfully glancing back over his shoulder at the pursuing police car.

Skippy gritted his teeth. "Don't tell me how to drive," he yelled. Leaving it until the last moment, he braked heavily, locking the wheels and causing the rear of the car to fishtail. Up ahead, a heavy stream of traffic was crossing his path, moving left to right and right to left. He knew they would be T-boned if he pulled out blindly, but if he could just get the timing right...

Spotting the smallest of gaps, Skippy came off the brake and stamped on the gas pedal. The Sierra responded sluggishly at first, but then it started to build up speed.

Letting out an involuntary shriek, G-Man instinctively dropped his gun into the footwell and wrapped both hands around his head as he braced for impact.

Somehow, Skippy managed to squeeze the car through the fleeting gap that had appeared between a bus and a lorry. As the Sierra bounced across the junction into Temple Mills Lane, he checked his rearview mirror and was delighted to see that the pursuing Rover had been forced to stop. He slammed the steering wheel with his palm and turned to his passenger with a triumphant grin. "Boom! That's how you lose the Old Bill!"

"I think I might have just shit myself," G-Man moaned, bending down to retrieve the gun.

Judging by the awful smell that was now coming from him, Skippy had no trouble believing that.

———

Inside the lead TSG carrier, PS Bobby Beach was sitting in what was known as the jump seat. This was the one by the side opening door on the nearside of the vehicle, from where he was guaranteed to be the first one out when it stopped.

PC Patrick Reeve was driving, and PC Ron Steadman was sitting beside him, acting as his radio operator. A second carrier was riding in their slipstream, and both vehicles were motoring along at a fair old speed, with their blues and twos on.

Up ahead, Beach spotted a long sloping left-hand bend. According to India 99's latest radio transmission, the bandit vehicle was going to come haring around this bend towards them in a few seconds time. He leaned forward and placed a hand on PC Reeve's shoulder. "Reevo, pull up here," he shouted above the siren. "Ron, tell the other carrier to draw level with us and stop, so that we're blocking the road. Let's see what the bandit does when he finds us in his way."

Steadman reached for the radio, twiddled the frequency knob until he came to the TSG's dedicated channel, and relayed Beach's instructions to the vehicle behind.

Reeve killed the two-tones and slowed to a halt, and as the other carrier drew alongside them, Steadman wound down his window and smiled across at its driver. "This should be interesting," he said.

At that moment, a yellow Ford Sierra came tearing around the bend towards them. Almost instantly, the front of the car dipped as the driver slammed on the brakes, bringing the vehicle to a screeching halt.

"Surprise!" Steadman said, waving happily at the occupants, neither of whom seemed remotely pleased to see him.

There was a fierce crackle of static from the Main Set, and then a slightly distorted voice spoke. *"MP from India 99, the bandit's been forced to stop in Temple Mills Lane, as his onward path is blocked by a couple of TSG carriers."*

Steadman scooped the mic up from the dash. "MP from Uniform 366, for India 99's reference, that's us and Uniform 367."

In front of them, the bandit car started manoeuvring.

"MP from India 99, the bandit's turning around. Stand by. He's now heading back towards Leyton High Road with the two TSG carriers in pursuit."

"So much for your genius plan, Sarge," Reeve shouted over his shoulder.

In the back, Beach shrugged. "Well, it was worth a try," he said.

Dan had now cleared the junction with Leyton High Road and was powering Juliet One along Temple Mills Lane, determined to catch the bandit car up before it reached the A12 dual carriageway.

"What was you saying about some local oik not being able to get away from a Hendon trained driver?" Janet said, acerbically.

Dan's face reddened. "Shut up," he snapped, wounded by the catty remark.

"...MP from India 99, the bandit has been forced to stop in Temple Mills Lane, as his onward path is blocked by a couple of TSG carriers..."

Dan slowed down as soon as he heard the broadcast.

"What are you doing?" Janet yelled, appalled by the sudden loss of speed. "This is our chance to catch up before they decamp."

To her dismay, Dan killed the siren and pulled into a little turning on the left. In one fluid movement, he swung the car around so that it was facing the other way, and positioned it at the mouth of the junction.

"Have you lost the plot?" Janet spluttered. She could see India 99 hovering above and a little way over to their right. It was so close that she could actually read the identifying numbers on its fuselage. The bandit car couldn't be more than a couple of hundred yards ahead of them, just around the other side of the bend. Her jaw quivered with anger as she addressed her driver. "Honestly, Dan Sergeant, if you're doing this deliberately to get back at me for dumping you, I–"

"Oh, get over yourself," Dan snapped, cutting her off mid-sentence. "Just be quiet and trust me, will you?"

Before she could respond, the Main-Set crackled into life again. "...*MP from India 99, the bandit's turning around. Stand by. He's now heading back towards Leyton High Road with the two TSG carriers in pursuit...*"

Dan gave her a superior smile and tapped the side of his nose. "See, little probationer, that's the kind of knowledge that comes from doing The Job for as many years as I have."

As the Sierra hurtled past them, Dan pulled out behind it, cutting in front of the two TSG carriers in pursuit.

"MP from Juliet One, we're back behind the bandit vehicle, which is now heading towards Leyton High Road," Janet transmitted.

From the corner of his eye, Dan picked up on the grudging look of respect she had just given him and smiled inwardly.

Inside the oppressively dark boot, Phoebe was being thrown all over the place. The tool box was sliding everywhere, and it had already struck her painfully in the side of the head several times. The smell of petrol from the car's dodgy exhaust was steadily contaminating her air supply, and all the bumpy movement was playing havoc with her injured ribs.

The sirens told her that the police were chasing the kidnappers, and the erratic and increasingly turbulent nature of the driving suggested that her captors were fighting a losing battle to escape. Phoebe had finally managed to dig out a screwdriver and a hammer from the tool box, and she was frantically trying to force open the boot by hammering away at the latch, but it wasn't easy, not when she was being tossed around like a rag doll in a tin box.

The car thundered over what could only have been a speed hump, and she was catapulted off the floor and into the ceiling, smashing her head into the damn thing. She landed with a jarring thud, scraping the side of her face against the sharp metal edge of the tool box. The landing expelled all the air from her lungs, and sent waves of agony through her injured ribcage. Coughing uncontrollably, Phoebe recognised the coppery taste in her mouth as blood. Despite the oven like heat of the boot, a chill spread through her. Had she just punctured a lung? Was she going to choke to death on her own blood? Panic mushroomed inside her and she closed her eyes, trying to regain control.

I'm strong. I've moved on and I'm getting my life back.

"We're almost up with them," Dillon shouted above the siren. It was a slight exaggeration; the chase was actually still about a mile ahead. They had just turned into Leyton High Road from Crownfield Road and, according to the commentary coming over the Main Set, the bandit was just driving past Coronation Gardens.

"Well done, Dill," Tyler yelled back. He had just come off the phone from speaking to Susie Sergeant, who was over at Manson's house. She had confirmed that the murder scene followed a similar pattern to the one that Spencer had set at Whitling's address, even down to his calling card of scattering candy coated chocolates around the body.

"Can you believe that I thought this was going to be an open and shut case?" he said, shaking his head in amazement at how wrong he had been.

"It's the girl I feel sorry for," Dillon told him as he accelerated past a slow moving van. "That poor little cow's been to hell and back this past week."

Hanging onto the overhead grip as his friend weaved the BMW in and out of traffic, Tyler nodded his agreement. Way up ahead in the distance, he spotted the blue flashing lights of a TSG carrier. "Look!" he said pointing excitedly. "I think that must be the tail end of the chase."

"This is hopeless," G-Man told him, angrily. "We've gotta find somewhere to bail out before we're overrun by the fuckers."

Skippy knew that he was right, and his heart sank. His big plan for becoming rich had come to nothing and, without the ransom money to save his skin, he would never be able to pay off his debt to Jonas Willard. In a few days' time, when the deadline arrived, Fred Wiggins and Casper Wright would be unleashed to hunt him down. They would cart him off to a deserted building site and feed him to a cement mixer. Of course, Casper would be allowed to have a little fun with him before then, which would probably involve him systematically breaking every bone in Skippy's body. Then, Willard's enforcers would drown him in concrete and his corpse would end up permanently entombed in the support strut of an underpass.

He doubted that anyone would miss him.

"Head for the Beaumont Estate," G-Man shouted, breaking his train of thought. "I know some people who live in All Saints Tower. If we can get into the block before the Old Bill catch us, I'm pretty sure they'll let hide us till the heat dies down."

"What people?" Skippy demanded, glancing at him suspiciously.

G-Man shrugged. "I know a couple of hippies who live in a squat on the eighteenth floor. We can crash in there till the Old Bill get tired of looking for us."

They were approaching the junction with Capworth Street, and Skippy knew he would need to make a left turn there if he was going to head for the Beaumont Estate. Leaving it until the last possible moment, in the hope that the pursuing police car would overshoot the junction, he hit the brakes and yanked the handbrake up, at the same time dipping the clutch and swinging the steering wheel hard left. With a screech of tyres, the Sierra skidded around the corner at a right angle, chucking up a cloud of smoke from the burning brake pads.

The car understeered onto the wrong side of the road, smashing into the side of a little Fiesta that was coming the other way. The impact was bone jarring, and the steering wheel was violently wrenched from Skippy's hands as the Sierra rebounded across the carriageway and collided with a parked car.

Somehow, Skippy managed to regain control of the steering and straighten the Sierra out. Glancing in the rearview mirror, he saw that the Fiesta had mounted the pavement and smashed straight into a brick wall. He found himself hoping that the pursuing police car would stop to provide assistance, but it didn't. It drove straight past the crumpled wreck, which now had acrid smoke spewing from its mangled bonnet.

The Sierra's steering wheel was vibrating crazily, the car was pulling violently to the right, and Skippy could hear a terrible scraping sound coming from underneath the offside front wheel arch. He realised that the collision with the Fiesta must have driven the wing so far inwards that it was now rubbing against the tyre, which meant that it was only a matter of time until he suffered a blow out.

Desperate to put some space between them and their pursuers before they bailed out, Skippy swerved the car into Bromley Road, which was the first junction on his right. This was a one way street for traffic travelling in the opposite direction, and it was always busy because motorists used it as a shortcut between Lea Bridge Road and Leyton High Road. Flashing his lights and leaning on his horn, Skippy barrelled his way through the line of traffic coming towards him. As he had hoped, the police car dropped back, following him from a distance and waiting for oncoming cars to move aside instead of ramming into them, as he was doing.

By the time he merged into Lea Bridge Road, he had opened a pretty substantial gap. Capitalising on this, Skippy turned left, and then left again, driving back towards Capworth Street via Westerham Road. Thick black smoke was coming out of the bonnet, and he knew the Sierra was on the verge of dying on him. "Come on," he encouraged, patting the dashboard affectionately. "Not far to go now." He turned left at Capworth Street and took the first right into Beaumont Road, finally entering the estate.

They were almost home and dry.

35

THE BEAUMONT ESTATE

By the time that Tyler and Dillon reached the junction with Capworth Street, there was no sign of the convoy pursuing the bandit car. There was plenty of evidence that the chase had come this way, though. To their right, a crumpled Ford Fiesta had smashed into a low level brick wall, and the elderly driver, looking shaken but otherwise unharmed, was talking to the crew of a Panda car that had attended to report the accident. Parked against the kerb of the opposite carriageway, a little further along the road, the side of another car had been transformed into the shape of a banana, presumably by the bandit smashing into it.

The Main Set crackled into life. *"...MP from Juliet One, the bandit has gone left, left, left into Westerham Road and is heading back towards Capworth Street..."*

"Isn't this Capworth Street?" Tyler asked, looking around for a road sign.

Dillon pulled over and killed the two tones. "Sounds like he's coming our way," he said, staring straight ahead and gripping the steering wheel tensely.

Sure enough, no more than two hundred yards from where they had stopped, the Sierra screeched into view, bursting out of a side road on their right and driving straight towards them before taking the first right it came to and disappearing into the council estate.

Tyler was shocked by the appalling state of the bandit vehicle. The car's bonnet, wings and side panels were all so severely dented that it looked like it had been used for stock car racing. The windshield was so badly cracked that it was impossible to make out how many people were inside, and Tyler figured that the driver's vision had to be almost non-existent. A terrible screeching noise was coming from the front of the car, and thick smoke was billowing from one of the front wheels and the bonnet. As it turned the corner, he saw that the exhaust had fallen off and was dragging along the floor behind, throwing up a trail of sparks.

The two detectives looked at each other, both fearing for the girl in the boot. "I hope that poor girl's alright," Tyler said, dreading to think what state Phoebe Cunningham would be in when they finally saw her.

Dillon threw the Beamer into a tight left turn and set off after the Sierra. "Hopefully, she'll be okay," he said through gritted teeth.

Tyler could only pray he was right.

―――――

Phoebe was suffocating from the acrid smoke and carbon monoxide fumes that were flooding into the boot. She knew that, if she didn't manage to break free within the next few seconds, she would lose consciousness, and that would almost certainly prove fatal. Wedging herself into position by planting her legs and one arm against the sides of her miniature prison, she smashed the hammer into the latch with all her might.

Thunk!

Nothing happened.

She hit it again...

Thunk!

And again...

Feeling her strength draining from her, she raised a shaking arm and put everything she had into one last blow.

Thunk!

Gasping for air, Phoebe suddenly felt too drowsy to continue, and the hammer fell from her grasp, narrowly missing her head as she collapsed in exhaustion. The urge to close her eyes was irresistible, and she gave in to it, resting her head on the rough carpet and resigning herself to her fate.

Maybe this is for the best...

As the detectives followed the badly damaged Sierra, it skidded around the next turn, clumsily mounting the pavement and losing a wheel hub in the process. A second later, it clattered back down onto the road with a savage jolt, and the boot sprang open.

A marked police Rover appeared behind them, lights flashing, siren wailing. Tyler assumed that it was Juliet One, and he wondered whether Dan Sergeant was driving it.

"MP from Juliet One, the bandit's driving through the Beaumont Estate service road towards the tower blocks. There's an unmarked BMW in front of us, but it's not a local unit, over." The female giving the commentary sounded narked, as though the detectives had committed a cardinal sin by relegating the Rover to second position in the chase. A wry smile flickered across Dillon's face. "I think she's got the hump with us for stealing her thunder," he observed, drily.

Tyler merely grunted. He had more pressing matters on his mind.

The bandit car was accelerating towards the centre of the estate. As it approached a tight bend, brake lights came on and the bandit swerved sideways to avoid a head on collision with a little Mini coming the other way. As the Sierra's driver brought the skid under control, a woman's head suddenly popped up from inside the boot.

"Look!" Tyler exclaimed, stunned by the bizarre sight of Phoebe Cunningham staring back at them with a blank expression on her bruised and bleeding face. He unclipped the mic from the dashboard. Perhaps the female operator in the car behind was right; perhaps he ought to start providing a commentary seeing as they were now lead car. As he opened his mouth, the radio speaker erupted into life.

"*MP from Juliet One, the bandit's heading straight for All Saints Tower.*" The female operator sounded even angrier now, he noted.

"He's going too fast!" Dillon exclaimed, easing off the gas and dropping back.

"Shit! He's going to stack it," Tyler said.

Either the Sierra's driver had left it too late to start braking, or the overheated brake pads had finally given up on him because, instead of stopping, the car careered across the tarmac at a frightening speed, flew over a speed hump, and then pummelled straight into a row of thick concrete bollards that had been erected to deter residents from parking outside the block's entrance. There was a loud smash, a mangling of metal, and a thick cloud of smoke.

As it sailed over the speed hump, moments before the final impact, the Sierra's wheels had left the ground, and the dazed young woman sitting in the boot had come flying out as though expelled from a cannon. Arms flailing as though she was trying to fly, she was propelled through the air straight towards the detective's windshield.

Dillon stood on the brakes and, as the car came to a juddering halt, the girl landed on the hard floor in front of them with a sickening thud and rolled beneath their car.

For a moment, both men sat in tense silence, too afraid to get out in case they found a mangled kidnap victim trapped under their front wheels.

"Please tell me you didn't hit her?" Tyler implored.

"I didn't feel anything," Dillon said, but his face was ashen.

Preceded by a pitiful groan, two trembling hands suddenly appeared on top of the BMW's bonnet, followed a split second later by a dishevelled tangle of hair. Then came a bruised and battered face as Phoebe Cunningham sagged onto the bonnet and started wailing.

Closing his eyes, Dillon breathed a huge sigh of relief.

Suddenly, the doors to the Sierra sprang open and two men piled out. Glancing fearfully back at their pursuers, they set off towards the block's entrance.

"Get after them," Tyler instructed, unclipping his seatbelt.

"What about the girl?" Dillon asked.

"Leave her to me," he said.

As he spoke, the angry female operator from the marked Rover ran past them, pausing just long enough to shoot them a withering glare of contempt.

Two TSG carriers were also pulling up on scene, and their crews were already spilling out before they had even come to a stop.

———

Dillon sprinted after the two men who had just decamped from the Sierra. Although they had a healthy start on him, he seriously doubted that either of them were particularly fit, and as long as he could keep them in sight he was quietly confident of overhauling them. He quickly overtook the female officer, who emitted a little growl of anger as he pulled away from her. She was certainly feisty, he'd give her that.

Up ahead, having reached the block, the two suspects were straining to pull open the entry door, but it was securely locked and didn't look like it was going to budge an inch.

Looking over his shoulder, Skippy's eyes widened in fear as he caught a blurred glimpse of a powerfully built detective hurtling up the ramp towards him. The cop's eyes seemed to burn with anger, and in the fleeting moment that their gazes locked, Skippy decided that this was definitely not someone he wanted to cross swords with. He hastily tapped G-Man on the shoulder. "Run!" he shouted.

G-Man ignored the warning, frantically pressing one buzzer after another in the hope that someone inside the block would let him in.

Knowing that he would be caught if he lingered a moment longer, Skippy heeded his own advice and legged it, abandoning G-Man to his fate.

Dillon slowed down as he reached the top of the ramp, aware that the uniformed female officer was hot on his heels. The TSG officers had all gone after Skipton, who had disappeared from sight around the back of the block.

"It's over, Gerry," Dillon said as he slowed to a walk.

Mangrove spun around, placing his back against the door and scowling at him like a wounded animal. "Do I know you?" he demanded, breathlessly.

"We met at the halfway house last Thursday," Dillon informed him. "You managed to avoid being nicked back then, but I promise you won't be that fortunate today." As he spoke, he reached behind his back and removed as pair of handcuffs from the pouch on his belt.

"Wanna bet, pig?" Gerry said, whipping his right hand up.

To Dillon's surprise, it contained a Luger pistol.

A malicious grin spread across Gerry's face. "Not so fucking full of yourself now, are you?" he gloated, releasing the safety with his thumb.

"Put the gun down," Janet said, stepping out from behind Dillon.

Brave and feisty, Dillon thought, feeling a grudging respect for her.

Gerry pointed the gun at her head. "Your ballistic vest won't save you from a bullet to the brain, soppy knickers, so stay where you fucking are."

Janet stopped, raised her hands, placatingly. "Just calm down," she said softly. "Don't do anything rash."

A low buzzing sound indicated that the door release had just been activated and, as it popped open, Gerry stuck his foot inside to prevent it from closing. "What I need now is a little distraction," he said with a vicious grin. "Eeny meanie miny moe," he taunted, alternatively swinging the gun from one officer to the other. "Looks like you lose," he said as it came to a halt directly in front of Janet's face. Squeezing the trigger, he quickly ducked into the lobby and pulled the door shut after him.

Skippy ran faster than he had ever ran before. Heart pounding, lungs searing, legs aching like hell, he glanced back over his shoulder and nearly crapped himself when he saw that half a dozen burly policemen were giving chase like a pack of rabid dogs. They all looked as fit as fuck, and they were steadily gaining on him. His heart sank as he realised there was no way that he could possibly outrun them, and there were no obvious little hidey-holes that he could duck into and give them the slip.

As he cleared the side of the block he spotted a young woman getting out of her car about thirty yards ahead of him. Leaving the driver's door open, she walked around to the boot and opened it. Amazingly, given the area they were in, the silly cow had left the engine running.

Skippy couldn't believe the lifeline he'd just been thrown, and he swiftly changed direction, veering off to his left and making a beeline for the idling car.

"Stop!" he heard an angry male voice call from behind.

Like that was ever going to happen!

The woman looked up from whatever it was that she was doing in the boot, alerted by his laboured breathing and the stampeding sound of heavy footsteps coming towards her.

"Oi!" she shouted as he jumped into the car.

Skippy ignored her. He hit the button to lock the door, and was just in time to prevent a panting policeman from pulling it open.

As he battled the gearstick to find first gear, the agitated copper started banging the window with the bottom of his fist. "OPEN THE BLOODY DOOR!" he yelled.

The woman who owned the car appeared by his side, pulling at her hair and screaming incoherently.

What the fuck was her problem? As Skippy reached for the handbrake, the policeman raised his baton above his head, ready to smash the window.

Several of his colleagues had joined him by now, and they surrounded the car, trying to get in.

One of them started to climb in through the hatchback's open rear, but Skippy saw this and floored the accelerator, sending him tumbling out of the back. As the car lurched away, the baton wielding policeman lashed out, only to find empty air where the driver's window had been a second earlier.

Two officers had positioned themselves in front of the car, and they were waving their hands to get him to stop. Gritting his teeth, Skippy drove straight at them, grinning wildly as they frantically dived out of the way to avoid being mown down.

He was laughing now, overcome by relief. As he drove towards the estate's exit, unable to believe what a fantastic stroke of luck he had just had, the baby strapped into the child seat in the rear of the vehicle started crying. Glancing back in shock, Skippy was confronted by a red faced toddler in full meltdown mode. "Shit!" he exclaimed, spinning around to face the front. What the hell was he supposed to do with a baby?

PC Jay Smith was silently fuming that he'd missed out on all the fun because his carrier had drawn the short straw and been ordered to remain behind at Adworth Road to help the murder squad gain entry while the other two wagons shot off after the kidnap suspects. He had listened to the whole thing on the Main Set while his carrier hurtled through the streets of Leyton in the forlorn hope of catching up before all the fun was over.

Smith, a stocky man who stood just under six foot tall and wore his short black hair combed back into a widow's peak, was a tough, no-nonsense Northerner, and he had a reputation for being a prolific thief taker, so missing out on the chance to arrest a kidnapper hadn't gone down well with him. As the carrier sped along Leyton High Road, a radio transmission from India 99 raised his spirits considerably.

"MP and all ground units from India 99, one of the suspects is attempting to carjack a blue Vauxhall Astra from the base of All Saints Tower... Officers are trying to get him out... Stand by, stand by... The vehicle is off, off, off, driving through the estate towards Skeltons Lane...For a visual reference, the hatchback is still wide open..."

"Skeltons Lane's just up on the left," Smith shouted excitedly to his driver, grinning at the prospect of seeing some action after all.

"*All units from PS36 North East,*" Bobby Beach's out of breath voice came over the airwaves, and it was uncharacteristically full of concern. "*I'm with the car's owner now. Be advised there's an eight month old toddler in the back of the car he's just nicked.*"

That wiped the smile from Smith's face. If a criminal wanted to get into a high speed chase with the police, that was one thing; recklessly endangering the life of a baby was quite another. "Skeltons Lane's quite a narrow road," he shouted, "so we should be able to block it off if we're quick enough."

Sitting beside him, PS Martin Brent was horrified. "We can't put a roadblock in," he objected.

Brent was a real stickler for the rules, unlike Beach, who was happy to bend them within reason if circumstances dictated. Being lawfully audacious was the phrase he used.

"If the fucker crashes into us and the baby's injured," Brent was saying, "we'd be hung, drawn and quartered for doing that."

They all knew that, by we, he actually meant him, as the senior officer on board. Using police vehicles to create roadblocks was strictly against police driver training policy, although in real life the difference between an official roadblock and a couple of police vehicles that just happened to be parked in such a way that they blocked the road was something of a grey area.

"We don't need to put in a proper roadblock," Smith argued. "If we can get far enough into Skeltons Lane, all we've got to do is stop where the road narrows naturally, and then the bandit won't be able to get past us."

Brent nodded, looking relieved. In those circumstances, Smith knew, he could argue their case with a traffic sergeant if the bandit crashed into them.

"Okay," Brent said. "Do it."

The carrier turned into Skeltons Lane and accelerated past a packed car lot on the right. It continued until it reached a point where the road started to narrow significantly. With cars parked along both sides of the road, there was absolutely nowhere for an oncoming car to go.

"Here's perfect," Brent called out.

As the carrier came to a halt, Smith slid the side door back and jumped out, rubbing his hands together in anticipation. As the rest of the crew debussed to join him, the sound of a high revving engine reached his ears. "Gotcha," he said, removing his baton and smiling gleefully.

Inside the stolen Astra, the baby's screams were driving Skippy insane. He decided that, as soon as he was far enough away from the scene to be sure of escaping, he would dump the car and continue on foot.

"Be quiet," he shouted over his shoulder, wondering why anyone in their right mind would ever choose to have kids if this was what they did all the time. His raised voice only made matters worse, and the red faced infant instantly took the noise level up another notch.

As the car accelerated along Skeltons Lane, Skippy was so busy looking back over his shoulder at the screaming monster that he almost didn't see the stationary carrier blocking his path, despite it having its headlights on full beam and its blue lights flashing. When he did clock it, he was forced to slam on the brakes to avoid imbedding the Astra's bonnet into the heavy crash bars that were mounted on the Mercedes' grill.

Skidding to a halt, he was aware of half a dozen angry policemen descending on him with batons raised. Almost immediately, the window to his right was obliterated by a strike that sent fragments of glass flying into his face.

"OPEN THE DOOR!" one of them shouted.

"TURN OFF THE ENGINE AND GET OUT!" another yelled.

Grabbing the gear stick, Skippy ignored them as he struggled to find reverse.

The baby's racket was deafening, almost drowning out the shouts of the officers, who were now reaching in through the shattered window and trying to drag him out through it.

Finally, the gearshift grinded into reverse. Looking back over his shoulder, Skippy was about to gun the accelerator when a marked police Rover appeared behind him, literally stopping a couple of inches shy of his bumper so that he couldn't build up the momentum he required to shunt it out of the way.

He was trapped.

"Shut up you horrible little bastard," he screamed at the infant, who was making so much noise that he couldn't think clearly.

And then one of the officers, a mean looking man with a widow's peak, managed to unlock the door. Leaning in, he grabbed Skippy by the scruff of his neck and yanked him out of the car. A moment later, he was face down on the concrete, face bleeding from where it had hit the floor, and the officer was twisting his arm so far up his back that he was sure it would be torn off at any moment.

"Argh!" he screamed.

"Pass me some bracelets," a Northern voice said.

One of the PCs standing around him produced a set of handcuffs and gave them to the brute who was pinning him to the floor.

"You're nicked, sunshine," the Northerner said.

Skippy didn't answer. Gritting his teeth in pain, all he wanted right then was for the screaming toddler to shut up.

Dillon reacted instinctively when he saw Gerry's finger tighten on the Luger's trigger. Moving quickly, he reached out and gave the ballsy female officer an almighty shove, sending her flying sideways out of harm's way.

As the gun went off, he felt a searing pain in his left tricep. Looking down, he saw blood ooze from the hole that had appeared in his shirt. Pulling the material apart, he was relieved to see that the bullet had merely caused a narrow furrow in the skin, and that it had literally just caught him a glancing blow on its way past. Satisfied it was nothing more than a minor flesh wound, he went after Gerry, only to find that the block's security door had locked on closing.

He cupped his hands against the glass panel inset and saw G-Man frantically pressing the button for the lift. As if sensing Dillon's presence, the fugitive suddenly looked back at the door. His eyes widened in fear and he quickly raised the Luger and fired twice in quick succession.

Dillon sidestepped away from the door as the two bullets thudded into it. Luckily, neither round penetrated the thick metal.

The female officer was back on her feet. As she stumbled over to him, radio clasped against her face, he could hear her requesting the assistance of Trojan units to provide armed support as they went after Gerry.

"Thanks," she said, when she reached Dillon's side.

"You're welcome," he replied, risking another glance through the meshed window. As he watched, the lift doors opened and an old women emerged. Brushing her aside, Gerry ran into the left and started jabbing at buttons.

The old woman ambled towards the door at a ponderously slow pace, with Dillon willing her to go faster. "Come on," he said through gritted teeth.

By the time she opened the security door, and they gained ingress to the block, the lift was already on its way up.

Dillon watched the floor counter climb all the way up to eighteen, where it stopped. After a few seconds, it started to descend again, coming all the way back down to the ground floor.

"What are you going to do if he's inside?" the girl asked, staring at him nervously.

Dillon glanced down at his injured arm and then looked her straight in the eye, grinning malevolently. "I'm going to rip his head off."

As the lift reached the ground floor, he signalled for her to move backwards, out of view, and they flattened themselves against the wall, one on either side of the door.

It opened with a ping.

Dillon counted to three and then jumped in, only to find that it was empty. "Bollocks," he said, his massive shoulders slumping miserably.

"Don't worry," the female officer said, treating him to a knowing smile. "

He must have gotten off on the eighteenth floor, and there's only one flat up there that he could have gone into."

36

THE ARMED ENTRY

As soon as there were enough Trojan units on scene at All Saints Tower, the flats on the eighteenth floor were quietly evacuated.

All but one.

The intelligence checks that Tyler had ordered be carried out while awaiting the arrival of a team of Specialist Firearms Officers from Lippits Hill hadn't revealed anything of significance about the squat Mangrove had taken refuge in. There was nothing in the system to suggest they would find any children or animals inside, which made life considerably easier from a risk assessment point of view. According to numerous complaints the local authority had received from other residents in the block about the squatters, which mainly related to noise nuisance and mess, there were four adults living there.

It seemed highly unlikely that Gerry Mangrove would be daft enough to try scaling down the outside of the building when Trojan went in but, as a precaution, officers had been deployed to the balcony of the corresponding flat on the floor below. In addition, India 99 was hovering above the tower block, and it was now beaming live-time footage back to Information Room at NSY.

The level One SFO team were preparing to breach the premises and conduct a controlled call out of everyone inside. The best case scenario was that all the occupants would comply with their instructions and come out peaceably. The worst case scenario was that Mangrove would take the squatters hostage and barricade himself in. If that happened, things would move into slow time; the armed containment would remain in place, and a trained hostage negotiator would be drafted in to talk him out.

The Technical Support Unit had been placed on standby, and were ready to insert covert probes into the address, either through the walls of the adjoining flats or via the ceilings of the one directly below. This tactic would only be used if the situation deteriorated into a siege situation, and it would provide live intelligence to help the incident Gold Commander to manage the ever changing risk assessment. The game plan was that, in the event of a siege, the premises would only be stormed as a last resort, should it become clear there was an imminent threat to the life of a hostage.

The SFO team leader, call sign Bronze Trojan, was a former paratrooper called PS Tim Newman. Tyler and Dillon had worked with him several times before, and they held him in high esteem.

As soon as Newman finished briefing the SFOs, they moved forward to engage the target address, replacing the Armed Response Vehicle crews who had put in the initial containment.

In addition to fire-retardant Nomex overalls, boots, gloves and balaclavas, each SFO wore a Kevlar ballistic helmet with integrated communications. Their bulging goggles, which gave them such a minacious appearance, would safeguard their eyes, while the Kevlar body armour they all wore would provide them with the best possible protection against incoming fire.

As well as their standard issue Glock 17 pistols, most SFO's were armed with Heckler and Koch G36C carbines, although four of them carried heavy ballistic shields, and one held an Enforcer at the ready, in preparation for crashing in the door.

Once he was satisfied they were all in position, Newman nodded for the operation to commence. Two SFOs immediately interlocked their shields and moved towards the front door, ready to step in once it had been breached. The PC carrying the Enforcer hoisted it up in one fluid motion, and then slammed it into the wooden door, which imploded inwards with a loud bang. He immediately withdrew, and the officers with ballistic shields moved forward seamlessly, filling the doorway. Two officers with raised carbines took up station behind them, ready to provide covering fire.

There were screams from inside the premises as the startled occupants were caught totally unawares.

"ARMED POLICE! COME FORWARD WITH YOUR HANDS IN THE AIR!" PC Danny Spears, one of the officers behind the ballistic shields, shouted.

A long haired male, clad in a creased T-shirt and scruffy denim jeans, cautiously poked his head out of one of the rooms. He had a large spliff on the go. "Shit!" he exclaimed, spitting it out and ducking back into the room.

"ARMED POLICE! YOU IN THE FLAT, COME FORWARD WITH YOUR HANDS IN THE AIR!" Spears shouted, even more forcefully than last time.

"Don't shoot, man. We're coming out," a terrified female voice called from within.

Almost immediately, the long haired man in denim jeans reappeared in the hallway, both hands held above his head. "You can't do this to us," he protested. "We know our rights. We're squatting in an unoccupied flat, which we're perfectly entitled to do, and you can't just order us out at gunpoint." His voice was slurred, and he seemed high.

"BE QUIET," Spears shouted. "STEP FORWARD. NOW STOP. TURN AROUND SLOWLY."

The stoner did as he was told.

"NOW, WALK SLOWLY TOWARDS ME," Spears shouted.

"Way uncool, man," the stoner objected, but he complied with the order.

"CLASP YOUR HANDS BEHIND YOUR HEAD AND LOOK DOWN AT THE FLOOR," Spears shouted when the terrified man reached the shields.

Once the squatter complied, the shield unit parted and another SFO stepped forward, grabbed him by the wrists and dragged him unceremoniously through the gap.

The shields slid back into position with practiced ease as the stoner was frogmarched away from the address to be secured and searched.

"What's your name?" Newman asked the squatter once he was out of the danger zone.

The man shook his hair from his eyes, and then flashed Newman a sullen look.

"What's your name?" Newman repeated.

A dejected sigh. "Pete."

"Okay, Pete. I need you to tell me, how many other people are inside the flat?"

"Four," Pete said, staring back at him with glassy eyes. His pupils were dilated to the size of dinner plates, and the stench of cannabis wafting off him was almost strong enough to give Newman a high.

"Four? Are you sure?"

Pete nodded, miserably.

"Are they all residents?" Newman asked.

Pete shook his head. "Me, Liz, Kenny and Cathy live there," he said, grimacing in pain as a set of plasticuffs was pulled tight against his wrists. "Easy man, there's no need for that," he complained to the officer who had applied them.

"Is Gerry Mangrove in there?" Newman asked, grabbing him by the shoulder.

"Who's that?" Pete asked, looking bewildered.

"You might know him as G-Man," Newman explained, using the street name that had been listed on Mangrove's PNC file.

Pete stared at him, sullenly, then nodded. "Yeah, G-Man's in there.

He's a friend of Kenny's. What's the deal, man? Why are you harassing us like this?"

"Did you see if he had a gun with him?" Newman asked next.

Pete's face contorted into a contemptuous sneer. "Gun? What gun? You're just making up shit about a gun as an excuse to evict us."

Newman ignored him. Leaving his colleagues to escort Pete to safety, he returned to the officers outside the address. "According to the first one out, there are four others inside. The first three are squatters, and their names are Liz, Kenny and Cathy. The fourth is Mangrove. Let's try calling them out individually."

Spears nodded his understanding. "OKAY, YOU IN THE FLAT, LISTEN CAREFULLY," he called out. "I WANT LIZ TO COME OUT NEXT. STEP INTO THE HALL WITH YOUR HANDS IN THE AIR. DO YOU HEAR ME, LIZ?"

"I hear you," a quivering female voice replied. A moment later, looking absolutely terrified, a slender female in her early twenties, with her waist length raven hair tied in a braid, walked hesitantly into view. She was visibly shaking with fear. Clad in a thin vest that exposed her exceedingly hairy armpits, and three quarter length shorts, she looked like she was about to burst into tears.

"WALK TOWARDS ME SLOWLY," Spears shouted. "STOP. TURN AROUND SLOWLY." He talked her through the same procedure that Pete had been put through. Within seconds, Liz had been escorted away.

Spears repeated the same routine with Kenny, a short, bald man with a pot belly, lots of piercings and masses of body hair.

So far, everything had gone smoothly, but when Spears called Cathy's name, there was no reply. "CATHY, CAN YOU HEAR ME?" he yelled. Again, no reply. Spears toggled his throat mike. "Bronze Trojan, we may have a problem, over."

Newman came over immediately. "What's wrong?" he asked, keeping his body flat against the building line so that he didn't stray into the line of fire.

"Cathy's not answering," Spears informed him, grimly.

Newman puzzled this for a moment. The most likely scenario was that G-Man was holding her captive. But, if that was the case, why let the others go? The answer was obvious: one hostage was easier to control than three. "Try calling Gerry Mangrove," he suggested.

Spears nodded, cleared his throat. "GERRY MANGROVE, CAN YOU HEAR ME?"

Silence.

Spears looked at Newman, shrugged. "MANGROVE, WE KNOW YOU'RE IN THERE. THERE'S NO WAY OUT. WALK INTO THE HALL WITH YOUR HANDS IN THE AIR. DO IT NOW."

The sound of sobbing reached their ears. Then, crabbing sideways, Gerry shuffled into the hallway, his left arm tightly wrapped around the neck of a distressed female with bright pink, spikey hair. This was obviously Cathy, and he was keeping her body in front of his, using her as a human shield. An old Luger was held in his right hand, and it was firmly placed against Cathy's right temple. "If you try to shoot me, I'll kill her," G-Man warned them. Nestling his face into hers, he proceeded to give her a big wet kiss on the cheek.

Cathy squirmed at the contact.

"No one wants to shoot you," Spears said, aware that his two colleagues had the sights of their carbines trained on him, and would be looking for a clean shot if the opportunity presented itself.

"That so?" G-Man taunted. "In that case, why don't you tell your frog faced mates to lower their guns?"

"That's not going to happen," Spears responded calmly but firmly. "Now, why don't you do us all a favour and put that gun on the floor so that this can end without anyone getting hurt."

G-Man laughed. "Like you said, not going to happen." As he spoke, he slowly backed along the corridor into the lounge at the end. Once inside, he closed the door, cutting off their view of him.

Spears glanced up at Newman. "I take it you heard all that?"

Newman nodded, glumly. It looked like they had a siege on their hands after all. "Guess we're going to be in this one for the long haul," he said with a disgruntled sigh.

An unexpected radio transmission startled them. *"All units from*

India 99, we have a white male on the balcony. Stand by... he's got a pistol in his hand..."

From inside the flat, the unmistakeable sound of two shots being fired in quick succession reached their ears.

"...Shots fired at the helicopter!" The man speaking over the radio sounded badly shaken. *"We're unhit, but we're relocating to a safe distance away..."*

Newman toggled the PTT for his throat mic. "India 99 from Bronze Trojan, where's the female?"

The sound of the rotors could clearly be heard over the helicopter operator's voice. *"The female's inside the living room, to the left of the door as you go in, and the gunman's still on the balcony, pointing his weapon at us, over."*

Newman signalled his team forward. There would only be a brief window of opportunity, and there would be a degree of risk involved, but if Gerry had opened fire on the helicopter, what was to stop him from doing the same to his hostage as soon as he re-entered the flat. "The suspect's out on the balcony taking pot shots at India 99, but the girl's still in the lounge. We're at State Green. Prepare to move in and secure the premises."

As Phoebe Cunningham was led to the ambulance that had arrived to take her off to hospital, a short woman with auburn hair and a plain but pleasant face hurried over to join her. Showing her warrant card, she introduced herself as DC Debbie Brown, and explained that she was from the Homicide Command. "DCI Tyler has asked me to accompany you to the hospital," she said with a friendly smile.

"I don't need anyone to mollycoddle me," Phoebe objected.

"I can see that, love," Debbie said in a brusque tone, "but he's the boss, and what he says goes."

Phoebe sat in the back of the ambulance while a paramedic gave her the once over. She was battered and bruised, her head was throbbing unbearably, and her ribs felt as though they had all snapped and were now sticking into various organs. Every breath brought excruciating pain, and she felt as though she could sleep for a year.

"Looks like you've been through the wars," the woman examining her said with a business-like smile.

"Feels like it, too," Phoebe admitted.

"Well, it looks like you've cracked a couple of ribs, and I think you've got a mild concussion," the paramedic said, putting her things away. "We'll pop you along to Whipps Cross and get you checked over properly."

"My parents will be worried," Phoebe said, looking imploringly at Debbie. "Can I call them and let them know I'm safe?"

"Don't worry, they've been informed," Debbie said, placing a reassuring hand on the girl's shoulder. "Let's get your medical needs addressed first, and then you can give them a call."

"Are you coming with us?" the paramedic asked.

Debbie nodded. "After what this poor young lady has been through lately, I'm not letting her out of my sight."

That really wasn't what Phoebe had wanted to hear. She needed to get away from the hospital as quickly as she could, to dispose of the incriminating evidence in the back of her car. She was fairly confident that she would be able to find it from what she'd overheard her captors saying. Hopefully, now that she was safe, the police would have no reason to search for it so, as long as it wasn't causing an obstruction, it should be okay where it was for a day or so longer.

If not, she was in deep trouble.

The hallway was too narrow for two shields to be deployed side by side, so PC Danny Spears took point, with PC Peter Carmichael perched on his shoulder, aiming his carbine into the flat. He was aware of the other two-man teams forming up behind them, each consisting of an officer carrying an 11.5 kilo ballistic shield like his, and a carbine wielding colleague whose job it was to provide covering fire.

Spears tensed as Newman's voice came through his earpiece. *"Standby! Standby! We go in three, two, one...GO! GO! GO!"*

Spears moved forward quickly, as he had been trained to do. With Carmichael behind him, he crossed the hallway to the living room door, intent on reaching their objective and trusting his colleagues to watch their backs. He was vaguely aware of the three other two man units storming in behind them, peeling off into each of the rooms. There was a lot of clatter and banging, accompanied by shouts of "ARMED POLICE! ARMED POLICE!" and then "ROOM CLEAR!"

Without pausing for breath, Spears pushed open the door and made entry into the lounge. As they crossed the threshold, he took in several things at once: a screaming woman was cowering in the corner off to his left; the balcony door was wide open in front of him, and a white male with a ponytail was in the process of climbing over the railing. The helicopter was visible, off to the right, having retreated to a distance that the pilot considered safe.

Behind him, Carmichael's weapon was sighted on the idiot on the balcony, who was clearly intent on descending the side of the building like Spider-Man.

"ARMED POLICE! SHOW ME YOUR HANDS!" Carmichael yelled.

It occurred to Spears that, for the suspect to do that, he would have to release his grip on the railings, which would probably result in him falling to his death.

There was no sign of the Luger pistol, and Spears assumed that the suspect had tucked it into his waistband to climb over the railings. A look of horror appeared on Mangrove's face as the rest of the SFO's spilled into the lounge, and his right hand dropped out of view, reappearing a moment later holding the pistol.

"GUN!" Spears cried out, dropping down beneath the shield.

"DROP THE WEAPON!" Carmichael shouted, his finger tensing on the GS36's trigger.

Gerry Mangrove ignored the order. Face contorted with rage, he squeezed off two rounds. The first shattered the window and imbedded itself harmlessly into the ballistic shield, while the second one went wildly astray, ending up in the celling. The reason for this was that the kick from the first shot had thrown Mangrove so badly off balance that he had lost his footing on the balcony and was now clinging on for dear life with just his left hand.

The gun was discarded as he desperately scrambled for a handhold, but his palms were so sweaty that he was unable to get a decent grip. "Help me!" he screamed, his voice full of panic.

Before any of the officers in the living room could react, he let out a piercing scream of terror and fell from view.

"Shit!" Spears said, lowering his shield and running out onto the balcony while Carmichael rushed over to comfort the terrified hostage. He peered over the rail, expecting to see a mangled and bloody mess splattered across the concrete eighteen floors below. Instead, he saw his colleagues on the balcony beneath them holding onto Mangrove's ankles as the suspect dangled upside down, arms flailing wildly.

Beneath his mask, a huge grin broke out on Spears' face, and he shook his head in disbelief. "Nice catch!" he called out to his colleagues.

Mangrove was crying like a baby as the SFO's pulled him up, and all the fight seemed to have gone out of him as they hauled him over the railing to safety.

"You're under arrest for kidnap, false imprisonment and discharging a firearm with intent to endanger life," Spears heard one of his colleagues tell the sobbing man.

Removing his mask, Spears walked back into the living room just as Newman walked in.

"All clear," Spears reported with a grin.

"They got the bastard," Newman said, smiling broadly. "Apparently he pissed himself with fright when he fell."

"I bet he did," Spears said, laughing. "I don't think I've ever seen anyone look so terrified as he was when they were pulling him back up."

37

Thursday 2nd August 2001
IS THIS YOUR PHONE?

It was two days since Gerry Mangrove and Thomas Skipton had been arrested. During that time, they had been interviewed extensively, but both men had remained stubbornly silent, replying 'no comment' to every question that had been put to them. It didn't matter. They were, to coin a phrase, bang to rights, and they both knew it.

Still recovering from her injuries in hospital, Phoebe Cunningham had been too unwell to provide a victim statement. That didn't matter either. Tyler was happy that they already had more than enough evidence to charge the two men, so her statement could wait until she was well enough to be released. It was coming up to lunch time, and he was sitting in his office with Tony Dillon and Susie Sergeant, discussing the charges.

"So, you're definitely happy to charge them both with abduction, false imprisonment and blackmail before we get Phoebe's statement?" Susie asked him.

She was looking much better today, Tyler noticed, more like her old self. "I've no qualms about that whatsoever," he assured her. "We've got Ben Cunningham's statement, which covers Skipton demanding money with menaces for his daughter's safe return, and we've got the CCTV evidence of both suspects carrying her in and out of the flat." The footage of the two men transferring Phoebe Cunningham from the boot of the Sierra into Skipton's flat during the early hours of Tuesday morning, and then lugging her back out again later in the day, was so incredibly powerful that it would probably be enough to convict them of her kidnapping on its own. "Then there's the evidence that me and Dill give, of her being still in the boot when we got behind them during the chase."

Dillon nodded. "Yep, and on top of that, we've got the call and cell site data from Skipton's burner." He held up a copy of the TIU report as he spoke. "The billing provides the date and times of both calls he made to Cunningham, and the cell siting confirms Skipton's burner was within the radius of the mast covering his flat in Adworth Road when the calls were made. As if that's not enough, the covert CCTV from our surveillance physically puts him in the flat at the time of the calls."

Tyler broke into a wide grin. "Apparently, the look on Skipton's face, when the burner phone was found on him in the custody office at Forest Gate, was priceless."

Dillon smiled, wistfully. "I wish I could have seen that."

"Me too," Tyler admitted. "Last, but by no means least, we've got the trace evidence that's been recovered from the flat in Adworth Road." The gaffer tape that Phoebe had been secured with, prior to her escape, had been found on the floor of Skipton's bedroom. Both his and Mangrove's fingerprints had been all over it, and the DNA results, which were due back later that day, would undoubtedly prove that it had been used to bind Phoebe.

"We were lucky there," Susie said.

Dillon grinned. "We were, but let's face it, we were long overdue a little bit of luck on this poxy job."

Tyler's face clouded. "Pity our luck hasn't stretched as far as arresting Spencer," he lamented.

Dillon nodded, and the smile vanished. "Him being on the run does cause us a bit of a problem."

That was an understatement.

"Is George Holland still moaning about the amount of overtime being incurred?" Susie asked. The Homicide Command were having to foot the bill for all the uniformed officers performing guard duty at the front and rear of the Cunningham residence, and for Phoebe's hospital guard, and the commitment was eating through the budget at an alarming rate.

Tyler grunted, despondently. "He's got the right hump about it, but there's nothing I can do until Spencer's caught."

Dillon became thoughtful. "I just don't get it, Jack," he said. "There's no way that he should still be out there, not with all the publicity surrounding the murders." The media coverage had been somewhat frenzied since news of Anna Manson's murder had leaked and, for the past couple of days, Spencer's ugly face had been plastered over the front page of every red top, and featured on every TV news bulletin. "Is the MIR still being flooded with bogus sightings?"

Tyler chortled. "Thankfully, that seems to have calmed down a bit," he said. "Although there was one this morning from a woman who reported seeing a man fitting his description working as a strippergram in Durham."

Dillon raised an eyebrow. "I'm surprised she even looked at his face," he smirked.

"What additional offences are we charging Mangrove with in relation to the gun?" Susie asked, dragging them back on topic before the smutty jokes started. "I think we should keep it simple and go with possession of a firearm with intent to endanger life and–" she sighed and pulled a long face, as though she had just stood in something unpleasant "–as much as it galls me, I suppose we'll also have to include a charge of attempted murder to cover where he tried to shoot PC Janet Husband-Stealer."

"Uh-Hmm," Dillon said, making a point of theatrically massaging his arm. "Don't forget, I was the one who actually got shot." Apart from having the wound cleaned and bandaged, he hadn't required any additional medical treatment.

Tyler grinned at him. "I'm sure we can add on a charge for you, too," he said affectionately.

"How about inflicting a scratch on a police officer?" Susie teased, and then became mock stern. "Personally, I think you only pushed her out of the way to annoy me."

"Ha-bloody-ha!" Dillon said, trying his best to look aggrieved. "I didn't even know her name when I performed my incredibly brave act of heroism."

"It was very brave," she conceded, smiling at him affectionately. "Just wasted on the likes of *her!*" She became serious again. "How's Andy's team getting on with interviewing Mangrove?"

When Mangrove's room at the halfway house in Hackney had been searched, the missing fourth bag of cash from the armed robbery that had resulted in PC Dawkins' murder had been recovered under his bed. Once Tyler's team had finished interviewing him about his involvement in the kidnapping, they had turned him over to Quinlan's officers, for them to question him about those matters.

Tyler grunted. "I spoke to Andy a little while ago," he informed them. "Apparently, Mangrove's still making no comment, but they've got more than enough to charge him with the robbery and a joint enterprise murder, so who cares?"

Dillon shook his head, dolefully. "You know, when Gurjit and I had our little run in with Mangrove the other day, while we were at the halfway house searching Spencer's room, I noticed that he had purple colouring over his hands. Stupidly, I didn't make the connection at the time, but now it seems obvious that this was dye from where he'd forced open the two damaged cash-in-transit bags we found at Higgins' flat."

"An easy mistake to make," Tyler consoled him. "Don't beat yourself up over it. Just make sure you put that information in a statement and let Andy's team have it."

"Already done," Dillon assured him.

There was a polite rap on the door and Reg Parker walked into the office. "There's been a development, and I thought you'd want to know about it straight away."

Tyler noticed that Reg's cherubic face was aglow with excitement. "Sounds intriguing," he said.

Reg grinned at him. "I've just had the call data back from that mobile phone we found at Skipton's flat."

Tyler raised an enquiring eyebrow. "And?"

"Mind if I pull up a pew?" Reg asked, handing over a printout.

Tyler shrugged. "Help yourself."

Clearing his throat, Reg looked at each of them in turn, his face suitably solemn. "Well, I think you're going to find this rather interesting," he predicted.

"We might, if you ever stop procrastinating and actually get around to telling us," Dillon chided, making a point of tapping his watch. "Time is money and we haven't got all day."

Reg's smile faltered for a moment, but then it was firmly back in place. "I take it you're all aware that Skipton's personal mobile ends in 137?"

Tyler sighed, trying not to let his impatience show. "Yeah, so?"

"And you all know that he's exchanged a number of text messages with Spencer's PAYG, which ends in 654?"

Tyler had no idea where this conversation was going. He glanced sideways at the others, and was pleased to see that they appeared equally baffled. "Again, so?

"Bear with me," Reg said, undeterred by their lacklustre response. "It turns out that the Motorola we found in Skipton's kitchen is none other than the 654 mobile that Spencer's been using."

That got their attention.

"But, that's impossible," Tyler said.

"I promise you it's not," Reggie told him, smugly. "Furthermore, at 00:20 hours on Tuesday morning, Spencer's 654 phone sent a text message to Skipton's 137 handset. It reads: 'I've done it. I've taken care of the last obstacle. I'm heading out of London till the heat dies down so don't worry if you don't hear from me for a while.'"

Tyler nodded, tartly. "I'm well aware of that. We believe it was a cryptic reference to his having taken care of Anna Manson."

"Yes, but what you're not aware of is that when this message was sent, both Spencer and Skipton's phones were within the radius of the same cell. In fact, they were in the same azimuth. Guess who's house that particular azimuth covered?"

Tyler could feel himself losing patience. "Reg," he warned, gesturing for him to get to the point.

Reg smiled, which only served to wind Tyler up even more.

"Reg!"

Parker raised his hands in surrender. "Okay. Okay. Both handsets were within range of the azimuth covering Anna Manson's house."

Tyler leaned back in his chair and steepled his fingers. For a while, he sat in moody silence, considering the implications. "Are you suggesting that the two of them met up, and that Spencer gave him the phone?"

Reg spread his arms in a blasé 'who knows?' gesture. "It seems probable. Perhaps, Skipton gave him a new handset, and took the old one away to dispose of it?"

"Why would he do that?" Dillon scoffed, clearly sceptical.

"I suppose Skipton could have been giving him a clean phone to go on the run with," Susie suggested.

"That's my take on it," Reg said.

Dillon stared at him for several seconds, deep in thought, then turned to Tyler. "What do you reckon, Jack? Maybe we should get the interview team to further arrest him for perverting the course of justice and assisting an offender. Then they could question him about those matters?"

Tyler shook his head. "No. Get them to arrest him on suspicion of having conspired with Spencer to commit Whitling and Manson's murders. Let's see if the prospect of facing a life sentence will encourage him to tell us about the phone."

Dillon nodded, stood up, headed for the door with a sense of purpose. "I'll give Steve Bull a ring now."

Tyler reached for his phone as the big man left. "While you do that, I'll have a quick word with Juliet Kennedy and ask her to get the handset fingerprinted and swabbed for DNA," he said. "Let's see what a full forensic examination throws up."

———

Colin Franklin wearily sat down opposite Thomas Skipton, staring at him across the bolted down table in the windowless interview room. For a moment, he studied the vague expression on the prisoner's face, wondering how he managed to tie his shoelaces without help.

"What you gawping at?" Skipton demanded, petulantly.

Franklin ignored him. He had spent a lot of time cooped up in the oppressive little room with Skipton over the past two days, and the order that had filtered down from on high, to further interview him about a murder conspiracy, hadn't been well received.

Leaning against the wall, Skipton folded his arms sullenly and stared down at his lap.

A sour faced woman of indistinguishable age, wearing a creased business suit that looked like it had been all the rage back in the 80s, sat primly beside him. She had an A4 notepad open in front of her, and an expensive looking fountain pen was poised in her wrinkly hand, ready to jot down every word that was said during the interview. Her name was Agnes Goody, and she was Skipton's solicitor. She was also quite possibly the most miserable person that Franklin had ever laid eyes upon. With a face like old parchment, Goody looked as though she hadn't smiled in the best part of a decade, and he suspected that her withered skin would probably crack and disintegrate if she tried.

Even with the air conditioner clunking away noisily overhead, the place felt unbearably hot and stuffy. Franklin attempted to make himself comfortable, but the wooden chairs they were all sitting on were hard and unyielding, with bits of foam protruding from the torn and frayed fabric of their flimsy cushions.

Jim Stone was sitting next to him, looking as stoic as ever.

"Okay," Franklin said, running a finger around the inside of his collar to loosen it. "If everyone's ready, we'll crack on."

"We've been ready for the past ten minutes," Goody pointed out in a voice that sounded like she regularly swallowed broken glass.

Franklin idly wondered how many cigarettes a day she had smoked over the past forty years to get it to that level. If her nicotine stained fingers were anything to go by, she had to be getting through at least forty a day.

Ignoring her narky comment, Franklin pressed the record button on the tape deck. The dull buzzing sound seemed to go on for ever. When it finished, and the lights on the machine started flashing in the correct sequence, he cleared his throat and rattled his way through the introductions and the caution. Speaking in a dull monotone, he dutifully read out the information that he was required to give prior to the interview commencing from the laminated idiot card that was sellotaped to the table in front of him. "Do you understand the caution?" he asked Skipton when he had finished.

Skipton yawned, closed his eyes. "No comment."

Franklin sighed wearily. This was going to be a long and pointless interview.

"Mr Skipton, you've been further arrested on suspicion of being involved in a conspiracy to commit murder. Do you understand what that means?"

"It means you're on a fishing trip," Goody said, pulling a face that made her look like she'd been sucking lemons.

"I'm asking Mr Skipton," Franklin told her, trying not to let his temper get the better of him.

Skipton lazily opened one eye. "What she said," he smirked before closing it again.

Wanker!

During the previous interviews, Franklin had questioned him about the evidence that they had found at his flat, which included the torn gaffer tape that Phoebe had ripped off when she made her escape bid. Skipton had squirmed uncomfortably when told that his and Mangrove's fingerprints had been found all over it. Of course, he had squirmed far more when he had been forced to watch the video footage of him and Mangrove carrying Phoebe Cunningham from the Sierra's boot to the flat and back again. Unfortunately, squirming during an interview wasn't considered admissible evidence of guilt at court.

Franklin slid an A4 sheet of paper across the desk so that Skipton and his hag of a brief could see it. "For the benefit of the tape, I'm now showing Mr Skipton a colour photocopy of exhibit DJ/12. This is a Motorola Pay-As-You-Go mobile phone that was found on your kitchen worktop. Is this your phone, Mr Skipton?"

Skipton didn't bother looking. "No comment."

"You might want to look at it first before replying," Franklin suggested.

Skipton sighed theatrically, opened his eyes briefly. "No comment," he repeated.

"Is it Gerry Mangrove's phone, perhaps?"

"No comment."

"Or is it John Anthony Spencer's phone?"

Skipton opened his eyes, glanced uncertainly at his brief, who responded with an almost imperceptible shake of her head.

"No comment," he said, but he sounded slightly nervous.

"Have you ever touched this phone?" Franklin asked, smiling sweetly.

Skipton looked at Goody, received another infinitesimal head of the shake. "No comment," he said, sounding like a broken record.

"Did John Spencer give you this phone?"

A sigh. "No comment."

"How did it get into your flat?"

"No comment."

"We've carried out a number of checks in relation to this phone, Mr Skipton. We know the number. We know the details of every call or message its ever made or received. We know where it was when it made or received those calls and messages. We've also recovered five voicemails that were made to this phone."

Skipton looked up, and his face drained of colour. "Voicemails?"

Franklin kept his face impassive, let the silence stretch on and watched as Skipton became increasingly agitated. "That's right," he eventually said. "Voicemails from you to your cousin, John Spencer."

Skipton swallowed hard. "No comment," he said in a shaky voice.

"I haven't asked you a question yet," Franklin pointed out.

"Oh." Skipton was perspiring, and it wasn't just because of the heat.

"When my colleagues visited you last Friday, you told them you hadn't had any contact with John Spencer since he'd been released from prison, but we can prove that's a lie. I'll go through each of the text messages and voicemails with you shortly but, for now, why don't you tell me why you lied to the officers?"

"No comment," Skipton whispered so quietly that Franklin had to lean forward to make out the words.

"And, likewise, you told them that you had never visited him in prison, but we've obtained his prison record, and we have a long list of all the visits you've paid him, the last one being three weeks before his release. Again, why did you lie?"

"I–"

"Mr Skipton," Goody interjected before he could say another word. "Please carefully consider my advice to you before you say anything more."

Skipton looked at her, nodded woefully. "No comment," he said.

For the first time in two days of interviewing him, Skipton was visibly rattled, and Franklin was keen to keep piling on the pressure. "As you know," he continued, "John Spencer is currently wanted for three murders. The first one occurred on the day of his release from Strangeways, after he got into a random argument with a stranger on a bus. You'll be pleased to hear that we don't, for one second, think you were involved in that."

A look of relief flashed across Skipton's face, but he said nothing.

"The second and third murders, however, were brutal and premeditated. The victims were people who were close to Phoebe Cunningham, the girl that you and Gerry Mangrove kidnapped. Interestingly, before killing Phoebe's fiancé, Martin Whitling, and her best friend,

Anna Manson, Spencer kidnapped Phoebe too, but she managed to escape from him. That makes us wonder if you and Mangrove were actually acting on his behalf. Were you?"

"No, of course not," Skipton said before he could stop himself.

"Did you conspire with John Spencer to commit the murders of Martin Whitling and Anna Manson?"

"No fucking way!" Skipton spluttered, slamming his fist down angrily on the wooden desk.

Goody reached out and placed a hand on his arm to calm him down. "My client denies any involvement in these matters," she said, calmly.

"If you're not involved," Franklin said, making a point of complete ignoring Goody's outburst, "why was your mobile number, which ends in the digits 137, and Spencer's mobile, which ends in the digits 654, both cell sited within the vicinity of Anna Manson's house at the time of her murder?"

"They can't have been," Skipton said, sitting forward in his chair and shrugging off Goody's hand. "I had nothing to do with either of them murders, and *that* can't be Spence's phone."

"And how do you know that?" Stone asked, speaking for the first time since the interview had commenced.

Skipton spun to face him, his cheeks quivering with anger. "How? Because it belongs to Phoebe-bloody-Cunningham. That's how!"

Franklin had expected him to come up with a rubbish excuse for having the handset in his possession, but this was just so implausible as to be ridiculous. "Oh, come on!" he scoffed. "Surely, you can do better than that?"

"It's true!" Skipton yelled. "That's her bloody phone, it was in her pocket when we–" he just about managed to stop himself from saying anything incriminating. "It was in her pocket. It's her phone, not mine. Why don't you ask her about it?"

"Has the phone been examined for fingerprints?" Goody asked.

"It's being done as we speak," Franklin assured her.

38

SNEAKY LITTLE COW

According to the clock on the wall above the nurse's station, it was almost a quarter to five. With a farewell wave to the Sister in Charge, Phoebe Cunningham hurried along the corridor towards the exit, her training shoes making little squeaking noises on the polished linoleum floor.

"Shouldn't you wait for the officer to come back?" the Sister called after her.

"That's okay," Phoebe said, eager to get away before he did. "I'm a big girl now. If he comes looking for me, tell him I've just popped to the café to grab a coffee. I'll be back shortly."

With a bit of luck, that would buy her a few extra minutes before he raised the alarm.

It was a fantastic stroke of luck that her police minder had popped off to use the loo a couple of minutes earlier, and she intended to take full advantage of his absence by doing a runner while she had the chance.

Phoebe had been delighted when the doctor who examined her this afternoon said that he was happy for her to be discharged. She had planned to spend the evening searching for her car, but her overeager police watchdog had jumped straight on the phone to DC Evans, and the obstinate detective had insisted on picking her up and taking her to the local station, so that she could make a key witness statement about the kidnap.

She knew that Evans would be pissed off if she wasn't there when he arrived, but she urgently needed to dispose of the incriminating evidence in the back of her car, and she wouldn't be able to relax until she had done so.

She would phone Evans later to apologise, explaining that she had needed a little time on her own to get her head together. After everything that she had been through over the past few days, she doubted that anyone would question her fleeing the hospital because she had experienced the onset of a panic attack. Her condition was well documented on her medical records, and her therapist would support her claim that she suffered from these debilitating episodes.

Kevin Murray pulled into the front entrance of Whipps Cross hospital and followed the service road around until he came to the car park at the rear of the A&E department. He found a convenient space, from where he could see the entrance, and killed the engine. "I'll wait in the car while you go and fetch her ladyship," he told Paul Evans.

"Hopefully, I won't be too long," Evans said, reaching for the door. Before he could open it, his mobile rang. Thinking that it was probably the PC looking after Phoebe Cunningham, calling to see how much longer he would be, he pulled it from his pocket and pressed the green button. "Paul Evans speaking."

"*Paul, Tony Dillon here.*"

"Hello boss, what can I do for you?" the Welshman asked.

"Have you collected Phoebe Cunningham yet?" Dillon asked.

"Not yet. We've only just pulled into the car park."

"Good," Dillon said, sounding relieved. *"Can I confirm that you're free to speak?"*

Evans frowned, wondering what was going on. "Yeah, go ahead. There's only me and Kevin here."

"Listen, Paul, I've just come off the phone from speaking to Steve Bull over at Forest Gate. Apparently, Colin and Jim have just come out of an interview with Skipton, and he's given them some very interesting, and rather concerning, information. As a result, there's been a change of plan and you need to be aware of a few things before collecting Miss Cunningham."

That sounded interesting. Evans put the call on loud speaker. "Go on then," he said. "What's Skipton told the interview team?"

They heard Dillon take a deep breath. *"Okay, before going into that, you need to be aware of a couple of other developments that have come to light today. Firstly, both Spencer's and Skipton's phones were cell sited near Anna Manson's house around the time of her murder. Secondly, the burner that Dick Jarvis found in Skipton's kitchen, when his flat was searched, has been confirmed as the mobile that Spencer's been using since his release from prison."*

"That doesn't make sense," Evans said, furrowing his brow in concentration. "Do we think that Skipton was somehow involved in the murder?"

"Well, we initially thought it was more likely that he'd met up with Spencer after the murder, given him a clean phone, and taken the dirty one away to dispose of it. We're having to reevaluate that theory in light of what Skipton's just told us."

"Which is what?" Evans asked.

"He's absolutely adamant that the burner we found in his kitchen belonged to Phoebe Cunningham. He reckons that she had it on her when they brought her to his flat."

Murray laughed at that. He just couldn't help himself. "Why would *she* have Spencer's phone?" he asked. "We know Skipton's a lying little shit. He's probably just trying to row himself out of trouble."

"*Maybe,*" Dillon allowed, "*but you might think differently when you hear where they abducted Phoebe Cunningham from.*"

"Where?" Evans asked, intrigued by the unfolding drama.

"*They grabbed her as she left Anna Manson's house.*"

Evans felt his jaw drop. "Shit!"

Murray was equally surprised. "That would certainly explain why they drove her car to Skipton's place," he said.

"It gets better," Dillon said. "According to her parents, Phoebe's car was booked into their local garage to have its annual service and MOT on Tuesday morning, and she told them that she'd dropped it off on Monday afternoon so that she wouldn't have to get up early the following day."

Evans briefly closed his eyes as he replayed the statement he had taken from Ben Cunningham in his mind. "Yep, I remember Mr Cunningham saying that to me."

"Well, Skipton reckons that the car was parked in a side road near her house on Monday night, and that she sneaked out of her house at about eleven p.m. He says they followed her to Manson's place from there. We've just checked with the garage. They say her Alfa Romeo was booked in for Tuesday morning, but she never showed up for the appointment."

"Sneaky little cow," Murray said, shaking his head in disgust. "And to think that I actually felt sorry for her."

Evans let out a low whistle. "So, what do you want us to do?" he asked.

"*I've spoken to the DCI, and we think we've got no option but to arrest her on suspicion of Anna's murder and then search her home and her car for evidence.*"

Evans groaned. "Her dad's going to go ballistic if we do that," he predicted. "And, if we're wrong, the publicity's going to be really harmful."

"That's for me and the DCI to worry about," Dillon told him, making it clear this wasn't a subject for debate. "*I need you to arrest her and take her to Walthamstow police station for interview. We can't take her into Leyton as Mangrove's being held there.*"

"Do you want me to come in with you?" Murray asked after the call had finished.

Evans shook his head. "No, you wait here with the car. I'll get the PC who's looking after her to give me a hand." This was going to be a job that required tact and diplomacy, neither of which were Murray's strongest points.

"Fair enough," Murray said, seeming perfectly happy to sit this one out.

"Wish me luck," Evans said as he set off towards the hospital reception.

"You're going to need it," Murray predicted. "Now, leave me alone and let me soak up some rays."

Emerging into the bright sunlight, Phoebe surveyed the hospital grounds in search of an official taxi rank, only to find that there wasn't one. She spotted an elderly Indian male, leaning against the side of a Vauxhall Cavalier that was parked in a no waiting area, and when their eyes met, he smiled at her. There was a magnetic sign on the car's door proclaiming it to be a minicab, and she wondered if he was hanging around in the hope of picking up a fare. She acknowledged him with a little nod, and he gave her a hesitant wave in return.

"Are you looking for a minicab, miss?" he asked in heavy accented English.

Phoebe nodded. "Yes," she said, hurriedly crossing the road towards him.

"Good, good," the man replied, opening the rear passenger door. He bowed politely as she climbed inside. "I can do you a very good rate."

"Thank you," she said, grimacing at the pain from her bandaged ribs.

After closing her door, the elderly man slid behind the steering wheel. "Where to, miss?" he asked, eagerly.

"I want you to take me to Adworth Road, just off West Ham Lane. Do you know it?"

She had wangled Skipton's address out of one of the probationer PCs who had watched over her during her hospitalisation. The naïve young man had taken a real shine to her, and a little flirting on her part had persuaded him to reveal everything that he knew about the case.

"I know it," the driver said, nodding happily. "Do you mind if I put the radio on?" he asked as he drove towards the exit in James Lane.

"Not at all," she told him. Hopefully that would deter him from speaking to her, because the last thing she wanted to do at the moment was have a conversation.

A few seconds after Paul Evans disappeared around the front of the building in search of the main entrance, Murray noticed a pretty female emerge from the A&E department opposite the car park in which he was waiting.

He didn't make the connection at first, but as she crossed the road towards a Vauxhall Cavalier that was parked in a no waiting area, he noticed that she was holding her ribs protectively. Sitting up straight, he removed his sunglasses and stared at her intently. "It can't be," he muttered, reaching into the back seat to retrieve his clipboard.

Opening it up, he flicked through a series of photocopied photographs until he came to the one of Phoebe Cunningham. These had been distributed to all officers working the kidnapping. He looked at the picture, then at the girl getting into the Cavalier, then back at the picture in his hand. "Shit," he said, reaching for his mobile and dialling Evans' number.

The call went straight to answer phone, so either Evans was talking to someone or his phone wasn't receiving a signal inside the hospital building. He pressed redial, but got the same result. He was about to ring the office when the Cavalier drove off. Tossing his phone onto the passenger seat, he started the engine and set off after it. Annoyingly, the pool car he was using wasn't equipped with a Main Set. Still, there was no need to panic. She didn't know that she was wanted, and she was in a minicab, not a getaway car. All he needed to do was follow her until she stopped, and then he could ring the office and request some backup. If an opportunity to arrest her cropped up, he decided that he would take it. After all, she was unarmed and she was injured, so she was unlikely to pose much of a threat.

He could not have been more wrong about that.

As the cab set off towards the Green Man roundabout, Phoebe sank back in her seat and retreated into herself. From what she could gather from the PC who had developed a crush on her, her kidnappers had been interviewed extensively since their arrest, but they had refused to talk. That was great news for her because, despite racking her brains non-stop, she had been unable to come up with a plausible explanation for coming out of Anna's house on the night of her murder.

Last night, she had tricked her gullible admirer into revealing the names of her kidnappers. Mangrove's name meant nothing to her, but she was convinced that Skipton had to be Spencer's cousin, the man he had told her about in the barn. Why Spencer's cousin would choose to abduct her remained a complete mystery, but as long as he didn't say where he had snatched her from or reveal where they had hidden her car, she didn't really care.

The most important thing, as far as she was concerned, was to retrieve her Tesoro before someone reported it as being abandoned or causing an obstruction.

Even though it was in a cool bag, she suspected that Spencer's severed hand would have started to decay by now, having spent a couple of days locked in her boot during a heatwave. That wasn't a problem; with Martin and Anna now dead, she had no further use for the gruesome prop anyway, and she planned to dispose of it at the earliest opportunity. There was also a holdall containing the kitchen knife that she had killed Martin and Anna with. That was wrapped in the blood stained tracksuit and ski-mask that she had worn for the occasion. She planned to burn the clothing and the hand, and throw the knife into the River Lea.

"The traffic is nice and light today," her driver pointed out cheerfully.

"Uh-huh," she responded, not wanting to be drawn into talking.

"Are you all better now?" he asked.

Phoebe's eyes narrowed. "What?"

Glancing over his shoulder, the driver smiled at her. "You were in hospital. Are you all better now?"

"Oh, yes. I'm much better now, thank you."

Thankfully, he didn't ask any further questions, and ten minutes later they pulled into Adworth Road. "What number do you want?" he enquired, watching her keenly in his mirror.

"Okay, so I don't actually want Adworth Road," she admitted, leaning forward to get a better look. "I'm actually looking for a secluded car park at the back of some flats in one of the roads running parallel with it."

Her driver seemed confused.

"I left my car there before my, er, accident," she told him, making a story up on the spur of the moment. "I was a bit drunk at the time, so I can't recall exactly where I parked it."

He glanced back over his shoulder and flashed her an understanding smile. "No problem, miss. We can try them all."

―――

When Evans strode into the ward that Phoebe was staying on, he found an anxious young constable pacing up and down by the nurses station. "Where's Miss Cunningham?" he asked, looking around for her.

The constable smiled nervously. "She, er, she popped down to the canteen to grab a coffee. She should be back shortly."

Evans glared at him. "If she's gone to the sodding canteen, what are you doing here? You're supposed to be glued to her side, not wandering up and down like a demented halfwit."

The young constable blushed. "She went while I was using the loo," he explained, unable to meet the angry detective's gaze.

Evans rolled his eyes. *Unbelievable!* "How long ago did she go?"

The constable shrugged. "Er, not too sure. Three or four minutes, maybe?"

"Wait here," Evans told him. "I'll go and look for her. If she turns up while I'm gone, don't let her leave again. I mean it," he said, pointing a warning finger at the officer's chest. "She's going to be arrested for murder, so grab hold of her and don't let her out of your sight."

The constable blanched. "Murder?" he spluttered. "I had no idea. I would never have left her unattended if I'd known."

"It's not your fault," Evans said, feeling guilty for having snapped at him. "I only just found out myself." Walking briskly, he set off for the canteen. With a bit of luck, he would bump into her on her way back and no harm would have been done. As the seconds ticked by, and there was still no sign of her, he began to fret. Eventually, he broke into a worried trot, unable to shake the feeling that she had absconded.

I knew there was something off about that bloody girl! I told the boss, but he wouldn't have it!

There was no sign of her in the canteen. "Excuse me, have you seen a young woman in here recently?" he asked the middle aged woman behind the serving counter. "She's in her early twenties, has wavy brown hair and blue eyes. She's very pretty and she might have been favouring one side from a rib injury." He mimed holding his ribs to demonstrate what he meant.

The woman stared at him blankly.

"About this tall," he said, holding his hand in the air at her estimated height.

She gave him a disinterested shrug.

"Shit!" Evans said, spinning around and breaking into a run.

Please be back at the ward!

When he got there, the young policeman stared at him hopefully. "Did you find her?" he asked.

"Shit!" Evans said, feeling sick. He pulled out his phone, saw that he had no signal. "Shit!" he muttered again. "Stay here," he told the officer. "If she comes back, she's to be arrested on suspicion of murdering her best friend, Anna Manson. If you need more information, call the incident room and they'll brief you." Without waiting for a reply, he ran out of the ward, intent on searching the hospital grounds.

Murray had followed the minicab along Leytonstone High Road, all the way up to Maryland Point. He could clearly make out the shape of Phoebe's head through the rear window. He glanced longingly at his mobile on the passenger seat. As soon as they caught a red light, he planned to call the office and get some back up organised. He had fully expected the mini cab to take her home, but it was heading in the complete opposite direction. Where the hell was she taking him, he wondered?

His phone rang, shattering the silence and making him jump. He scooped it up and glanced at the caller ID. It was Paul Evans. "You took your bloody time," he snapped.

"*Kevin, shut up and listen,*" Evans retorted angrily. He was breathing hard and he sounded stressed. "*The girl's done a runner. I need you to come in and help me search for her.*"

"Calm down," Murray told him. "I've got the girl in my sights. She took a minicab from the hospital, and they're in Leytonstone High Road heading towards Stratford. I tried to call you but your poxy phone kept going to answerphone."

At the other end of the line, Evans breathed a huge sigh of relief. "*Sorry, mate. I don't get any signal inside the hospital.*" There was a pause. "*What's she doing, going to Stratford?*"

"How the hell am I supposed to know that?" Murray asked in a sarcastic tone. Up ahead, the minicab stopped at a red traffic light, and Murray glided to a halt two cars behind it. "Listen, I've got to go. I need to call the office and get some back up sorted." He hung up without saying goodbye, and immediately dialled the number for the Major Incident Room.

39

I HAD TO KILL THEM!

Susie Sergeant was sitting in a hardbacked plastic chair in a little canteen in the back yard of Leytonstone police station, where she had come at the behest of her husband. Across the table from her, Dan was looking utterly miserable. "But surely there's a way we can sort this out and give it another go?" he asked, staring at her with puppy eyes.

That might have worked once, but not anymore.

"It's over, Dan. The sooner you get that into your thick head, the better."

Dan looked like he was about to burst into tears.

When he had rung her a little earlier, Susie had been under the misapprehension that he wanted to meet her so that they could discuss their joint finances and work out what to do about the house, but Dan clearly had a different agenda in mind. He had opened the conversation by telling her that his fling with Janet had been a terrible mistake, and he had spent the past fifteen minutes trying to convince her to put it behind them and go back to normal.

"Look, Susie, I know I acted foolishly, and you have no idea how much I regret my actions but–"

Susie's phone rang. She held up a hand to cut Dan off, glad for the excuse. Now that she had made her mind up that their relationship was over, she was feeling much better in herself, and she had no intention of going around in circles with him, just because he wanted something else. He should have thought about that before going off with another woman.

"I've got to take this call," she said.

"*Susie, it's Kevin. Listen, are you in the office? Only I've been trying to call the MIR and the phone's permanently engaged.*" There was an edge to his voice, like he was under pressure.

"I'm sorry, Kevin, I'm over at Leytonstone at the moment. Is it urgent?"

"*You could say that! I'm in Leytonstone Road, driving towards Maryland Point. I'm following Phoebe Cunningham. The sneaky little cow did a bunk from the hospital before we could arrest her, and I need some uniform assistance to stop her.*"

"Can't you just radio for help?"

An awkward pause. "*Didn't bring one.*"

Typical!

Susie glanced up at Dan. "I need you to blue light me to Maryland Point," she told him. "One of my lads is behind Phoebe Cunningham, and we need to arrest her for murder."

Dan stood up, eager to please. "Of course," he said, reaching for his radio. "408 from 186, we've got a call. Where are you?"

There was a long pause. "*Er, I'm in the ladies room at the moment. Be with you in two minutes, over.*"

From the acute embarrassment in her voice, and the echo around her, Susie suspected that she was probably sitting in trap one.

"She'll be back in a minute," Dan said, covering for her.

Susie glaring at him, green eyes blazing with anger. "We can't wait for your strumpet," she said, icily. "I'll be your operator for this one. You can pick her up when we've finished."

"But–"

"Come on," she snapped. "That's not a request, constable. It's an order from a DI."

Dan blushed at the rebuke. "Yes, ma'am," he said, staring at her grudgingly.

"Kevin, keep the commentary going," she said as Dan started the car. "We're leaving Leytonstone nick now, and we should be with you in a few minutes."

As the pursuit car pulled out of the rear yard, lights flashing, siren screaming like a Banshee's wail, a dishevelled female PC ran out of the female toilet block, frantically adjusting her clothing and trying to fasten her utility belt around her waist. "Wait for me!" Janet called, only to see the pursuit car zoom off at a great rate of knots.

The elderly minicab driver seemed content to pootle along at a snail's pace, and that was fine by Murray because it made following Phoebe Cunningham that much easier. His mobile was clamped between his jawline and shoulder, which was really uncomfortable but allowed him to use both hands for driving. "We've just turned into West Ham Lane," he told Susie a few moments later.

"*We're just coming up to Maryland Point now,*" she informed him.

To Murray's astonishment, the Cavalier pulled into Adworth Road. "You won't believe this," he told her, "but her cab's just pulled into Adworth Road, where Skipton lives."

"*Why on earth would she be going there?*" Susie asked. At least that was what he thought she had said. It was hard to tell above the wail of the siren.

"Okay, so they've just driven past Skipton's flat," he updated her.

The minicab turned left into Tennyson Road and then left into Romford Road. A few seconds later, the cab turned left into West Ham Lane.

"I haven't got a clue what they're playing at," Murray complained. "They've just driven in a complete circle and now they're turning left again, into Adworth Road."

"*They must be looking for something,*" Susie suggested.

"You think!" Murray replied with heavy sarcasm. "And here was me thinking they were going to be driving in ever decreasing circles until they disappeared up their own tailpipe!"

"*Don't be a wanker!*" she told him.

Murray smiled. He liked Susie Sergeant, even when she was having a go at him, which was actually most of the time. He was just about to fire back a witty riposte when the cab suddenly turned left into a little turning called Elliott Close. "Hang on, Susie," he said, almost dropping the mobile. "They've just turned into Elliott Close."

"*We're almost with you.*" Susie responded. "*Just turning into West Ham Lane now.*"

"The cab's stopping," Murray told her. "And I can see her Alfa Romeo parked up just ahead of it."

"*Wait for us to get there before approaching her,*" Susie instructed.

Murray snorted. "Don't worry, I think I can handle a silly girl on my own," he mocked, opening the door to go after her.

———

When the cabbie had suggested trying Elliott Close, Phoebe hadn't been overly hopeful of finding her car parked there, so she was ecstatic when she spotted it tucked away in a corner spot. "There's my car," she exclaimed, leaning forward to point it out to her driver.

"Good, good," he said, giving her a grandfatherly smile. "I knew we would find it for you."

Luckily, her parents had thought to bring her up some money and a fresh change of clothes when they visited the previous evening, so

Phoebe wasn't short of cash, and she slipped him an extra fiver tip on top of the fare as a reward for his kindness.

His old eyes lit up, and he accepted the money with a gracious bow of his head. "Thank you, young lady," he said. "Do you want me to wait and make sure it starts?"

"That won't be necessary," she said with a strained smile.

As the cab pulled away, the driver stuck his hand out of the window and waved farewell to her. Waving back, Phoebe walked over to the rear offside wheel arch of her car and reached underneath. After fumbling around for a couple of seconds, she removed a small magnetised key holder. Opening it up, she removed the spare ignition key it contained.

"Yes!" she said, resisting the urge to punch the air in triumph. Instead, she dusted her hands off and walked around to unlock the boot.

She recoiled at the vile stench that greeted her as soon as it was opened. She hadn't closed the cool bag properly, and the severed hand it contained had fared badly in the oven like temperatures of the boot.

"Phoebe Cunningham?" a harsh male voice startled her.

Phoebe spun around to find a skinny white male, with brown hair and a goatee, standing about ten feet away from her. Hands on hips, head tilted to one side, he was regarding her with a mixture of curiosity and disdain. The man's eyes were hidden behind wrap-around sunglasses, and he was wearing a crumpled suit.

"Who are you?" she demanded, warily.

He flashed his warrant card at her. "I'm DC Kevin Murray," he informed her while reaching behind his back to remove a set of handcuffs from the pouch on his belt, "and I'm here to arrest you for the murder of Anna Manson."

Phoebe felt her legs go weak at the knees.

They knew!

But how?

"I-I don't know what you're talking about," she said, backing away until she collided with the open boot. Licking her lips nervously, she glanced around for a way out.

On seeing this, the detective raised a condescending eyebrow. "Don't be silly," he said. "It's bloody hot out here and I'm already sweating worse than a sailor's armpit, so please don't make this any harder than it has to be."

It struck her that he was alone, which seemed odd. Didn't they usually work in pairs?

"I'm not afraid of you," she told him, reaching into the boot as she spoke. Trying her best not to gag at the overpowering stench coming from Spencer's rotting flesh, she unzipped the holdall containing the knife that she had used on her fiancé and Anna. The policeman represented a threat to her freedom, and that made her incredibly angry.

I'm strong. I've moved on and I'm getting my life back.

The smirk on the detective's face, as he took a casual step closer, triggered the irrational rage that had become her default response to any threat.

"Hold out your arms for me," he said, sounding bored, "so I can handcuff you."

Phoebe stiffened. "No," she said, defiantly.

He let out a little sigh of irritation before shaking his head like a disappointed parent. "Don't be daft."

In the distance, the faint wail of a siren reached her ears.

Phoebe casually reached inside the holdall, rummaged around until she found the hard plastic of the knife's handle. As the detective reached out to grab her wrist, she withdrew the knife from the bag and lunged at him with it. Her face twisted into a grotesque parody of its former prettiness as she tried to run him through.

Murray was standing too close to avoid the blow completely, but he reacted surprisingly quickly by pivoting his slender torso to one side. It was a move that undoubtedly saved his life, for instead of gutting him as she had intended, the keen blade merely sliced through the external oblique muscles of his right side. Squealing in pain, he instinctively jumped backwards, clutching his side. In doing so, he lost his balance, stumbled backwards and fell onto his rump.

Snarling with rage, Phoebe advanced towards him, knife raised to finish the job.

Murray scuttled backwards. "Drop the knife," he shouted, eyes bulging with fear.

Phoebe found herself strangely intoxicated by his reaction. *Was this how Spencer had felt when he had me at his mercy?*

As the detective retreated, she followed him, grinning wickedly. "I'm sick of men like you trying to bend me to your will," she snarled. "You're all the same. You all want to control me, or rape me, or tie me up and beat me."

"I don't want to hurt you," Murray said, clumsily crabbing backwards and leaving a trail of scarlet behind him.

The siren was getting much louder now, but she didn't care anymore. This man had tried to hurt her, and she was going to punish him for it.

A marked police Rover pulled into the close, wheels squealing, lights strobing, siren blaring. As it screeched to a halt, the doors flew open and two officers jumped out. One was a man in uniform, the other a woman in a business suit. Phoebe snarled at them like a rabid animal, then turned and fled in the opposite direction.

―――

Susie was out of the car before Dan had even undone his seatbelt, and she set off in pursuit of Phoebe Cunningham like a terrier going after a rat. "Look after him," she bellowed, pointing at Murray, who was sitting on the pavement and bleeding profusely.

"Susie, wait!" Dan called after her, but she ignored him.

Luckily, she was wearing flats, so she didn't have to worry about accidentally twisting an ankle.

"Phoebe, stop!" she yelled at the fleeing figure. The haunting expression she'd seen on the girl's face, as they were pulling up, had been frightening in its intensity. It had been feral, leaving no doubt in her mind that Phoebe had intended to kill Kevin Murray, even though, injured as he was, he no longer represented a threat to her.

Susie had had the foresight to grab her gravity friction lock baton from her shoulder bag before setting off after the girl, and its weight felt comforting in her hand. She was confident of catching Phoebe, who was injured and already struggling to maintain her pace. The problem was, how would the girl react when she did? Would she calm down and surrender, or was her mental capacity now so diminished that she would behave irrationally and go on the attack, as she had with Kevin Murray?

"Phoebe!" she called again.

This time the girl glanced back over her shoulder, baring her teeth like a wild animal.

"Leave me alone," she screamed.

Susie didn't have a radio with her, and she had left her mobile in her shoulder bag, so she had no way of calling for help, but she knew Dan would have done that for her by now, so she was confident that units would be flocking into the area to assist her.

Phoebe was running aimlessly, and there was a desperation about her that reminded Susie of a wounded animal looking for somewhere to lay down and die.

Phoebe turned into Elderflower Way and then cut across the car park into Victoria Street. Behind her, Susie settled into her stride, relaxing her body, getting her breathing right, and pumping her arms to drive her forward as she ran. If one good thing that had come out of Dan leaving her, it was that she had become something of a gym junkie, and she had clawed her fitness back to a level she hadn't enjoyed since being put through her paces as a new recruit at Hendon.

Phoebe's breathing had become noticeably more ragged, and her steps were becoming shorter and more laboured. Clutching her side, she was clearly in considerable pain, but she refused to give in.

Susie was content just to keep pace with her, confident that the girl was running out of steam and would soon stop of her own accord. "Give it up, Phoebe," she called as the converging sirens grew steadily louder. "You can't get away."

With a scream of frustration, Phoebe slowed to a walk. Breathing heavily, she turned to confront Susie, her distressed face the colour of beetroot.

It struck Susie that she seemed totally detached from reality, almost as if she was sleep walking. Did this mean that she was going into shock or having some sort of mental breakdown? Maintaining a safe distance, Susie raised her hands to calm the girl.

"Phoebe, listen to me," she said, speaking gently. "No one's going to harm you, but you need professional help. Put the knife down and let's get you somewhere safe."

"No," Phoebe said, shaking her head violently. "I know you're all in this together. You're just as bad as Spencer and his cousin. Why won't you all just go away and leave me alone?"

"We can't go away," Susie said, smiling apologetically. "You've already murdered your best friend, and you just tried to kill a police officer. You need to let me help you."

Phoebe was on the verge of hysteria. "I *had* to kill her!" she cried, gesticulating angrily. "I *had* to kill them all. Don't you see? They *had* to be punished for hurting me. And the policeman... he was going to hurt me, too." A note of paranoia crept into her voice. "You *all* want to hurt me."

Susie was taken aback. *Kill them all?* What had she meant by that? The working assumption was that she had only murdered Anna Manson. The question would have to wait until later.

"Phoebe, you need to calm down..."

"No! What I need is to be left alone." Nodding to herself, as though she had reached a decision, Phoebe began backing away from Susie, holding the knife out in front of her to deter the detective from following. "I'm warning you," she said, "if you come after me, I'll punish you, too."

A TSG carrier slewed into Victoria Street from West Ham Lane, its blue lights flashing, its two-tones ear-piercingly loud, and screeched to a halt a few feet away from the two women. The doors immediately flew open and the crew alighted.

Susie was immensely relieved to see them. The TSG had vast experience of dealing with scenarios like this one. "She's got a knife and she's delusional," she called to them.

"Liar!" Phoebe screamed, frantically looking around for a means of escape.

A TSG officer ran to the back of the carrier and started handing out short shields to his colleagues.

"Form up," their sergeant shouted, and Susie immediately recognised him as PS Bobby Beach.

"She's already stabbed one of my DCs," Susie told him.

Beach acknowledged the information with a curt nod. "Miss, put the knife down," he told Phoebe. "There's no way you can get away from us, and if you put up a fight, you'll only end up getting hurt." As he spoke, the six PCs who made up his crew took up positions around her, cutting off her escape route.

"Keep back!" she wailed. Turning in circles and holding the knife out in front of her.

Keeping his eyes on the girl, Beach unclipped the pouch containing his CS gas cannister.

With the TSG officers now containing her, Phoebe seemed to withdraw into herself.

Susie walked forward, signalling for them to hold back from engaging her further. "Phoebe, please listen to me," she implored. "Put the knife down and let us get you some help."

Phoebe's head shot up at the sound of Susie's voice, but she seemed to stare straight through the detective, as though she wasn't there. She stood as immobile as a statue, staring into space, and Susie began to wonder if she had entered a catatonic state.

Beach took several steps forward, gently easing his thumb inside the trigger guard of his CS in readiness for use, should the opportunity present itself.

"Stay back!" Phoebe screamed, snapping out of her stupor.

Beach froze.

Worryingly, Phoebe raised the blade of her knife and held it dangerously close to her own throat. "I - I mean it..." she sobbed, hysterically. "If you come any closer I'll slit my own throat."

"No!" Susie shouted, raising her hands to stay her. She could see that the girl was becoming increasingly unstable, and she wasn't sure how much longer they had until she lost the plot completely. "Please, Phoebe, don't do that," she pleaded.

Phoebe licked her lips nervously. "Okay, but tell them to move back."

With a jut of her chin, Susie signalled for the TSG officers to retreat a couple of steps, which they reluctantly did.

All but Beach.

He waited until Susie fired him a questioning look, and then casually glanced down at the canister in his hand and then across to the girl.

Susie nodded her understanding. The TSG skipper wanted her to keep Phoebe engaged long enough for him to get closer. It was a risky strategy, but Phoebe was so volatile now that it was only a matter of time until she either used the knife on them or herself, so there was nothing to lose.

"Look, Phoebe," Susie said with an all-encompassing sweep of her arm. "the officers have moved back, just like you wanted them to. You can lower the knife now."

Phoebe hesitated for a moment, and then her arm fell to her side.

Two marked police cars pulled into the road, making a hell of a racket, and one of the TSG lads walked towards them hurriedly, making an urgent slicing motion across his neck for them to kill the lights and noise. As the newcomers alighted their vehicles, he waved for them to keep back, so as not to agitate the girl any further.

Ignoring the background distraction, Susie placed her baton on the floor. Holding her hands up to show that they were empty, she took a tentative step towards Phoebe. "It's okay," she soothed. "I know it feels like everything's coming apart, but we can help you if you'll let us."

Phoebe was shaking her head with increasing desperation. "Stay back, stay back, STAY BACK!"

And, suddenly, something inside her snapped.

Several things happened all at once.

Accompanied by a sudden, bone chilling scream, the knife in Phoebe's hand flew back to her throat as she screwed her eyes shut and pressed the blade into her flesh.

Susie rushed forward, arms outstretched in a desperate effort to reach the knife before it could cause catastrophic damage.

"NOOO!" she yelled as she ran.

Several of the TSG officers surrounding Phoebe, reacted in a similar fashion, all dashing in to try and save her from herself.

Bobby Beach was standing closer to the girl than any of them and, as soon as the knife began moving upwards, his right arm extended in a blur. As it did, a concentrated jet of liquid shot from the CS canister's nozzle. The jet stream hit Phoebe square in the chest, and then rose up until it was squirting directly in her face: Mouth first; then nose, and lastly eyes.

Screaming in unbearable agony, Phoebe instinctively dropped the knife and started clawing at her face, trying to scrub the debilitating chemical away.

Scarlet began to stream from the thin line that had appeared across the side of her neck but, thankfully, the cut hadn't been deep enough to sever an artery.

Phoebe staggered around, clawing at her face and howling in pain until she finally lost her balance and fell to the floor.

"Phoebe, listen carefully to me," Beach was shouting. "You've been sprayed with CS incapacitant. Do NOT touch your face. Turn into the wind and let the air blow it away. The effects will pass quickly if you do as I say."

It was impossible to tell if she was listening, or if she was even capable of processing the information he was giving her, but they couldn't go any closer for fear of being harmed by the CS themselves.

One of the officers recklessly ran in and kicked the knife away from Phoebe, who was still rolling around on the floor in agony, but he immediately succumbed to the effects of the CS and had to be given aftercare himself.

As Susie watched on, powerless to help, Dan came running over. "Are you okay?" he asked, clearly worried for her safety.

"I'm fine," she said, still staring pitifully at the anguished girl on the floor. "How's my injured DC doing?"

"He'll be fine," Dan said, dismissively. "Turns out it was a superficial cut, and the LAS are on scene with him now."

Susie nodded, relieved. "Good," she said, suddenly feeling utterly drained. Phoebe Cunningham would live, that was for sure, but Susie couldn't help wondering if it might have been better for her if she had managed to kill herself. At least her suffering would have been over; now, all she had to look forward to was a life sentence. The only question was, would she serve it in a high security prison or a hospital for the criminally insane?

Susie walked over to Bobby Beach. "Nice shooting, Tex," she said, affecting an American Midwest drawl.

Beach grinned, bashfully. "I think I might have gotten a bit carried away with how much CS I used," he admitted, shaking the now empty container, "but I was really worried that, unless I gave her a really good dose, she might manage to kill herself."

Susie patted him on the back. "You did good. You stopped her from topping herself."

She wasn't sure that Phoebe Cunningham would share her view.

40

Friday 3rd August 2001
THE CONFESSION

Phoebe sat in the interview room, shoulders slumped, head hanging down to her chest. Resting in her lap, her hands relentlessly worried away at the cuticles of her nails. A large strip of surgical gauze was plastered across the left side of her neck, covering the stitches that she had received to her self-inflicted wound the previous day. She had large bags under her eyes, which were red rimmed from crying, and she seemed to have withdrawn into herself, as if that was her only way of coping with the situation she now found herself in.

Debbie Brown was reminded of a broken doll, and she really wasn't looking forward to putting the poor girl through the turmoil of an interview in which all her painful memories would be dug up and raked through in fine detail.

The FME had examined Phoebe, and he had declared that she was physically fit for detention and interview. The local Mental Health Team had also been called out to perform an emergency assessment, and they had concluded that Phoebe was more likely to be suffering from complex PTSD and depression than psychosis. There were clearly underlying mental health issues dating all the way back to her teenage years, the team leader had pointed out, and the admissibility of anything she said during interview was likely to be challenged by her legal team once they had the benefit of a full forensic psychiatric assessment at their disposal but, for the here and now, she was lucid enough to be detained and interviewed.

"Are you ready to begin?" Debbie asked her.

Phoebe nodded lethargically, like she was under heavy sedation. She had hardly said a word since her arrest the previous day.

"Do you need some water?" Debbie asked.

Phoebe gave an economical shake of her head.

Debbie glanced across at the duty solicitor who was sitting next to the prisoner. "Are you ready, Mr Kincaid?"

Kincaid was a rotund man in his mid-forties, with a drooping walrus moustache that completely hid his mouth, and a greasy combover. "Aye, I'm ready," he said in his rough Geordie accent. He opened his legal pad to a blank page and scribbled down the date, time and location of the interview, daintily holding his thin biro between thick, nicotine stained fingers.

Debbie glanced sideways at Colin Franklin, who was conducting the interview with her. An almost imperceptible nod from him told her that he was ready to go.

After being detained in Victoria Road the previous day, Phoebe had been whisked off to hospital in order to receive medical attention for the gash in her neck. She had been released later that evening but, by then, it had been too late to realistically commence the interviews, and it had been decided to let her get some rest and make a fresh start first thing the following morning.

A solicitor had been arranged and, after having a brief telephone consultation with him, Phoebe had been placed straight into a mandatory sleep period.

Because of the ongoing concerns over her mental state, and bearing in mind that she had tried to kill herself prior to her arrest, the custody sergeant had placed her under a constant watch. This had necessitated dragging a constable in off the streets in order to spend the night shift sitting in the doorway of her cell watching over her.

The rotting severed hand had been found in the boot of her car, which had been searched once all of the drama relating to the arrest had finally died down.

The blood stained tracksuit that she'd worn while committing the two murders had also been recovered in a holdall, as had the empty packet of candy coated chocolates that had been scattered around Manson's body. Along with the knife that had been in her possession upon her arrest, the tracksuit, candy wrapper and holdall had all been shipped off to the lab for an urgent forensic examination.

After being photographed in situ, DNA samples and fingerprints were taken from the rotting hand, which was then sent to the local mortuary, where it had been placed in a freezer to await a post mortem examination.

There had been a lot of skin slippage on the hand, due to the hot weather, but the prints had come back late last night, and they had been confirmed as belonging to John Anthony Spencer.

At least the reason for Spencer evading arrest for so long now made sense. He hadn't outsmarted them as they had all feared; he had simply been dead. A Home Office Forensic Pathologist was currently examining Spencer's severed hand, and they had been assured that they would receive a report regarding how long ago it had been amputated within the next couple of hours.

It now seemed pretty clear that Phoebe Cunningham had killed Spencer back at the barn, and that she had then gone on to murder both her fiancé and her best friend. That scenario fitted in with everything they now knew, and made perfect sense of what Phoebe had said to Susie, just before to her arrest, about having to 'kill them all'.

Debbie pressed the button on the tape deck, and waited patiently for the irritating buzzer to stop. When it finally did, she formally commenced the interview, explaining how everything would work, getting everyone present to introduce themselves, and finally reading out the caution to Phoebe from the idiot card in front of her. "Do you understand what that means, my love?" she asked when she had finished.

Phoebe nodded, a slow ponderous movement that seemed to take forever. "Yes."

"Can you tell me what you think it means?" Debbie asked. "Just so that I'm happy you really do understand."

Phoebe slouched down in her chair and let out a long sigh, giving Debbie the impression that just being alive was taking all the energy that she had.

"It means that I don't have to tell you anything, but whatever I do say will be admissible against me at court," Phoebe replied in a depressed monotone.

Debbie smiled encouragingly. "Well done. I know this isn't easy for you, and if you need a rest at any time, all you have to do is say so, and we can take a little break. Is that okay?"

Phoebe nodded wearily. "Thank you."

"Now, Phoebe, you were abducted from a car park in Diss town centre on Wednesday 25th July 2001. Can you tell me who abducted you?"

Phoebe's face clouded over and she lowered her eyes as she spoke, as though she was ashamed of what she was about to tell them. "His name was John Spencer, and he was an evil rapist. He deserved to die for what he did to me."

Debbie said nothing, waiting to see if Phoebe would feel obliged to fill the silence.

She did.

"When I was fourteen years old he kept me a prisoner at his nan's cottage in Kent for a whole week, and during that time he repeatedly raped me..." Her voice cracked, and a tear ran down the side of her face as she forced herself to remember.

Debbie magically produced a pack of tissues and handed her one.

Phoebe accepted it with a strained smile. "He was sentenced to twelve years in prison, but only served eight." Her features twisted with pain. "How can that be justice?"

Debbie remained silent. She could hardly say that she didn't think it was.

Phoebe dabbed at her eyes with the tissue, sniffed loudly. "The bastard was released on the Tuesday," she said in a tremulous voice, "and by Wednesday evening I was his fucking prisoner again."

Debbie had to resist the urge to reach across the table and give the poor girl's hand a reassuring squeeze. "It must have been terrifying," she said quietly.

"Terrifying!" Phoebe snorted. "You have no idea!" She paused to take a deep breath before continuing. "At first I thought I was going to die, and all I could think about was Martin and my parents, and how sad they would all be. And then I thought I was going to be raped again, and suddenly death didn't seem quite so bad. Something in me changed that night, and I decided that if anyone was going to die, it was him, not me." Her face hardened, and so did her voice. "I tricked him into retying my hands in front of me, and then I forced myself to sit down beside him while he talked utter garbage about us spending the rest of our lives together." She shuddered. "When he popped out of the barn, I searched around and managed to find a heavy pipe, which I hid. Later in the evening, when he went out again to phone his cousin, Skippy, I retrieved it." A cruel smile spread across her face. "When he came back, I hit him with it and tried to escape. All I wanted to do was call for help and have him arrested." She shook her head sadly. "He chased me out of the barn, so I hit him again, and this time he stayed down for good." A mirthless laugh. "That was when I realised that, if I called the police, he would go back to jail for a little while, but then he would be back out and he would come after me again…"

"Go on," Debbie encouraged as Phoebe stalled.

The tears were flowing again, and she seemed to shrivel in her seat as she said, "And that was when I realised that there was only one way to be free of him for good, so I hit him again, and I didn't stop hitting him until his brains were splattered all over the floor."

"So, you're saying you deliberately killed him?" Debbie asked softly.

"Don't you see? I had to," Phoebe wailed, burying her head in her hands and sobbing uncontrollably.

Tyler was making himself a hot drink when someone shouted that his office phone was ringing. Thanking them, he hurried back, being careful not to spill his coffee all over himself.

"DCI Tyler speaking."

"Boss, it's Debbie here. We've just broken so that Phoebe can have another consultation with her brief, so I thought I'd better let you know what she's said so far."

She sounded drained.

Tyler took a quick sip of his drink. "I take it she's talking, then?"

"*Is she ever! It's almost like she's finding it therapeutic and she can't get the words out quickly enough.*"

"I bet her solicitor's loving that," Tyler laughed. He reached for a pen and opened his daybook. "Okay, tell me everything, but don't talk too fast as I'll be making notes as I listen."

"*So, she's admitted to killing all three of them: Spencer, Whitling and Manson.*"

"That's a good start," Tyler said, scribbling away. "Has she said anything about where Spencer's body is?"

"*Yep. It turns out that the barn she took the local plod to, after she escaped, wasn't the one where Spencer had been holding her captive. That one's a couple of miles in the other direction, and it has an old abandoned well next to it so it should be relatively easy to locate. She told us that Spencer's body, minus his severed right hand, is in the bottom of the well, along with the piping she used to bludgeon him to death with and her mobile phone.*"

"Did she say why she killed him?"

"*Basically, it was him or her as she saw it and, to be honest with you, a part of me can see her point.*"

"And how did she manage it?"

"While Phoebe was being held prisoner at the barn, she found a lump of heavy piping. She waited until Spencer started to relax his guard around her, and then she whacked him over the noggin with it. Having stunned him, she made a run for it, but he came after her so she hit him again, knocking him out this time. As he lay on the floor, the poor cow had what she describes as an epiphany. She realised that he would never stop coming after her and that she would never be safe. At that point, or so she claims, something in her snapped. Apparently, she experienced a vivid flashback to the horrors he had inflicted on her when she was a teenager, and this caused her to lose the plot. The next thing she remembers is staring down at his corpse and wondering how his brains had ended up splattered all over the floor."

Tyler grunted cynically. "So, she's already laying the grounds for a diminished responsibility defence," he said. "What a surprise."

"After realising that he was dead, Phoebe hid the body in the barn, scooped up the gaffer tape that her wrists and ankles had been secured with, along with a white floppy hat that had been used to gag her, and then drove the stolen BMW to another abandoned barn a mile or so away. She dropped the gaffer tape and hat off there, and arranged it so that it would look like the barn he'd taken her to when she fetched the police. After that, she cleaned herself up and drove the Beamer to another derelict barn and parked it up out of sight. Then she hitched a lift to the police station."

"How does she know about all these places?" Tyler asked.

"She knows the area inside out from all the exploring she's done to find the best beauty spots to paint in," Debbie explained.

"Hmmm. These hardly sound like the actions of an irrational mind to me," Tyler said. "In fact, it all sounds rather well thought out and deliberate."

"She's a highly intelligent girl," Debbie agreed, "and there's no doubt that what she did after killing him was designed to prevent her from being caught. She even took his mobile phone and started sending messages to Skipton to make him think that Spencer was still alive."

Tyler shook his head in wonder. That was an incredibly clever touch, and it had certainly fooled them into thinking Spencer was still on the run. "How the hell did she know to pull a stunt like that?" he asked.

Debbie chucked. "*Ah, well, I asked her that exact same question, and she told me that she got the idea from DCI Craddock, who helpfully explained in great depth all about the way mobile phones work, and how we can track them by the masts that they shake hands with when they make or receive calls.*"

"You have got to be kidding me!" Tyler said, wondering what the hell Craddock had been thinking when he'd told her that.

"*Sadly not,*" she replied.

There was an awkward silence. He couldn't think of anything to say that wouldn't be derogatory and, as Craddock was a fellow DCI, he didn't think it would be appropriate for him to start slagging him off to a junior officer. "So, what happened to make her kill her fiancé?" Tyler asked.

"*Ah, well, it seems she caught Whitling and Manson having a snog when she got back from Diss police station on Thursday and realised that they were bonking each other. Hell hath no fury like a woman scorned, and all that.*"

"Is that all there was to it? A bit of old fashioned jealousy?" Tyler was strangely disappointed. He had half expected Phoebe to say that she had been hearing voices in her head, telling her that Martina and Anna were lizard people, and that she had to kill them. If she had topped them simply because they were having an affair, her barrister was going to have a very hard time arguing diminished responsibility.

"*Not quite that simple,*" Debbie said. "*Although he doesn't think it's likely, the doctor from the Mental Health Team said it's hypothetically possible that the head injuries she received from being knocked out by Spencer could have led to a change in her personality. He reckons that her defence team will argue that she suffered an acute stress reaction, after being exposed to constant trauma, and this triggered disassociation and emotional detachment, which resulted in her having poor impulse control from that point onwards.*"

Tyler grunted, dismissively. "Sounds like a load of old baloney to me."

"I think he was just trying to be helpful, pointing out the line of defence that her barristers will have to go with. Bottom line is, he doesn't think Phoebe's suffering from acute psychosis, although he does accept that the way she behaved when Susie confronted her, and the things she said leading up to her arrest, could be construed as delusional. In his opinion though, it was more likely just a stressful reaction to her having suddenly lost control of the situation."

"What about when she tried to slit her own throat? Does he think that's a sign of mental illness?"

"The MHT doctor thinks her doing that is consistent with her documented background of suffering from stress, depression and complex PTSD. In other words, it was a fight or flight reaction, born out of panic. It isn't necessarily a sign of psychosis or schizophrenia."

Drumming his fingers against his desk, Tyler frowned, deep in thought. "So, basically, her justification for killing Spencer and trying to stab Kevin Murray was that she was protecting herself, and the reason she killed the other two was that she was punishing them for hurting her, is that correct?"

"That's about the size of it," Debbie confirmed. "*The MHT doctor doesn't consider her to be delusional or psychotic. In fact, according to him, people with severe psychosis don't plan well and are much more disconnected from reality. Phoebe's actions in killing Martin and Anna were cold and calculating. That said, he does concede that the paranoia she seems to have exhibited upon arrest isn't consistent with the actions of someone who is entirely well, so who knows.*"

Tyler sighed. "In other words, he's saying the case could go either way at court, depending on the forensic psychiatric reports, how she presents over a number of months while on remand, and her legal teams' arguments?"

"Yes, I'm afraid so. Whatever way you look at it, I thinks it's safe to say that this one isn't going to be clear cut, and I reckon the jury will have a pretty tough time deciding whether she's mad or just bad."

Tyler took a moment to digest this, concluding that he had more immediate priorities to focus on, rather than worrying about what might happen months down the line at court. "So, when did she cut

Spencer's hand off? Surely not before she rocked up at Diss police station in the early hours of Thursday morning?"

"*No. At that point, she had no intention of killing anyone else. It was only after she caught Martin and Anna snogging at the cottage, later that day, that she got the idea of knocking them off and blaming Spencer.*"

"So, when did she chop his hand off?" Tyler repeated.

"*She returned to the crime scene the following day to dispose of the body. Manson had driven up to stay with her, so she had to pretend that she was going off to do some painting. She drove back to the barn in her Alfa. Before hiding the body, she chopped Spencer's hand off with a hatchet she had taken from the cottage, and put it in a cool bag stuffed full of ice to stop it from deteriorating. Then she kept it in the freezer between kills.*"

That would be the cool bag that the decaying hand had been found in, inside her boot, Tyler surmised, making frantic notes. He would need to get Craddock's team to search the cottage and seize the hatchet for him. He would also need to identify what clothing she been wearing on the day that she had 'gone painting' and have it examined for microscopic traces of blood. The Alfa had already been taken to Charlton car pound, and he would have a word with Juliet Kennedy and ensure that the vehicle's interior was treated with Luminol as well as the boot. That would show up any blood that she had tried to wash away.

"How did she get the body into the well?" he asked. On films, they always made it seem so easy to lug dead bodies around; in reality it was anything but.

"*She reckons that it was back breaking work to drag the corpse from the barn, and then hoist him over the edge of the well. And before she could do that, she had to use bolt cutters to break off the padlocks securing the wood panelling that had been put over the well's mouth to stop people from falling in.*"

Tyler shook his head in disbelief. "It's an incredible story," he said. "I can't wait to hear the rest of it."

"*Well, as soon as their consultation ends, which should be any minute now, I'm going back in for another round of interviews to try and put some* flesh on the bones that I've already given you," Debbie said. "*If anything significant comes up, I'll let you know straight away.*"

―――

"Hello, Jack," Barty Craddock said with a contented smile. He was standing beside the well that contained John Spencer's body. "Just thought I'd give you a quick ring and let you know that we've found the blighter." He glanced down into the hole and turned his nose up at the mangled corpse lying below. The smell of decay was barely noticeable all the way up here, but he certainly wouldn't want to be the Crime Scene Examiner who had been roped down to examine Spencer's remains a half hour ago.

"*Was he where she said he would be?*" Tyler asked from his office in London.

"He was," Craddock confirmed. "Good job Spencer picked this particular barn to take her to," he chortled. "It's the only one with an old well next to it for miles around, so it was a doddle to work out where you meant from the description you gave us."

"*Well, with Spencer dead, your kidnap case is nicely sown up,*" Tyler said. It would be shown as a clear up, leaving Craddock's team free to move on to a new job.

"Indeed," Craddock confirmed happily, "and it hardly made a dent in my overtime budget, so that's a result all round as far as I'm concerned."

Spencer's murder was technically a Norfolk job too, so they would get the clear up for that as well, but with the Met lads already interviewing her about the two London based murders, it had been agreed they would retain control of the entire investigation and deal with his murder as part of a linked series.

"*The girl reckons that she bludgeoned Spencer to death just inside the barn's main door. Can you get someone to check the floor for me, and see if there's any blood visible?*"

Craddock glanced over at the dilapidated barn. "I'll have a mosey over there right now and do it myself," he offered. "I've arranged for copies of all the statements and forensic reports to be prepared in readiness for the handover," he said as he walked. "I'll get one of my boys to run it all down to London for you on Monday morning, if that's okay?"

"*That'll be perfect,*" Tyler said.

Craddock reached the barn and forced open the groaning door. "Ah, yes," he said. "There's clear evidence of blood spatter here, and what looks like bone fragments and bits of dura mater. I'll get the Crime Scene Examiners to process and photograph it as soon as they've finished recovering the body."

"*You might need to call a Blood Pattern Analyst out,*" Tyler said. "*I need to know if the blood is purely from where she hit him over the head, or if some of it comes from where she chopped his wrist off.*"

Craddock knelt down, wincing as his knees clicked. "I reckon there's a bit of both, from what I can see," he told his London colleague, "but we'll get it photographed and examined by a BPA boffin and see what comes out of that."

"*I take it the well was a good hiding place for the body, then?*" Tyler asked.

Craddock nodded, then remembered that Tyler couldn't see him. "Yes, it was," he confirmed. "It might never have been found down there if she hadn't told us where she had hidden it."

It was getting on for ten p.m. when Debbie Brown went to collect Phoebe from her cell in order for her to be charged. All the available evidence had been put to her during an exceedingly long day of interviewing and, as Debbie led her through to the custody sergeant, she thought that the girl looked close to exhaustion.

Phoebe's fingerprints had been found on Spencer's burner, along with microscopic traces of Anna Manson's blood. She had listened to this information without displaying any emotion. Likewise, the revelation that they had found traces of her DNA on the shiny surfaces of the candy coated chocolates at Whitling's flat had failed to evoke a reaction. She hadn't lied; hadn't tried to make excuses for her actions. She had told them everything. Worryingly, Phoebe seemed to think that, under the circumstances, all three murders had been perfectly justified, and she struggled to understand why no one else could see this

The custody officer was leaning on the raised dais, and he looked down at Phoebe with indifference as she arrived. To him, this was just another prisoner to charge, one of many that he had dealt with during his busy shift. He cleared his throat and then read from the computer screen in front of him. "There are three charges against you, Miss Cunningham," he said, adjusting his reading glasses so that he could see the small print better. "The first charge is that, on or before Thursday 26th July 2001, at an abandoned barn in Norfolk, and within the jurisdiction of the Central Criminal Court, you did wilfully murder John Anthony Spencer. This is an offence contrary to common law." The custody officer then read out the charges relating to Martin Whitling and Anna Manson's murders. "In answer to these three charges, you do not have to say anything, but it may harm your defence if you do not mention, now, something that you later rely on in court. Anything you do say may be used in evidence against you." He glanced at his watch. "Charged, charges read over and cautioned at 21:56 hours," he said for the benefit of the witnessing officers and Phoebe's solicitor, who all made a note for their records. "Do you wish to make a bail application, Mr Kincaid?" he asked her solicitor.

Kincaid shook his head, wearily. "I think we all know that would be a waste of time," he said, pragmatically.

"What will happen to me now?" Phoebe asked Debbie Brown as she was led away to have her fingerprints and DNA taken.

"You'll stay here overnight," Debbie explained. "In the morning, you'll be taken to Waltham Forest Magistrates Court. The chances are that they will remand you into custody, and you'll be sent to a prison to await trial. While you're there, you'll receive a full psychiatric evaluation, and that will help your solicitor and barrister to decide how best to prepare the case for court."

"I had to kill them," Phoebe said, as though she felt the need to justify herself. "They all hurt me and I had to protect myself." Her bottom lip trembled as she spoke, and she seemed strangely vulnerable as she stood there, hugging herself and looking terrified.

As Debbie ran the DNA swab against the inside of Phoebe's mouth, she had to remind herself that this wasn't a frightened child. This was a dangerous woman who had brutally murdered three people during the course of the past week. She had also attempted to kill Kevin Murray yesterday, although Debs suspected that anyone who knew Murray would undoubtably have a degree of sympathy for her in regard to that. "Phoebe, I really can't discuss the evidence with you anymore," she said gently. "It just wouldn't be right, but you need to try and stay positive. At least where you're going, you'll be safe, and we can get you some professional help. Hopefully, the doctors will help you to see things a little more clearly over time."

"Will I be able to see my parents before I go?" Phoebe asked meekly. Her eyes were brimming with tears.

Debbie sighed. She really was too soft to be doing this job. "I'll see if I can persuade the custody sergeant to allow you to have a supervised visit," she promised, "but it won't be for very long."

Phoebe's parents were waiting outside. They had been there for most of the day, and Debbie had been regularly popping out to update them. It had broken her heart to see how devastated they had been by the shocking news that Phoebe had confessed to three murders. The revelation had all but destroyed them, and she really didn't know how they were going to cope with everything that was yet to come.

"That would be so wonderful," Phoebe said, wiping away the tears that had started to fall.

After the fingerprints and post charge DNA samples had been taken, Debbie led her back to her cell. As she handed Phoebe over to the care of the PC who would be sitting with her all night, she felt an intense wave of sadness wash over her. Putting murderers behind bars normally gave her great job satisfaction, but today all it did was make her feel physically sick. Debbie watched in silence as Phoebe was ushered into her cell. The girl seemed somehow diminished as she walked listlessly over to her cot. Laying down with her back to them, she pulled a threadbare blanket over herself, curled up into a foetal position and lay still.

"I'll go and speak to the custody sergeant and see if I can arrange that visit," Debbie told her.

"Thank you," Phoebe murmured quietly.

With a final glance at the demoralised girl, Debbie turned and set off back down the cell corridor towards the main custody area.

EPILOGUE

Sunday 5th August 2001

The christening had been a great success. Everything had been perfect: the weather, the venue, the turnout. Little Ralph had been on his best behaviour and he had charmed everyone that he had come into contact with.

Tyler had found his role of godparent nerve wracking to the point that he had been aware of his knees knocking as he and Kelly gathered around the font for the baptism with Eddie, Jenny and the ever smiling Reverend Saunders. Even though he was well versed at public speaking, he had heard the warble in his voice as he uttered his lines in front of the assembled congregation. After all, he was volunteering to look after young Ralph's development and be there for him if anything ever happened to his parents, and it was a big responsibility.

At the conclusion of the church service, everyone had gathered outside for photographs before retiring to Eddie and Jenny's house, in nearby Chingford, to continue the celebrations in a more relaxed environment.

Tyler wrapped an arm around Kelly's shoulders and grinned at her. He had been doing a lot of that since she had returned from her trip to France on Friday evening. "Have I told you how much I missed you while you were away?" he asked, pulling her in close and kissing her cheek.

"Only about a thousand times," she replied with a broad smile, "which is nowhere near enough."

He giggled and kissed her again. "Then I shall keep reminding you until you tell me to stop," he promised, clinking his glass against hers.

They were standing under a giant parasol in the Maitland's large rear garden, surrounded by a sea of people, many of whom they had never seen before today. Doing a quick head count, Tyler estimated that there had to be at least fifty people present.

"They've put on a fabulous spread, haven't they?" Jenny's mother, Sylvia Parker, said as she joined them to get out of the sun. Sylvia was in her mid-sixties, but she looked much younger, and there was a vibrancy to her personality that always seemed to light up a room whenever she entered.

"You're looking particularly splendid today, Sylvia," Tyler said, going over to give her a hug. She was wearing a grey and silver chiffon dress, the bodice of which was adorned with delicate lace and shimmering sequins.

Kelly smiled at her with genuine affection. "Yes," she agreed, enthusiastically. "I absolutely love that dress."

Sylvia curtseyed, graciously. "Thank you my dear," she said with an equally warm smile. "You look positively stunning, too. Doesn't she, Jack?"

Kelly was wearing a figure hugging, pink Ted Baker knee length dress, with 'off the shoulder' sleeves. An intricate woodland print rose up from the hem, and she carried a pink handbag with a matching pattern.

"I think she looks amazing," he said, smiling at her goofily.

"How long have you two been together now?" Sylvia asked.

"We started dating about twenty months ago?" Tyler said, shooting Kelly an uncertain glance.

She rolled her eyes. "We've been seeing each other properly since November 1999," she told him, peeved that he didn't remember the exact date. *Typical man!*

Tyler grinned sheepishly. "That's roughly twenty months," he said, taking a sip of champagne.

"Then, isn't it about time you made an honest woman of her?" Sylvia asked with a mischievous twinkle in her eye.

Tyler spluttered and almost choked on his drink.

Seeing his unease, Kelly blushed. "We've got plenty of time ahead of us to think about that," she said, eager to change the subject.

"I'm going to grab us a refill," Tyler said, taking Kelly's glass from her. "What about you, Sylvia? Can I get you anything?"

"I'm fine," she said, smiling sweetly. "In fact, I'm going to go and check on Ralph, make sure he's not getting up to any mischief." Leaning in, she gave each of them a peck on the cheek. "And I meant what I said," she told Tyler, wagging a finger at him as she walked away. "You could do a lot worse than put a ring on this wonderful girl's finger."

Tyler smiled awkwardly, and set off for the bar, leaving Kelly alone.

"Well, that was uncomfortable," she said to herself as she watched him go. Deep down, she was desperate for him to propose. She knew that he loved her with all his heart; he demonstrated that on a daily basis, but she often wondered if he would ever feel able to commit to another marriage after what he had been through with Jenny.

"Has he abandoned you already?" Jenny said, appearing at her shoulder like an apparition. She was carrying a huge glass of white wine and she already looked half cut. Despite that, her appearance was impeccable; not a crease in her clothing, not a hair out of place, and Kelly didn't even want to hazard a guess how much her fancy designer label dress had cost. Her Jimmy Choo shoes were probably worth more than twice what Kelly had paid for her entire outfit.

"Jesus!" Kelly exclaimed, almost jumping out of her skin. "You shouldn't go sneaking up on people like that!" After swallowing her heart back down into her chest, she turned to face her hostess, forcing a pleasant smile onto her face. "Little Ralph seems to be having a wonderful time," she said, eager to fill the silence. Kelly never felt comfortable around Jenny, who didn't seem to like her for reasons that she had never been able to fathom.

"Yes, the little dear is enjoying himself enormously," Jenny said, looking around the garden in an effort to spot him.

In the background, music started to play.

"Sounds like the DJ is setting up," Jenny said.

Kelly nodded politely. "Uh-huh."

Jenny took a large mouthful of wine and then swilled the remainder around her wide bottomed glass. "I wanted to thank you and Jack for agreeing to be Ralph's godparents," she said.

"Our pleasure," Kelly assured her.

A smile pulled at Jenny's cheeks, but it stayed well clear of her eyes. "I think it's lovely that we can all be friends," she said.

"Me too," Kelly agreed, wondering how much longer Jack would be.

"So, tell me, are you two thinking of tying the knot anytime soon?" Jenny asked, trying to sound casual.

Inwardly cringing, Kelly put on a brave smile. *What's wrong with people today? Why do they keep asking me that?*

"Only, now you're our son's godmother," Jenny was saying, "I want to make sure that you're going to be around for the long haul."

Kelly wasn't sure what to say to that. "Well, er, we haven't exactly discussed it yet."

"You do love him, I take it?" Jenny asked, staring at her intently.

Where the hell was Jack?

Kelly nodded. "Of course I do. Falling for the boss is so cliché, isn't it," she said with an embarrassed grin. "It's the sort of thing that you only expect to happen in romantic comedies, but that's exactly what happened with me and Jack."

"It's what happened with me and Eddie, too," Jenny said, waving across the garden to him. Maitland blew her a kiss and then resumed the discussion that he was having with his friends.

"That would have been quite romantic," Kelly observed, and then her voice hardened, "if you hadn't already been married to Jack at the time." Without giving Jenny time to form a reply, she spun on her heel and went in search of Tyler.

Why did I just say that?

Now regretting her outburst, she wandered over to the bar in search of Tyler, but there was no sign of him there. She hoped he wouldn't be too hacked off with her when she told him what she had just blurted out to his ex-wife.

Jack had made peace with Jenny and Eddie, and they were all 'friends' now. The pain that the acrimonious split had caused him was water under the bridge as far as he was concerned. The trouble was, Kelly knew how much Jenny's betrayal had hurt Jack, and she wasn't quite so forgiving.

I've obviously been spending far too much time with Tony Dillon.

Jack still couldn't mention Jenny's name in front of him without the big man launching into a tirade of abuse.

She walked up to Jenny's father, Brendon Parker, who was standing at the bar. "Excuse me, but I don't suppose you've seen Jack anywhere, have you?"

Parker smiled at her fondly. He and Jack were very close, and since finding out about their relationship, he had always made it abundantly clear that he wholeheartedly approved of Kelly. "Hello, my dear! How lovely it is to see you. He was here a couple of minutes ago, and then he went off in search of the DJ."

Kelly was surprised to hear that. "Oh, okay," she said, squeezing Brendon's hand affectionately. "I'll go and look for him there."

As she started walking over towards the DJ's booth, she spotted Tyler leaning in to talk to a long haired man who was wearing the largest set of headphones that she had ever seen. Reminding her of a Cyberman from Doctor Who, the DJ was standing behind his sound deck, playing with the controls and dancing on the spot. A large promotional sign had been erected next to the booth, and it read: *DJ STAN THE MAN!*

As she drew nearer, the music was suddenly switched off and

Tyler started addressing the crowd through a microphone that Stan the Man had just given him.

"Good afternoon ladies and gentlemen," he began. "If I can just have your attention for a couple of minutes, I promise I'll leave you alone to enjoy the rest of the afternoon and evening in peace."

There was a ripple of polite laughter as the crowd turned to listen to him.

"Can I just ask Eddie and Jenny to join me here by the sound system," he asked, and then waited for them to come over. Both looked confused, and Kelly realised that this speech hadn't been scripted, which was strange, because Jack wasn't the sort of man who liked being the centre of attention, so she couldn't imagine him making an address unless he had to.

"I'd like to start off by thanking Eddie and Jenny for asking me and Kelly to act as godparents," Tyler said, waving at them. Eddie gave him a little salute in return and Jenny blew him a kiss.

"We promise to take our responsibilities extremely seriously, as long as Ralph doesn't turn out to be a Tottenham Hotspur supporter," he said with an impish grin. Everyone knew that Tyler was an avid Arsenal fan and Spurs were their North London rivals. "If that happens, he's on his own."

Laughter broke out.

One man, obviously a Spurs fan, booed.

"I'm only joking," Tyler said, making a point of crossing his fingers in front of them to show that he wasn't.

More laughter.

"I also want to thank them for laying on such an incredible spread for us all to enjoy, and for going to great lengths to make us all feel so welcome. I think the least we can do is give them a big round of applause to show our appreciation, don't you?" Tyler started clapping and the crowd all joined in.

Eddie and Jenny lapped it up, bowing and curtseying respectfully.

"Okay, so there's one last thing that I need to do before I go," Tyler said as the applause died down. He looked around until he spotted Kelly and, to her astonishment, he beckoned her over to join him.

Epilogue 481

When she reached his side, he wrapped a protective arm around her and addressed the crowd again. "I'd like to introduce you all to my girlfriend, Kelly Flowers. We've been going out together now since November 1999."

Feeling everyone's eyes on her, Kelly blushed with embarrassment. What was he doing? He'd only had one glass of champagne, so he couldn't be drunk.

Everyone was watching them, wondering what was going on. Most people were smiling, but she noticed that Jenny was glowering at her, no doubt still sulking over her earlier barbed comment.

"I know this is Ralph's special day," Tyler continued, "and I really don't want to steal his thunder, but there's something important that I need to do, and I was hoping you would all give me a little bit of moral support as I do it." Lowering the mic, Tyler reached into his trouser pocket and withdrew a small box. "Kelly," he said, kneeling down and taking her hand. "Would you do me the very great honour of marrying me?" With that, he opened the box to reveal a sparkling engagement ring.

She noticed that his hands were shaking.

Kelly's hands flew to her face. "Are you serious?" she asked, unable to take her eyes from the gleaming gem.

"I should bloody well hope so," he whispered. "That little ring set me back three months' worth of wages." Smiling at her, he carefully prised it out of the padding that surrounded it and slipped it onto the ring finger of her left hand, breathing a huge sigh of relief when he saw that it fit.

Everyone started clapping as he stood up.

"I haven't said yes, yet," she pointed out.

That wiped the smile from his face. "But I–"

She threw her arms around his neck and kissed him hard. "Yes!" she said, feeling deliriously happy. "Of course it's a bloody yes!"

FURTHER READING

TURF WAR

May 1999.

An out of town contract killer is drafted in to carry out a hit on an Albanian crime boss.

That same evening, in another part of town, four Turkish racketeers are ruthlessly gunned down while extorting protection money from local businessmen.

As the dust settles, it becomes apparent to DCI Jack Tyler that the two investigations are inexorably linked, and that someone is trying to orchestrate a gangland war that will tear the city apart.

But who? And why?

The pressure is on. can Tyler can find a way to stem the killings and restore order to the streets, or will this be the case that destroys his career?

Available on all Amazon platforms

―――――

JACK'S BACK.

October 1999.

When a horribly mutilated body is discovered lying beneath a taunting message written in its own blood, it quickly becomes apparent to DCI Jack Tyler that he's witnessing the birth of a terrifying new serial killer.

With the relentless media coverage causing panic on the streets of Whitechapel, Tyler is put under increasing pressure to bring the case to a rapid conclusion, but the murderer is scarily smart; a ghost who always seems to be one step ahead of the police.

Tyler knows that this case could make or break his career, but he doesn't care about the bad press, or the internal politics; all he's interested in is finding a way to stop the killer before he strikes again...

But what if he can't...?

Available from all Amazon platforms

THE HUNT FOR CHEN

November 1999.

Exhausted from having just dealt with a series of gruesome murders in Whitechapel, DCI Jack Tyler and his team of homicide detectives are hoping for a quiet run in to Christmas.

Things are looking promising until the London Fire Brigade are called down to a house fire in East London and discover a charred body that has been wrapped in a carpet and set alight.

Attending the scene, Tyler and his partner, DI Tony Dillon, immediately realise that they are dealing with a brutal murder.

A witness comes forward who saw the victim locked in a heated argument with an Oriental male just before the fire started, but nothing is known about this mysterious man other than he drives a white van and his name might be Chen.

Armed with this frugal information, Tyler launches a murder investigation, and the hunt to find the unknown killer begins.

Download the e-book for free at: Markromain.com

UNLAWFULLY AT LARGE

January 2000.

When DCI Jack Tyler put Claude Winston behind bars, he was convinced the psychotic killer would never breathe fresh air again. Then the unthinkable happened and Winston escaped, leaving behind a trail of death and destruction.

Recapturing Winston won't be easy. He'll be better prepared this time around and, due to the bad blood that exists between them, he'll be itching for another chance to see Tyler lined up in the crosshairs of his gun.

Tyler doesn't care. With a colleague dead, this case has become personal, and he'll do whatever it takes to see justice done, even if that means putting his reputation and his life on the line.

Available from all Amazon platforms

DIAMONDS AND DEATH

October 2001.

When an ex-squaddie who's struggling to keep his failing business afloat discovers that a local thug has been entrusted to look after a small fortune in diamonds, he senses an opportunity to get rich quick. But there's a snag. The gems belong to a notorious East London gangster, and he's not a man you steal from if you want to continue breathing.

When an unidentified body is found floating in Regent's Canal, DCI Jack

Tyler is tasked with solving the sinister mystery. A difficult and frustrating case from the start, it doesn't help that he's been saddled with a TV crew who are making a documentary about homicide investigations.

It hasn't been a great start to the week, and things are about to get a whole lot worse...

Available from all Amazon platforms

WOLFPACK

November 2001.

It's bonfire night, and Gabe Warren, a fourteen year old runaway from Bristol has just arrived at London's Victoria coach station. He is homeless, penniless and friendless, which makes him ripe for the plucking.

When Gabe accepts the offer of a hot meal and a place to sleep for a few nights, he is unaware that he is about to set foot along a dark and twisted path that will lead to murder.

That same night, two young boys are snatched from a busy fairground in Chingford.

DCI Jack Tyler is tasked finding the boys, but he knows that time is against him. If they were taken by a paedophile, as seems increasingly likely, the chances of them being found alive diminishes with every passing minute...

Available from all Amazon platforms

ACKNOWLEDGMENTS

Edited by Yvonne Goldsworthy

Cover design by Woot Han

I'd like to say a very special thank you to my brilliant team of Beta Readers, not only for taking the time to read the first draft of the manuscript, but also for all the great feedback and helpful suggestions that they provided. They are: Clare R, Danny A, Cathie A and Darren H.

I'd also like to thank Dr. Karen Romain for her extensive input on the complex subject of mental health. This was invaluable to me and it helped me to have a much better understanding of how Phoebe would be feeling and reacting, and what she would have gone through at various points in her life. I must say, it's very handy having a psychiatrist in the family! Naturally, any mistakes I made on the subject were entirely my own! Thanks again, Karen – you're a star!

GLOSSARY OF TERMS USED IN THE DCI TYLER THRILLERS

AC – Assistant Commissioner
ACPO – Association of Chief Police Officers
AFO – Authorised Firearms Officer
AIDS – Acquired Immune Deficiency Syndrome
AMIP – Area Major Investigation Pool (Predecessor to the Homicide Command)
ANPR – Automatic Number Plate Recognition
ARV – Armed Response Vehicle
ASU – Air Support Unit
ATC – Air Traffic Control
ATS – Automatic Traffic Signal
Azimuth – The coverage from each mobile phone telephone mast is split into three 120-degree arcs called azimuths
Bacon – derogatory slang expression for a police officer
Bandit – the driver of a stolen car or other vehicle failing to stop for police
BIU – Borough Intelligence Unit
BPA – Blood Pattern Analysis
BTP – British Transport Police
C11 – Criminal Intelligence / surveillance

CAD – Computer Aided Dispatch
CCTV – Closed Circuit Television
CIB – Complaints Investigation Bureau
CID – Criminal Investigation Department
CIPP – Crime Investigation Priority Project
County Mounties – a phrase used by Met officers to describe police officers from the Constabularies
CJPU – Criminal Justice Protection Unit (witness protection)
CRIMINT – Criminal Intelligence
CPS – Crown Prosecution Service
CSM – Crime Scene Manager
(The) Craft – the study of magic
CRIS – Crime Reporting Information System
DNA – Deoxyribonucleic Acid
DC – Detective Constable
DS – Detective Sergeant
DI – Detective Inspector
DCI – Detective Chief Inspector
DSU – Detective Superintendent
DCS – Detective Chief Superintendent
DPG – Diplomatic Protection Group
DVLA – Driver and Vehicle Licensing Agency
ECHR – European Court of Human Rights
Enforcer – a heavy metal battering ram used to force open doors
ESDA – Electrostatic Detection Apparatus (sometimes called an EDD or Electrostatic Detection Device)
ETA – Expected Time of Arrival
(The) Factory – Police jargon for their base.
FLO – Family Liaison Officer
FME – Force Medical Examiner
Foxtrot Oscar – Police jargon for 'fuck off'
FSS – Forensic Science Service
GP – General Practitioner
GMC – General Medical Council
GMP – Greater Manchester Police

Glossary of terms used in the DCI Tyler Thrillers

GSR – Gun Shot Residue
HA – Arbour Square police station
HAT – Homicide Assessment Team
HEMS – Helicopter Emergency Medical Service
HIV – Human Immunodeficiency Virus
HOLMES – Home Office Large Major Enquiry System
HP – High Priority
HR – Human Resources
HT – Whitechapel borough / Whitechapel police station
IC1 – PNC code for a white European
IC2 – PNC code for a dark skinned European
IC3 – PNC code for an Afro Caribbean
IC4 – PNC code for an Asian
IC5 – PNC code for an Oriental
IC6 – PNC code for an Arab
ICU – Intensive Care Unit
IFR - Instrument Flight Rules are used by pilots when visibility is not good enough to fly by visual flight rules
IO – Investigating Officer
IPCC – Independent Police Complaints Commission
IR – Information Room
IRV – Immediate Response Vehicle
JL – Leyton police station
JS – Leytonstone police station
KF – Forest Gate police station
KZ – Hertford House, East London base of the Homicide Command, also known as SO1(3)
Kiting checks – trying to purchase goods or obtain cash with stolen / fraudulent checks
LAG – Lay Advisory Group
LAS – London Ambulance Service
LFB – London Fire Brigade
Lid – uniformed police officer
LOS – Lost Or Stolen vehicle
MIR – Major Incident Room

MIT – Major Investigation Team
MP – Radio call sign for Information Room at NSY
MPH – Miles Per Hour
MICH/ACH (Modular Integrated Communications Helmet / Advanced Ballistic Combat Helmet)
MPS – Metropolitan Police Service
MSS – Message Switching System
NABIS – National Ballistics Intelligence Service
NADAC – National ANPR Data Centre
NFA – No Further Action
NHS – National Health Service
Nondy – Nondescript vehicle, typically an observation van
NOTAR – No Tail Rotor system technology
NSY – New Scotland Yard
OCG – Organised Crime Group
OH – Occupational Health
Old Bill – the police
OM – Office Manager
OP – Observation Post
P9 – MPS Level 1/P9 Surveillance Trained
PACE – Police and Criminal Evidence Act 1984
PC – Police Constable
PCMH – Plea and Case Management Hearing
Pig – Derogatory slang expression for a police officer
PIP – Post Incident Procedure
PLO – Press Liaison Officer
PM – Post Mortem
PNC – Police National Computer
POLACC – Police Accident
PR – Personal Radio
PS – Police Sergeant
PTT – Press to Talk
RCJ – Royal Courts of Justice
RCS – Regional Crime Squad

Glossary of terms used in the DCI Tyler Thrillers

Ringer – stolen car on false number plates
RLH – Royal London Hospital
Rozzers – the police
RTA – Road traffic Accident
RT car – Radio Telephone car, nowadays known as a Pursuit Vehicle
QC – Queen's Counsel (a very senior barrister)
SCG - Serious Crime Group
Scruffs – Dressing down in casual clothes in order for a detective to blend in with his / her surroundings
SFO – Specialist Firearms Officer
SIO – Senior Investigating Officer
Sheep – followers of Christ; the masses
Skipper - Sergeant
SNT – Safer Neighbourhood Team
SO – Specialist Operations
SO19 – Met Police Firearms Unit
SOCO – Scene Of Crime Officer
SOIT – Sexual Offences Investigative Technique
SPM – Special Post Mortem
SPOC – Single Point of Contact
Stinger – a hollow spiked tyre deflation device
Tango – Target
TDA – Taking and Driving Away
TDC – Trainee Detective Constable
TIE – Trace, Interview, Eliminate
TPAC – Tactical Pursuit and containment
Trident – Operation Trident is the Met unit investigating 'black on black' gun crime
TSG – Territorial Support Group
TSU – Technical Support Unit
VODS – Vehicle On-line Descriptive Searching
Walkers – officers on foot patrol
Trumpton – the Fire Brigade
VFR – Visual Flight Rules - Regulations under which a pilot operates an aircraft in good visual conditions

AUTHOR'S NOTE

I really hope that you've enjoyed reading The Candy Killer. If you have, can I please ask that you to spare a few moments of your valuable time to leave an honest review on Amazon. It doesn't have to be anything fancy, just a line or two saying whether you enjoyed it and would recommend it to others. I can't stress how helpful this feedback is for indie authors like me. Apart from influencing a book's visibility, your reviews will help people who haven't read my work yet to decide whether it's right for them.

Many readers have told me that they like the detail and gritty realism of the DCI Tyler stories, which is great to hear because I really do try to keep my writing firmly grounded in the real world and ensure that all the police procedural matters are described as accurately as possible. Of course, there are unavoidable times when, to keep the flow of the story going or to maintain the intensity of the drama, I'm forced to apply a little sprinkle of artistic licence, but I really do endeavour to keep these occasions to the minimum.

The Candy Killer is the fifth DCI Tyler story that I've written. It's safe to say that I've grown rather fond of Tyler, Dillon, and the rest of the team – even Murray – over the years, and I sincerely hope that you'll grow to feel the same way about them that I do. I'm already fleshing out the plot for the next book, and I look forward to being able to share that story with you in the not-too-distant future!

I'll sign off by saying that if you haven't read them yet, why not give the other books in the series a try? And while you're at it, pop over to my website, www.markromain.com, and grab yourself a free copy of The Hunt For Chen.

Best wishes,

Mark.

ABOUT THE AUTHOR

Mark Romain is a retired Metropolitan Police officer, having joined the Service in the mid-eighties. His career included two homicide postings, and during that time he was fortunate enough to work on a number of very challenging high-profile cases.

Mark lives in Essex with his wife, Clare. They have two grown-up children and one grandchild. Between them, the family has three English Bull Terriers and a very bossy Dachshund called Weenie!

Mark is a lifelong Arsenal fan and an avid skier. He also enjoys going to the theatre, lifting weights and kick-boxing, a sport he got into during his misbegotten youth!

You can find out more about all Mark's books or contact him via his website: **Markromain.com**

Printed in Great Britain
by Amazon